ALSO BY ANDREI BITOV

The Monkey Link

A Captive of the Caucasus

Pushkin House

Life in Windy Weather

THE
SYMMETRY
TEACHER

THE
SYMMETRY
TEACHER

ANDREI BITOV

Translated from the Russian by Polly Gannon

Farrar, Straus and Giroux
New York

Farrar, Straus and Giroux
18 West 18th Street, New York 10011

Library of Congress Cataloging-in-Publication Data
Bitov, Andrei, author.
[Prepodavatel' simmetrii. English]
The symmetry teacher / Andrei Bitov ; translated from the Russian
by Polly Gannon.
pages   cm
ISBN 978-0-374-27351-4 (hardcover) — ISBN 978-0-374-71209-9 (ebook)
I. Gannon, Mary Catherine, 1953– translator.   II. Bitov, Andrei.
Prepodavatel' simmetrii. Translation of: III. Title.

PG3479.4.I8 P7413 2014
891.73'44—dc23
                                                          2013048088

Designed by Jonathan D. Lippincott

Farrar, Straus and Giroux books may be purchased for educational, business, or
promotional use. For information on bulk purchases, please contact the Macmillan
Corporate and Premium Sales Department at 1-800-221-7945, extension 5442, or write to
specialmarkets@macmillan.com.

www.fsgbooks.com
www.twitter.com/fsgbooks • www.facebook.com/fsgbooks

1   3   5   7   9   10   8   6   4   2

ИНСТИТУТ ПЕРЕВОДА

AD VERBUM

Published with the support of the Institute for Literary Translation, Russia

THE SYMMETRY TEACHER

A Novel-Echo

Translated from a foreign tongue by Andrei Bitov
Retranslated into English by Polly Gannon

Close your unholy lips,
And attend the priest's words as he reads from the Book:
What did He say on the Tuesday?
He told them all to get lost,
And render unto Caesar what was his, and to the Pharisees what was theirs.
Clean the vial from within
Instead of polishing the sides—thus He spake.
Then will I believe you.

—Lauren, 2006

A. Tired-Boffin

THE TEACHER OF SYMMETRY

A Novel

LONDON, 1937

1859–1937

We believe that the translation of *Tristram Shandy*, like that of Shakespeare, will remain unfinished. We live in a time when the most unusual works are attempted but do not succeed.

—Voltaire on Laurence Sterne

"I believe, señor," said Rebecca, "that you have studied the workings of the human heart inside out, and that geometry is the truest path to happiness."   —Jan Potocki, *The Manuscript Found in Saragossa*

It was by dint of hearing a great many such sneers at faith that Brother Juniper became convinced that the world's time had come for proof, tabulated proof . . .   —Thornton Wilder, *The Bridge of San Luis Rey*

A NOTE FROM ANDREI BITOV

I suppose I ought to forestall the reader's surprise at what follows by providing an explanation. Long ago, in my pre-literary youth, during my remote "geological" past, I came across a book entitled *The Teacher of Symmetry* by an obscure English author. I took it along with me on a lengthy geological expedition, with the salutary goal of self-education. Whether due to laziness, overexertion, or the withering glances of my companions, however, I never opened a page the entire summer.

Suddenly, it was autumn. The weather had turned foul, our helicopter was delayed, and we were waiting for the skies to clear. All our reading matter had been read and reread, all our games had been played and replayed. To my misfortune, someone recalled having seen me with a book in a foreign language, and even though I did not fully understand either the language or the subject, it nevertheless fell to my lot to recount its contents amid the unremitting rain.

Without a dictionary, hazarding guesses to the point of fabrication, I jotted it all down in a notebook—one story a day. Like Scheherazade. My ordeal was over when our helicopter was finally able to land. I was glad to surrender both the book and my torment to the oblivion of that sodden taiga.

About ten years later, something extraordinary, something that beggared belief, happened to me. I found that only a certain story from that forgotten book could offer the solace and support I needed. The story rose to the surface of my consciousness with such clarity and force it seemed I had read it just the day before. Today I can no longer recall the extraordinary event in my own life that prompted my memory of the story.

I rummaged in my attic through a flotsam of stray oars and skis for the manuscript of my desultory "translation." As I began remembering some of the other stories in the book, the book thus recounted took firm hold of my imagination. I then vowed that I would find the original text—but I had forgotten the name of the author. There was something non-English about it. Perhaps Dutch, or even Japanese? No, I just couldn't remember. I tried asking the experts, dredging up the contents for them, but to no avail. No one had ever heard of it.* Years have passed since that sudden mental "reread" of the book, and still I cannot put it out of my head. Alas, I never found it again.

To cope with the importunity of the phantom book (I hadn't thought it all up myself, after all!), I began little by little to "translate" it, not as one translates texts but as one applies waterslide decals. There was, to be sure, conjecture involved. (Let the passages that falter somewhat be mine alone.) After I had recovered a few of them, I forgot the original once and for all (as I had forgotten that unspeakable event in my own life). There was no making heads or tails of it anymore. Now, instead of recollections about a lost book, I was burdened with the responsibility for the manuscripts it had spawned. And so I decided to rid myself of them, too, and thus to forget about the whole business.

I knew nothing of the author's biography. Perhaps he had endowed his protagonist (Urbino Vanoski), also a writer, with some features of his own life? Born in the early 1900s. Random, mixed origins (Polish, Italian, and a dash of Japanese). Belated entry into the language of his future literary oeuvre†—hence, certain linguistic quirks and a style that is somewhat *recherché*. For example, the author perceived the complex system of tenses in English in a very literal manner, and ascribed

---

*In Washington, D.C., Lord Billington, the director of the Library of Congress, asked me (purely out of politeness, I'm sure) what I was working on. He was tall and thin, and reminded me somewhat of the protagonist of *The Teacher*. So I blurted out that I was doing a remake of something by an obscure English writer, but that I couldn't for the life of me find a copy of the original. "Oh," Lord B. said, "if it was published even once, we are sure to have it in our collection." When we met at a reception a few days later, he seemed rather abashed to have to tell me that the book didn't exist. I felt even more awkward. *(Andrei Bitov's note [hereafter: A. B.])*

†Had Tired-Boffin's contemporary, the future author of *The Real Life of Sebastian Knight*, read him? *(A. B.)*

each fragment of text to a corresponding temporal category, organizing his titles according to a table he had devised.

I managed to pen it down:

	Present	Past	Future	Future in the Past
Indefinite	Freud's Family Doctor	The Talking Ear	The King of Britannica	The Inevitability of the Unwritten
Progressive	Pigeon Post	Future in the Past	A Couple of Coffins from a Cup of Coffee	Doomsday
Perfect	Bach's Spring	The History of Histories	The Centennial of Abolishing the Calendar	No Idea
Same Author	My Father in Paradise	The Monkey Link	Nothing About Japan	Back from the Earth

Altering the names of works is the first liberty a translator is permitted. And this was the first thing I did:

	Present	Past	Future	Future in the Past
Indefinite	O: Number or Letter?	The End of the Sentence	The Battle of Alphabetica	Posthumous Notes of the Tristram Club
Progressive	The Last Case of Letters	View of the Sky Above Troy	The Absentminded Word	Emergency Call
Perfect	Mozart's Ear	The History of the 2Xth Centuries	The Centennial of Abolishing the Calendar	The Gospel According to the Tempter
Perfect Progressive	Something About Love	The Burning Novel	Auto-geography	Buried Alive

That was just a diversion. Russian grammar resists such pecu-
liarities—which are, by definition, untranslatable.

Now the only thing that remained for me to do was to translate the
elusive book into Russian. I offer my efforts to the sophisticated reader
with trepidation, taking recourse in a passage from my favorite author:

> However this may be, in anticipation of my celebrated quarto
> I intend to share several excerpts from my notebook with you. I
> should like to warn you in advance that it is rife with theft: for
> every page of my own it happens that there are sometimes ten
> pages of pure translation, and then as many pages again of ex-
> tracts. It would be pointless to grace the pages with references
> to the sources from which I have purloined. Some of the works
> you would never be able to find; others you would not wish to
> read. The books are manifold—some sensible, some senseless:
> medical, mathematical, philosophical, and some falling into
> none of the aforementioned categories. I make a deep bow in
> advance to all those victims of my plunder; few in our time are
> capable of such candor. [from V. F. Odoevsky, *Letters to Countess
> E.P.R. on Apparitions, Superstitious Fears, Deceived Emotions,
> Magic, Cabbalism, Alchemy, and Other Mysteries*]

Each chapter of *The Teacher* may be read as a stand-alone piece. The
reader is free to take the chapters on their own merits as individual
stories; but if one manages to read all of them in sequence and hears
an echo carrying over from each story to the next, from any one story
to any other, one will have discovered the echo's source—and will be
reading instead a novel, not merely a collection of stories.

1971, Rybachy settlement (formerly Rossitten), Russia

P.S. 2008
The 1970s were upon us. In Russia, no one heard anything, saw anything, or traveled anywhere outside the country. Myself included. This
was why my companions were eager to sit through my oral account of
the book, however inexactly I quoted from it, thinking: Well, how about
that? The world is full of peculiar things. I would ask the modern

reader to respect the translator's labors to the same degree and in the same manner that the translator respects the efforts of the reader: from the first word to the last.

The author of this translation would like to express his gratitude to the places where it came into being:

The Rybachy Biological Station, Russian Academy of Sciences (formerly Rossitten), Kaliningrad Oblast, 1969–1975;
Peredelkino House of the Arts, 1967–1977;
The village of Goluzino in the Antropovsky region of the Kostroma Oblast, 1978–1985;
Petropavlovskaya Street and Dostoevsky Street in Leningrad, 1986;
New York and Princeton, U.S.A., 1995–1997;
The Baltic Centre, the island of Gotland, Sweden, 2007;
Hotel Alpengut, Elmau, Bavaria, 2008.

I would also like to thank Zuger Kulturstiftung Landis & Gyr, Zug, Switzerland, who offered me material support for completing my translation.

Andrei Bitov

PART I

VIEW OF THE SKY ABOVE TROY

(Future in the Past)

A flash of lightning,
A drop of dew,
An apparition—
A thought about oneself.
                    —Prince Ikkyū

I am the only person in the world who might have been able to shed light on the mysterious death of Urbino Vanoski. Alas, it is not within my power. What makes a legend a legend is its immutability.

This is the way he died, or, rather, was reborn in the minds of readers and critics—in complete obscurity, ignorant of his own fame, and poor as a church mouse (I would not resort to this idiom if it were not literally true: according to legend, he lived out his final days as a churchwarden, selling devotional candles). His grave is unmarked, and this is only fitting. Obscurity during one's lifetime fans the flames of posthumous glory, and the nonexistent gravestone gives off a scorching heat. For him, the literary prize for lifetime achievement remains forever posthumous. Having established a foundation in his honor, we—Vanoski scholars all—began to meet annually on the Adriatic Sea. After each session, we publish a volume of our proceedings that we ourselves read, leaving no trace of our efforts which might be of any benefit to potential geniuses languishing as churchwardens.

Vanoski, an obscure author from the 1930s, enjoyed a veritable boom at the end of the sixties. This was due solely to the efforts of the permanent chairman of the foundation, V. Van-Boek. I would be banished in disgrace from the close-knit ranks of my colleagues if I so much as raised an eyebrow about the veracity of the myth he has so carefully constructed. No one would believe me. I would be refuted categorically, and accused of fabrication. And then where would I take my annual vacation?

Incidentally, Urbino Vanoski was not a churchwarden. He was an elevator operator, and died (or perhaps he is not dead at all?) fully aware of his sudden fame and his Grand Prize. Fully aware. For it was I who found him before his death (or not before, whatever the case may be). I was the last one to see him, to pass on the happy news to him. And I was the last one to interview him. It was not even so much an interview as a confession. I do not know why he chose me for this task—perhaps because he disliked me the moment he laid eyes on me. One is well advised not to believe everything that was revealed in the course of this confession. I have grounds to suspect that his mind was no longer absolutely sound. When I asked him how he felt about receiving such a high prize, he answered that he expected a higher one. "Which might that be?" I asked him. "Death," he said. He became particularly irate when I asked about what he was working on just then. "Thank God I have never been a worker!" he spluttered. I tried to rectify matters by asking what he was writing. "I'm not. I'm painting! Landscapes. Why do you bother to ask me what I'm writing, anyway, if you haven't read what has already been written?" I took this to mean that there was an unpublished book in the works. "Don't get your hopes up," he broke in. "I know, of course, that every decent writer is supposed to leave a respectable posthumous work in his wake." I couldn't resist the temptation to swoop down on this morsel. "Well, yes, as a matter of fact there is," he said reluctantly. "There is an unfinished novel. It's called *Life Without Us* . . . or *Buried Alive*? I don't remember the name myself! Besides, it's unlikely I'll finish it . . . Life will."

"Is it about life in the beyond?" I said, pondering.

"About life here and now," he said, angered. "How can one possibly know which side is beyond, and which is here?"

It is likely that I looked somewhat deflated. He regarded me as though I were a child, and again his eyes blazed.

"There is one novel, perhaps nearly finished, but I can't find it. I'm not surprised, however, for it is called *Disappearing Objects*. It's about—well, no. I won't try to retell it. That would be 'tasteless impropriety.'

"Have you ever clean forgotten a word? You know the word, but your tongue is incapable of catching hold of it . . . You say that happens to everyone? But then you remember the word eventually. What if you forget it for all time, and can never recover it? I was once in the possession of such a word—a key word. I recalled it on one occasion, but at that very moment I was caught in a storm and forgot it once and for all. To this very day. It is, of course, significant that it was that particular word, and that I was the one who forgot it. Have you ever observed how sunflowers remember the sun, so they won't forget it before morning?" The old man's eyes glittered. "Perhaps you would like me to paint you a landscape? Very well, then. I will. It will be a landscape that no one apart from the ancient Greeks has ever seen."

"Such sunflower fields must surely have existed in ancient Greece. Dika and I saw them when we were together in Italy. No, not the ancient one," he said, pointing to his calf. "Right there, in Umbria. There was an enormous sunflower field. We passed it on our way up into the mountains to watch the sunrise and sunset. Everyone knows that sunflowers always turn toward the sun. They drink in every little ray. They've even copied it onto their faces, like children. We walked past them, smiling, and they smiled back at us. At sunset, however, they looked more organized, more preoccupied, like a regiment of soldiers waiting for orders. It seemed they wanted to catch the very last drop of sunlight. Then, suddenly, the whole regiment would turn away from the sun, showing us the backs of their cleanly shaven heads. Uncanny. Did they feel insulted by the sun, as though it had done them some injury?

"I was only able to explain it to myself in this way: They were preparing to greet the first ray, and not to see off the last. They use the energy of the setting sun to turn and face the rising sun. They must derive more benefit from the light of the sun as it is coming up. Dika rejected my theory. Unlike me, she knew a thing or two about biology. But she was always more drawn to fauna, whereas I was attracted by flora. I spoke to her of sunflowers, she spoke to me of goats. 'Why,' she said, 'do they always go up a slope in a single direction? It must be awkward, always the same way. They never turn around.' I explained to her that she was referring to a special breed, a mountain goat. The right legs are shorter than the left ones. 'But what happens when they come back down?' Dika fretted about them. 'They'll topple over!' 'They just go round in a circle their whole lives' was the solution I offered her. And she believed me. She was so very gullible."

The old man suddenly grew stern. He continued.

"You see, life is a piece of writing that the living never read to the end. But writing is alive, too! Every line contains the secret of the line that follows. So it is in life—the next moment is always To Be Announced, always in abeyance. We're not sunflowers, we're mountain goats. In America she wondered about how the Americans found enough turkey legs to go around on Thanksgiving Day. I told her that the Americans had bred a special four-legged turkey to prevent a shortfall, and this satisfied her." He blew his nose and mopped his teary eyes.

I have reason to suspect that he was no longer in his right mind. Could I later publish all this nonsense? I could. It would cause a sensation, at the very least. I was young, I dreamed of fame. Fortunately, one seasoned reporter dissuaded me, warning me that I would lose my job if I did. And, really, who was ı? My sensational article was sure to founder on the cliff of the myth that had grown up around Vanoski. Sometimes it seems to me that the myth had shattered the poor elevator operator himself. As if his own elevator had snapped off its cables. It could so easily have crushed him. But, then again, who would have wanted to take his life?

Perhaps the other story would be better after all—in the church, selling votive candles, cherishing no thoughts of grandeur? An easy, light-filled death.

"So it's nothing out of the ordinary when some stranger—fat, bald, sweaty—sits down next to you in the Garden Park. In fact, he doesn't so much sit down as flop down beside you, with a 'Phew! Made it, for once.' He composes himself, airing himself out, his sweat drying in the April sun, and says, still panting a bit, 'Now then, Urbino. There isn't a whole lot I know how to do, but I *can* show you a photograph of yourself . . .' If something like that ever happens to you, as it did to me, don't register surprise, and don't give it a moment's thought. Simply send the gentleman packing. Sending someone packing is always a sound philosophy. It's the wisdom of dignity. This is something I came to understand only much later. Though despite understanding it, it's a kind of prowess I have never been able to muster to this day."

Here, old Urbino Vanoski heaved a deep sigh, raising his beautiful eyes to mine. Never had I seen a gaze of such directness and such meekness rolled into one. Still, he averted his eyes in consternation the very next moment, lest I think that his philosophy held true for me, as well. Though how could it not? As a correspondent for the *Thursday Evening Post* and *Yesterday's News*, I was interviewing him. We sat in his tiny lair, which was so clean and empty that it felt spacious. The only real piece of furniture was a dilapidated plywood wardrobe.

It would have been a bona fide prison cell, had it not been for the subservience of the surroundings: he was not the prisoner of the room, but rather the tiny room was the prisoner of his gaze. The room was the frame of its dweller's face, and his face framed his own eyes. Their relationship to one another was somehow reversed—a face in a gaze, a room in a face. His little shoebox of a room nestled right under the roof, and through the slanted window neither the courtyard nor the roofs beyond were visible, just a scrap of sky with a cloudlet floating in the frame. I sat on a solitary bentwood chair, quite rickety. Vanoski sat on a narrow folding cot. His long, perfectly clean-shaven face was as spare as his room. He had a youthful expression that for some reason accentuated his age, lending depth to it. Ah, how empty, how pristine, how well-considered it all was, so that he could part with every moment of existence, leaving no outstanding debts to the world at large. This room accommodated nothing else but me—but my body, despite its robust plumpness and the impropriety of my health and desire to exist, felt a sensation like heat from a kitchen hearth, or maybe it was the coolness of a crypt. Either I had arrived here from another dimension, or my body was itself another dimension . . .

Something in my perception had shifted. I kept confusing the external and internal planes of objects and phenomena—quite an unpleasant feeling. I stared with hostility at this maniac, who, nevertheless, had written *The Last Case of Letters*, a book so remarkable that only I could have written it, if I could have . . . With what enthusiasm I had

thrown myself into this unenviable task—to seek out the grave of the
mysterious Vanoski. And what do you know, I found it! Not the grave
but the man himself. And alive, to boot. Or was he? I found him—only
to freeze in the proximity of this minus-man, to marvel at the irony of
the foresight that offered me the ability—or, rather, the opportunity—
or even the hint of a possibility to create such a book . . . such power—in
the dead loins of a moribund man . . . with hot, pulsing envy to stumble
upon the futility of that envy, and to experience a painful awkwardness
besides, because you are pestering someone who has consciously removed
himself from life, as if this were your role—to cause him his last, living
pain. Any movement of mine would rend his fragile, ashen-gray cocoon,
like a child crushing an empty wasp's nest.

It now seemed to me that from the first glance, after I had stepped
inside the elevator with him, the old man saw his executioner in me—
his expression was so mournful, within the bounds of propriety and
good breeding, yet nearly bursting these bounds. He couldn't possibly
have looked at every passenger in that way. In other words, he was expecting me. At the same time (I was aware of this), he couldn't have
been waiting for *me*, because he no longer expected anything to come
from his books, no consequences thereof. He was anticipating someone
who could have been me but turned out not to be—this much I understood by how quickly his fear left him when I explained to him why
I had come. When it left him, however, I sensed that he felt not simply
relief but disappointment, in the same breath. He seemed bored, agitated, and bereft, to a degree that I could only guess at but never quite
grasp. I had no notion of that abyss of absence that swallows an author
who has evoked things so intimate and familiar to us all.

Vanoski said that he couldn't spare any time for me until the end of
his shift, so I decided to arrange for it to end immediately. Timid and
frightened, he tried to stop me. I announced that it would not trouble
me in the least. With the self-assurance of a young fool, I assumed that
this impoverished, unsung genius of an old man would be pleased with
the flurry of courtesy and servility his superiors would show upon learn-
ing of my mandate and credentials from *Yesterday's News*. And, indeed,
everything was as I had predicted: the supervisor began rushing
around—Certainly, by all means!—and let the old man take the whole
day off, finding a replacement for him without further ado. But the

pangs of torment in the old man's face from all this fuss and bother, from the fawning curiosity of others, from the cannibalistic lip-smacking at the gratuitousness of fame—the very anguish of his gaze—was something I didn't expect. It was the gaze that meets visitors to the zoo from inside the cages. I had destroyed the old man's balance of energy. The damage was done, and he knew it.

He was poised for a predetermined spectacle: the sensation of a new star—launched from the penury of nonexistence into the august ranks of great artists—overshadowed both the artist and his poverty. The hoopla was the content. Thus, the poor old man could not become himself in any sense of the word but had to remain that Vanoski whose legend had been born without him. The legend had to develop and grow while there was still time, but only according to the simplest rules of a fixed plot. The masterpiece created in poverty presupposes the poverty that creates a masterpiece—and positivism triumphs. I asked him how he had been able to write *The Last Case*, and he answered, "I don't know." I asked him what he would do with twenty thousand dollars and he answered, "I don't remember."

I might have called it quits then and there, because the old man couldn't be of any use to me. He had no needs himself, so he wouldn't appease me for our mutual advantage; and the newspaper wasn't interested in anything close to the truth. The truth might have intrigued me personally, but truth was far to seek, and time was short. There wasn't even anything to hold the gaze, not a thing for it to rest upon, in this clean-swept grave. There was only one object that ornamented the room, and a rather strange one at that, if one paid proper attention. It was a large-format photograph behind glass in a thin metal frame. For all intents and purposes, the photograph depicted nothing. It was empty, save for something that resembled a small cloud in one corner. The picture hung above the bed over the old man's head on the wall opposite the little window—like a second little window I could look out of, at the same time that the old man, sitting across from me, looked through the real one. This photograph could also have served as evidence of the oddity of genius: placing above the bed a view of one's own window, from which, in its turn, nothing is visible except a scrap of sky. Under the picture frame was a bronze nameplate with a florid engraved inscription. Would some vainglorious photographer really want to take credit for such a paltry work, I found myself wondering. Another object that would not have interested me in the least, had it not been for the behavior of the old man toward it, was something resembling a doorbell, also located above the bed, but slightly lower than the "picture." The doorbell was set flush into the wall so that only a button protruded from it—round, smooth, white, and fairly large for a doorbell. Apparently, the device had been installed just recently, because the patch of plaster encircling it was still slightly moist. Now and then the old man glanced at the button with something like trepidation, at the same time trying to conceal this from me by awkwardly pretending it was only by chance that his eyes had strayed to that place. I easily satisfied myself with the explanation that the doorbell was actually some sort of intercom, a means of summoning the old man to the elevator that required him to answer back. I interpreted his sidelong glances at it as the sign of a downtrodden wretch with a self-abasing nature.

"Your supervisor is not going to trouble you anymore today," I said to him as gently as I could, so that he would stop worrying and ignore the doorbell, though I already despaired of extracting anything useful from him.

"Thank you, I realize that," said the old man. Heavens, how that gaze inserted into his face astonished me! I couldn't help but think how sociologically predetermined perception is; for I had known very well whom I was seeking while my search was under way, but once I had found the object of my search, I lost track of the original. In this little shoebox I assigned to him a level of understanding characteristic of the lowliest rung on the social ladder. My God! If he had indeed written that, how clearly must things have appeared to him, how transparent must I have seemed to him all this time. I was suddenly so abashed about my own condescension that I leapt up out of my chair. To justify the abruptness of this action I pretended I had gotten up to read the inscription under the photograph. What I read was very peculiar. It said: VIEW OF THE SKY ABOVE TROY.

"Have you been to Troy?" I said.

"How could I have been there?" the old man said with a faint grin. "I wasn't around back then."

"Of course. I meant . . ." I muttered, stumbling over my foolishness. "I was referring to the spot where they recently discovered Troy had once been . . . I meant the modern-day Troy."

"No, that sky is the one in the other Troy, the other sky," the old man said in a monotone.

A chill ran down my spine. Like all young men, I had a horror of madness. What am I saying? I had never seen a single dead man in my entire life, not counting accident victims—and they aren't true corpses, not like one's own dead. And mad people? Only comical shadows amid the faceless crowd in the streets. But half-wittedness or dementia isn't the same as madness. Now I grew afraid of Vanoski. I averted my eyes and stared at his clothes cupboard.

In *The Last Case of Letters* (a novel about a poem) he has a passage . . . Oh, what a passage it is! I can't explain why it stirs me so every time; and I've reread it many times, playing it over and over like a favorite record, so . . . In it the protagonist is waiting for a letter to arrive from his beloved. It doesn't come, and, consumed with fear and passion, he walks through a wasteland by the shore of the sea. Suddenly, on a dune, he sees a dilapidated plywood cupboard, apparently washed up by the surf. In his agitation and haste he opens the door, and there's a letter. He frantically rips it open, fastens his eyes on it, sees that it begins: "Dear Urbino . . ." But it's impossible to read it through to the end. The page is covered with what look like words, letters of the alphabet, in her handwriting, and he drinks it all in, but—he can't seem to read it, and he tries to read the letter again and again, and can't. Then he rushes home, takes a seat, and dashes off a reply. And now—my God, what a description!—the words swirl around, the ink smokes, the text into which he pours all his passion flows—but at the end of every line the text disappears. His passion hangs poised in midair and disappears without a trace beyond the margins of the page. Instead of the phrases he has just uttered, something entirely different appears on the page, some nonsense about Aunt Clara and her parrot. Poor Urbino sobs with helplessness and drenches Aunt Clara in his tears; and when he is comforted he raises his transparent, flowing head, and recovers his strength and equanimity and writes a letter, now calmly and quickly, efficiently, but in fact he's just tracing out wavy lines—like a child painting the sea . . . Then his neighbor arrives, and they start conferring about a small mutual concern of long standing. They come to an agreement and go to the city of Taunus. And the passage that follows is so strong that I always make a singular effort to grasp the transition, but I just can't manage—I can no longer find the passage in the book, however much I leaf through it.

And now it seemed to me that I was standing on the brink of his madness, which whirled around in a vortex, so smoothly, so imperceptibly and seamlessly—a funnel that consciousness pours into like sand—that you don't even notice how you end up inside it, sliding along the breathtaking mathematical curvature, and peering out of a place from which there is no return . . .

"Yes, yes. I understand. That sky," I said, as though backing up warily within his gaze.

The old man grinned. "I have grounds to believe that this is the case. You are young . . . Also, does not the very same sky cover that Troy and this one, and us, and all those who come after us? There you have it, at least in a metaphorical sense."

"That's the truth!" I said, nodding, overjoyed at Vanoski's return to our mutually accepted stomping grounds of logic.

"I'm curious why figures of speech—an image, a metaphor—while distancing themselves from their object, seem to approach the truth, whereas the reality surrounding us seems to be senseless, littered with trivia, as though insufficiently generalized and abstract, and therefore untrue. It's quite the opposite! I don't think the time has come for you to understand this yet. I can only warn you—and, apparently, in vain. It is hardly likely that my personal experience will be of any use to you. Experience never is. And it's unlikely that you will meet with such an open-ended fate. In any case, my advice to you is, never agree to any tempting offers. You are a simple and selfless man"—the first epithet jarred me, and I was about to take offense, but at the second I nodded benignly—"and for that reason you accept everything offered to you as a gift, or as an adventure, or as fate. You grab hold of it like an unselfish person who is usually left empty-handed. Refuse any offer—it's always of the devil. That is why this is the real sky over Troy."

This was when he repeated the words of the fat bald man in the Garden Park—and, once again, I failed to understand him. It was also when he said that sending someone packing was always the best bet, and on his face was that look of anguish, a look of "Why did I fail to do it this time, too?"

"There is something you need from me, for *I* am certainly not what you need. Rather, you desperately need something you suspect to be here, in my place. Everyone is a tyrant over reality nowadays, a practitioner of progress. Assume, therefore, that I'm no longer here. But since you want something from me (even though I'm not what you need, and this is precisely why I keep the life around me at bay, because I always feel answerable to it), I am now obliged to respond, insofar as you are life, since you have come to me. But since you couldn't care less about me but are intent upon something you purport to need, I reserve the right to repay you in the only way I can. And this utter imbalance, albeit equal in weight, is the essence of the question and the answer.

"I will tell you about the picture. I have reason to want to draw closer to it now." Here again he pretended not to be looking at the button on the wall. "I think about it now unceasingly, so it will be fairly easy for me to relate it to you. Whether you need me to or not is up to you. You came to me yourself, of your own volition, so it's not at all surprising that I am the one here in front of you—though you are of no concern to me whatever."

"So was he the devil?" I said, growing angry at this sermon.

"Must there always be horns?" Vanoski said, frowning impatiently. "And his eyes were as blue as blue can be—not burning coals. Even his baldness seemed intentional, as proof there were no horns to speak of. Fat. Corpulence disarms suspicion—that's folk wisdom. Only later did I come to appreciate the extent of his good nature. He was not at all insistent. He didn't try to deceive me in the least—temptation has nothing to do with deception. We are tempted solely through our own devices. Perhaps he really did sit down beside me just by chance—to take a breather, as it was so hot.

"The English, as everyone knows, are garrulous. Perhaps this is why we spread the myth of our reserve and taciturnity: we try to cover up that particular vice of ours. In any event, I didn't fail to take exception to the stranger's audacity, saying I didn't believe we had met, and so forth.

"He seemed somehow unwelcome and out of place in every way—to me in particular. And, overall, that's how he looked: unseemly and inappropriate. I was young, like you. I had strong notions about myself—the vaguer and more obscure they were, the more I fancied them. Especially when I didn't have a farthing in my pocket. Notions of love . . . of fame and glory. I was quite carried away by my own thoughts. And it was all the more unpleasant to catch myself in the middle of them . . . At that particular moment some shadowy beautiful creature, for some reason dressed in an Indian sari, standing on the shore of a turquoise

sea, was pressing my rose to her breast . . . And I took exception to him
with the icy dignity of a true Brit.

"'What do you mean—you're not Urbino?' the fat man blurted
out. Only then did the awkwardness of the situation that my diffidence
had created dawn on me. He had, however, already opened his shape-
less, beat-up briefcase and dropped his fleshy thief's paw into the contents. It seemed to me that he was rummaging around and stealing
from his own briefcase.

"'Perhaps this isn't you, then?' He plucked out a photograph like
something from a flower bed, and thrust it under my nose in triumph.

"But it was *not* me at all! That is to say, it could have been anyone.
Half the face was obscured by some apparatus that looked partly like a
camera, partly like a fantastical weapon whose muzzle resembled a rifle.
In any case, the character in the photograph seemed to be aiming at
something, and the half a face that wasn't obscured by the apparatus in
his hands was wincing and distorted. And he was dressed queerly, in a
whimsical, foreign style. I said, mastering my recent confusion, that it
was certainly not me.

"'Not you?' the fat man said, finally taking a good look at the
photograph. 'Drat it, what an old fool I am!' His disappointment was
unfeigned. 'I do beg your pardon.' Here he began to cringe in annoyance, as if giving himself a slap in the face with the photograph.

"'Stop this improper clownery,' I said coldly.

"'You cannot imagine what an unpardonable mistake I've made,
and how I will have to pay for this!' he wailed. 'Never in my life has
this happened to me before. Truly, this is not you. This is a photograph
of one of your future acquaintances. But yours is here, too. Honestly . . .
I swear it . . . None other than the devil has mixed everything up.'
Again he gestured toward himself, but more gently now. 'Don't be angry.
Just give me a moment.'

"He rummaged and rummaged through his briefcase, pulling out
thick piles of photographs of various sizes and eras, as though they
had been purloined from myriad amateur photographers and family
albums—underexposed and overexposed, stained with developer,
with jagged blobs of glue stuck to them and torn-off corners.

"'Where could it have gone?' A rare sampling of artistic ineptitude
passed before my eyes: here was a client without a head, though wearing

a coat of armor; then there was a single hand holding a glass; next there appeared a bush with one blurred branch, as if the picture depicted an attempt to photograph a bird as it flew away. 'You are very observant,' he said, continuing his search, 'which is why I sat down beside you. It is uncommon for someone to spy a bird on that branch right off the bat. One has to be a born poet for that. And that happens no more than three or four times a century. Well, like you, for example, or . . . But you're not an admirer of the Lake Poets, are you? By the way, it was precisely this bird that inspired . . . Well, never mind, it doesn't matter. What I mean to say is that these are all absolutely random shots. They mean nothing at all. This one, for example, is Shakespeare. And don't think it's the moment when he wrote his "To be or not to be" monologue. Nor is it a meeting with the Dark Lady, or with Francis Bacon. Here he is, looking tired after a performance.' In the photograph was a faience basin with a broken rim, certainly outmoded in shape; but from it protruded two ordinary naked feet, either crooked themselves, or placed crookedly in the vessel. One toe stuck out in such a way that it looked like the legs it belonged to were busy at something down there in the basin, and a stream of water was pouring from the upper-right corner of the photograph into the mouth of the vessel. That was all.

"'No, I am not a madman, still less a photographer or dreamer, which you have just suspected me of being. These pictures are, in fact, capable of far less than the actual possibilities of fantasy allow. These things I'm holding in my hands are historical originals, believe it or not. Ah, now you have hit upon a wonderful thought: Why should histori-cal fact appear more precise or attractive than what I have in my hands? History happens right in front of our eyes, I must agree with you there.' He was quite deft at guessing all my thoughts, and he did this just when I was either about to call him out and put him in his place, or simply stand up and leave, thus throwing off his unbearable obtrusive-ness. But his angle on things, which you would later call the close-up shot, was very amusing from a poetic point of view. Here a line of poetry pecked its way out with heady facility: mud under the hooves of Alexander the Great's troops, waves closing down over the *Titanic*, clouds floating past above Homer's head . . . What did that mud know about the triumphant hoof? What did the water care about the trea-sures of the Spanish Armada? What need had the sky of verse?

"'And here is the chink in the floor where the light squeezes through,' the purveyor of pictures muttered to himself, but simultaneously with the line that had just before entered my head. 'Not bad. Not bad at all. You see? I knew you were the very one I could trust. Possibly the only one, in our day and age. No, this isn't flattery. I am not your garden-variety medium or swindler. Honestly, what is so special about anyone's head that it should be considered a miracle to guess what's inside it? Then again, what would I gain from it? Indulge my own talents by leading astray a gullible mind? That is a consideration, of course, but I am not so petty in my conceit. I have more humble, though less romantic, models than a Mephistopheles or Cagliostro. Now science fiction is all the rage. H. G. Wells, for example—*The Time Machine*. No, you scoff because you are still young. His style isn't bad at all. I would even go so far as to say its Englishness is quite pleasant to the ear. It's rare nowadays. It's a childlike pleasure . . . He's no Dickens, of course. But then again, begging your pardon, you and I are no Dickens, either. What do you mean boorish, when it's only the truth? But I must agree with you that there is always a tinge of vulgarity in the truth. Because not everyone has the right, although, not everyone has the gift, either . . .

"'Take a look, however, at this highly curious photograph: a box with the head of Mary, Queen of Scots. I can vouch for its authenticity. Both the box and the head. No, no, it's not just the box *for* the head. At the moment it was photographed, the head was inside. Calm down, don't get so upset! Just imagine, in the spirit of fantasy, albeit poor, of the H. G. Wells you do not approve of, that such a thing is possible, that I am the inventor of a time machine . . . Can you imagine the difficulties one runs up against before one achieves anything? A dearth both of parts and of finances. No livelihood. They kick you out of your apartment. On the pilot flight you don't even have an amateur camera, let alone a professional one. No money even for a sandwich to take along for sustenance! Ah, at last. Here it is. But I warn you—no, on second thought, I'd rather you didn't see it. I shouldn't have insisted, you'll take it the wrong way.'

"I was already clutching the photograph when he tried to snatch it out of my hand again. I grew really angry. I was on the verge of punching the lights out of this impertinent gentleman.

"'Oh, no, young man, let's not succumb to brutality. Or else I might

decide not to show you. But have it your way. I won't go back on my
promise, if you will be so kind as to hear me out and remember what I
am about to say to you. And it is mandatory that you believe me. And
I swear on I-don't-know-what, since you seem to reject everything about
me, that I am not deceiving you. I am holding a photograph of you. It is
from your future, a not too distant one. When? I know, but I won't tell
you, for then you'll be expecting it, and I don't wish to spoil it ahead of
time. You do have a future. I know both the year and the day. What do
you mean, when? How impatient you young ones are! Well, not in five
years, let's say . . . You're now just about twenty-one. You dream of love
and glory. Oh, I know what kind! Top-notch. You have the right to it;
and, what's more, the opportunity is yours, now, and in the future. So,
not in five years but fewer than ten, certainly . . . No, I'm not talking
about success, I'm talking about this picture. It's just as random and
meaningless as the others you have seen. Just as authentic, but also just
as random, as the others. You may consider me a poetry worshipper
who was unable to hold out and depict you as you would one day become. All right. Here, take it . . . But mark my words. This is a random
moment, not biographical fact. For your amusement, as it were . . .'

"I no longer heard his admonitions. I fixed my eyes greedily on the
image, which happened to be much clearer and sharper than Shakespeare's legs or the Lake Poet bird. The face of an unfamiliar young
man reflected in a shopwindow stared back at me. He was older than
me by some ten years, perhaps a bit less, but he looked far more mascu-
line. His face was attractive, albeit distorted by the kind of sorrow and
shock that one rarely sees in a living face, much less one captured in a
photograph. It was like a mask suited to a myth in which the hero turns
to stone from an encounter with a monster. Perhaps even Medusa herself
wore such an expression when she beheld her own reflection. In short,
the reflection was striking, though it originated in the display window
of an ordinary shop selling ready-made clothing, between two mannequins, male and female, who seemed to be striding toward one another
with outstretched arms. Their arms, however, bracketed something
horrible, something that the One Who Was Reflected saw, as well. The
One Who Was Reflected saw Her. And She could not possibly have
inspired that kind of horror. There was nothing horrible about Her.
Nor was there anything benign.

"Sometimes beauty can astound or shock. That's what books tell us. That was not the case here. A pale moth—that's what I said to myself in the first moments. I couldn't take my eyes off her, however. What did He see in Her? Perhaps this is what it's like to peer into Fate? Perhaps this is what Fate looks like? Her garments were unprepossessing, too— the clothes of a woman who was indifferent to her appearance: comfortable, but no more. On her arm she carried a shopping bag. Long, ash-colored hair, tousled, as though it was rearing up. A slattern. That's what a slattern looks like, I said to myself. I was fascinated. Those eyes! I couldn't unfasten my gaze from hers. A wide forehead, pale thick brows, eyes that were more gray than blue (the photograph was black-and-white)—but large, luminous eyes, eyes that were somehow rectangular, and spaced enchantingly, at an improbable distance from either side of the bridge of her nose. Her cheekbones were also impossibly wide; but this you wouldn't notice, so wide apart were the eyes. They almost looked out of different sides of her face, like a fish. A fish, I said to myself. A moth, a slattern, a fish, that's what I said. But no one was as slender underneath her clothing as she was . . .

"No. I can't recount it. I don't recall what I saw first, and what I only discerned afterward, in what order it happened . . . That's very important, the order. The first thing I registered was the shocked expression on his face. Then there was perplexity about hers: it didn't contain anything that would elicit such shock. Then her reflected face, more pallid and washed-out than his, but also surprised. Then his reflection, as though distorted from horror of itself—horror from witnessing its own shock. For a fraction of a second the photograph came to life and turned around, as if someone else entered or left the store at that moment, and the glass door swung open . . . But first he looked at her, and she looked at the window; then he looked at the window, and she looked at him.

"The photograph is fixed in my memory, I see it before me now, as we speak. Oh, I studied it as I never studied anything before in my life. But perhaps there were altogether three photographs, like frames in a film. Or for a fleeting moment the photograph became stereoscopic, so that you seemed to see behind the backs of the people in it . . .

"'Don't attach any meaning to it . . . Pure chance . . . Just a detail . . . Don't believe anything . . . I shouldn't have . . . I didn't think you'd . . .'

"His prattle grated on my ears and forced me at last to unfasten my gaze from this admittedly rather insignificant picture. But the madman was gone.

"I thought I caught a glimpse of his back at the end of the park, though perhaps it was no longer him. I wanted to run after him, but for some reason I remained sitting. I don't know how long I stayed there, staring at the end of the park, hypnotized by his disappearance; but when the photograph dropped from my hands onto the ground, I came to. So there *was* a photograph! I bent over mechanically and picked it up . . . It wasn't the same photograph. But I had caught a glimpse of this one, too, when he was rummaging through his brief-case: a cloud . . . *View of the Sky Above Troy*. Yes, the very picture that hangs in my room.

"Does it not seem to you that the plot of the *Iliad* is somewhat strange? Even contrived? I understand that now it's beyond discussion. The *Odyssey*, as the follow-up to the story, is more recognizable to us. There's nothing more to do there but sail and sail. Waves . . . But Helen . . . The paeans to Helen through the centuries are far more real than she is. No, it wasn't her indescribable, or, rather, never yet described, never yet depicted, beauty that thrilled and still thrills poets, but the very fact of her existence, the fact that she lived at all. There has never been any proof of this, except that she was the reason the Trojan War was waged. The war must be explained somehow, don't you think? The war happened, but was Helen the cause? And was there a Helen at all? It is not Helen whom the poets love, but the cause that resides in her. The reason her image can be summoned up ad infinitum is because she her-self never really was. Naturally, I immediately dubbed the stranger in the photo Helen; but it was initially only because of the incomprehensible cloud. At that time I didn't think about things in the way I am explain-ing them to you now. Not about the *Iliad*, nor about the *Odyssey*. I didn't know that the war was already lost, that I was already sailing away . . . Isn't it strange that you and I can see clouds that Homer couldn't see? Have you ever imagined yourself blind? Everyone imagines it . . . What does a blind man see? Night? No. Endless waves."

Vanoski's face went blank. I was no longer there in front of him. It even seemed to me that I saw waves in his gaze; but this was fear. He was again staring at that absurd white button on the wall. Was it the button he feared, or was he afraid I would ask him its purpose? In any case, that was precisely what I intended to ask him, but he made sure to interrupt me just then.

"You ask what the upshot of all this was?" I hadn't asked, but he seemed to want to bring the narrative to a close. "After that everything happened very simply, and too smoothly. Without a hitch. No, I didn't fall in love with her immediately. I'm not a soldier, I don't fall in love with pinup girls. Besides, I was already in love. I laughed at myself with the mockery of youth, which is the way youth tries to free itself from the embarrassment that someone might notice its ineptitude. No one noticed. And shaking off the devilish delusions as something so irrelevant to my charmed, resilient life that they could, therefore, never have happened, I thrust the 'cloud' carelessly into my notebook and hurried on to where I had been heading from the start—only I was running ahead of schedule, which is how I had ended up on the park bench. I hurried off to meet my Dika.

"She was Eurydice. Eurydika—though Dika was what I called her. No, she was not yet mine. You think this is all too Greek? But her father actually was Greek, although she didn't remember him, or her birthplace, for that matter. She had grown up with her mother in Paris. I didn't remember my father, or my birthplace in Poland, either. Now we had both become dubious Britons. This bound us together. We studied in the same department. She first, and I joined later. She was younger but outstripped me by a mile in scholarship, while I was trying my hand at poetry. She coached me in the history of poetry so that I could pass from year to year, by the skin of my teeth. She liked teaching me, and I liked being her slow-witted student. Our own subject evolved slowly. We had already started kissing. Oh, we had a world of time back then!

"And now, half a century later, when I need nothing but dull, unremitting calm, I suppose that there is such a thing as happiness. Because that's what it was! With our heads buried in our books in Eurydice's tiny room, time had no ending and no beginning—it simply was. It lived in this room like a warm, languid cat, and had no intention of leaving. It was true, I had no special liking for the Lake Poets. I remember we struggled over them for a long time—but nobody had lips or voices sweeter than our own. If only we had known then how precious it all really was! They were the most minuscule living quarters

I had ever seen. Believe me, it was half the size of this little shoebox of mine! The apartment was located right next to my old grade school, and I felt that we had grown up together. We remembered childhood games we had both played: tic-tac-toe, kick the can, battleships . . . We got lost in our games until long past midnight. 'Sleep! Sleep!' her beloved African gray parrot shrieked. How did he get here? I wondered. Where did he find room to fit? The room was piled high with books of erudition I couldn't grasp, and small souvenirs, impossibly naïve. They had a habit of spilling over and spreading. I threw myself into the task of picking them up, but she tried to discharge me from my duties. She said I mixed everything up. We would crawl around on our hands and knees, gleaning together, though crawling there was difficult. Between the table and the bed there was no room to pass each other, and we bumped heads. That was what led to our first kiss."

Vanoski was overcome with emotion. Witnessing his childlike raptures, I felt uncomfortably aware of my own youth, of the freshness of yesterday's kisses on my lips.

"Bookishness and tenderness," he babbled on. "Oh, she was the most enchanting bluestocking that ever lived. Though, incidentally, she didn't like blue. She liked all kinds of red—roomy sweaters, long skirts . . . beads, bracelets; at home she even wore them on her ankles. I crawled around on the floor and picked up books whose very titles made me cringe, and I loved them—as long as they were closed. I gathered up this debris: a jumble of castanets, bast shoes, African masks, tea tins, generic greeting cards and postcards she loved receiving from distant parts of the world, and photographs of herself that were very dear to her, because she felt she looked better in pictures than in real life. But how wrong she was! I picked it all up, then let it drop and scatter again, pretending to pluck a volume out of the middle of a pile by mistake, only to cause another avalanche. Then she would tear herself away, flushed and lovely in her shy embarrassment, and begin to make coffee for us. She prepared it over a camp stove in some forlorn Turkish—not Greek—saucepan, and I sneaked up behind her. The coffee boiled over, of course, and she was angry with me, because she was especially proud of her secret coffee-making method, which she always bungled.

"She was rather lofty with me whenever we met, and we continued to address one another formally. The books were arranged in neat piles up to the ceiling, poised for their next tumble. We were sitting sedately at the desk, which doubled as a dinner table.

"'What is that stone?' she said, opening up my notebook. I had completely forgotten about it!

"'That isn't a stone. It's a cloud.'

"I wanted to tell her all about the recent episode, but I couldn't. Another photograph took shape before my very eyes, and there was the face of the stranger looking out at me.

"'Hello,' Eurydice called to me. 'Anybody home?'

"'Oh, you mean that photograph,' I said, turning red. 'That's your homeland, by the way. A view of the Trojan sky.'

"'You are a true poet,' Eurydice said. 'Did you mean for me to have it?'

"'Of course it's for you,' I rushed to say. Yes, she was the one who had it framed. That's how it all began. Or, rather, how everything eventually ended, too.

"Believing in the impossible is the easiest thing of all for us. It starts out as a bluff, an absurdity, mere delirium—and then it becomes an enticing mirage, a seductive vision. At the same instant that I wrote off the ridiculous meeting in the park as something that had never happened, I believed unconditionally in the authenticity of the photograph I had seen. The cloud may not have been the same cloud, but it was without doubt my reflection in the shopwindow, so the one who was reflected in the window was also me. Consequently, the woman who had been reflected in the window was the one I had seen. And it was She! Because it was undeniable that it had been me. The longer I stared at the picture—and it was pinned to the inner side of my forehead, as though on a screen—the less doubt there was about it. Even the slightest shadow of one.

"It was me, only some seven years older—and I found myself quite appealing, like an object I might want to possess. During those seven years I had traversed a clear path as yet unknown to me, and by the end of that time I had a certain face—and not the kind of pleasant, unassuming countenance that might have appealed to anyone else but me. I was particularly impressed with the slightly sunken cheeks and sprinkling of gray in my hair. It's nothing new, but it's a fact: in our youth we rush headlong toward our final days, and, indeed, cover most of the distance toward death in a flash. Then, just before the finish line, we hit the brakes with all our might. But what chance do our doddering, old man's brakes have against the momentum of the youthful energy we had when we threw ourselves into the race?

"There could be no doubt that it was me in the photograph, and my future face was quite to my liking—but why on Earth was it so contorted? What could have shaken me so profoundly? For as far as my experience went, and insofar as I could imagine my future, there was no reason for me to wear such an expression. Indeed, even on other faces I had never seen the like—except, perhaps, in literature, in some children's fare: 'His face was contorted with indescribable pain and torment, despair and horror.' But I scrutinized this photograph through and through, and grew convinced that the provincial stage set, the pretend scenery of the outskirts of town, were this time not in the least counterfeit. They were genuine. If something like this could happen to someone—and not just anyone, but to me—then what was it? Here there was no longer any uncertainty, anything equivocal, in the matter: it was She. Call her what you will: the woman of one's dreams, or Fate itself. I didn't like her. She was not to my taste. I couldn't take my eyes off her. I never thought about how lovely 'my' Dika was. I had no need to account for this to myself. I wasn't aware of how very lovely Dika was; for everything about her was lovely. It didn't matter to me what she looked like. One 'looks like' something for others, and I sought no comparison, for she existed only for me. An inability to judge is the benediction of love. It didn't matter to me what she looked like. But oh, how it mattered what this Helen—who was not 'mine'—looked like! For if Helen was not destined for me, then whom was she meant for? She must be somewhere, even though we had yet to meet. A sharp pang of jealousy gripped me. I didn't know her, I didn't like—much less love—her, but I was already jealous. I was certain I would meet her in the coming days. Because how much would one have to experience with another person before a chance meeting at a shop could unhinge one so? What could be so unimaginable that life without it would henceforth be impossible?

"'Did you mean for me to have it?' Dika said, looking at the 'cloud' with a doomed expression.

"Looking at her through the pale transparence of Helen, I suddenly

saw an unfamiliar girl before me, not the one I had come to visit at all.
Before this I had always come for Dika alone, and it was a source of
happiness to me that she was always the one I found. Now I scrutinized her unfamiliar face, comparing it for the first time. The comparison was, without doubt, in Dika's favor! The difference was to her
advantage. Everything in her was tinged with vibrant hues, in contrast
to the photograph—a downpour of light versus light stanched. Early
summer, young leaves, clear wind, shadows of clouds passing over tender shoots of grass, splashes of sky through the dappled foliage—that
kind of face. For the first time I feasted my eyes on it—when it was no
longer mine. It belonged to no one, like that summer day. A forsaken
Paradise. Tempter! It was no ordinary apple you slipped me . . .

"I took a bite from it without noticing it. I could embrace and kiss
Dika—she was right here, waiting for me. She wanted to be mine. But
this paper Helen, who didn't exist, was mine already. 'Idiot! Madman!'
I cursed the fat stranger in the Garden Park who had started it all, and
realized that these curses were directed at myself. How I dreamt of
meeting him once more to shake a name and address out of him, or an
admission that he had lied, or proof of his insanity, or his secret, or his
soul—but he, of course, no longer ventured into the Garden Park.

"He looked as much like the devil as a photograph of an apple resembled a real apple. I wandered through town in search of Helen,
peering into all the faces and shopwindows, but I couldn't find the one
I was seeking—and my own reflection vexed me with its monotonous
sameness. I had never come across it so frequently. I was sick of it, I
didn't recognize myself, I began to see myself as a faceless crowd.

"Everything around me reminded me of something else. I made
an effort but couldn't recall what it was. Every something took on the
likeness of another something. The whole world rhymed and multi-
plied its reflections. Everything conjured up some other thing, and it
was never the right thing. I wandered around like a nearsighted man
who had misplaced his spectacles, like one blinded by mist and fog.
The asphalt stretched out before me like a smooth sheet of water, and
waves fell away into the distance behind me. What kind of deck was
this, what kind of stern? Where was my vessel bound? Waves, photographs, mirrors . . . Oh, how blind I was! Blind man, blind singer. I
stumbled across my own reflection and shuddered, as though it reflected

someone else, and was surprised by a poem unknown to me—penned, nevertheless, by my own hand.

"What I had heretofore only dreamed about while scribbling my paltry verse came to pass: I became a Poet. You can't fool yourself: it's either poetry or it isn't. I had always had an unerring sense for it, and for this reason was never flattered by my own attempts. Now there could be no doubt about it. I wasn't aware of how the verses arrived. They were alien to me, as if written by someone else. I could evaluate and judge them as words that were not my own—and they were deserving of admiration. But, my God, how little comfort they brought! The price of those lines was too dear, however beautiful they might be—a price too dear for Dika, for me, for Helen . . .

"My jealousy over Helen knew no bounds. At first this virus assumed only light, Proustian forms. Unable to find her among passersby, I ventured into museums, bookstores. I discerned the outlines of her face through the strata of centuries in portraits, in the dust of the Renaissance. On my walls at home, in my student digs, I hung up successive pictures of my elusive Helen's predecessors: a Botticelli replaced a Ghirlandajo.

"Poor Dika. She was eaten up with jealousy at these reproductions. Then she would make peace with her rival, and even approve of my choice. But no sooner had she done this than another picture would take its place, one whose resemblance seemed to me even more striking. Dika accepted my poems, however, without a murmur.

"She would come to visit me in a new dress—'Pretty, isn't it?'— wearing new bracelets . . . Always breezy and carefree, as though nothing had happened, chirping on about some university nonsense. She brought flowers, and went searching for a vase . . . and found a page of verse. 'It's remarkable how little you understand your own poetry.' Tears of what appeared to be ecstasy welled up in her eyes, and her voice trembled. And through her ecstasy I glimpsed some deep torment that she would never have survived had she realized that the muse of these poems was not herself but another.

"But Dika didn't betray so much as a hint of this. I couldn't bear it: her expression, her voice, her ecstasy, her feigned nonchalance—and the better she kept it up, the more it smacked of fortitude, self-denial, meekness. I couldn't bear her suffering and became gruff. I didn't need her praise, her favors, her urge to put things in order. Could she not understand that there are times when a person has a right to be alone? She paid no heed to my gruffness but instead asked me to forgive her, and slipped away, snatching the page up off the floor as she left. She was the one who salvaged them all, else they would have been lost. I could appreciate them but never attach value to them—and, indeed, I almost hated them, as I hated Helen when I finally drove Dika away. Oh, I hated Helen so intensely at that moment when the door shut behind Dika that if I had chanced to meet her then, I would have strangled her, like Othello. I hated Helen perhaps even more for the torment I caused Dika than for her absence.

"But Dika did leave, and I diligently banished her from my mind. I was alone again with the absence of Helen. I ripped the current reproduction off the wall. Where had I seen a resemblance? Again I wandered through the streets, studying every stranger I met, until weariness and poetry felled me again at night. Waking up in the morning, I gave the poems their due and tossed them away. Then Dika would collect them again, surreptitiously and lovingly.

"Oh, I knew Helen's face by heart. I knew it as only someone lost in the woods knows the trees he circles round and round; as someone dying of thirst knows the desert. I can't describe its fatal charm. Even then I couldn't, even though, at the time, the ineffable easily succumbed to my words. In my verses anyone can sense her but will never see her— she was here one moment and gone the next. Slattern, fish, moth . . . Her face was paler than the most washed-out photograph. It was not just a matter of the poor quality of a botched print—only the most unskilled photograph could convey her characteristic vagueness, that elusiveness of expression and feature, and then only partially. Some Polish women look like that, I believe.

"Have you ever had the chance to visit Poland? They are renowned for their beauty, Polish women. Their beauty is distinctive. That's it— distinctive. And this notion alone was enough to lead me on a journey to the land of my ancestors, a place where I had never before set foot, and had never felt drawn to in the past. Really, I thought, what made me think that the shopwindow in which we were both reflected had to be located in the place I lived? That shopwindow could be anywhere. The world grew in my mind to dimensions that only despair can assume. Only the ocean and the desert offered me solace—places where there were no stores, no shopwindows, no reflections to be found. But I knew that in seven years this shopwindow would appear, all the same: I would hear the faint click of the diaphragm, the magnesium would flare, and a shot would result. I knew, and nothing could stop me. Wasn't it all the same, what end of the Earth I sought her in? It is a commonplace that beginners win in the game of roulette, and experienced players, who have built a system from their experience, lose. Why not Poland?

"I traveled its length and breadth. There were thousands of them like her. This is how it is with Polish women. At first you feel puzzled. Where are all those renowned beauties? Their faces are astonishingly inexpressive, impassive. You are geared up, you are ready to behold them, you focus your crystalline lens again and again, reproaching yourself for being inadequately perspicacious. Finally you leave, disappointed. You leave—and then they come to you. You begin dreaming about them at night. Independence and deference, compliance and proud inaccessibility: the essence of womanhood. They submit; but, as it turns out, not to you. They remain, but you are no longer there. An odd sensation. I saw thousands of them like her, but she was not among them. I would have recognized her out of a million—but out of a thousand she was nowhere to be found. I would have stayed there forever for her, if she had been there. But she wasn't there, since I had already departed . . .

"By now it had become clear to me that she was not in Poland. With my return ticket in my pocket, not knowing how to spend my final day there, I wandered into the celebrated municipal cemetery. Perhaps I wanted to justify my defeat; but in the cemetery I sensed that I had made this journey to find my ancestral homeland, and for no other reason. The beautiful September day was waning into evening. The cemetery was not a haunted graveyard but an ancient, well-tended park. The leaves of two-hundred-year-old oaks and maples blazed like national banners. The trees stood tall, but the nation lay in the ground underneath them. Little flames flickered among the tree trunks— women in black mantles carrying candles in their hands moved toward the graves that I could not yet make out. All at once, the trees thinned, and ancient, moss-covered stones began to appear. They stretched out in an endless line like a glacial moraine. Then the trees closed ranks again, only to give way before the gravestones one more time: the eighteenth century had arrived. Little candles burned here and there on individual gravestones, but the rest continued to gleam up ahead. I followed close behind the candles, aware of the emptiness in my hands. The silence thickened and the sense of expectation grew. I seemed to hear a roar in the distance ahead of me. It swelled—and the next long ridge of graves lay down at my feet like the last breaker of the surf. I was in the nineteenth century. War, uprising, war, uprising—defeat, defeat, defeat . . . And again—uprising and war. It was just like a sea; history was frozen here in undulating billows of common graves—somewhere up ahead, not yet visible, boomed the ninth wave . . . Its time was due in my own, our own, century. Now more candles burned and guttered on the gravestones, more flowers had been laid on them, more often a solitary figure was to be seen standing nearby.

"I didn't notice right away that my hands were no longer empty—they grasped neither a candle, nor a flower, but the flaming banner of a maple leaf. The copse grew younger before my eyes; an expanse opened up in front of me. It was a timid, childlike undergrowth—but the future already seemed to be digging in, making preparations there. I turned to go back, now and then stopping to read the name of a young officer. In one common grave, in an alphabetical list of names, I read out my own: U. Vanoski. I had no knowledge of this legionnaire of the Polish forces, First World War. That was where I laid my leaf. Suddenly it seemed to me that I wasn't seeking a woman at all, but my homeland in her image. A strange feeling of delight in defeat gripped me: my homeland, the people, had not vanished.

"Someone was watching me. I sensed this from behind and for some reason felt frightened. 'Pan polak?' a throaty woman's voice addressed me. I didn't know any Polish, but I knew she wasn't Polish, either. I could make out a distinct accent. At last I turned around—it was HER! We met on the Day of Remembrance of the Deceased by the grave of my possible relative.

"But, no, it wasn't her. I realized this only the next morning, waking up in a strange bed, staring at a strange ceiling. Dressed for travel, she was sitting in an armchair and examining me. I even had the impression that there was a packed suitcase standing in the corner. 'Dzień dobry,' she said with an accent. 'Kawa [coffee]?' Those were the only words she knew in Polish. I drank coffee, she rolled one cigarette after another and smoked them. She was from Holland, and besides her native Dutch knew only German and French. I only knew English and Italian. So we maintained an eloquent silence, as though we knew everything already. The Dutch woman was considerably more beautiful than my Helen, and it was difficult for me to recognize the resemblance that had seemed so obvious to me the day before. She was darker, stronger, with a richer color, I suppose. There was a certain heaviness, a seriousness in her pose and movements. This monumental being smoldered and percolated, smoking in silence. Her enormous eyes were in the habit of changing color, or, rather, light—they lived a stormy life of their own amidst her bulk; for, suddenly, I was able to see her. She was huge! She sat there like a cast-iron kettlebell. Her eyes grew dark in their depths; she kissed me awkwardly and said in broken English: 'I want be your husband.' I burst out laughing, and she was offended. I promised to come visit her in Amsterdam.

"But I was already in a hurry, rushing back home to my Dika. Begone, phantom!

"For this was the devil's plan—to plunge me into incessant expectation, deprive me of real time . . . that is to say, real happiness. And Dika was the most real happiness to me. How delighted she was at my return! How glad I was . . . Here, under the blows and the dull thud of scholarship falling all around us, through the parrot's shrieks of 'The coffee's boiling over! The coffee's boiling over!' amidst the frenzy of our kisses, it all happened. Suddenly, Dika grew somber, tore herself from my embrace, went into her diminutive bath-kitchen-hallway-toilet, brushed her teeth long and furiously, came back, marching like a soldier, pushed me into a corner behind a curtain, covered the parrot's cage with a skirt, restored the books to their places, then folded out the bed with abrupt, angry motions I didn't recognize, skillful and unattractive, like those of an elderly charwoman, made the bed, and began to undress with fierce and deliberate abandon.

"She removed everything from herself, then folded it up on a chair—timidly, as though she had hated the clothing that covered her, then regretted its loss. After folding everything and placing it on the chair with the utmost accuracy and care, as fastidious as a schoolchild in a German primer or a soldier in his barracks, she lay down. I remained standing in the spot to which she had banished me, merging with the curtain, evaporating into the darkness, almost unaware of myself. It was a strange sensation—I wasn't there. Dika was lying motionless under the white sheet; next to her, the pile of her clothes, like someone else's, like the clothing of a dead person that has been returned to the relatives. The light from a streetlamp pierced through a slit in the curtains, pouring over everything like moonlight. Such was the silence, the stillness, the absence, and the dearth of feeling, that I didn't know how many ages, minutes, seconds had passed before I heard from over there, from the white blur, someone else's lifeless voice: 'Where are you?'

"The following morning we had coffee and hurried to the university as if we had done this every morning for many years. And never again did we kiss each other as we kissed then.

"How I tormented her! The ruse was that it was my creative quest, some grand conception, that gripped me—and *this* was tormenting *me*, not *I* tormenting *her*. I told her everything, but not as the truth—rather, as the plot of a novel that was born in me suddenly when I chanced to come across that photograph of the cloud (which was now hanging over our bed). I told her about the quest of my protagonist, about his experiences, everything just as it was, except for one detail: my protagonist did not have a Dika. He was solitary, alone with the image he pursued. There was no betrayal. It would be a new tale of chivalry, I told Dika, like the Knight of the Mournful Countenance. Through his fidelity and love, this knight triumphed over the devil who had tempted him with the image. The knight overcame temptation by believing in it as the truth, by not calling it into question. Dika was shattered each time I enriched the plot with some fresh detail, or unexpected but convincing twist. She disguised her jealousy with flights of rapture over my creative mastery, and found parallels in world literature through her philological erudition, thus refining and honing my mythology.

"I kept up my search, whether for another fleeting resemblance, or for another twist in the plot of my novel. I could no longer tell which took precedence—whether the literary concept modeled the events, or the events drove the novel. I only had to imagine something and it would happen, altering everything I had anticipated. When something happened, it would be mangled by my memory and assume fabulous shapes to suit the plot. I traveled a great deal. My travels were not so much long and unbroken as short and frequent. Flight and return. This was my narcotic. I thieved and collected days of departure and arrival: on these days I was happy, because I didn't exist for anybody. Oh, the glorious last day—the first day that you are free!

"Dika and I traveled to Greece together. This was the first time she had been to her ancestral homeland. In contrast to me in mine, she felt immediately at home in that place she had never before visited. How proud she was in my presence of everything around us! As soon as she alighted from the train, even her gait changed. We bought each other sandals right there on the platform. We exchanged them like rings. She was happy, and I suddenly felt that in Greece we were as we had been in our first room, when we had done no more than kiss. No more than . . . ! Maybe we should move here, I caught myself thinking. Maybe we should just stay here, and everything will be as it was before.

"We paid a visit to the local university. We thought Dika might be able to teach there someday, and I could have devised some special seminar. Dika posted a notice about me in a university publication, and on the eve of our departure for home I gave a poetry reading to a smattering of devotees. I don't think anyone understood a word of it, but for some reason the reading was a success. And then I saw Her, coming down the aisle toward me, with a yellow flower in her hand. It was Helen again. The likeness was striking—the Dutch woman paled in comparison! This time, however, I realized it was only a likeness. Nevertheless, later that evening at a small restaurant, where Dika and I had gathered with friends to celebrate our imminent departure, the new Helen and I exchanged addresses and agreed to meet again. She had plans to travel to England. She promised to write me care of poste restante to let me know when. A soothsayer with a fortune-telling bird approached us. The bird picked out scraps of paper with fortunes that promised happiness to me; beauty to Helen—but Eurydice refused to tell us what her future had in store for her.

"The mussel soup we ordered was marvelous. Surrounded by admirers, I was witty and jovial, and somewhat drunker than usual from the red wine and the heady proximity of the French Helen. I felt I was standing on the prow of some ancient galley ship like Odysseus, fanned by the wind, sailing through the night toward the stars, the sirens, and the waves. I sailed and sang. Suddenly we seemed to founder on a reef, and the galley split in half. I fell into the hold, which turned out to be a pub that I entered—I remember this well—with a large group of people, though I ended up alone with Dika. She had a swollen nose again. She often had a swollen nose in those days—a sure sign of jealousy. This time I was not sure whether my actions had triggered it, so I grew especially angry and went on the offensive. 'What did your fortune say?' I demanded savagely. She remained, as always, resigned and uncomplaining. She pacified me and spoke conciliatory words. Still, she didn't produce the fortune and told me she had thrown it away.

"How I made her suffer! I was in a foul temper because she prevented me from making definite plans with Helen. I would dash off to the post office in secret—there was nothing there, of course. I wrote impassioned letters to Paris, recounting them to Dika as rough sketches of scenes for the novel, and always returned from the post office empty-handed. I told Dika that my irritation was the result of writer's block.

"The novel, meanwhile, continued to grow in my head. It was called *The Life of a Dead Man,* and told of a man who lost his soul and blamed life itself for his ruin. He vowed to take revenge on life, destroying his useless, soulless body not by an ordinary act of suicide, but in the manner of a Japanese kamikaze, blowing himself up like a bomb. This bomb-man prepared long and hard for his final act, and his life acquired at least some semblance of purpose. He now achieved quickly and easily everything he had strived to achieve so unsuccessfully while his soul was still alive, while happiness and glory was still something he wanted. Now that he no longer wanted it, his career took an instantaneous and vertiginous upturn, because the only thing that attracted him was the success of his future detonation. He intended to blow himself up at the apex of his career, thus taking by surprise the prevailing evil. He had been hapless and weak when his soul was alive, but suddenly he became mighty, exacting, and impeccable in his attempts to achieve his soulless aims. He was afraid of nothing, he wanted nothing—his automatism overcame every obstacle. He got what he wanted. Now, after laying to rest all his worldly affairs, leaving no outstanding debts, he set out for a grand international affair as an invited guest, with two grenades fastened by a special strap (I borrowed the strap from Dostoevsky) under his genitals.

Here I faltered before the further development of the plot. The dénouement was still unclear to me. I knew that his plan wouldn't fall through for some external reason. No one would catch him, unmask him, disarm him; but he might well be afraid to carry out his plan. There wouldn't be anything to prevent him from reaching his goal, but for some reason he wouldn't enact it. I balked at continuing, as though some insurmountable obstacle interfered. It was like a black mirror that cast my creative efforts back to me like my own dark reflection.

"And then, when I no longer hoped, and had sat down before a blank sheet of paper as listlessly and mechanically as I asked for mail at the poste restante window, I received a telegram from Helen in Paris that named a rendezvous at the very same post office, at such-and-such an hour. As you might have expected, I arrived an hour early, with the emblematic yellow rose in my hand, the same kind she had once given me. She never appeared. I went to the information window at the station to inquire about the train—all the trains had already arrived, and there was no telegram from her that warned of a change in plans. Late in the evening, I returned home distraught, and only when I was face-to-face with Dika did I realize I still had the damn rose in my hand. I dissolved into rage. Another second and I would . . . 'Did she come?' Dika said, without a tremor of emotion. 'No,' I replied, suddenly just as calm as she was. 'This is for you.' I handed her the rose and embraced her, exulting. 'I've got it! I've got it! Now I know how it all ends!'

"I rushed over to the table and scribbled away until sunrise, and all the next day. My hero didn't blow himself up—and for a good reason. Because there wasn't one. Every goal exists for the sake of continuity, to justify its own sequel; and there was no possible sequel here. He had accounted for everything—and there was nothing left. There was nowhere else to go. It wasn't because he took fright, it wasn't because someone interfered—it was because there was no more reason. So he doesn't blow himself up, but quietly leaves the reception to wander through the night, finally on this side of life. I was especially pleased with the last scene. He goes down to the shore of the sea, the night is starless and moonless, thick with mist. Standing in front of the inky blackness, as though before an abyss, he unbuttons his fly, takes the grenades out one by one, and flings them into the sea. They burst out there in the mist like burned-out lightbulbs. This symbolism was very fine, I thought, because in fact he threw away his . . .

"I collapsed fully dressed on the bed and slept for sixteen hours straight. I had a strange and beautiful dream in which I was in Japan with a group of tourists. The wonderful thing about dreams is their incongruity. Although it was Japan, we stood in front of a bay I had seen in Greece. The bay was surrounded by imposing cliffs, and we descended them in single file, making our way down to the sea. The path was extremely intricate and unpredictable, which, it seemed, proved that I was in Japan; although the reason it was Japan was perhaps because my great-grandfather had married a Japanese woman. The path evolved in such a way that we gradually found ourselves jumping from stone to stone. It became clear that we were in a kind of Japanese garden, and that these artificial stones, placed illogically, in the Japanese manner, were tiles paving the pedestrian pathway. Leaping from tile to tile, now left, now right, sometimes even backward, one had to step very gingerly, because between the tiles there was not simply grass, or little bushes, but infinitesimally small Japanese gardens, living ikebana that it would have been a shame to destroy. Carried away by this task, I discovered that I had gotten lost. I was lost, to be exact, in one of the lilliputian gardens; because, suddenly, between two of the tiles, the one on which I was standing and the one onto which I was supposed to spring, I saw underneath me that very bay, that very sea we had been descending to . . . But 'we' was not the right word, because the whole group was down below already, scattered along the narrow strip of shore, getting ready, most likely, to take a dip in the sea, while I was still there above them on the cliff. I raced down after my companions at breakneck speed, in leaps and bounds—it was easy and pleasant, almost like flying. What was strange, however, was that I didn't seem to get any nearer to them.

"On my way down I came across a strange contraption that vaguely resembled a reflecting telescope. It was blocking my path. I clambered up its trusses, slid down a short flight of steps, and came to a stop when I hit the mirror. It reflected the very same bay, the same shore, the same sea, but my companions were already walking along, farther down the shore. I realized I really had to hurry to catch up, turned away from the mirror, looking for a passage leading out of the contraption, and stumbled across another mirror. I started to run, searching for an exit, but everywhere there were mirrors blocking my path. I kept rushing about and running into them, until I noticed with horror that I was circling around and around in one spot that was lined with mirrors. I was immured in a prism of mirrors.

"I woke up with a sense of panic, thinking that I had been left behind and would never catch up, and then I saw Dika. She kissed me, and congratulated me. Why? I had forgotten everything. She had read the novel. 'It's wonderful.'

"What a blockhead I was! I had forgotten about everything. I slapped myself on the forehead, saw that I was already dressed, and, without washing, ran down to the post office. There was a telegram for me from Helen. She wrote that she had waited for me the whole day, then left, and that I shouldn't write her anymore. When I reread the first telegram, I realized I had mixed up the dates, that in my impatience had gone to meet her a day earlier than she was to arrive. Thus, she had been waiting for me all the next day, while I was finishing my novel . . . For some reason I resigned myself quite calmly to the loss, telling myself that she wasn't the real one anyway, and hadn't even resembled her very closely. I rubbed my chin—it was overgrown with three-day stubble. Have you ever noticed that when you write through the night your beard grows twice as fast? It was positively improper to appear in public like that—now I understood the perplexity on the face of the postmistress. I set off for the nearest barbershop.

"Not paying attention to anything around me, I simply plunked down in an empty chair, threw back my head, and closed my eyes. 'Are you asleep?' a gentle voice said. I opened my eyes—I had lost track of whichever dream I was now in. There in front of me was a mirror. Well, no wonder, it was a barbershop! But at the same instant I was so unnerved by it, it was so unexpected, that I couldn't fathom it. In the mirror I saw a crumpled, unshaven face that seemed to belong to a stranger. And this strange face reminded me very urgently of someone. Everyone has experienced this exasperating tickle of incomplete recollection. All of this happened, mind you, in the first fraction of a second, which was pulverized by the second; for, to the right, above my head, hovered HER face. Not once more, not all over again—because this one matched the original completely. It was an exact replica. And since nothing can match something completely, it could only have been HER.

"Two things confirmed this beyond the shadow of a doubt. First, my own face. Talk about an expression! It was just like the one in the photograph. Second, when I shifted my gaze away from my own likeness, I saw that both of us were being reflected from the back, in the mirror behind us. The mirror that we were facing revealed a regressive series of reflections. This was my morning dream! A dream—come true. Prophetic. I looked at her. She was smiling brightly and tenderly, almost laughing. I only had to turn my head to the right to see her in the flesh! My neck grew stiff, my heart was pounding, I couldn't take my eyes off her reflection for fear she would disappear.

"It didn't disappear—it changed before my eyes: it smiled, looked amazed, perplexed . . . It came to life! I heard my neck crunch as I turned to her—she didn't disappear. I can't say what I felt at that moment. Relief? Devastation? Joy? Disappointment? Freedom? . . . That was it, I felt freedom. We were surrounded by mirrors, repeating hundreds of times, one inside the other, an endless chain into eternity. Our reflections laughed, because we laughed. At first I was moved to laugh by the very word 'freedom'; and she, for some reason, laughed in response. Perhaps she really did find it amusing. I laughed at myself, she laughed at me, the mirrors laughed at both of us. Well, so what if she was wearing a white robe instead of a dress? She was a hairdresser! So it wasn't a store, but a barbershop. So what? A barbershop is a kind of store. It wasn't a shopwindow, but a mirror. So what? It's still a reflection. Both these arguments led to a fresh bout of laughter. The photograph matched like a parody. But what was a parody of what? I doesn't matter, I thought with relief. There's a third corroboration here: she's the third. The magic of the number three was self-evident. I burst out laughing one last time, and it seemed to me that she responded to me with laughter that was not only cheerful, but happy. That meant that it was not just me laughing at myself, but her laughing at me—WE were laughing! Together.

"No, her name was not Helen. That would have been too uncanny. Then she might as well have been called Calypso. What was her name? Have I forgotten it? Her boss gave her permission to leave, and we took off for the country. I don't think we conversed about anything at all— we were as happy and playful as children. We swam and ran about naked, chasing after each other like we were in Eden, like Adam and Eve. That's it! Her name was Eve. Definitely. Or was it . . . ?

"I had never felt so comfortable with anyone before. And never would again (I know that now). We didn't have a penny to our names. We didn't have to live by the sweat of our brow, though: her numerous admirers supported us. No, of course not! I wasn't her pimp. Perhaps it wasn't very proper, but believe me, it was absolutely pure. In Italian jargon there is even a word for it: *dinamo*. And so we hoodwinked others. She would make plans with someone, saying that she wanted to drink and was absolutely famished. The admirer rolled up in a car packed with wines and delicacies. She set the table, lit candles—and then I made my presence known. She was terribly embarrassed, took me off to one side and whispered to me guiltily (the admirer didn't know what she said). Then she took the admirer aside and whispered to him in secret. (I knew what she was saying: he's just a boy, a greenhorn—Italian blood. And the most persuasive argument: I had promised to marry her; but the admirer hadn't.) Then we sat down to dinner together.

"No one is as obliging as the man next in line to his predecessor, or the deceiver to the deceived. It was very amusing to watch. At first I would sulk and scowl, but I didn't play the part to the end. I was too hungry. You should have seen how courteously I was served—you can't find a better waiter than a happy rival! He also regaled me with conversation to dispel any awkwardness . . . The longer I remained silent (my mouth was full), the more he talked, trying indirectly to convince me I wasn't a cuckold. Oh, it was the sweetest sort of vaudeville! Such delicate word choice, it was like dancing between knives. I would eat my fill, then fall into a sulk. The rival left at the first opportunity, usually without even tasting his own offerings—and we fell into one another's embrace.

"I must admit, they were pleasant people, and I wasn't at all jealous of her past. (Funny how I fell into the same logic as my rivals.) They seemed to acknowledge us as a couple. Only one of them saw through us—and we became friends with him, since we all liked each other so much. Fat, bald, lively, he perspired constantly. He had a strange profession: he was a master of ceremonies. He was always on the move. Prone to boasting, he never demanded that we believe him. A good man . . . There was only one thing he kept insisting on—he said he was a close friend of Charlie Chaplin's, which he tried to prove by fishing around in an abyss of tattered receipts and documents. In the end, he never found the calling card. So we didn't believe him; and he was genuinely upset.

"I don't know how many days passed—probably as many days as

there were admirers. We started on a Sunday, that much I know for sure. Either the admirers grew fewer, or the days grew longer. Suddenly I had a dream about the novel. A new ending. A new version. My hero, before he went to commit 'the deed,' after he had paid all his debts and destroyed his receipts, after he had carefully washed, shaved, and strapped on the grenades . . . Just then, right before the banquet, he goes to discharge one more duty. He goes to say goodbye to the only person on Earth who wasn't indifferent to him: naturally, to the woman who is devoted to him. (You have already guessed that my solitary avenger, who considers himself very callous and unfeeling, is secretly very sentimental—but the one does not exclude the other.) He enacts a scene in which he takes leave of her forever, confesses to his own heartlessness, says that he has the right, etc., and then, won over by the honesty and persuasiveness of his arguments, she finally believes him—this is it, this is the end—and sets him free. And when he decides not to blow himself up, when he has flung his burned-out lightbulbs into the dark expanse of ocean, he ends up, finally and absolutely, alone. He has nowhere to go. He no longer even has a home. He has sold it. He doesn't even have money: he gave it all away. What need would he have for money after blowing himself up? He has no one to turn to. He has no relatives, and he has just parted ways forever with the only woman who could put up with him. His soul is gone, but he still has a body. And so, having wandered the whole night through, shivering and hungry, he finds himself standing at the abandoned woman's door, unable to decide whether or not to ring the bell. Suddenly the door opens of its own accord. She is not at all surprised that he has returned. She expected him. Dinner is still warm . . .

"I thought I had returned to pick up the manuscript. How much time had passed? Three days? Three years? I felt my face blazing with fire, I was covered in perspiration. It wasn't shame, or pain, or fear, or pangs of conscience, or repentance . . . It was . . . There are no words for the sense of irreparable damage I felt, and felt I had caused. 'Dika!' I screamed, and started running.

"The lock didn't fit the key, the door opened in the wrong direction . . . and there was no Dika. Everything was pristine and empty. It was more empty than when Dika simply wasn't home. The parrot was gone, too. The cage was empty—that was it. Three days? Three years?

I groped around on the table, searching for a note. The blinds were pulled, and there was no light to see by. My hand couldn't find the switch . . . Finally, there was light. The note shook my hands, the lines veered past my gaze. I put it back on the table, on the exact spot where it had lain, and, gripping the edge to steady myself, I made out the words: *Jacko flew away. I went to look for him. The porridge is on the stove. Love, E.* This should have reassured me, but it didn't. 'Three days? Three years?' I mumbled, circling the room. I brushed up against a pile of books and knocked them over. They spilled and spilled, and scattered about like oatmeal flakes. 'Porridge!' I exclaimed, and rushed over to the stove. The porridge was still warm! It couldn't have stayed warm for three days, much less three years. Time contracted violently, like a living thing, like a heart. I should have felt reassured by all of this, but I didn't. Time contracted to today, to this moment, to a point, and then stopped, like a heart. A needle, finer than the sliver of an instant, pierced my heart like time. I closed my eyes and imagined I saw the chair, the one from our first night, with a pile of folded clothes on it, like the clothes of one recently deceased. I opened my eyes in alarm— the chair was empty. And, still, my heart wasn't beating.

"Then I rushed like a madman in the direction of the Zoological Gardens. Why the zoo? I don't really know how to explain it. I was certain she was there, that's all. It was only later that I was able to imagine how it must have been . . . How she waited and waited for me . . . How she forgot to lock the cage . . . How it grew stuffy in the room and she opened the window . . . How suddenly, with the ineluctability of insight, she understood that I was gone and wasn't coming back, understood because Jacko had flown away . . . How she rushed after the parrot, as though rushing in pursuit of me . . . How she dashed through the streets, crying, 'Jacko! Jacko! Have you seen my parrot?'

"What came next? An automobile? A streetcar? 'No! No!' I screamed as I ran. The conjecture gripped me so suddenly that I was absolutely certain, just as she had been when she realized in her despair: Of course, Jacko had flown away to find his OWN! Where else? So she ran, joyfully, almost flying, gasping with happiness that he was there, in the zoo. Where else could he have gone . . . ?

"For the hundredth time she combed the Zoological Gardens— oh, that overpopulated desert where there was no Jacko! 'My dear! My dear! Please come back!' she called. But he wasn't there. His absence seemed to grow. Little fool! What a little fool you are, Dika! You can't find him; he can only return to you. He's sure to return! He's flying home already . . . Dika! It's me! I've come after you . . . Where are you? Dika wasn't there. Suddenly I saw a crowd, a small crowd, on the edge of the park where the chamois were, and after that the ape house . . . I made my way toward them. Most likely the little fool ran first of all to the parrots. Of course there was no Jacko there. Or, rather, there were hundreds, but none of them answered to her call, or else all of them would at once. But just at that moment, several zookeepers ran by in a panic with nets and boathooks, as though a fire had broken out. No doubt they're after my Jacko, thought crazy Dika, and she dashed off after them.

"I tore off in pursuit of the invisible Dika. You can see into the future more quickly at a run. The crowd parted silently to let me pass. A doctor in a white coat stood there, smoking indifferently. Next to him stood one of the zookeepers—in a gray uniform, with an inconsolable monkey in her arms. On a stretcher lay . . . No! Never! What do you mean? You're out of your mind . . . Dika! Wake up! It's me, I'm here . . . I made it!

"She had raced right behind the people with nets and boathooks. No one tried to stop her, either because they were too distracted by other matters, or because they took her for a fellow zookeeper, a novice, in their panic. Straight toward Dika, with a shriek, hurtled a monkey— a little chimpanzee, just a babe in arms. Tame, and used to being lavished with caresses . . . Why did he choose her out of all the others? She so wanted a child. The little chimpanzee so wanted to be saved. Who else would save him? Everyone else scattered helter-skelter to avoid him, as though they were running from the plague or a leper. They knew what was happening. Dika didn't know. Even if she had known, would she really have jumped aside, turned away from that little tyke hurtling toward her with its terrified shrieks and yowls, desperate for help, for salvation? At the last minute, the little chimpanzee leapt. He flew like a cannonball at breakneck speed straight toward Dika. She didn't see that behind it, stretching out in a transparent gray thread, something else was flying through the air . . . Like a goalkeeper, Dika caught the warm, living ball of terror. The little monkey, sobbing and howling, threw its arms around her neck and pressed itself to her, trembling uncontrollably . . . And the gray unseen thing fell short of its goal and plopped down at her feet with a naked gray thud . . . and began twining itself around her. And the little monkey kept whimpering and clasping her neck, covering her with kisses. That was her last embrace on this Earth."

. . . Vanoski went quiet. Tears streamed down his face—literally streamed. I had never seen anything like it. An unbroken stream. He didn't wipe them away.

Why was I so angry with him? I didn't know. I wanted to tell him that I had read it already in a book—moreover, his book. I wanted to. But I couldn't.

"I know you find it implausible," Vanoski said with a sigh. "But that doesn't matter to me. I prefer it this way. She's waiting for me there. I've had a slight delay; but that's all right. She waited for me here even longer. You'd like to know how it really was? It's hard for me to remember what I have written and what I have lived. I think it all really happened, because this time I recounted everything from memory. I didn't invent anything. Perhaps you're right, I'm—a writer . . . An unhappy creature! Everyone thinks that choosing what to write about is the hardest thing. No, the hardest thing is to think up the one who's writing. All the writers we read and revere were able to summon up within themselves someone who writes for them. And who are they, then, besides the ones who write? It's horrifying to imagine this solitude. Only other people are happy: they labor, love, give birth, die. Those who write can't die, either. They aren't cut out for it. They are like actors, only they play one role their whole lives: themselves. For others. Their lives don't belong to them. They are slaves of others, slaves of those who love them. They don't know how to love, just as monks don't know how to believe. If you love and believe, why write or pray? You love a living woman—and it's an image; you reach toward God—and it's words; you fall to Earth—and it's your homeland. If you're a writer, the Earth shoves you out, larger than life, like a monument, like relics, so that you don't linger on Earth but in your homeland, unburied after all . . .

"I have always dreamed of one thing only: giving up writing and being able to live. Oh, I could have! And I wouldn't have written another word. With the utmost satisfaction. To my profound delight. I almost

managed to love! Fate took it away. We were already leaving the altar
when she trod on that gray, unseen . . . It was raining, and we were
running, clasping each other by the hand, laughing, away from the city
hall to the car. She got tangled in the hem of her wedding dress, lost
her slipper . . . and landed with her heel on the bare electrical cable . . .
But there had been a way out! I had always had a way out—to *love*. I
could have vanquished the one with the briefcase and the photographs
through love alone, as in a fairy tale. Could have sent him on his way,
and not attached any meaning to this forgery . . . because it *was* a forgery! I forged my whole life according to it. If only it had been just
mine . . . If only I were a scoundrel. If only I had abandoned Dika, or
the Frenchwoman, even the Dutch woman, for love. But no. Not one of
them! I could definitely have loved the hairdresser . . . But I only loved
ONE: that paper Helen. I had a dream about that, too.

"After Dika's death, I burned the novel and refused to leave the
house. Someone brought me my meals. Maybe it was even the hairdresser, but I don't recall any woman. A year later I dreamed I was
flying over a painting or an etching of a country, perhaps Greece, which
looked like one of Picasso's graphics on a mythological subject, only it
was more conventional, and more parodic. There below me reigned a
bacchic idyll: sheep, goats, shepherds, shepherdesses . . . And they were
all making love. They were also made of paper, like children's dolls cut
out of the lined pages of a notebook. It was like the dream itself was on
lined notebook paper. The vision of their paper love made me laugh at
first, then it amused me, then it intrigued me. I felt I was just as papery,
but just as capable of love as they were. I flew around looking for a girlfriend, but they were all engaged. My ability grew, but there was no
girlfriend to be found. Finally, I saw one. I descended; she opened
herself to accept my embraces. I swooped down on her . . . and then I
became myself, no longer paper, but flesh and blood, and I felt myself
rip bodily through this page from a school notebook.

"That was the day I went out into the city for the first time. I wandered aimlessly, peering again into faces, but no longer in search of the
mythical Helen, not differentiating between women and men, just studying people's faces: What are they like, and who are they, these people?
I stopped into cafés, stores, parks—and left without sitting down, without eating, without buying anything. I was tired, so I decided to go home.

Then I found I was no longer walking, but standing, standing in front of a display window and looking dully at two mannequins, male and female, who seemed to be striding toward one another with outstretched arms, to embrace at last, only something prevented them. Was it my reflection between them? And then, through the display window, between the mannequins, I saw her: Helen from the photograph. For this time it was she, down to the minutest detail. How could I have failed to notice this shop before? I had passed this place thousands of times in my life during my quests! But it was new, a store that had just opened during the past year, while I was secluded in my room. I calculated—exactly seven years had gone by. And while I was standing there, dumbstruck, turning over these simple calculations in my mind, Helen emerged through the glass doors, dressed as she was in the photograph, with a shopping bag, like the one in the photograph . . . She glanced at me, as she had in the photograph, without registering any feeling, as though glancing at a thing, and walked on. I kept standing there, rooted to the spot. Then, in the display window, I saw my own ghastly face from the photograph, with snakes growing from my head instead of hair. I screamed, and rushed after her—to kill her. 'Kill' is not the right word here, though: I thought I could rip her to shreds, like a photograph, so certain was I that she was made of paper. It wouldn't have been murder—just scraps of paper scattered about on the street. But SHE was gone. She had disappeared.

"Ripping her up—that was nothing. It was still not the end. When she vanished, and I was unable to catch her, I understood that I had yet again fallen into temptation by the one with the briefcase, that I should have caught hold of her and held on for dear life. I should have urged myself on her and fallen in love with her at last, unto death. This was my last chance to revive fate, and I had missed it. Oh, how blind I had been my whole life: waves, mirrors, paper, photographs . . .

"I embarked on a new quest then, though I knew it was doomed from the outset. I wrote something called *The Burning Novel*. It was a novel in which the characters didn't say a word. No, you couldn't have read that one, either, for the same reason . . . I don't know what you've read of mine—I have been writing these two books my entire life, nor have I ever finished writing either of them. Perhaps they were in fact one novel and not two. In the sequel the protagonist returns to his first love and to his first, abandoned, novel . . . In that book it turns out he had a son, a grown-up boy who is a deaf-mute. His mother hasn't spoken to him, out of solidarity with her son, for fourteen years. The protagonist settles down with them again and finishes writing his very first novel, amidst this embodied muteness. In this novel he . . ."

I think Vanoski recounted his novel to me to the end; but he no longer saw me. I quietly slipped out of his little shoebox. My God! How wonderful life is! How sweetly the dusty urban lilacs smell of benzine! Of what use are success, money, and glory to him? Why do they come to those who not only have no more need of them, but who never needed them to begin with?

And then I recalled Vanoski's words, the ones he had spoken when I was feeling such antipathy toward him that I had stopped listening:

"All the same, he didn't conquer me. I know that for sure now. He only conquered me in this life; but in *that* one he can't vanquish me. In *that* one I'm stronger. My Dika is there with me . . ."

And I realized why I had turned against him: it was because of his Dika. Because she is his, and not mine. What good is my youth to me without her?

0: NUMBER OR LETTER?

(Freud's Family Doctor)

FROM *A Fly on a Ship*, A BOOK BY U. Vanoski

"Did you fall from the Moon?"

"Yes," he said.

His "yes" was calm and bore no trace of challenge. The laughter that followed in the wake of his answer no longer injured him. Had he been aware of it, this circumstance would even have gladdened him. But he wasn't aware of it, and was somewhat abashed that he hadn't fully lived up to their expectations. For some reason, though, they guffawed even more than usual. This put him on his guard. He stared in wide-eyed surprise at the encroaching, wobbling surface of unfamiliar faces—at the mounds of cheeks and foreheads, the chasms of eyes, the clefts between teeth. This carnival-mirror surface of faces reminded him of another surface, another landscape. Then he recalled where he had been going, excused himself, and set off down Sunday Street toward where it ended, merging gently and imperceptibly into a faded meadow. Here, the laughter straggled behind, then died away altogether. Invisible insects began their chirring, and identical butterflies hovered and dipped in haphazard motion. A dirigible—a phenomenon whose novelty would disappear almost overnight—floated in the sky. The sun had been warming the meadow all day, and now the grasses released a lazy, parched heat. Once he had passed the meadow he was just a stone's throw away . . . there, where the brown cow was grazing . . . He moved as though he were walking through shallow water, lifting his feet high and planting them down into the motionless heat, the pungent smells, the chirring. He screwed up his

eyes in satisfaction. He was quite happy: he had something to tell
Dr. Davin today, and even something to show him. In his hands he
carried a bicycle handlebar.

Toni "Gummi" Badiver had shown up in these parts not too long ago.
He was found on the side of the road, on the Northern Highway, three
miles from Taunus. He was unconscious, bleeding, and covered in
scratches. Samuelsen the night-soil man, who picked him up, concluded that he was dead drunk and, out of a sense of camaraderie,
delivered him to the police station. On the way there, due to the jolting
and lurching of Samuelsen's mode of transport, the injured man came
to and began babbling incoherently about some Brother Hom Laoshan
who had beaten him up when he interceded on behalf of the singer
Tieng. At the station, however, they were quick to figure out what was
what. They locked up Samuelsen in the adjoining cell for his testimony.
The man he had delivered could be none other than Toni Badiver,
they thought, after finding this name embroidered in crude, red block
letters on the lining of his flimsy, mouse-colored jacket. They were
somewhat at a loss to explain why not so much as a whiff of alcohol
clung to him, however.

They called in the medic. He let some blood.

"Nothing serious. Let him sleep it off. You'll have time to interro-
gate him later." The medic was not overly fond of policemen and was
ashamed that he worked for them. He dreamed of one day working in
Dr. Davin's clinic. Well, that was his business. To each his own.

The newly delivered Badiver (if that was indeed who he was) slept
through the evening, the night, and the following morning. Smogs, the
officer on duty, spying on him through the peephole, kept repeating
his favorite little joke:

"Sleeping like a murderer."

The station was all aflutter over the arrival of Badiver. When the
newly-delivered-Badiver-if-that-was-indeed-who-he-was finally turned
over onto his other side, Sergeant Cups, who had relieved Corporal
Smiles, who had relieved Officer Smogs—though Smogs and Smiles,
instead of going home, were still hanging around, waiting to see how
it would all end, which was rare, if not unprecedented, in their tenure

as policemen; they didn't go home, and were standing right next to Cups when he peered through the peephole and saw the above-mentioned Badiver turn over onto his other side . . . Sergeant Cups said, "Oh!" so loudly (and Smiles, who shoved Smogs, who had shoved Cups, so that he could crowd up to the peephole and see, too, said, "Oh, my!" even louder) that the newly-delivered-Badiver-if-that-was-indeed-who-he-was opened his eyes.

At that very moment the door groaned, and all three of them tumbled into the cell. Behind them, blocking the doorway, thronged all the other officers who happened to be on duty.

Badiver-if-that-was-who-he-was sat up on the plank bed and stared at his visitors.

"Badiver!" barked Cups, poking Badiver in the chest with his fat finger, in a tone that brooked no doubt. "Don't try to get out of it!"

"We know everything!" Inspector Glumet announced. He was referring to the wanted poster of the murderer from three days before, boasting a portrait that was strikingly unlike the verbal description of the suspect that appeared underneath it. "We know everything," Glumet said logically, because Badiver didn't look like either the portrait or the description.

"Stand up, detainee!" shouted Lieutenant Homes from behind the throng in the doorway. He couldn't see over their heads. He was short in stature, and he didn't want to miss out.

Overwhelmed by the confusion of the moment, the individual-suspected-to-be-Badiver started fidgeting on the plank bed and frowned. Then his face broke into a series of such hilarious, mutually exclusive expressions and grimaces, conveying at the same time such simplicity and goodness, that Smogs smiled, Smiles grinned, Cups burst out laughing, Homes roared with laughter, and even Glumet contorted his face so that he looked like he was suffering from a toothache. This was in fact the moment when the individual-who-very-likely-could-be-Toni-Badiver was dubbed "Gummi," because of his resemblance to a toy that was all the craze following the hullabaloo surrounding Brazilian rubber. (The toy was modeled after an old Scottish tippler with a pipe between his teeth, and when you stuck your fingers in two holes at the back of his head and wiggled them around, the old geezer winked and smirked.) Gummi—such was the name bestowed on Toni-no-doubt-about-it-Badiver by our brave policemen, who were famed all over Taunus for being quick with the tongue if slow on the uptake.

Embarrassed by the laughter at his expense, Gummi-who-else-could-it-be hung his head and rubbed the toes of his snub-nosed boots together—his feet didn't quite touch the floor—and for some reason this was such a perfect complement to his most recent grimace that old man Samuelsen in the next cell longed to join in the gales of laughter and started banging on his cell door, shouting, "Let me see, too!"

On Homes's orders, the goodhearted Smiles sighed, then went over to give Samuelsen a good punch in the ribs. Then Gummi said, "Did he fall yesterday, too?"

That was when it became clear beyond the shadow of a doubt where Gummi had come from . . .

To give them their due, the clever Taunus policemen managed to put two and two together in no time. No one was reported to have escaped from an asylum within a two-hundred-mile radius. Inquiring at the Daruma Monastery, where Gummi's earlier delirium suggested Badiver might have come from, didn't seem sensible; all the more since, judging by his blathering, it might be located in Tibet, if not Cambodia. (Added to that, Gummi had clean forgotten about the monastery when he finally came to, and, indeed, remembered nothing at all except his last landing. Apparently, the blow had temporarily wiped out his memory.) Gummi was vouchsafed to the shy medic, who promised to take personal responsibility for him. Samuelsen, charged with riotous conduct, stayed locked up in his cell for two more weeks.

Dr. Robert Davin, Esq., made the acquaintance of Gummi in the train station.

The doctor was seeing off his fiancée, who was traveling to Cincinnati to visit her parents. As soon as the train pulled away, the doctor realized how very weary the past week of unbroken happiness had made him. Only when it was clear that he could no longer be seen from the window of the train, even with binoculars, did he relinquish his smile. A pleasant sensation in his relaxing facial muscles made him realize he had been smiling the whole week nonstop, even in his sleep. (Thus, if his fiancée had happened to wake up in the middle of the night, she would have seen him happy.) This was not Joy's fault, of course. She was a charming, kind girl, and he loved her deeply. Yet now, waving his handkerchief for the last time, he might have entertained the thought that since their betrothal, the inexorability of future happiness had become a burden. He didn't think this, however, perhaps because of that habit of inner disingenuousness people call propriety.

So the doctor didn't notice the change that was about to pounce on him until the very moment he abandoned his smile and sighed, almost demonstratively, on the empty platform. And a thought came to him all at once, as though it had broken off a leash: How I miss my work! Such was the intensity of his sigh, and the determination in his first giant step along the platform, that he called it freedom. He managed to think about all of this in the space of a second—about the loss of happiness, the acquisition of freedom, about the subsequent emergence of that startling thought . . . It seemed to him that a thread of something else, something greater, attached to this triad. He immediately got carried away by the effort to determine the relations among these parameters (happiness, freedom, thought). Unable to find in his vocabulary the many terms now fashionable and known to one and all ("sublimation," for example), he pondered: substitution, transfer of energy, disengagement—no, transference, i.e., distortion . . . displacement? . . . Oh, come now, not these stupid reflexes. Reasoning with considerable intrepidity for those times, Dr. Robert Davin, an outstanding young man of his epoch, to whom we ourselves are greatly indebted, discovered with all the literal force of that particular verb that he was standing in front of a stranger, and staring at him so fixedly that it was downright improper. That person was, of course, Gummi.

Before drawing Dr. Robert Davin, Esq., into our narrative, it would be well to say a few words about him. The narrator is particularly agitated, and his speech somewhat hampered, by the fact that he is already aware of the fame and notoriety that the doctor's affairs, fresh and hardly raising an eyebrow at the time of our story, will gain in the not-so-distant-future. For the time being, suffice it to say that although the young man of science has fixed his gaze on the future and is doing everything possible to ensure his own recognition and immortality, he is not in the least preoccupied with it, and, unbeknownst to himself, it is the thought of outer space, something truly vast, and as yet unconquered, that has captured his imagination. He had not stopped yet. He did not even know that he already knew why his name would be celebrated, even reviled, in the future. And the fact that he didn't know allows us to treat him with the maximum degree of objectivity, and sympathy.

Dr. Davin was the scion of an ancient English family, one branch of which had bent outward and reached across the Atlantic. It then split off, and, despite the skepticism of the remaining tree, took root. (We will leave out of consideration the baseless claims of later biographers about the doubtful purity of his ancestry—a full quarter of Negro blood; the cruelty of his sham father; the various garret dramas of his sisters, which were allegedly a direct consequence of this cruelty. What we do know with a strong degree of certitude is that his father was one of the outstanding horse breeders of his day. And back then horsepower was still supplied by horses!) The future doctor received, it must be said, a decent education, which he finished across the sea, in Heidelberg and Vienna. A brilliant future beckoned him. Maître Charcot invited him to work for him. But the young psychiatrist resisted the temptations of success and fashion, and returned to his birthplace.

His homecoming was in part necessitated by, and certainly clouded by, the mysterious death of his father. As sole heir, the young doctor, who for a man of science was endowed with a surprising degree of shrewdness and practicality, disposed very profitably of his father's horse-breeding enterprise. With the proceeds from the sale he was able to purchase a small clinic on the edge of Taunus, where he took up residence. The windows of his study commanded a beautiful view of an open field. The unusually small number of patients that our hidebound, old-fashioned town could provide him with (indeed, there weren't many who lost their minds in the county, the state, even the whole of America in those simple and stable times) prevented Dr. Davin from being touched by the decadence that psychiatry, prematurely believing its recent history to be its Renaissance and Classical Era, had already fallen into. Dr. Davin based his system on truths—simple, sad, fundamental—like God's Green Earth, and we are glad to have been able to contribute to the formation of these wholesome principles. In other words, his thinking was far from bourgeois, and it never resorted to pallid notions of "liberty."

In short, Dr. Davin could not help but occupy a prominent position in our town when he settled here. He stood out head and shoulders above the rest of us, as they say. Indeed, he was a tall fellow; refined as a European, illumined slightly by the far-off glimmer of his future glory, he was a magnet for the gaze of the prosaic, docktailed townspeople, who were preoccupied with getting rich, and burdened by good health that was even greater than their riches. The latent power his every glance and gesture held for the Taunusians, however—the only semblance of intuition that they could have been said to have developed—forced them, by way of exception, not to hate the young doctor, but to step aside and make room for him, hoping (it was possibly Davin who first introduced the term "the unconscious," though he wouldn't dispute its origins with the one to whom it is ascribed) that it was the first and only time they would have to.

And so, Dr. Davin was twenty-eight years of age, tall, somewhat lean, with a fine build. He had a large, pallid countenance framed by an extremely black beard—that rare combination of the pale and the dark that is attractive in its own way. The hearts of the local young ladies came to a standstill under his stern gaze. A glance from those enormous and also very dark eyes, sharp as anthracite, made their little hearts skip a beat, and—oh, but if only our young ladies could grow pale! There is, however, much that is unknown to our small town, and pallor is one of those things. You might say that Robert Davin was, in this sense, the first white man in these parts. Having finished with their trembling, the young ladies confess to one another, in a whisper, that he frightens them. One of them, just a smidgen paler than usual, corrects them by sighing and remarking that he is "frighteningly handsome." (She was our town's first intellectual of the fair sex.)

But his gaze, however penetrating, was not malicious. Dr. Davin seemed extraordinarily attentive, as though he could look into your soul, which made some people take heed and draw back from him. This attentiveness was nevertheless also something of an illusion. In essence, the doctor didn't notice anything except that which he intended (perhaps in spite of himself) to see, wherever his gaze happened to fall—which also boded well for his future greatness. Maybe it wasn't so much that he actually saw "through" people as that his vision accommodated and made room for each person. This inspired others to be on their guard, while fascinating them at the same time. And they were right to be cautious: he was drawing up a verdict. For about a hundred years he would dictate his own insights about who they really were, deep inside. Again—*shh!*—for the time being, no one was aware of this; not even the doctor himself.

The doctor stared straight at Gummi. He might well have been the first person in Taunus who had looked at Gummi without tittering. The doctor, who found nothing laughable in his appearance, stood there immobile, while one thought drove out another, edging out the one before it. Something in Gummi's appearance captured the doctor's attention. He wasn't able to pin down Gummi's cast of mind with his perspicacity, and, funnily enough, the quotidian appearance of this simpleton just did not fit within our hero's established frame of perception. The doctor's professional persona got down to work before his conscious mind did, but, flipping through his vast mental card index, he found no corresponding card for anyone like Gummi. There were certain constitutional alterations in Gummi (though the doctor did not yet know this was he) that were not entirely in keeping with the classical interpretation of this type of underdevelopment. It appeared that if he were indeed an idiot, he had not been one from birth, but had been reborn one, regenerated, so to speak, and that the constitution of an idiot was an acquired trait in him. In this case, however, the regeneration had been very strong, quite improbable; something he had never before encountered in his practice.

Gummi, surprised, obeyed some internal imperative and raised his head, fixing a gaze of blue-eyed simplicity on Dr. Davin (though Gummi did not yet know that this was he).

Now a few words, if you will allow me, about Gummi, whom we left behind at the police station.

The times about which we are speaking were still uncomplicated times. A person who lived in them, of course, believed them to be modern and unprecedented. They used the word "progress" and were surprised by the rapidly accelerating tempo of change. The Age of Steam was reborn as the Age of Electricity before their very eyes. But although they thought they lived in the most modern of ages, we, of course, know that they lived in the good old days, which are, alas, gone forever. We believe that they were able to live their lives without much ado, in concert with one another, not yet departing from the dictates of nature with regard to humankind. Life fit fully and neatly into the time allotted to it—that is, time still managed to catch up with life.

As we have already said, the youthful blush had not yet faded from the century in this nature reserve of time. There was enough room in life for children, weddings, deaths, visitors, a tiny prison and simple crimes, the church, and the city cemetery. A cow or a sheep could still wander down Main Street, and people still knew whose cow or sheep it was. In this life there was a place for a town idiot, a vacancy that was not filled until the moment Gummi "fell" into our midst.

He managed to surprise the town only once—when he was asked where he had fallen from, and he said "the Moon." This set them laughing, and also reconciled them to him. When the police had become convinced that Gummi (the presumed Toni Badiver) wasn't a wanted man, nor was he on the run, they decided that he couldn't be suspected of having any other secrets worth knowing and stopped questioning him. People asked, got the same answer, and were satisfied. So Gummi from the Moon became Gummi from Taunus, and assumed his proper place among us, a place that would otherwise have gone empty.

He was given shelter by Carmen, a fat, old Spanish woman with a mustache. This was accepted as something completely natural. Carmen lived on the outskirts of town and gathered herbs, and she had a glowering and inhospitable countenance. But however hard it might have been in a small town such as Taunus for each person to choose a tailor-made and congenial fate, loose ends still managed to get tied up in those days. And although Carmen did not really treat Gummi like a human being, all the same she was thoroughly humane toward him. She did his washing and kept him fed. Moreover, it must be said that insofar as Old Woman Carmen didn't treat anyone like a human being, she was more humane toward Gummi than she was toward anyone else.

Toni soon became renowned as a first-rate woodchopper and as such justified his existence with a vengeance. He conversed with the firewood, and was so persuasive that it seemed pleased to split itself at his slightest touch. Then he arranged the logs in stacks that were a beauty to behold in both size and elegance. He was quick-witted and agile when it came to the firewood, but decidedly inept at any other task that was even slightly more demanding.

Gummi's existence was thus settled and serene. He was mocked only with moderation. The cruelty of the Taunusians was as straightforward as their humanity. They couldn't think of more than one joke, and laughed at this one with unfading delight. "Did you fall from the Moon?" And he answered "yes," affording the Taunusians sincere merriment and pleasure. It upset him very much that they didn't believe him, and that their disbelief remained as adamant as it had been the first time. This was in part what prevented the joke from going any further. He tried to elaborate, to explain to them that he really could fly, that he had even been to Tibet, where he carried water for half a year for the Daruma Monastery; but no one listened to his words. People saw in them only an unsuccessful elaboration of the joke that had incited their laughter the first time. Thus, the Taunusians were quick to edit Gummi's tales, pruning them down to the laconic and precise formulation: "Did you fall from the Moon?" And he answered, "Yes."

Gummi was a meek man, and although it saddened him that these people didn't want to believe him, he understood that it would be useless to grumble and argue about it with them. This was an example of how an awareness of one's inferiority can, in some respect, make even an idiot wiser than normal people.

In his spare time, when he wasn't working (and in those days there was less spare time, but what there was *was* truly spare, nearly a void), Gummi loved walking to the Taunus Railroad Station, where there were always a few newcomers who had not yet learned to run their jokes into the ground. He loved looking at the steam engine, which he found very amusing. He watched how it snorted and thrashed its knees rhythmically, and spewed out sparks from under its wheels, which spun around but wouldn't move an inch. Its temperamental nature and lumbering heaviness appeared ridiculous to him, and he seemed to want to show it a thing or two, but then thought better of it and turned away with a sigh.

In addition to these two pleasures, not entirely comprehensible to us, he also had an attachment to the commerce of Crotchety Joe, who lived up to his name. The fact was that everyone settled their debts for Gummi's labor through Carmen. Only Crotchety Joe paid Gummi "in kind." Gummi chopped enough firewood for him to last him till the twentieth century. Crotchety Joe paid Gummi back with pictures and postcards from the newspaper and magazine kiosk he ran at the station.

Gummi, who had no work to do on this particular day, had been loafing around the station since morning. Crotchety Joe, whose firewood was already piled up to the sky, but who had a soft spot for Gummi, notwithstanding his own nickname, couldn't refuse him a stack of pictures—stars of the Broadway stage. But presenting them to him for nothing didn't seem right, either. For this reason he found it necessary to repeat the joke about the Moon three times, enjoying Gummi's discomfiture, and to reward him just one more time with a harmless cuff on the noggin (which Gummi did not resent). After this, he could satisfy his unspent kindness and present Gummi with the stack of postcards as something well earned.

Gummi resisted the urge to examine the pictures straightaway. Hiding them in his pocket, he deferred the main pleasure for later and went to see off the train to Cincinnati. He laughed at the steam engine. All the non-local people had already left, and the ones who remained on the platform didn't interest him. He sidled off, then gingerly removed the photographs from his pocket. After he had looked at the first two, however, he realized that this place was not quiet and deserted enough for beholding something so beautiful, standing there casually as he was. So, demonstrating admirable restraint, he stuffed the whole packet back into his pocket, without shuffling through them or peeking at the others.

When he had made sure that they were all safely tucked away, he raised his eyes and met those of Dr. Davin, who was staring at him intently. He didn't yet know this was Dr. Davin. The doctor led a secluded existence and seldom ventured out of his yellow castle into Taunus. It was clearly the first time Gummi had seen this person, but strangely enough there was something vaguely familiar about him. Gummi was surprised that all the new people had not gone away on the train, that one still remained. This person looked at him attentively, intelligently, and kindly. Gummi easily distinguished this gaze from the others, because everyone else, with the exception, perhaps, of Carmen, looked at him in the same way, which was very different. He was struck by the way this person looked at him, and it turned something inside him upside down. He felt like drawing close to him and nuzzling his chest. This person was not laughing at him, nor had he any inclination to laugh. Gummi understood this instinctively. This man looked at him with an attentiveness that was dearer to him than caresses. Never before in Taunus had Gummi seen such a handsome and noble gentleman. As is often the case with idiots, Gummi had a very refined aesthetic sensibility, and the appearance of this gentleman, especially the corner of his handkerchief peeping neatly out of his breast pocket, made a deep impression on him. He was filled with absolute trust.

"Good day," Gummi said politely. When he said this, his face did not crumple up into the usual accordion. Neither did he wince or wink.

Davin looked at the placid face, in which only an expression of unparalleled trust betrayed simplemindedness. The doctor did not consider himself to be a sentimental man (that was perhaps the reason he was) but caught himself watching this face with pleasure. His own face seemed to grow more mellow upon seeing Gummi; it shook off the solid, stern beauty it wore like a mask, and found itself again, after a long absence. Gummi appeared to him to be an elderly boy.

Gummi greeted him, and regarded him steadily.

"Good day," said the doctor. "Allow me to introduce myself. Dr. Robert Davin." And he extended his hand.

"Gummi," said Gummi, and touched the doctor's hand in confusion, unable to take his eyes off the snow-white cuffs and the cufflinks in the shape of little golden birds.

"Please excuse me for taking the liberty to approach you like this," the doctor said. "But you were just examining something extremely interesting."

"You like them, too?" Gummi said happily. "Want me to show them to you? I haven't looked at them yet myself," he said in a mumble, rummaging around in his pocket. The postcards, as though to spite him, kept getting stuck. He was unable to remove them, but he was no longer afraid of crushing them, for the doctor said, "I'd very much like that." He moved closer, bending over Gummi's shoulder from his own greater height. Gummi finally managed to extricate the packet.

The doctor, a man who moved in the best circles, had probably never had the opportunity to see such brazen vulgarity before. The tawdry chromolithographs showed faces that were coarse and depraved, tired, and equine. Lifted legs, in black stockings, cascades, flounces; smiles as seductive as dried sweat . . . The doctor looked politely at Gummi. Such a heated, holy ecstasy lit up his face that the doctor felt somewhat unwell, a slight dizziness. Again he turned his gaze to the pictures, and saw something completely different. In each of the faces Davin read an unfulfilled dream, a primordial purity. Not a drop of smut clung to them; only weariness, the fatigue of hope. The doctor saw them through Gummi's eyes and was taken by surprise by a notion that seemed absurd to his lofty and irreproachable mind— that he himself was the one who saw the vulgarity, that the capacity to perceive it lay in him. He looked at Gummi with the delight of a scientist after a successful laboratory experiment: such a capacity for love he had never witnessed before in anyone.

"Heavens!" the doctor said to himself. "What kind of sin could a person like this possibly have on his soul? None, except, perhaps . . ." But even that sin, of such an innocent variety, was out of the question, he realized at once.

He stood there in rapt admiration of Gummi's purity and beauty. The elderly boy grew younger by the minute, illumined by the beauty his eyes feasted on. Gummi lingered for a long time over one portrait. It was by far the least provocative image of all those he had examined: a homely face, plain and not too bright, seemingly unsuited for the stage—mediocrity not cut out for theatrical wickedness. Gummi sighed rapturously. "Do you like it?" he asked. "Very much," said the doctor in all sincerity. His heart sang. He loved Joy again. He was seized with a feeling of exhilaration. He noticed that the air around him had become more transparent, revealing cleaner lines and more vibrant colors. Of course, it's autumn again, Davin realized. The world rushed along, rapid and precise, like an image, and again ended up in the same place. The world returned again and again, without ceasing, and escaped the notice of awareness for only a fraction of a second, so that it could be itself, unburdened by cognition and drab egotistical reflections. Davin drank it in like the rarest, most ineffable, water—like water that was more than water.

Most likely Paradise, too, is blessed with no special marvels other than streams, groves, and skies, he thought. But what streams, groves, and skies! My God! And the town—the town! For the first time he became aware of the town's layout and situation, and realized, too, that they were very pleasing.

They walked out together from under the overhang. Standing on the little promontory of the railroad platform, they saw the town wreathed and whorled in mist, still chilly and not quite awake yet; they saw how it curled itself up into a ball in the bend of Cool Palm River. There were clouds floating in the water, as though they were running away from a laundress who had dropped them into the river. Way over there, on that little bridge . . . She really *is* rinsing laundry . . . My God, how clear it all is! Even the train that had just left, way off in the distance. And, closer, the throng of red brick, becalmed by green crowns of trees just starting to turn pale, dust at the end of the road, cowbells modestly ringing out the good news. With what equanimity, what elegant simplicity, everything has settled down and arranged itself; it has no need to conceal, to hide, to muffle itself up. Suddenly it seemed to Davin that he had to hurry to love, because . . . such love . . . soon . . . would never again . . . be.

He took out a cigarette case, his fingers trembling. Gummi was reflected in the polished lid, and Davin, recollecting himself, offered him a cigarette.

While Gummi, touched and flattered, kneaded the cigarette with an unpracticed hand, strewing tobacco around, Davin came to his senses abruptly. The town had lost its radiance and was overlaid with a dull gray film. It was a different train, because it was going in the other direction; a garbage can, tipped over on its side, disgorged its abundance . . . Damnation, I forgot! . . . Davin tried to recall that cardinal thought that had dawned on him when he was seeing off his departing betrothed. It seemed the idea had followed Joy into the distance, leaving no trace. What was it again? Feeling, thought . . . no, no connection . . . Drat! It was imperative that he remember it—without it, he couldn't continue his work.

> Mental activity is nothing other, and cannot be anything other, than the distribution of movement, originating in external impressions, between the cells of the cerebral cortex. The words "soul," "spirit," "sensation," "will," and "life" do not refer to essences, nor to actual things, but only to a quality, an ability, or an activity of a living substance or result of the activity of substances that are based on material forms of existence.

Dr. Davin reread and then crossed out what he had written, skewering the page with his pen. He didn't tear it up or throw it in the wastebasket, however. He leaned back in his chair, rubbed his face wearily, thus wiping something *off* his face—something weak and angry—and stared out the window. Mountains of firewood were growing up around Gummi, and new logs were flying merrily through the air like little birds. At this hour, the sun illuminated the yellow gaiety of the freshly cut wood as though it were shining from within, as though it were burning with the anticipation of its eventual combustion. How neat and precise its death is, Davin thought. For it is already dead . . . Evolution is connected with permission to oneself, with the dissolution of the aesthetic principle. How foolish it is to say, "What an ugly tree has taken root there." The tree's nobility is obvious: it is devoted to its place of birth, it leaves no excrement . . . No, no! To the

capital! To Europe! Davin howled to himself in alarm. I'll lose my
mind here! The provinces . . . Who would have thought that it's not the
absence of theater premieres, not the stagnation, but this . . . This hyp-
nosis, or whatever one might want to call it. Happiness—of all the nonsense! What a meaningless category! And I, a scientist, whose sound
reason . . . How can such a word come out of my mouth—"happiness"!
The provinces are . . . happiness *is* the provinces. The provinces are
anti-science. They're blurry features, the inane smile playing on Gummi's
face . . . Gummi—now *that's* the embodiment of the provinces.

Why am I suddenly so tired? It seemed that today my soul had
finally found some repose. For the first time, perhaps, I allowed it to
rest, but it is so fatigued. Why? Perhaps for the first time I let it be?
And it became overtired, like babies from the fresh air, like convales-
cents when the sunlight streams through the window. My untrained,
frail, infantile soul. What, am I still saying the word "soul"? Davin
laughed out loud. I have water on the brain! Sentimentality has dis-
placed sanity. Could it be that sentimentality is actually an absence of
education, a lack of exercise of the soul? . . . Damnation, damnation!

He went over to the window and flung it open. He was greeted
by the smell of freshly chopped wood and the cool evening, a scent
slightly redolent of wine—autumn again . . . Behind the heaps of wood,
only Gummi's foolish head was visible. It appeared and disappeared in
concert with the ax. Gummi was singing, and by attending closely,
Dr. Davin was able to make out the words.

Viewing the land
from a wooden Moon
I see a maiden
like the Moon from the back.
One of them can't see
another one who sees
them both. But she sees only
half the Moon.
Oo, Oo, Oo . . .

He sang this sad little ditty with lively gusto, refuting whatever
idea one might, with great effort, extract from it. The doctor grinned,

and his envy faded. I can't truly envy Gummi for how easily his fire-wood flies when my words are so constrained, he thought. These are certainly two different spheres of activity.

Dear Joy, he wrote.

I am consumed by new thoughts that will overturn the state of contemporary psychiatry. Does this not mean that the new foundations of psychiatry are now being laid? I think that if we submit our practice to the sacred individual analysis of each separate case, science would fall apart into the sum of all these individual cases, one to every life. It is only a crudeness of approach, monetary rewards, practical mediocrity, and the practitioner's negligence that lead to the generalization and grouping of psyches according to the most approximate and rough-hewn symptoms and signs. Besides the exercise of crim-inal justice or a guardianship function in the case of obvious pathologies (which we carry out in a far from Christian man-ner), one must admit that our science has no right to treat peo-ple so. No one has the right to try to cure a soul except for those who love and have souls themselves,

he continued, submitting the delicacy and purity of these ideas to the benevolent judgment of Joy.

We are capable of destroying a primitive ideal, but are not capable of erecting in its stead a more capacious one that would include what we have ruined. If a person were paid money for what is characteristic of him, and not for those distortions and aberrations by which he accommodates himself to success, the prime minister and great scholar would experience the com-fort of their places, and so their happiness, like Gummi out there chopping wood. If everyone, having discovered his in-most secret wish, could be allowed to engage in the simple pastime that made him happy, the world would descend into idiocy and a golden age would reign on Earth. It is only due to the fear of loneliness that people are not all mad—and they are all mad because they accept the conventionality of social existence while failing to examine it in their minds. The therapy of real work is possible only in Paradise. The only explanation for what I as a person have done is that it is "peculiar-to-me"; but this peculiarity can be ascribed to me by myself alone. Otherwise, why is it so difficult for me, why does it take such effort, to do all those things I consider it not only my duty but also my vocation to do? Only because other people are doing things just as uncharacteristic of them in a worse manner than I? But doesn't this mean that they are simply more normal than I am in their inability to act uncharacteristically with enthusiasm, that they, the loafers and hangers-on, are closer to Gummi in this sense, truer to their own natures, even though they refrain from coercing those natures? The inertia of the philistine is natural. And the clarification of the world, that higher "naturalness" that I justify through my purported genius, is vain poppycock, depraved nothingness.

He reread what he had written, and was surprised by it. "What a poetaster I've become!" he said, and frowned in chagrin. "What drivel! I've become an A-1 bumpkin. How shameful . . . No, Joy is right. We're leaving. To someplace in Europe, if only to St. Petersburg. How, in my wildest dreams, could I ever have supposed I'd experience a creative breakthrough here, that isolation and solitude, the removal of all distractions, would be conducive to my work? Balderdash! Outside the small circle of those who take an interest in my work, all my efforts are senseless and truly futile . . . Back! Albeit to Monsieur Charcot, and his harebrained douche . . ."

Finally, Gummi's good-natured character had delivered him happiness. Life wasn't all about caressing logs, after all. Now he had a why, a whom, and a for-whose-sake—not to mention a where and a wherefore. His life had acquired a purpose, as they say. He was able to share his loneliness, thereby halving it. He was happy.

He didn't notice himself how, from the first time he accompanied Dr. Davin from the station to the doctor's yellow house, he managed to tell him everything: his whole life, everything he knew, and even everything he thought about. This surprised him, too. Even more surprising was how quickly he recounted it all, how small his own life was—like a newborn's. He felt stunned, and his jaw dropped when, halfway down the road, he caught up with the present moment in his story, and the two synced up: here he was, walking with the doctor down this very road . . . And that was where his story ended. It was crowned with success. He shook his head, laughing at himself, and closed his mouth.

The doctor took an interest in all that Gummi had to say. He believed him implicitly. Why, otherwise, would he have begun asking him so many questions?

Truly, the case fascinated Davin. He explained the ease of interaction, the novelty and unexpectedness of his own thoughts and insights in Gummi's presence, in purely professional terms. He didn't know how to explain it otherwise, and the sense that it was simply and inexplicably pleasant to be in his company mounted, until the cumulative vagueness of it all suddenly irritated him, and he was surprised at himself. What was wrong with him? On what was he wasting his precious genius? But here his thought turned back on itself, drawn by the good nature and ingenuousness of his interlocutor, and was reborn before he was able to understand it—a feeling of exuberance and joy. And the conversation flowed on.

He had never been able to discover anything about Gummi's past. Gummi himself seemed sincerely baffled about it. He didn't even know his exact age. He was not much older, but certainly no younger, than Dr. Davin. Of this span of years, he could remember only the part of it he had spent in this small city of Taunus. But how to account for the rest of the time? . . . Gummi's eyes grew wide from strain, as though he saw something in front of him, but this something was so unutterable that words had yet to be found for it. His own words, at times smooth and mellifluous, at times even eloquent, tangled into a ball, crumpled, melted, and turned into a characteristic idiotic mush. All that Davin was able to gather from Gummi's strained mumbling was that he had spent his whole previous life lying down, rolled up like an embryo in some sort of large membrane, through which the sky was always visible and was never obscured by anything. Sometimes Gummi said he was swaddled; sometimes he said that he had lain on something like a bed, a sofa, with his eyes open, under a transparent bell jar without a roof.

"Maybe the bed was standing in a field?" Davin said.

Gummi looked at him with alarm, then, brightening, said without a trace of irony, "Maybe it was in a field . . . I remember that kind of smell."

He could no longer recall anything about the Daruma Monastery, either. The memories had been wiped out. Before the monastery, he had probably slept with his eyes open, but in the monastery he had lived maybe a year, maybe two—maybe no more than a week.

"Did you chop wood there?" the great diagnostician-to-be asked with surprising acumen. This was a pointed question, and it jolted Gummi's memory.

"No. There was no firewood there. There were mountains. I carried water."

That was all. Davin couldn't come up with another, equally astute question. Instead, he brushed aside Gummi's past. And he began asking him about the Moon.

Gummi glanced at the doctor warily, but again caught no signs of anything but sympathy and genuine interest.

"Yes, I've been to the Moon," Gummi said.

"But how did you manage that?" Davin said. He overacted, and even though he knew nothing about irony, Gummi picked up on it. He noticed, and grew glum.

"You don't believe me."

"That's not true," Davin said with urgent sincerity. "As far as I can tell, you are incapable of lying. But you must agree that no human being has ever accomplished such a feat."

"You're just like them," Gummi said.

"I assure you—"

"You also say I'm not human."

"I never said that!"

"You said 'no human being.' Carmen says the same thing: 'You're not human.'"

"You have misunderstood me . . ." Davin began. Just at that moment he started thinking about the relationship between madness and the capacity for logical thought. Perhaps perfect logic is a sign, a symptom. Normal thought is, on the contrary, illogical. The mechanism of healthy thought boils down to knowing how not to notice, how to ignore or overlook, to change the sequence . . . skipping, shifting . . . There has to be a word for it . . . Maybe there already is . . . Thought flows on two levels, as it were, not suspecting its own parallel existence: in the depths is the mute knowledge of the ages, with a sheen of logic in the interests of self-delusion on the surface, like a garment . . . The ineffable is covered with an unruly layer of names, words . . . How empty it all sounds, indeterminate, all wrong. But there *is* something, a regularity, a mechanism . . . To name it, to announce it! . . . Think, think about this! he said to himself peremptorily, with an eye toward the future.

"They just don't know what flying means," Gummi said. "Birds, of course, fly, too. But people are not birds. People fly differently. They are not equipped like birds. People don't know how they are equipped, and think that only birds can fly. Of course, you shouldn't think that people fly like birds. And so they laugh at me. But I don't flap my arms like wings when I fly. That's not how it's done."

He's remarkably subtle for an idiot, Davin thought. There is no equivalence . . . As always, there is no equivalence! What is equal to what? What is sense, what is nonsense? It's just a conventional arrangement, the cynicism of which is obscured by yet another agreement, which in its turn is forgotten. Oh dear! Davin became angry with himself. Will I ever be able to get to the end of a single thought today?

"It's as easy as any other ability, if one has it. And just as impossible, if one doesn't. It's an ordinary ability, like any other. Is being able to smell something any less remarkable? Is there anything given by God that isn't remarkable or wondrous?"

Heavens! Davin thought. He can't be saying this! Did he say that, or was I just thinking it? No, madness is positively contagious.

"Well then, show me," he said without softening his tone.

"You don't believe me." The sorrow that suffused Gummi's face in an instant was so deep that the doctor gasped and nearly howled in despair. This was more than he could bear.

"How can you say that!" Davin said, losing his temper for the first time. "Of course I believe you!" he shouted, sharing in the delusion of many people, equal only to their guile, that rudeness is a display of sincerity. "I believe you!"

"I see," Gummi said with sad humility, nodding. "You believe me, but you don't believe *in* me."

"Listen, Gummi, you are a remarkable person. I say this in all seriousness, I am not laughing—you are a remarkable person. You don't even understand yourself how much you . . ." The more verbose and modulated his speech, the more confused he became: how many words did you have to resort to to make a person believe what you don't believe yourself? Actually, the only thing required here was words. The rest just—was. Necessary and sufficient, he thought, and sighed. I should have become a mathematician rather than trying to pin down imprecise thoughts about life. "I assure you!"

Gummi believed him and all but purred from joy. "I believe you," he said.

"Did you learn to fly in the monastery?" Davin's perspicacity and abrupt about-face produced an unexpected effect. Gummi seemed to recall something. He stared, round-eyed, his gaze fixed in front of him, at something that was not there.

"Yes . . . The Teacher . . . He drank water . . . I was supposed to grasp the empty . . ." Once again, words that had miraculously just found each other stuck together like warm candies in a pocket. "He drank the water, put me in a corner . . . Beat me a little with a stick . . ." Something seemed to burst forth out of Gummi's eyes. "He said to me, 'Where in this cup is that water I drank?' I said that it was in him. Then he beat me hard. After that he put the empty cup in front of me and said, 'Think about what is in it.' Then he left, locking the door behind him. I was there for three days, and I thought."

"Hmm," Dr. Davin said.

Gummi's face grew brighter. "You gave me a hint, and I remembered. That's how it was. I looked at the cup for three days."

"That's strange, to say the least," Davin said, sighing.

"Let me try to explain it to you. I think that's when it happened the first time. I became numb and cold. Then I warmed up all of a sudden, and everything became colorful. I was still in the same room, though. I began to feel curious, frightened, and cheerful. I was cheerful and happy, but I didn't laugh. I looked around me, and the numbness in me began to heat up, and to buzz like a cicada. Everything was what it was, and at the same time not what it was. Suddenly I noticed that the cup was in the other corner. I didn't believe it at first. I probably just hadn't noticed that I had moved into another corner, away from the one with the cup. I went back to it—I had to obey my teacher. I knelt down before it. Again I felt that something wasn't right. The only window—a small, narrow one—was directly above me, in the corner where my teacher had placed me. Now, after I had moved, it turned out to be right above me again—the very same window. I glanced at the corner I had just left to rejoin the cup, and screamed— for I was scared: there I was, still in the same position, kneeling. Little by little I recovered from my shock and grew bold enough to glance at him again. He was me, that was certain, and my fear began to melt. I looked at him more and more boldly, and sensed that he was waking up.

"I don't know how I understood that he was aware of my existence and was letting me get used to him. He made an effort not to look in my direction. I sensed that he avoided looking at me on purpose. I don't know how he made me understand this. Finally, he turned to me and looked at me mockingly, then winked. And suddenly, when he got up off his knees after winking at me, it wasn't him, but me. In a flash, he was standing over the former, empty me. Then I somehow leaned over to the side and tore myself away from the floor and for a short time floated above that self who stayed behind in the corner, timidly and without the least bit of interest in watching what was happening to me. He became boring to me, as though I realized that everything was all right with him. I hovered above him for a second, limp and bent over, then straightened myself out and soared up to the ceiling. And I was seized by intense joy! I knew that I had been flung wide open, and my incarceration in a rigid and heavy world was finished. Hastily trying out all my newfound possibilities, spinning around and turning somersaults through the room, and, somehow mastering all this instantaneously, I glided over to the little window. I remember noticing that it was dusty."

Typical drug-induced delirium, the doctor thought. Could he really have been in Asia?

"What happened next?" Davin said with childish impatience, no

longer surprised at Gummi's narrative abilities. "You tell it marvelously well. Then what happened?"

"I saw the monastery and the mountains from above. I fluttered
about like a crazed butterfly, and suddenly I discovered that I had
drifted off very far, that the sea was underneath me, and I began to
fall. Just at that moment, the teacher burst into the cell with a shout:
'Who gave you permission? How dare you?' He began to beat the one
in the corner, striking him on the head with a stick. That one didn't
budge, he was like an earthenware figure. The teacher kept beating
and beating, saying, 'Don't you dare! Don't you dare! It's a sin! You'll
be punished!' As though he wasn't punishing yet, only beating. Slip-
ping in unnoticed through the window, I returned to my corner in
front of the empty cup and obediently refrained from looking at them.
It seemed to me that once or twice, however, he threw a glance at me.
And then beat 'that other one' with even greater fury. For some reason
I didn't feel sorry for him. Then the teacher left 'that one' abruptly,
turned to me, and, staring directly at me now, said, 'Have you regained
your senses? Is it painful? Pain is empty.' And he left." Gummi again
fell silent. He was far away.

"What about the Moon?" Davin insisted. Gummi's cheeks quiv-
ered, as though he had jumped from a great height, and he wrinkled
up his face. Gathering his wits, he went on, but now somewhat wearily, and his words fell from his tongue more and more listlessly.

"I woke up on the floor . . . beaten and bruised . . . There was a
cup of water . . . I drank it." And he stopped.

"The Moon," Davin said harshly.

"I flew to it."

"When?"

"After that."

"After you drank the water?"

"Yes."

"But how? You were drifting. That's a very slow means of propul-
sion. It's around four hundred thousand kilometers to the Moon. Ten
times around the Earth."

"That doesn't matter," Gummi said with difficulty, as though he
couldn't get his tongue around the words. "Soaring is pleasure, it's an
indulgence. You can also just find yourself there."

Dr. Davin was tired, like Gummi's tongue, as though it was he himself who could hardly find his way out of his mouth. "Well, what's it like? The Moon?" he said offhandedly. Gummi's eyes grew glassy and mute. Something was approaching him headlong, coming ever nearer, until it shattered his stare. He seemed to see something directly in front of him, so close and so clear that he lost the gift of speech, because he wasn't remembering, he was truly seeing. For a moment Davin even imagined that something was reflected in Gummi's irises that wasn't there in front of them (they were walking through a field). He gave his head a shake. "So? What was it like," he persisted.

"Brown," Gummi said faintly, and a bubble of saliva appeared on his lips.

Good gosh, he's epileptic to boot, the doctor thought.

. . . When Gummi came to, he saw the alarmed, guilty face of Davin bending over him. Davin rubbed Gummi's temples. He was so relieved when Gummi regained his senses that he smiled with ingratiating tenderness.

"Please, Toni, forgive me. I overtaxed you with my questions. I believe absolutely that you were on the Moon that time."

Gummi looked at the doctor with love and indulgence, as one looks at a child.

"But I was just there again," he said, picking himself up off the grass.

Davin lay down to take a nap in his study and seemed to collapse. He woke up from the sun bearing down on his eyes. He felt unusually wide awake, and alarmed that he had slept so long. Nowadays the sun came to visit him on the couch when it was already after five, getting toward evening. He sat up abruptly, feeling out of sorts, and vibrating and ringing like the metal spring in the couch underneath him. He sat there for a moment while the sparks and black specks cleared away from his vision, then stood up just as abruptly. He stretched energetically, with a crunch. What kind of nightmare was I having? Rubbish! Time to *study* the nature of dreams, yet I'm experiencing them instead of working. He shook his head once more, laughing and chaffing himself: sensitive soul, beloved gone, Gummi, Toni, the Moon . . . Stuff and nonsense!

He sat down at his desk with confidence, ready to resume his manuscript on the nature of dreams. He loved the view from his window, loved to gaze out of it when he was concentrating. He looked—someone was out there, chopping wood. And that person was Gummi.

In the provinces in those days, everything fell easily into a rhythm. A random event today is, by tomorrow, already something familiar. By the day after tomorrow it is already expected, and by the day after the day after tomorrow it has become a ritual.

The residents of Taunus were used to meeting this strange couple walking along the Northern Highway, to town and back, toward the end of the day. What did they need to talk about that was so important? So as not to have to raise Gummi in their own estimation, the Taunusians lowered the doctor. The idea that the doctor also "had a few screws loose" returned everything to its proper place. Was it any surprise, when there were thingamajigs like *that* dangling in the sky? And they pointed at the dirigible. Here one should note that the provinces experience a paucity of events not because they don't happen, but because they have no need for them.

Rare objects are thus brought together because of their lack of utility. (It's the same story in museums.) Gummi and the doctor developed a need for each other, as though they were lying side by side in the same display case. That Gummi adored Davin, for his handsome looks, his astute mind, his humaneness, we can understand. But what did the doctor see in Gummi besides a curious clinical case? It is easiest to believe that the doctor's progressive mind was trying out particularly humane methods of treatment, unprecedented in the asylums of the day, on Gummi. Methods such as kindness, respect, attention, trust, an effort to inspire self-confidence, and so on—a whole array of them. This is most likely how it appeared to Davin himself, and this is what he wanted to see. But we have already mentioned that he was sharp, and observed the behavior not only of others but also his own. In so doing, he did not find this explanation of his relationship with Gummi to be fully exhaustive. He seemed to be unable to find a satisfactory answer to the problem, or to avoid it altogether. A simple explanation of this reciprocal attachment as a feeling of satisfaction from the righteous fulfillment of his doctor's duties (when it comes right down to it, people like acting kindly, otherwise it would be completely disadvantageous), and even the assumption of a certain degree of normal human attachment to a weaker, more innocent creature (a dog or a cat) didn't quite explain the phenomenon. Davin wasn't *attached* to Gummi; he *needed* him. He himself didn't know why. He tried not to understand, because in some way his contemplation of the matter turned against him: accepting Gummi's love for him, he understood that he didn't love back. And if it had been only about Gummi! But catching the reflection of Gummi's love, he began to understand that he was unable to love, as if it was impossible to love anyone *on principle*. Joy was no exception. In and of itself, this would not have devastated his soul so profoundly, had he not caught himself thinking that with Joy he didn't experience the same inequality of feelings that he experienced with Gummi. Did that mean that Joy didn't love him, either? No, that was not at all acceptable to the ingenious doctor.

So it won't do to think that their relationship was cloudless and serene. Only Gummi was cloudless and serene.

On top of everything else, Gummi had fallen in love with Joy. He was, it seemed, not in love with her portrait, as the doctor assumed, given Gummi's passion for cheap postcards; he was in love with *her*. The photograph had been taken on Joy's last visit and had turned out well—though it was rather a failure, technically speaking. It was Davin's first experiment with photography. He had adjusted the focus improperly, and hadn't kept the negative in the developer long enough, and the result was . . . a miracle. It was a bright white blur of hair and smile, merging with the dazzling foliage of a bush behind her. "Don't you dare move! Do not stir an inch!"—but that made her laugh and turn her head, and this motion and her smile were captured even as they slipped away. The moment was not stayed, but what remained was beautiful. It seemed as though Joy would turn back again any moment now, and happiness would ensue. Because her face looked like happiness at that moment. Not in the sense that it was "beaming with happiness"—if you looked closely, that certainly was not what you saw. There was even some sort of alarm visible in the blur amidst this flood of light. She herself was happiness. That which exists only now, but not at the very next moment; what exists somewhere, but not for you, and is not within your reach.

"Gummi? Come in, come in. Don't hover in the doorway like that. Come in and take a seat. What is it, Gummi?"

"I wanted to say that I can't find another stone like the first one."

"What stone?"

"You liked that stone I brought you yesterday so much, I wanted to find another one for you."

"Never mind, Gummi. You'll find another."

"No, I won't."

"Don't be sad, Gummi."

"I realized that you can't do it on purpose . . . You can't find something on purpose, because finding happens by chance . . . You can't find what you want—"

"What do you mean by that?"

"Finding something—you can't set out to do it . . . it's—" Here Gummi's voice began to tremble, then broke off. Davin's fountain pen came to a standstill. What was going on? "I would give my life."

"What? What are you talking about?" Davin said, perplexed. Gummi blinked as if he were staring directly into a bright light somewhere above the doctor's head. Davin turned around and saw Joy. It was Joy he saw, and not her portrait. She was there, in the garden, in the bright sunlight, as though he had a window there above his head and she was smiling because her Robert didn't know this yet. Davin rotated his head back around and was again confronted with Gummi's prayerful gaze—*he* illuminated Joy. The portrait dimmed.

"What would you give your life for?" The doctor's voice was dry.

"For such beauty I would give my life," Gummi repeated in an unsteady voice, his words turning to mush again in his mouth.

Davin remembered the postcards at the station and smiled disagreeably.

"All right, Gummi. That's enough. You're keeping me from my work."

Dear Joy, he wrote. *You can't imagine what an impression you've made, or, rather, your portrait has made, on my Gummi . . .*

•

"Look, there goes the doctor with his idiot!" the Taunusians said the first time they saw them together. "Look, there goes the doctor with his idiot!" they said the second time.

And if they had overheard (and they did overhear) what this small, bald Don Quixote and his tall, passionate Sancho Panza were saying— what they would discuss with one another, this arrogant bookworm and a bona fide idiot—their assumption that the doctor himself could have used some treatment would have been borne out so unequivocally that no other confirmation was needed.

"So you suppose"—for every two and half steps made by the doctor, Gummi made four blunt-nosed steps—"that it isn't the outer surface, but the inner?"

"Always the inner," Gummi said with conviction. "It's just that people only look at the outside."

"But if we turn everything inside out?"

"Exactly," Gummi said, beaming. "That's what you'll get."

"I see," the doctor said, deliberating the matter. "In other words, people's vision is inverted—they perceive the outer as the inner, and vice versa? Just as newborns see the world the other way round?"

"Almost, yes. Only nothing is really outside at all."

"I can agree with your argument, but not with your certainty about it, Gummi. So, there's an interior, and that is all?"

"That's the way I see things."

"But when you look at a steam engine, for example, isn't it outside you? Do you really see the boiler and the firebox?"

Gummi groaned, voicing an inexpressible chagrin.

"You wish to say that I have again muddled the argument? That you were talking about another spatial dimension?"

Gummi nodded vigorously, visibly relieved. "You said that on purpose. But I see the firebox, and I see steam—it doesn't have enough room."

"You simply have a rich imagination, Gummi."

"I don't have any imagination. I can't make up things that don't exist."

"Fine, I withdraw my example. You're right, it was a primitive one. Let's move on to a more complex machine. Let's talk about ourselves. You and me."

"I think the machine is less primitive than you think," Gummi said sadly.

"Well, I'll be darned!" the doctor exclaimed. "You were just arguing the contrary, I thought. That there is nothing complicated about human inventions, that they are lower than living things by several orders of magnitude." Gummi couldn't get any words out, and chewed his lip. "Did you not understand? Orders, Gummi . . . That is to say, levels . . ."

Gummi nodded. "I understand order. Order is when things are right. And right is when things are in their proper places. Machines, human beings, and the sky . . . I said that a machine was more complicated because it isn't on the outside. It isn't itself. It's more complicated than it seems to us on the outside, because . . . part of our complexity is inside it. We are not more complicated than it is; it is simpler than we are." Gummi was puffing like a steam engine from the effort of speech. "I can't express it in words."

"You can't deny that a human being became human because he evolved—learned, invented, gained knowledge? A person is the most complex of all things on Earth, precisely because he began from what was simple. Without the wheel, the lever, the sail, he would have remained at a very primitive level."

Gummi was straining. They seemed to be digging a tunnel from two ends, unable to see each other. The doctor sought words that were simpler from his side, and Gummi was unable to find words for what was already clear to him.

"They're even more complicated," he murmured.

"In what sense? I don't understand you, Gummi."

"The wheel, the lever—they're more complicated."

"More complicated than a steam engine?"

"Absolutely."

"I'll try to understand . . . This is interesting . . . Doesn't your idea suggest that the brick is more complex than the house, the atom is more complex than the molecule, the cell is more complex than the organism, that any single element is more complex than a combination?" Gummi nodded enthusiastically. "But *how* are they more complex?" the doctor blurted out.

"There is more mystery in them."

"Ah!" Davin was struck by this. He even seemed to understand, but couldn't quite trust himself. Gummi couldn't possibly be expressing ideas of such complexity, could he? Surely that strange idea—wherever it had come from—had simply flitted into his mind and then flitted out again.

"But a steam engine, a camera, a telephone . . . you don't understand how they work, do you? It's a mystery to you, isn't it?"

"It's not a mystery, it's a secret. Because someone knows. A mystery is something no one knows."

"Just now they don't know; but eventually they will. They'll discover what an atom is made of. They'll discover the mechanism of a cell. They'll discover everything, and it won't be a mystery anymore."

"The mystery will remain."

"I think," the doctor said, "we have just arrived at the question of the existence of God again." The doctor grew angry, and was all the more angry because he didn't understand the reason for his ire, as if it were as elementary as an atom, and no system of words could capture it. "You don't go to church, you don't believe in God, you have already agreed that God doesn't exist."

"I didn't say there is no God. I don't believe in your God." Gummi's eyes grew glassy, and foam began bubbling in the corners of his mouth again. "He's your machine. He's part of you. A person can't believe in God because God isn't on the outside. Because we are inside belief. We are a particle of belief in God." He began to mutter unintelligibly. The doctor checked himself, ashamed of his cruelty.

Just at that moment Carmen caught up with them. She was dragging a goat behind her.

"Gummi, let's go home," she said sternly. She led the submissive Gummi, and Gummi led the goat. Gummi followed behind her like a blind child. "It's a sin, doctor," Carmen scolded Dr. Davin. "You should be ashamed, doctor," she said, turning to fix her eyes on him one last time.

The doctor stood watching them for a long time after they had left.

•

Davin was ashamed. To be more precise, he was angry at a certain alien feeling that was either truly uncharacteristic of him, or that he considered to be uncharacteristic, as every forward-thinking individual does who rejects everything innate as atavism. Strange, but it was just this self-assured man, with the courage of his convictions, who was at loose ends in the company of Gummi, a man who didn't know the meaning of intellectual competitiveness. It would have seemed more fitting for Gummi to experience this feeling in his life and in the world: the perpetual inability to participate in the general course of events or common life—whether it be games or dance—in any collective activity at all. (We are all familiar with the sense of failure, when in childhood we were not picked during a game, with that feeling of abandonment and envy, watching from the sidelines all that elation— and that was nothing compared with the feelings of apprehension, even panic, or tormenting awkwardness, we endured if they invited us to play the game, and at that very second our dream was realized as violence against ourselves.) So it was not Gummi but Robert who felt this inadequacy, possibly for the first time since childhood, and there, in Gummi's presence.

He almost envied him, which was unusual in the extreme for him, for he envied no one, sharing his sense of superiority with no one but himself. Yet here he was, feeling envious of the most superfluous specimen of all humanity: a simpleton. Envy knows an endless array of shades and colors. Let's say, in a brief moment of particular sensitivity, when one feels an urgent tugging in the region of the heart, he could even imagine that his sympathy for Gummi was the result of a certain kind of kinship: "He reminds me of myself as a child"; or, "I was like him in my childhood"—something of that nature. *Recognition.* Or, regret: "Now I am no longer like that"; or "Most likely, I used to be better than I am now"—not going so far as to say in what way he was now worse. "I killed the idiot in me," he even whispered to himself once. But he checked himself. He was in fact constantly checking himself, drawing himself up short. "You mustn't, you mustn't," he exhorted himself. "That could lead to . . ." What? "Foolishness is indeed contagious," he posited. He was embarrassed for himself, as if he had

said something compromising in public. But no one caught him thinking this thought, and he would never allow his words to give him away.

Of course, if we peer back into those distant days, we discover far
more decency in practices and habits among people than we are likely
to see nowadays. That the doctor, with his advanced worldview, was
still incapable, not only of cursing, but of striking, offending, or insult-
ing, cannot be attributed to an excess of tact and delicacy. The time for
that had still not arrived. Thus, despite his lack of delicacy, he could
not help but feel some discomfort at what felt like voyeurism in his
contact with Gummi. Gummi was there, and Davin was not. He
tested Gummi, and experienced discomfort, something akin to shame
for himself, for his cold gaze of objective observation. Gummi didn't
play games. When Robert encountered his unique unambiguousness,
his self-sufficiency, or, more simply, his sincerity, Robert felt a sharp
pang of guilt. His thoughts acquired a tinge of moral feeling alien
to science, and became sharper. The doctor, of course, generalized,
broadened the terms (thinking in broad terms is a tried-and-true exit
out of a moral dilemma: I thought, therefore I did something); he
thought about the nature of human interaction, about the inequalities
of nature, about the psychology of interaction among unequal indi-
viduals, about the amorality of unequal interaction.

There was no way that people could come together in an appropriate way, it seemed. Accommodation didn't work. But how, then?
What about love? Only love rendered different natures equal and
made contact possible, because all communication, all contact, was unequal. Not one thing was equal to another. Love! Only that. How
else? Love . . . Joy . . . a son (who didn't exist, but might someday). As
a result, he caught himself each time afresh doubting what wasn't subject to any doubt: Did he love Joy, and did she love him? The latter
possibility was absurd. Joy was love itself, she could not help but answer his, for he . . . His interactions with Gummi led him yet again
to this suspicion of his own indifference. Yes, unequal interaction was
a crime. With this thought (which was almost a feeling) he sat down to
write his usual letter to Joy. *Underlying the inequality, besides the feeling
of pity that it elicits*, he wrote, *there is also Nature itself. What will the
victory of the democratic ideal look like if the Nature over which it triumphs rises in rebellion? We don't know* . . . After talking to Gummi he

found the emotional strength to write his fiancée about it, supposing that the explication of his innermost thoughts was sufficient proof of his passion.

We have already touched briefly on another aspect of the relationship between the doctor and Gummi. The doctor came away from every "idiotic" conversation with a fresh idea that called him to work with renewed energy. Gummi was now superfluous, and, as such, irritated him. The doctor needed to remove Gummi from his field of consciousness. Davin sent him away under some pretext, then planted himself in his chair and hastened to come to grips with these fresh ideas. He did not assume, naturally, that the glinting nugget of an idea had been transmitted to him by Gummi. He couldn't deny, however, his role as a catalyst.

Gummi used every opportunity to gaze at Joy. He dropped in and forgot the reason, standing in the doorway and staring spellbound at the portrait.

"Ah, Gummi," Davin muttered with waning tenderness in his voice. "What's that in your hand?" Gummi held out a stone with a hole in it, or a bird's banded claw, or a faded butterfly. "Well, well, well. Very interesting," the doctor said through clenched teeth. "Keep it."

If only the doctor had known that neither that stone, so far from the sea, nor the claw, banded in another hemisphere, nor the butterfly, native only to South Africa, could ever have been found in this state . . .

"But I'm not an ornithologist or an entomologist," he objected, reining in his agitation. "Get going, now, I've got to concentrate." But Gummi kept gazing at the portrait. "If only you'd bring me something from the Moon," Davin said then, laughing. And Gummi felt wounded each time afresh that the doctor didn't believe in his Moon. Exchanging a final sympathetic glance with Joy, he went away, downcast. But after a time his enthusiasm rebounded.

"Well, what have you found?"

"Nothing. I just wanted to ask you something."

"Yes?" But Gummi, lost in reverie, continued to gaze at Joy. "Go ahead and ask."

"Ask what?"

"What you came here to ask me."

"Me?"

"Yes, you. Who else?" Gummi turned around to look. There was no one else there. "Either go away and let me work in peace, or ask your question and then leave."

Gummi threw a beseeching glance at Joy. Then something dawned on him. He joined the tip of his thumb and his index finger together, showed the resulting circle to the doctor, and blurted out triumphantly:

"Is ———— a number or a letter?"

It must be said that he was right about this. The full phrase cannot be uttered without stumbling. Because, of course, *0*, when it is a zero, and *O*, when it is a letter, are two different things. And the question "Is *O* a number or a letter?" is easy to read silently to oneself but cannot be read aloud without some hesitation. The phrase contains a picture, like a primer or an ABC book.

The doctor was taken aback and didn't understand right away. Then Gummi drew an O in the air with his finger and repeated:

"Is ———— a number or a letter?"

Now it dawned on Davin, too. He laughed until he grew weak, and for a long time couldn't suppress the lingering mirthful hiccups. "You mean to say . . ." He was already shaping his lips into an O, when he faltered, realizing the trap for what it was. He was overcome by another bout of laughter; and, unable to pronounce *O* in either one of its meanings, and already succumbing again to another attack of mirth, he choked it down, sighed roundly, and repeated: "Is ———— a number or a letter?"

And while he spluttered and again exploded into guffaws, Gummi felt flattered, abashed, and distressed. He clarified, again joining his thumb and his forefinger together to form a little circle:

"This here"—he held it up to view—"a circle or a hole?"

The doctor gasped for breath, and his eyes bulged. He was unable to laugh, nor could he breathe. His face grew brown with blood and then turned a dangerous blue. Finally, he managed to breathe out in relief, and then, weak with exhaustion, grew gloomy. He looked at Gummi in a new way. A thought that he didn't understand, didn't recognize, flitted across his face, and in his expression there appeared something of a decision that he didn't make. A wordless, unconscious finality took shape. And his expression evinced that final pain of parting—the farewell—that is forever. Perhaps this is the way one looks at a leg once it is already severed. Or maybe not a leg but an arm. Isn't it all the same, once it's gone?

The doctor sensed all this without being aware of it. Gummi, however, was aware of it; and he was frightened. He loved the doctor, and every love lives for *something*. Where can it go once it already exists, but when the last crumb of this *something* is gone?

Parting is always mutual. Only one takes leave with the body— and the other, with life itself.

Gummi watched the doctor fearfully. He lifted his eyes to Joy. The pain and grief of his final surmise almost broke his heart, and he looked at the doctor in horror. "You don't love Joy . . ." he said in a whisper.

"Get out of here," the doctor said in an icy voice. "I can't answer your stupid question."

Gummi slinked away. He ran his gaze over the yard, the woodpile—everything had lost its meaning. Alone, alone again; but now he could no longer bear it.

Gummi's clear mind dimmed (we did not misspeak). His expression contracted and flattened out, his features grew lax, a weak smile trembled on his lips. Gummi's thoughts jostled one another and took on forms that were uncharacteristic of him. In some sense he became more normal, quicker on the uptake. The customary mode of a human being—sensing danger and trying to avoid it, or to flee from it— filled him with panic-stricken bewilderment due to the bifurcated simplicity of its impulses. "I have to do something, I have to undertake something immediately. It's not that bad, everything will turn out all right," he tried to persuade himself, but his doomed smile gave him away. "The doctor is just angry that I didn't bring him anything from the Moon. I'll bring him weighty evidence, I'll find something heavier. He'll forgive me, and his love will return to Joy. He's really very kind . . . Yes, it's decided!" And Gummi quickened his pace and his spirits rose. He cheered up, with a paltry human cheerfulness.

The doctor's pen couldn't keep up with his thoughts, nor the hand with the pen, which vigorously dodged the answer to Gummi's question about O.

Matter and spirit are not distinct from one other, nor are they heterogeneous. Objects of the so-called external world consist of known combinations and relationships of the same elements of sensation and intuition that in other respects comprise the soul. Material objects and the soul are, in part, woven out of the same basic material, so to speak.

The duality of life, or the unequivocalness of madness? The quiver of existence or the fanaticism of the idea? Life unfolds on the temporal plane, surging vertically in relation to this plane, touching something higher, retreating, and touching it again, trembling and gleaming with a double reflection. In essence, this is a metaphorical system with a reverse sign: life is a reflection of an image. Image and reality . . . As in poetry, to give birth to the image, both naming and the removal of the name simultaneously are necessary (so the flow can be captured, but not stopped).

Division is the condition of wholeness. A healthy personality is clearly split or divided. But the splitting of the personality as illness is the cleaving of an unequivocal, i.e., monolithic and hard, yet fragile, relationship to reality. No violence of the idea or relationship can accommodate or reconcile those two planes, in relation to which each particle assumes its being. Natural division is in a state of constant and unquenchable merging: division as an illness is the triumph of life over the petty effort to find a system in it (or, not finding it, to satisfy itself with an intermediate version, to come to believe in it, and then, reversing, to try to pin down life again . . .)— the natural erosion of a lifeless nature.

Dr. Davin, in raptures, sketched out his "homonymic theory," found among his papers after his death. It gave added life to his name in a new field that had only recently announced its independence, like the next Latin American democracy.

Why are homonyms rare in language? Because their occurrence points to a technical blunder in the system, the exception that proves the rule. Homonymy between two terms is the word gone mad; for every word is a homonym only of itself. Every word contains the spark of division into a sign (a stop) and the current meaning of what is signified (life).

Meanwhile, Gummi was striding through a field in active anticipation, lifting his feet up high so as not to disturb the stagnant heat in the grass. Grasshoppers flew out from under his feet. He smiled; he believed in good fortune. In his hands he held a bicycle handlebar.

Rhymes are another matter, Davin wrote. *They initiate an elusive interrelation of meanings, thus dissolving them again in life. In this sense, poetry* . . .

He was just about to formulate the meaning of poetry, which, one must admit, no one had ever before succeeded in doing. Right on the heels of this definition of poetry glimmered the dawn of the almost ineffable notion of "life." And we ourselves are very disappointed that, just at that moment, Gummi prevented the doctor from uttering this truth. The doctor was even more upset than we are.

"What is the meaning of this!" Davin spluttered. After getting stuck momentarily in the doorway, a triumphant Gummi tumbled into the study with a clatter, gripping a rusty bicycle handlebar in his hands.

"This," Gummi announced, somewhat perplexed at the way he had been received, "I have brought to you from the Moon."

The doctor seemed to spread out, puff up, and then to hover above the desk, as amorphous as a storm cloud.

"No, really, it's exactly the same kind . . ." Gummi prattled, plunging into a chasm of despair and clutching at invisible ledges of fate. But all was lost. Remorse strangled him. For the first time in his life he had acted like other people, not like himself. The doctor understood this immediately—he is wiser than anyone on Earth, of course. But Gummi's falsehood was such a small and innocent one . . .

"I was very nervous today and couldn't fly," Gummi said. "But last time on the Moon I saw one just like it. I kept wanting to grab something just for you, but I didn't find anything interesting. And then I saw this: exactly the same kind. I'm wondering if maybe I myself didn't grab it and bring it back with me last time."

The doctor didn't hear his excuses. He didn't hear anything at all. The eternal definition of poetry had just disappeared for good. He darkened in fury.

"Just a minute. I'll be back in a jiffy. I'll bring a real one."

The doctor flew into a rage and couldn't even hear his own voice. Gummi wafted in front of him like a ghost, like madness, a brown mist. Now he drifted in again, this time with the propeller of a future airplane in his hands, now with the leg of a giant grasshopper, the size of a horse . . .

And, seeing nothing, piercing the cloud of sobs and childish sniveling with his blind fists, slamming the door with all his might, then locking it and making it doubly secure by ramming an alpenstock through the door handles, and wrapping it with twine to secure it— after all this, Davin recovered somewhat. He still rushed about the study—there was something he hadn't done to make his isolation complete. He dashed over to the window, then flung it shut with exaggerated haste so that the breeze couldn't carry in even a spore, even a faint reminder . . . And he caught his fingernail in the latch. Jumping about on one foot in pain, swearing crudely and shaking his finger, his eyes met Joy's.

For a long time he stood there in the middle of the room, feeling completely hollow and empty, and something began to hum in this emptiness. He stood there for an eternity—whether for an hour, or a second, he didn't know. He walked up to the window like a transparent vessel, trying not to break or harm himself. He opened it gently, without a sound. The world looked at him. The grass, splashes of sunlight, the woodpile.

The grass is always greener . . . How much wood would a woodchuck . . . the doctor thought.

Gummi wasn't in the yard. In the region of his heart, Dr. Davin felt an unfamiliar, incomprehensible warmth of love. Gummi . . . he thought. Just at that moment, his warming heart was seized by something external and cold. Something alien and invisible struck his compressed heart from the outside. It rang from the inside like a jar.

"My God! I must hurry! Just let me make it in time!" the doctor pleaded, stumbling as he ran.

•

At the police station they heard him out three times: first Sergeant Cups, who sent him to Officer Glooms; and then Officer Glooms, who sent him to Lieutenant Homes. Homes returned him to Cups.

"Blockheads!" the doctor said. "You don't understand a thing. You have to initiate a search! He could be anywhere."

"So," said Cups, "what did he steal from you?"

When he returned to his yellow castle in the evening, exhausted from his fruitless search, he ran into Carmen, who was already half-dissolved in the twilight from her long wait.

"Gummi," she said, and held out a scrap of paper. Davin snatched it from her hand and pored over it, long and myopically, trying to make out the words in the darkness. Finally, he struck a match.

> No one needs me—
> but someone needed my gift.
> It is very simple to find yourself on the Moon—
> but the Moon isn't visible from it.
> If you manage to love—
> you lose love in yourself.
> On the Moon no one will ask me about the Earth.
> The Earth can be seen only from the Moon—
> but only I saw it.
> No one needs my gift—
> and no one needs me, either.
> Forgive me, Carmen . . .
> I'm not a human being.

Davin burned his finger, and shook his hand. "Do you understand any of this?" he asked.

"You killed him," Carmen said. The accusation didn't offend him. "Where is he?"

They found him there, a charred bag of flesh. He was strangely flattened, pressed into the succulent water-meadow in a bend of Cool

Palm River. He was half-buried in the earth, like a cannonball. They recognized him by the bicycle handlebar, tied up in a bundle.

The doctor examined the body. The nature of the injuries was such that from a purely technical point of view, no sadist could ever have inflicted such damage. Only a fall from a great height could have resulted in this. But there was no sense in searching the empty field for an Eiffel Tower. Nothing of that sort was to be found in the entire state.

Davin looked at the sky in anguish. What he felt was neither pain nor grief. It was the horror of reason, the crackle of consciousness, the despair of a shipwrecked man in the middle of the ocean. He looked at the sky, calculating the trajectory of Gummi's fall—the sky was clean, empty, silent. There was nothing up there. Then, his eyes roving across the impenetrable blue dome and coming to rest on a point at the far end of the meadow, at the edge of the woods, he saw the blue, cigar-shaped dirigible.

Davin clutched at his head like he was trying to crush it, and let out a howl. Stumbling and falling, and still clutching his head, he set off on a crooked course. He ran and ran.

While the investigation was going on, Davin fell into a deep depression. His colleagues were alarmed at his condition. He lay in one spot, his face turned toward the wall, and refused to talk or answer any questions. The investigation independently came to several conclusions, and he was cleared of the suspicion of murder (a suspicion universally held by the Taunusians). But these very conclusions led the case into a dead end.

A commission of experts corroborated that no human being was capable of inflicting that kind of injury on Gummi. Physical trauma of that kind could be caused by only one thing: a fall from a great height. The position of his body when they found him, not to mention the nature of the deformed ground beneath him, supported this conclusion. A person would have been incapable of falsifying the details of the event, as he would have had to crush the victim's bones in just that manner and sequence. (And this was a time when forensic science had reached unprecedented heights, when its fame rang out, when the experts, before the very eyes of the admiring public, poured out a substance from one test tube into another, hung charts showing ballistic trajectories, and reversed the course of the most notorious cases: victims and defendants changed places, justice triumphed, and the careers of criminal investigators flared up and burned out like Edison's light-bulbs.) No, the experts insisted, the corpse was not dragged to the field from the place of the murder. But why were the clothes charred, while the flattened grass was not? And then, excuse me, but where could he have fallen from?

If something like this had happened in our time, with its air-planes—or in an even more modern age, with its helicopters and rockets; or in the yet more distant future, with its extraterrestrials and flying saucers—the ordinary citizen's imagination would have a small chink somewhere he could stuff the mystery into. Every age has its vulgarity and its superstition. Say, on an undiscovered planet in the Alpha-Beta galaxy, a planet-wide gala celebration is taking place in honor of the successful return of Astronaut 1 from the inhabited (though at a very low level of development) planet Earth. None of the dwellers on the planet mourn the unknown hero Astronaut 0, who perished while carrying out his mission and never returned from Earth but who had blazed the trail. No one cries over poor Gummi in his homeland, because no one knows about him, just as they would never have known about Astronaut 1 if he hadn't returned. In that case, Gummi's strange babbling about spending a long time in an in-explicable transparent membrane, his uncanny ability to travel through space, his claim that he wasn't a human being, would make sense to us. One could elaborate on any number of theories and claims, in par-ticular about his death, that he was, for example, an extraterrestrial who fell out of a flying saucer; or that he was not an extraterrestrial but had been picked up by one and, having mastered a few of the knacks of future civilizations, had damaged his normal human mind.

But all of this is the vulgarity and superstition of our future, the twentieth century; and at the time described herein, the end of the nineteenth, both vulgarity and superstition worked a bit differently. This was a time when the natural sciences were so triumphant that their claim to be able to explain everything they scrutinized could have been considered the only superstition. Any supernatural explana-tion elicited the contempt of the enlightened public. For this reason, all explanations of a decadent-mystical bent, which would come into fash-ion a bit later (in the era of "liberty") as a pre-catastrophic spasm of the intellect—those connected with Tibet, magicians, and the like, ideas which would help us to imagine Gummi's ravings about a monastery in Cambodia, the splitting off and flight of the detached incorporeal substance, in the spirit of H. Rider Haggard or Jack London—were dismissed.

Notions such as this, therefore, must be dismissed as irrelevant and inaccessible to forensic science. Not venturing outside the framework of a materialist perspective, then, the only thing left to do is to seize the dirigible by the gills, as it were, since it has drifted into our story so conveniently. Yet everyone who had any relation to the dirigible had an airtight alibi. The dirigible hadn't moved from its position and couldn't have been located above the spot where Gummi's body had been found. The ninety-degree angle of his free-fall descent was beyond any doubt—the authority of Newton was still indisputable—and the imaginary vertical line projected from Gummi's point of landing led only to an indisputably nonexistent God. The proposition of an expert in ballistics who suggested that Gummi's body had been shot out of a cannon was also rejected, and the elderly retired colonel of the artillery was judged to be senile. The hypothesis that Gummi could have been struck by lightning was rejected with deep regret, due to the absence of thunderstorms for the duration of the previous one and a half months. The dirigible remained the only plausible explanation. But this was the era, not only of the triumph of materialist explanations, but also of the law's supremacy in such matters as the presumption of innocence. It was an era when, due to a lack of evidence, poisoners and sexual maniacs were released from custody in droves. And the enlightened public applauded the prevailing legality.

Gummi had no one—no friends, no relatives—who might have appealed the case and demanded that the investigation be renewed. Carmen, his only executor, arranged to have him buried in the exact spot where he had been found, where the grave had already been partially dug by his own body. At his head they placed the bicycle handlebar, as later they would place the propeller of an aviator who perished in a crash.

Dr. Davin continued to lie on his divan with his face to the wall, and we would be hard-pressed to describe the kind of suffering that lacerated

his—well, mind, rather than soul. It was neither regret, nor repentance, nor doubt: the brain itself, as everyone knows, does not experience pain. A certain empty bubble containing a single thought had
formed there, which resembled a dirigible. It had floated into his consciousness back then on the edge of the field, and refused to float away.
What did he want with this dirigible? What tormented the mind of
this great scientist was that the only explanation of what had happened to Gummi that held water—the dirigible—did not satisfy him.
The only possible explanation—that is, the only precise, logical, materialist, and, consequently, true explanation—was that Gummi somehow ended up on the dirigible and then fell from it. It did not satisfy
him, not because he could refute it, because he could not. After all, he
was the first person to see Gummi, and then the dirigible, and then to
connect them in his mind as cause and effect as the only solution to the
problem. But this connection grew in his head and burst like an ab-
scess, unable to sustain itself as an explanation. It would not serve as
such for Davin. It would not serve him for the simple reason that he
did not *believe* it. And this *disbelief* in the only rational explanation
implied, it would seem, that he did believe in Gummi's inexplicable
fall from a great height; that it was not a murder; and that he had
taken his own life (the indirect reason for which he clearly acknowl-
edged, but which seemed to him, in his cerebral torment, immaterial).
Since it was suicide, there was also a Moon, moreover a brown one, with
a bicycle handlebar that had lain about in its deep layer of dust. But this
wasn't what tormented him, either. What was unbearable to him in his
disbelief of the dirigible was the very fact of *belief.* Without the *dis.*

He never told this to anyone. The selfless Joy came to fetch him,
ready to wipe away his spittle till the end of his days. He rose from the
couch in silence, stuffed his manuscript into a suitcase, and they left
for Europe. The doctor's departure made a deep impression on the
Taunusians. Because nothing happened after that for a good decade
and a half before it all began—and how!—and they found themselves
suddenly in the true twentieth century, with its progress, wars, and
crises, and the departure of the doctor, the only preceding event in living memory, marked the boundary between the good old days and the
new. "That was before the doctor's departure," they sighed. Or: "That
happened after he left."

But they are not our concern here. Nor, indeed, is Robert Davin, who achieved global renown in Europe and produced students and theories galore, almost exceeding those of Freud, whom we will also not concern ourselves with here. We would not have remembered him at all, were it not for the fact that some materials came to our attention not long ago that were connected with the Shroud of Turin. This is not the time or place to recount the story, which boils down to the question of the authenticity of the cloth on which is imprinted, like a negative, the image of Christ. (Those who are interested may consult the widely known articles by Dr. P. Villion and Dr. D. Falk, et al., on the subject.) At around the time of our story the Shroud was photographed for the first time, and the negative revealed a positive image. This sensation led to numerous strictly scientific verifications of what people had not doubted over the course of almost two millennia. The discussions, research, and articles surrounding the controversy reached their apex in precisely the year that the Shroud was exhibited to the public. I will cite just two arguments in favor of the authenticity of the image depicted on the Shroud and the reality of the story of Christ. These arguments present an especially heady psychological challenge. The first argument was that the idea of a negative image became known only with the discovery of photography, and that no artist, even one familiar with the photograph, would be capable (technically) of creating a negative from the positive image. The second was that the Shroud itself, and the linen bands in which it was wrapped, were preserved in the shape of a cocoon. Their covering had not been touched, and no natural processes can explain the fact of their integrity and wholeness except the Ascension. Christ was not unwrapped. He disappeared from them.

Going over these materials, we came across a response by the well-known Dr. Robert Davin. It is strange that he descended from the heights of his authority and deigned to consider something that for scientists of his stature was extremely dubious and lacking in prestige, if not dangerous for his reputation (which every authority cultivates, the greater his authority). More curious still was that Dr. Davin failed to maintain his composure as a man of science and lashed out in a most inappropriate manner. Alluding to the classic "Gummi syndrome," described by himself, he accused even such an absolutely

skeptical and upright scientist as Dr. Howell, Professor of Anatomy, of
abnormality. This expert had merely observed, in his capacity as an
anatomist, that no attempt at extricating the body of Christ from the
Shroud could possibly have left the cloth in the state in which it is preserved up to our day. Moreover, it was curious that logic—a tool that
Dr. Davin had always deployed powerfully and irresistibly—seemed
to betray him. His arguments are imposed on his opponent by direct,
importunate pressure, and his deductions ring with a pathos that
boiled down to the formula: "That cannot possibly be, because it could
never possibly be."

But we are not really concerned about his views on the infamous
Shroud here. It was the fact that he took the matter of the Shroud so
personally that gave us pause, compelling us to try to understand it.

THE END OF THE SENTENCE

(The Talking Ear)

FROM *A Fly on a Ship*, A BOOK BY U. Vanoski

IN MEMORY OF ANTON O.

> When everything moves equally, nothing moves apparently; as,
> for example, a fly on a ship.   —Pascal

Yesterday was still sunny, and I witnessed a lush sunset. The sun dropped directly into the sea. It flattened out, became oval in shape, and all but sizzled. The birds, somehow joyous and panicky at once, chirruped and twittered about it. I know they do this each time, as if they don't believe that the sun will rise again tomorrow. I know very well why they make such a racket; although how much more seldom did I witness a living sun than the birds did!

This is what's hard to keep track of: what is the first time, and what is the last. People really have no true concept of time. It has set, but will it rise? We sink into sleep. Will we awaken?

I woke up again to the chirping of the birds, which sounded not so much happy as surprised, or even frantic: no sun, no sea, no sky. The gray walls of the fortress and the other ruins merged with the absence of everything else, and dissolved like salt. Only the barely delineated mass of the Church of Our Lady floated in front of my window, like the prow of a ship running up against a reef. Like a ship's bell, the belfry announced the damp morning hour—five o'clock. And with each stroke, the outline of the branch of a tree with indecent young foliage and a fat non-songbird grew more clearly defined. Songbirds, on the other hand, were always smaller, and stayed hidden in the foliage.

At seven bells the birds ceased their morning work, and silence returned.

I am on an island, albeit a Swedish one, and here I understand everything. I sailed here to be closer to my Russian subject. Russia is directly in front of me.

I just don't seem to be able to come up with the plot. Perhaps it's because it's Russian? Russian—or from Russia?

Russia has no plot—only space. It's the same with the ocean. The ocean has no plot, either. Defoe or Stevenson notwithstanding—they marooned their plots on islands, like us Britons. The ocean has no subject, just as Russia has no subject: there is no experience to rest on. There are no edges. It's an abyss. For a subject, the first thing one must do is close off space. Like theater. Like Shakespeare. True, recently we discovered a remarkable American writer. That's where there should be no literature by definition, and yet . . . He yearned to make it to England, but never did. So they browbeat him at home, never recognized him, those Yankees. Now he knew how to write about the ocean!

That's because he divined a protagonist—the hero of his story is a whale; a white one, no less.* As huge and solitary as an island. A sort of living, floating island that one must destroy, because such a thing simply cannot be allowed to exist. Truly, an island is a must! A ship is also a floating island, though a female one, so all our pirate literature is not about the ocean, but about islands torn away from Great Britain.

In Russia there are no islands. Out there where the islands begin, it breaks off, this Tartaria Magna. Somewhere in Japan. That is why Russia lost the war.†

Admittedly, I have never been to Russia, so it's not for me to judge. Maybe nomads view their steppe as an ocean, and their horses as boats? That would mean they are always sailing, and all their literature, if it exists, is also of the pirate variety—or at least about bandits. I haven't read it, I admit. I did read *War and Peace*, an unparalleled book, of

---

*Herman Melville, in other words (1819–1891). (*Translator's note [hereafter: A. B.]*)
†In the years 1904–1905. (*A. B.*)

course; but very big. Like Russia. They say the women there are beautiful. Helens and Natashas everywhere. But why do they keep speaking French?

I've never been to Russia, but I spent some good times with a certain Russian. He told me so much about it that the country coalesced in my mind into a little island, drifting along in a still unfathomable space. This memory troubles me, and I wish to unburden myself of it, turning it into a more or less ordinary plot.

My narrator—let's call him Anton, after the Chekhov who is suddenly all the rage in these parts—disembarked on the eve of the First World War, and made his way to a London pub that I also used to frequent when I managed to write at least something to the end, and where I would take a drop or two as my heavenly reward.

Anton spoke English quite well, and he delighted me with the strange music of his accent, as well as, it turned out, his mind. Listening to him over a pint was magical. It was like entering a universe that was not so much Russian as Carrollian. If truth is realized as fiction in Lewis Carroll, with my Russian friend it was the opposite. Every untruth was confirmed by his own life, and fiction suddenly became reality. I will attempt to expand upon this incoherence. Perhaps out of the resulting kasha (Anton loved the expression "to boil kasha," i.e., "porridge," apparently a Russian calque) it will be possible through patient and steady stirring to boil up a nonexistent Russian plot.

At the time of our first meeting, this Siberian who hailed from the village of Fathers (Batki, in Russian) announced himself as a member of Captain Robert Scott's expedition.* Oh, the yarns people spin in pubs! The whole of Britain was shocked by the circumstances of his death and the arrival of the remainder of the expedition. I didn't believe my drinking mate; and I was a fool not to. At our next meeting, Anton modestly showed me a medal that had just been presented to him by Her Majesty. "And she gave me a valuable gift, too!" he said, now with pride. He refused to show me the gift, however, or to elaborate on its value. "Otherwise I'll drink it away and never make it back

---

*This is how I am able to date our first meeting to February 14, 1913, after the memorial service for Robert Scott in St. Paul's. We both attended it, then went to the pub afterwards to "memorize" him (Anton's term). (*Author's note—A. T.-B.*)

to Fathers," he explained. But by that time I no longer doubted that
the gift existed.

In Vladivostok, Lieutenant Bruce hired him to purchase Manchurian
horses for the expedition in Harbin, then a Russian city. He was knowl-
edgeable about the sturdy, compact, frost-resistant horses, since he had
spent several seasons herding sheep—either to or from Mongolia . . .
Mongolia—is that in Siberia?

"No, it's in Poltavshchina," he said, and the irony of the joke was
lost on me. So Mongolia is in Poltavshchina? "He doesn't know where
Poltavshchina is!" Anton guffawed. "It's in the same place as Fathers!"
My head started spinning, and we drank to Fathers. "Well, all right," he
said graciously. "Now, Mongolia isn't China. Understand?" "All right."
"Alright? You mean okay, fine?" "Okay is American. We prefer all right."
We clinked glasses.

My God! Where is the subject? Every subject should begin with a portrait. But just try to describe my Anton . . . His portrait has no subject,
either. He resembles no one else, and nothing else. Just a towheaded
lump. An extremely smart one, by the way.

He seemed to lack even the slightest reserve; but the more he opened
up to me, the blurrier his image became, blending with the image of the
country he came from.

Everything seems to lose its substance in Russia, to become insubstantial,* spilling its contents in the course of the discourse (the more
one expounds on it, the more weightless it becomes). And as it reaches
its conclusion (in Russian, the word for conclusion and imprisonment
is the same: *zakliuchenie*), it becomes so insubstantial that it disappears
altogether.†

Some of Anton's observations and tales remain fixed in my mind,
as though he nailed them there. Now, the whole of that exorbitant and

---

*The Russian words for this, *plotnost'*, *besplotnost'*, contain, most appropriately, the English word
"plot." *(A. B.)*
†So in Russian, a conclusion (*zakliuchenie*) is the end of a discourse, and imprisonment (*zakliuchenie*) is
ending up in jail. *(A. B.)*

excessive country of Russia seems to be hanging on those nails like a bedsheet, with far-flung stations of destiny, where yet another pint marked a thought, or a thought gave birth to yet another pint: conclusion as the end of thought, and conclusion as imprisonment.

"If prison is an attempt to exchange space for time and then foist it upon an individual, Russia is an attempt by God to exchange time for space."

I liked this formulation; but I began to object, citing Newton's laws.

"Right, next you'll be recalling Archimedes and his bathtub," Anton said, interrupting me. "That's just what I mean: there is a boundary between space and time. And this is nowhere more clear than in Russia."

This kind of scholasticism unnerved me utterly. "Well, where exactly is this boundary of yours to be found?" I said.

"That's the thing, it moves. Like a piston, or a membrane. It's most stable in the Urals or the Caucasus. Although sometimes it runs through Moscow, too . . . But then it's a crack that time falls into."

"What? How can that happen?"

"Easy. A century or two just disappears."

"I beg your pardon, but this contradicts all common sense, not to mention the laws of physics."

"The laws of physics don't apply everywhere."

"How can that be?"

"Because I saw Lieutenant Evans vanish before my very eyes! Have you ever seen how ice cracks? Who knows, maybe time is a lump, and not a current."

Here I lost my composure altogether, which is fairly distressing for an Englishman.

Anton calmed me down and said, "The laws of physics operate here because human laws are also observed, pulling everything into shape. You drive everything into mind."

How I loved these literal turns of phrase from Russian! To "drive into mind," to "drive forth from mind" . . . He drove me out of my mind, but without any coercion—that was what astonished me.

"Yes," he said, conciliatory. "It's a misfortune for a country when the law doesn't operate but is still imposed."

"Who are you talking about now?" I was ready to parry the blow.

"Russia, of course. Everything is in order with you. Here, *pre-ce-dent* reigns."

"There are no precedents in Russia?"

"In Russia, everything is a precedent. That's why you defer to it."

"Who imposes it on you, in that case?"

"Which who would that be?"

"The law."

"Oh, I see. You mean whose side is the law on? On the side of the power."

"But what is this power?"

"The most unbridled form of passion."

"Passion?"

Anton launched into a homily about the hierarchy of senses (the power vertical), but I had already had enough. I refused to understand and went off to sleep without having grasped why we have not five senses but seven, like musical notes or colors in a spectrum.

"Russia isn't a backward country, by any means. It's a country ahead of its time."

"How can that be, since it already exists?"

"Maybe it exists, and maybe it doesn't."

"How do you mean?"

"Perhaps it is merely stored up for future use, not for present consumption."

"The whole length and breadth of it?"

"Any way you slice it. Makes no difference. The main question is: Why did we seize so much land, if not for future use? We made it all the way to California! We could have snatched up your Canada along the way. Easy! Only we had already forgotten where we had come from, and then we turned back. And regurgitated Alaska. What a misfortune. Giving it to you wouldn't have been so bad—but to the Americans?"

"And what are you going to do with this territory you have so much of?

"Look whose cow is mooing!"

"What do cows have to do with it?

"You grabbed half the globe, and now you're stealing it black, blue, and blind!"

"Are you referring to the slave trade?"

"And that's not all! The whole thing's a disgrace. But we don't do anything with all our land—we keep it on hand, just in case. That's what I meant when I said 'for future use.' Just wait until we've panned enough gold. Then we'll buy out Alaska along with India. We'll over-pay, of course; we're profligate."

"According to that logic, Anton, you're the most calculating of all nations. Who are you Russians, anyway? Tartars? Mongols?"

"Not at all. I explained it to Scott this way: Russians are half-baked Germans, half-baked Jews, and half-baked Japanese. All rolled up into one. One and a half people."

"Why Japanese?"

"Because."

"Because why?"

"Because you didn't ask me about Jews and Germans."

"Fine. Let's take them one at a time."

"It will take too long. You'll get tired."

I took offense at this. "Don't you think we're speaking two differ-ent languages here?"

"You just noticed?"

I laughed out loud. He had caught me out.

"Where you use one word, we use two, and vice versa. An exam-ple? Well, 'earth'; or 'birthplace.' Earth, *zemlya*, for us means both land and the planet Earth. But 'birthplace' means different things in Rus-sian, depending on whether it's written as one word or two. It's either a mineral deposit (*mestorozhdenie*) or the place one was born (*mesto rozhdeniya*). Let's say I was born in Fathers, in my father's place. That's my birthplace. But I panned for gold at a birthplace in Zabaikal. You wouldn't talk about a birthplace of gold, would you? But that's what we say."

I liked Anton. And he sensed this. "Here's the thing: the Russian is like a mineral deposit, like gold. You just have to prospect for him, dig him out, wash him off, and enrich him. Then there's the language. We have one, of course. Quite a respectable one, at that. No worse than yours.

You don't have to dig it up, enrich it, or wash it off—only prospect for it. Our word is a nugget. It hasn't yet decayed into synonyms. Ours is a word of unbroken ambiguity."

"How do you mean?"

"Well, what do you suppose is the most important thing in your language?"

"Umm . . ."

"Well, who governs whom? Who's the boss?" It took me a while to realize he was talking about parts of speech. "Why, the verb, of course!" Anton was thrilled by my lack of acumen. "No wonder you have so many tenses."

Say what you will, a compliment to your mother tongue is as pleasant to the ear as caresses to a cat. And I agreed that it was the verb.

"And what do the Germans have?" Anton said.

"Do you mean to say you know German, too?"

"I don't even want to! I only know that every thing starts with a capital letter, and that they bow down before all their things: der Table, der Chair, das Book, das Ladle."

"An interesting observation," I said. I wasn't offended on behalf of the Germans. "I quite like Russian, too. It's musical, like Portuguese. Those shushing sounds alone . . ."

Now Anton was pleased.

"Yes, we have a good imagination. *Zhopa* ('rear end'), *shchaste* ('happiness')," he said, savoring the sounds. "Strange that in this case we do take things to the end, bring them to a full stop. That's the one thing that all languages have in common—a period. The end of the sentence must be marked by a period.* Do you sense the difference between a sentence† and a proposal? Here you have the fissure between freedom and the deed! Mohammedanism . . ."

"What do Russians have to do with all this?"

"I'm getting there." Here he swung around like a boomerang. "With us it's not verbs or nouns—just adjectives. Even the Russian word *russky* is an adjective; maybe it modifies the noun 'man,' but that

---

*In Russian, of course, the word for sentence (*predlozhenie*) means both "proposal, offer" (of a hand; a heart; a drink; etc.) and "a grammatical arrangement of words in a phrase." (A. B.)

†In English, a "sentence" can mean both a punishment handed down by a court of law and a grammatical arrangement of words in a phrase. (A. B.)

word is missing." Anton's face grew markedly sad. "No man." This "no man" sounded particularly tender and musical, almost like "know-men" or "noumenon." It almost seemed to me that it was accompanied by a sob.

I didn't understand what he meant by Mohammedanism, and we parted, each returning to our different languages. *Na pososhok.**

Here's what we spoke about the next day: the same thing.

When I expressed somewhat strongly my surprise at the paradoxes in his thinking, Anton reddened, slightly embarrassed, then looked at me with downcast eyes and muttered, "It's not really me, it's my Tishka."

But "Tishka" was neither his double, nor his nickname; nor was it some intimate part of himself. It was his closest friend, Tishkin, a great scientist who had invented a contraption for flying to the Moon.

Although I was wary of not believing him by now, since everything he related had somehow turned out to be true, I wished to know a bit more—not about the Moon, but about the circumstances of the death of Robert Scott. Anton balked and clenched his jaw.

He said, "You're the one who says that a live dog is better than a dead lion. And I say to you: if a lion were a fox, he would be cunning." (As I have already said, Anton liked to flaunt his English, though in this case he had no idea he was paraphrasing William Blake.)

"I'll kill him!" he announced.

"Who?"

"That Finn!"

It turned out he was referring to Roald Amundsen.

"What for?"

"He had better dogs. And he took advantage of it . . . Ah, Robert, Robert! Why didn't you listen to me? Why didn't you take me along?" Anton burst into tears.

I had no choice but to believe in his sincerity, as well.

This is the story as I eventually came to understand it.

---

*Pososhok—a small stick, or "one for the road" (Russian). (Author's note.)

•

Anton purchased, very economically, the right horses, and Lieutenant Bruce recommended him for the expedition. Scott liked him, too, and Anton was taken on as a member. He was entrusted with the task of meeting and seeing off those setting out to the South Pole. He longed to follow them all the way but was left with the horses because of his youth. ("Again because I am Russian," Anton moaned. "Though what kind of Russian am I, anyway, when I'm a *khokhol*?" I won't belabor the distinction, but it seems that a *khokhol* is just a Russian with a different haircut.) Even with the horses in tow, he reached 84 degrees south latitude. "I just had six more degrees to cover!" he said. "Although I did climb a volcano. Almost made it to the top, but I got scalded."

This also appeared to be the truth, though he did call Mount Erebus "Elbrus." (There is a dormant volcano by that name in Russia.)

For his exploits he was decorated by Her Majesty. For these, too, he was barred from the next expedition and now had occasion to grieve the death of his idol Scott. News of the tragedy drove us to the counter of a pub that bore the name A Tired Horse.

"But where's the plot?" you will ask. "*Tyoo-tyoo!*"* I answer, recalling my lost friend's favorite little word. "I'm getting around to it."

And that's just what happened to Anton. Pfft! He disappeared just as suddenly as he had appeared, as though he had drowned in one of the mugs.

Anton had many favorite little words and expressions, some of them even English. Not only was there "knowmen," but also "know-how." "Neekhuyaneeknowhow-knowhowneekhuya," he intoned sadly, and this rang very pleasantly in my ear.

"*Neekhuyanee* . . . means 'nothingdoingness'?"

"More like 'doingnothingness.'"

"A subtle difference! So, which one is more correct?"

"Both are worse than *neekhuja*!" (You can imagine my surprise when I learned some years later that his expression meant, more literally, "Nofrigginknowhow-nohowfrigginway.")

Tyoo-tyoo—untranslatable, like *dao* (but recalling an exclamation, like "Poof!" or "Pfft!"). *(A. T.-B.)*

"Again," he said. "You have 'network,' together, but it's separate for us: 'net work. No work.'"

But if I had a fairly good grasp of everything he told me when I was on the bar stool, a grasp that increased the longer I was on it, that didn't mean I understood even a smidgen of what he wrote me in a letter I received a few years later.

Deap fpehd! Raitin English fyurst taim in mai laif! I rite uyo in zaimke, haunting uan Amerikan. Zei a not rial soldgeps! Bat weri welll ekvipt! We a hauntin zem laik kuropatok—smol Rasshn vaild hens—uan prope shot end sri aurs ken bi dresst. Its raze kold tu veit—I dreem abaut a guud shot of Whiskey—luuk! I remembe hau it voz rittn on ze botel!—viz uyo, mai Dalink! Bat tuu fa iz yoz Anton! Drug (vor-frend) creep op ti-khoi sapoi viz samogon (aue Whicky) . . .

I won't try your patience or mine by copying out the whole missive. Even with the help of a friend of mine, a Slavist by profession, it was not easy to decipher. At first I thought that since Anton had been fighting the Germans he was mixing up the two languages: these "deep horses"* as a form of salutation were somewhat bewildering. The Slavist got stuck on *zaimke* and wandered around for a long time in his "castle" (*zamke*), until he was finally mired for good in *tikhoi sapoi*. Even when it was translated into something resembling English, it still didn't make a great deal of sense:

Dear Friend, I'm writing in English for the first time in my life! I'm writing you from a pit, I'm hunting for an American. They are not real soldiers, but very well equipped! We are hunting them down like *kuropatkas* (small Russian wild hens): you can dress three with one good shot. It's quite cold waiting here—I'm dreaming of a good gulp of Whiskey (look how well I can spell that—I remember the word from the bottle!) with you, my dear

---

*Apparently the author read this as "deep Pferd." *(A. B.)*

friend! But your Anton is too far away. My fighting friend (drug) crawled quietly into the trench with moonshine (Russian whiskey) . . . to your health! . . .

I was very touched when it was finally deciphered for me, and I immediately drank to Anton's health, while trying to fathom the Russian turn of phrase "to hunt for an American."

I sent him a concise and friendly reply, saying that I was awaiting a more detailed dispatch from him, and that he should rather write in Russian, since I had a translator on hand.

Ten years later I received a hefty parcel. Throughout its long years of wandering, it had accumulated multiple layers of torn wrapping paper, miles of twine, and pounds of sealing wax. Unsealing it and fishing out its contents, I felt like my friend Howard Carter when he entered the tomb of King Tut.

The letter was as long as it was incoherent. Some things, however, were more clear than others. It was almost as if, while not understanding the Russian language, I began to understand things in a Russian way. Now the initial incoherence took on the semblance of a plot. I lost the ability to understand anything in the English way.

The bulk of the parcel consisted of the manuscript of Dr. Tishkin, which was entrusted to my safekeeping, and which I was supposed to pass on to "the most scientific society in England." Not only did I understand nothing of the Russian language and the accompanying scientific formulas, but the pages of the manuscript were mingled with Anton's own notes on Dr. Tishkin and himself. I had no recourse but to sort through it all meticulously to find out what had happened to the two in Russia (or was it what had happened to Russia itself?).

I replied to Anton, assuring him that I had received everything and that I would do my best to carry out his request in regard to Dr. Tishkin, but that it might take some time. I never received an answer.

My Lord, how tired I am of all of this! Of these footnotes, of this whole pseudo-translation . . .

I did have a life of my own, after all.

It ended when I became a widower.

Now, during this forced, albeit sad, leisure, I will try to assemble a plot out of the bits and pieces of this veritable bird's nest; to splice together our semi-drunken ramblings in the pub with the semi-coherent epistolary information. If a plot does not emerge, let it then be a sequence of events.

Before Lieutenant Bruce picked him up in Vladivostok, Anton spent quite some time in the city of Tobolsk, the birthplace of Dmitri Ivanovich Mendeleev (1834–1907), whom the Russians consider to have been the first to discover the Periodic Table of the Elements. I checked the *Britannica*,* and it wasn't quite true that he was the first. Ours, of course, were the first; but he was the seventeenth [*sic*] son in the family, and he received a whole column, which is a great honor for a Russian. In any case, he was finally able to complete the Table with the help of valencies (I haven't the faintest idea what those might be). Anton, as far as I remember, revered him not so much for this, as for the fact that he determined unequivocally that Russian vodka must be forty percent alcohol (no more, no less). This scientific discovery of his is not even mentioned in the *Britannica*; therefore, it may turn out to be true.

Do not think that I am so besotted by Russia that I am again getting sidetracked. This time I am already grappling with the subject—for the subject concerns precedence. Anton and I argued a great deal over this. It turns out that Russians thought of everything first: the dirigible, the steam engine and the locomotive, the telegraph and telephone, the electric lightbulb, the radio, the airplane—only they never brought it to fruition ("drove it into mind"). (He named a few more inventors, but I never found one of them in the *Britannica*. "Our encyclopedia is different," Anton parried breezily. "It's newer.") "Could someone with a name like Polzunov† ['Turtleson'] really have invented the locomotive?" Anton once said indignantly. "Instead of rolling like an engine, he crawled like a turtle. That's why we ended up sitting in front of the Russian stove and

**Britannica*—not a ship but an unparalleled English encyclopedia founded in 1768. (*A. B.*)
†Ivan Ivanovich Polzunov (1728–1766)—Russian inventor of the locomotive, not mentioned in the *Britannica*. (*A. B.*)

the samovar for years on end. Now, Stephenson* is another story alto-gether. A wise man." At that point he became agitated and broke into a "Dubinushka."† I liked the song immensely, especially the part that went: "Hey, green one, you go on your own!" What green one? Where is it going?

"You see," Anton said, having cheered up after the third *Hey, whoop!,* "you Englishmen are, of course, wise men . . . Still, everything that burns from the inside is ours. And when we finally manage to combine our Russian stove with the samovar, my Tishkin will show you! The Moon will become ours, just like Antarctica!"

Who is this Tishkin, you might ask? It's not Anton himself, is it?

Alas, no. But Tishkin is the hero of our story.

Tishkin was a bombist (what we would call a terrorist), but not a warrior or a fighter. He was a man of science who developed the technology for making bombs, for which he was exiled to Tobolsk. After he had liberated himself from his primitive tinkering with ex-plosives, he took a post as a teacher in a technical college and devoted himself entirely to his beloved Science. He invented a rocket for fly-ing to the Moon. He was inspired by the fact that Mendeleev was also from Tobolsk. The scientific interests of Dr. Tishkin were, how-ever, too heterogeneous not to distract him from his primary pursuit: local flora and fauna, mineralogy, astrology, folklore . . . He delved into everything, and concentrated fully on nothing. He was tall, broad-shouldered, pale, with a black beard. The local maidens fell in love with him on sight. But he paid no attention to them, since he himself was already head over heels in love. His chosen one, in her turn, paid no attention to him.

She was not one of the beauties, and not one of the maidens. She was small, round, red-faced, and taut, like a turnip. One would never have suspected that such a powerful voice resided in such a tiny body. She sang in a church choir but was more celebrated for her ancient folk

---

*George Stephenson (1781–1848)—Englishman who introduced the locomotive as a means of civilian transport in 1825. (Sir Isaac Newton first put forward this idea in 1680.) *(A. B.)*
†Dubinushka—not a weapon (like the Kalashnikov) but a clever Russian folk song. *(A. B.)*

chants, which she learned from various old grandmothers and remembered note for note, word for word. Initially, Tishkin took an interest in her as a folklorist with a natural talent. She was a natural talent in the sense that when she wailed and keened, she turned every heart upside down. But they called her Manya, and a mania she certainly created. She was considered to be rather light-headed: she liked to tipple, and she didn't shun suitors. No one could say for certain whom she preferred. Therefore, they all lived in hope, and this would promptly reach the ears of our Tishkin. He had, as we say, fallen for her; but he was one of those for whom jealousy was the primary source of his passion. The deeper he sank into one emotion, the more another one increased.

I rolled on the floor with laughter each time I listened through the wall to Tishkin declaring his love to Manya. (The room had an especially creaky bed and floorboards, and they produced sounds in different keys: *poing-poing* and *skreek-skreek*, respectively.) Having satisfied his uncontrollable primary urges, he poured himself some Russian whiskey, handed her a glass in bed, puffed—to mark the degree of his satisfaction—on a pipe (the kind with a long mouthpiece), and then began pacing about the room, making the floorboards creak.

"You see, my dear Manya, on that day Mercury was especially close to your Moon. (You remember, that was the day I found the Coitus Necropolis, very rare in these parts.)"

"You mean the day you killed the bedbug?" Manya giggled. She was easily tired by his talk, and just as easily grew tipsy.

"A bedbug!" Tishkin was indignant. "Bedbugs don't live in gazebos. What I want to know is, where did you run off to when you left the gazebo? You told me you went to a rehearsal, but what kind of rehearsal could it have been, when I found you the next morning in a disheveled haystack, in a likewise disheveled condition?"

"What was I supposed to do? Listen to you talk about your arthropod earsnouts? You pay court to them for all the world to see, but you have no sweet nothings to say to me."

"What did you say? Earsnouts?" Tishkin's voice sounded smug. "Is it possible that you're jealous of a bedbug?"

"And how!" Manya laughed. "Get over here, quick! Now I've caught a real one."

And the squeak changed key again.

He seemed to be an intelligent fellow, but the closer he came to an obvious fact, the less capable he was of accepting it. As a scientist, however, he believed only in facts, which Manya could easily strip him of.

"Look," he said, beginning to simmer, "I ought to know when you're lying and when you're telling the truth."

"As if I know myself," she chortled. "Don't listen to anyone else. Look at me. Can't you see that I love only you? Who else is there to love in a hole like this?"

If that didn't calm him down, she laid siege to him: "Heel, my little rabbit! Heel!" Although this pet name offended him, it always had a transformative effect—he seemed to press his ears back against his head. As she knew he would. The victory was always hers. A lean compromise is always better than a fat lawsuit. Let's have a drink, let's strike up a song! When she broke into "You Are My Sweetheart," he was ready and waiting to take the bait, poor old chap. How much feeling she invested in the song! He, naturally, took everything at face value, to his own detriment. He wept from happiness.

She laughed it all off with well-honed expertise. He, to her: "Don't torture me, don't become my mania!" And she, to him: "What kind of mania? I'm Manya! And my surname is fitting: it's Grand. I'm your delusion of grandeur. Do you suffer from megalomania?" "What kind of megalomania could I suffer from, when I'm a hopeless loser?" Tishkin objected. "In that case you have a persecution megalomania. Persecution by Manya Grand! Take your pick: either persecution megalomania or Manya Grand. Which do you prefer?" "Manya's better," Tishkin agreed. "At last. You chose correctly." And she kissed him. And Tishkin bloomed. The floorboards began creaking again.

"Manya, you are a science; and science is my mania. Manya! There's an idea. True science is nonlinear, like romance. There's a novel in there, too, Manya. Romance, as in novel, *capice*? What other Roman? What do you mean—you're having a romance with Roman? Who is this Roman? A baron! Oh, come now. Eyewash! I'm talking about a novel. A novel is nonlinear, too, like scientific discovery. Everything in it has to be revealed, uncovered anew, you see? This is how I explain it to myself: in real scientific discovery, the interesting thing is the nonlinearity of becoming, and not the results, however astounding they might be. That's why I say it's like a novel, romance or otherwise. I beg you, stop pestering me with your Roman! Oh, so there was a Roman? Well, all right, so he's a baron. A baron is also a result, it's a hereditary title. It's passed along, transmitted like a disease. Aha, I see! So that's where they came from. You brought them! From him!"

The scuffle turned into sobs and squeaking in the dominant key. Followed by the floorboards, again . . .

"You see, Manya, if the romance is a book, and the discovery is nonlinear, it's already worth writing a real novel about. You realize that the book was also discovered, don't you? No, no; a book needs covers, of course. That's part of what makes it a book. I mean discovered, like electricity, like America . . . No, in science only the path is interesting, not the actual achievement."

Poing-poing! Skreek-skreek!

"That's why you are a science, Manya. Or a mania, as you wish. And if it's love? Passion? . . . Will you stop nattering on about that baron? The kerosene worked, didn't it? You washed, and that was that? But kerosene also had to be discovered! Oh, that's a long story, how it was discovered . . . More interesting by far are these whatchamacallits from the order . . . What are they? Okay, crabs. By the way, how did you pick them up? Ah, you don't know. You don't remember. You didn't count. Of course, why count crabs? When I'm going to strangle you with my bare—!"

Poing-poing! Skreek-skreek!

You be the judge—an intelligent enough fellow . . .

But she had only to sneak out and disappear into the night for him to get all fired up again: Why so sudden? What was the hurry? At night, unable to get a wink of sleep because of his jealousy, he devoted himself to his other beloved—Science. But Science betrayed him, just like Manya. Even so, he defended it, too, with all his powers. He laid it out on a large tabletop, like a game of Patience: newfound minerals, plants, beetles, spiders, and butterflies, trying to align them with the disposition of the stars, and the stars with the sequence of the chemical elements. All with one goal: to expose Manya in a concrete act of infidelity. And each time, it turned out to be something that resembled a crossword puzzle more than a science experiment, but with a single, ever-recurring word: Manya. The links didn't connect up—Manya slipped away. She left him bit by bit: now a hand, now a foot, now an ear . . . Manya became a mania.

Vacation time drew near, and in his despair he decided to set out on an expedition to a distant region, with the goal of building his flying contraption. He needed an assistant, and he bumped into Anton at that very moment. They suited one another to a tee: Anton called Tishkin Tishka, and Tishkin called Anton Toshka.

Thus, Tishka and Toshka set out on the expedition. They rafted down the Irtysh, far from civilization, set up camp on a little offshore island, and there began assembling the contraption. The parts all fit together perfectly; but instead of a rocket, they ended up with a moonshine distillery.

Toshka quickly put it to good use, and assigned the head of the expedition to watch over the process while he went hunting for victuals to accompany it. He returned with a small wild boar, and found the chief sound asleep, with his head almost inside the firebox. "He's tasted his fill," Toshka surmised. Placing a vessel under the dripping firewater, he began slicing up the little boar for shish kebab. When everything was ready, he woke up Tishka with the words, "Let's do the test launch." And they started drinking.

"How is it," Toshka said to Tishka, "that the most beautiful dame in town is in love with you, but you fell for the frog? I don't get it."

"Go ahead and kiss her," Tishka replied, laughing. "You know the story of the Frog Princess."

"Did she tell you that herself? But that one was a talking frog; this one sings. I just don't get it."

"Is it possible to understand someone who really wants to understand?"

"You speak the truth," Toshka agreed. "What about science, then?"

"That's the point. Manya and Science are one and the same. I'm not seeking a general answer, a correct one, but my own. Whether or not I posed the problem to myself, I'm the one who has to solve it. And if I do, only then will it be solved for others. It never works the other way round. It's not something you can do better or worse—not a stool, or wool that you must spoil before you spin it well. In those cases the substance they were made of stays the same. Only a singular, unique solution changes the substance. Oh, how well I understand the alchemist! He wasn't seeking profits from gold or the elixir of life but the very birth of the substance. For thought itself is a substance. This is not within the power of man, however, but only of . . . I won't even say whom. The One who Created Water!"

Like a devoted student, Toshka knew how to sleep with his eyes open.

"His thought is his most precise instrument. A true scientist cannot be a nonbeliever, just as a real believer cannot help but be a materialist. Render unto God what is God's. Otherwise we will always fall victim to scientific error—face-to-face with a soulless instrument and a drunken lab assistant who didn't wash the test tubes. There has to be a third: an observer. Without a point from above, the experiment is impossible. Who's going to oversee the experiment? Who's going to oversee the overseeing of the experiment? Hey, I'm talking to you!"

"I always wash your dishes," Toshka mumbled.

"I'm not reproaching you. 'What could be more fascinating than following the thoughts of a great man?' our Pushkin once said. Manya, you say. Beauty, you say. But I say that beauty is the elaboration of our vision, not an objective category. What do you know about the feelings of a blossom when it is visited by a bee? Oh, if only the ear could utter what it hears! I will create a Talking Ear!"

"A talking ear? An ear you can hear? Ah, you mean an echo!"

"No echo. Just an ear," Tishkin said impatiently. "Without belief in something, life is meaningless—this is what I believe. It's impossible, it's perfidious, it's terrifying, it's nausea! Without belief, our attempts to understand life become a dangerous temptation. And God forbid that our approximate idea were ever confirmed by the imprecise reading of an instrument—then it would be a double mistake! (A good name for a book . . .)"

Whether they drank for a long time or a short time, when they sensed the approach of autumn they hurried home. Tishkin had managed to collect only a small sampling of lichen, but, in addition, he had come to suspect that there was a sizable diamond deposit in the vicinity. He decided to call it Beckandcall (Zamanilovo), in honor of Gogol, Manilov, and Manya.

They returned with this scientific baggage, and despite his precipitate return, Tishkin did not catch Manya in any compromising activity. This made him suspect her even more, and he persuaded himself of the certainty of the diamond deposit. He laid out the new exhibits on the tabletop, adding to them exhibits that were already present in the collection, and the stars tending toward autumn burned more brightly. He perceived the simultaneity of all these phenomena—lichens and stars, minerals and butterflies, Tobolsk and St. Petersburg, Mendeleev and Manilov, diamonds and Manya. Feeling a wave of nausea welling up in him from all this temporal coexistence, and unable to find a formula for it, or an exit from it, he took a swig from the bottle they had brought back with them from the expedition and wrote down the title of his opus in big block letters:

A BRIEF INTRODUCTION TO A COURSE ON THE THEORY OF UNIVERSAL SYMMETRY

... and woke up with the precise feeling that yesterday's arrangement of scientific exhibits would at last bring an end to the anguish of his ignorance, because he would be able to prove scientifically his betrayal by the full-throated Manya. He rushed over to the tabletop and saw, as clear as day, the Periodic Table of the Elements, the very same Table that the world's greatest minds, including Dmitri Mendeleev himself, had been sweating over for many a year.

Not only Manya's enigmas but also a great scientific law were concealed in yesterday's arrangement. Forgetting his passion, Tishkin threw himself into the task of writing down his discovery in scientific form, and was brought up short by the news that Mendeleev had just announced it as his own, claiming as well that the long-awaited solution to the problem had appeared to him in a dream. Tishkin's discovery was, again, belated.

Overcome by the same attack of nausea that always accompanied a surge of genius, he suddenly saw that Sir Isaac Newton was not really so unshakable, that he, too, was relatively relative—to Tishkin, let's say. That everything in the world was relative in relation to relationship. Clear-cut mathematical definitions suddenly lay themselves down easily on paper, definitions not of a universal theory of symmetry but a universal theory of nausea. This time he didn't rush to broadcast his discovery but verified it, and verified it again; and everything checked out and shone even brighter, with more promise—until he discovered that some German named Einstein had stuck out his tongue on the same grounds.

He summoned his loyal Toshka, and they drank together, not in an expeditionary spirit this time but in a domestic spirit: they went on a binge for the whole winter. Toward spring, he announced that it was over, that he had done a complete about-face, that he was finished with science and drink forever, that Manya was going to marry him and bear him six children—the same number Pushkin had. He'd had enough of the crosswords, he was moving on to the jigsaw puzzle! What the jigsaw puzzle was he couldn't explain to Toshka—it seemed to be a novel about science unlike anything world literature had ever known. He found the title straightaway—*Simple Solutions*. And the first one was to lock up the bottle in the cupboard and throw away the key. Soon he was calling Manya and Toshka to come hear the beginning. While still not drinking himself, he wanted to treat them to a drink, just to guarantee his success; but the key was gone. With her shoulder pressed against it, Manya heaved the cupboard aside (it turned out not to have a back panel) and easily retrieved the bottle. Tishkin, delighted with her exploit, was nevertheless surprised by the obvious lightness of the bottle. There were only a few drops left sloshing around on the bottom. There was enough for one glass each, however. They drank, cleared their throats, and sat down, placing their hands on their knees as though for a photograph.

And so Tishkin began reading.

I don't know why I don't have a single idea in my head, I thought. And everyone considers me to be intelligent.

Mrs. Down in particular. I am deeply indebted to her. If it weren't for her authority over Mr. Down, our chancellor, the university would long ago have learned to do without me.

But here I am, sitting in a boat and rowing, and Mrs. Down is blocking the view with her hat. For this reason I am thinking about how I am not thinking. These gray curving threads with facets hardly noticeable in their breadth cannot be considered thoughts, can they?

Whether something runs along them, or I am clambering up them . . .

As though it's possible to see something inside your skull. But, then, why not? Consciousness is thought, is it not?

How much better it used to be, not so long ago: you sit in a bathtub—a law; an apple falls—another law. Newton hands Archimedes an apple.

Something knocked against the side of the boat, and I imagined the whole lake filled with apples, that I was rowing, and having a hard time shoving the oars through them; but it turned out that it was Mrs. Down asking me to turn back. I thought that now I would be able to see the view, but the hat turned around with her, with the view, that is; with Mrs. Down, that is; with the boat, that is; that is, with me . . . But how could it be otherwise? Only, what is inside what? The hat isn't the issue, it's all old hat now . . . I have to remember that idea.

And I forgot everything forthwith. As soon as I thought it, I promptly forgot it. Why do I never think about anything? I looked out the window in annoyance. It turned out I wasn't in a boat. If a thought is expressed in words, and between every word, even between every sound, time passes, what kind of thought is that? It's a length, a distance measured by words. And every word keeps its own distance. What a collision ensues when they try to express something! The distance the word "Cosmos" keeps is far less than that of "fly." No, not harmony! One must listen to the cacophony. Brownian motion—in that, at least, there is something besides a bathtub with apples.

Chaos is the most uniform condition.

It turned out I wasn't rowing at all but playing the violin. At least in music the distance between sounds is measured out. That was when I laid the violin aside in vexation to look out the window.

Just yesterday, the nineteenth century was in full swing. Today it's already the twentieth century, and nothing has changed. Has time changed? But what in the world is time, after all?

Is it not just the measure of our annoyance at our absence within it? What prevents us from being happy?

And again my mind is a blank. I see the two girls again: one very fair with brown eyes, the other dark-haired with blue eyes. It doesn't count that I am thinking about them, does it? What kind of thought is that? On the other hand, I am thinking about them, not about the twentieth century. If one were to swap their eyes around, nothing good would come of it . . . but this way it's impossible to choose between them.

Equality is transient. All of this is extremely relative. Except perhaps symmetry.

The stamp of the Creator is everywhere, like the fingerprint of a criminal. A fish skeleton and a leaf. A blossom and a woman's secret places . . . No, that could go on forever; and we won't get started on that! We are not yet ready. The crystal is more symmetrical than the human heart. Living and unliving . . .

Adequate perception is impossible. It is not within the power of consciousness, only of God.

It is impossible to perceive God. That is why we come up with laws, using them like steps on a ladder leading to Him. We clamber up a ladder; but there is a Way. It is considerably more accessible than gradualness—another trajectory or speed. And if we ourselves are a point on this trajectory, we coincide with the velocity, and cancel out time.

Cursed rhythm! It exists.

Where was I? Oh yes, fair or dark? Blue or brown?

It's not as simple as it seems. Choice—is it a rhythm?

I'm getting mixed up. I've lost my train of thought. Or was it still just the beginning?

Yes, precisely. Mrs. Down took a fancy to me. I don't know how I had acquired my fame, but fame was already mine. Most likely because I had capsized in the boat . . . I had been invited to a party and everyone was expecting something of me. I was supposed to toss off a little number for them. Alcohol was alien to me, and I was sick of it all. Their tablecloth was sumptuous, like something out of Windsor Castle. "Bring me some scissors," I said. They were glad to, they bustled around, they brought them to me. Silver ones, on a silver platter.

I began to snip—everyone watched, thrilled. I snipped and snipped . . . I reached the middle of the table. And again I got sick of it all. Everyone watched me expectantly. "I forget the rest," I said.

I put the scissors down on the table and left.

It was all so silly . . . On top of everything else, I stuck out my tongue at them.

But what do you know? They were all very pleased, and my fame only increased.

Now, stupidity is not relative. It doesn't depend on anything, because it's too rational.

They wanted to be entertained, and entertained they were—no madness there at all.

Everything is static, there is no velocity, no time. One has to find the stupidest of all solutions. You don't need to solve, you need to re-solve, so that if you gain renown it will be once and for all, and you'll never have to do anything again! Otherwise it looks like everyone keeps slaving away, and I'm the only loafer around here. "With your talent," they say to me. "If we were in your place, we would long ago have . . ." Oh, how I hate these go-getters!

Who are they? These chancellors, vice-chancellors, department chairs, division heads, editors-in-chief? Conductors and directors of talent that is not their own! Politicians and businessmen.

No, they're not the same—serious fellows, those crooks. They get to boss the go-getters around.

It's good at least that they take me to be a Jew. I won't try to deny it.

Fine, then. But what can I resolve to do? Something mad and beautiful . . .

The stupidest thing of all is the simplest thing of all. The simplest—single-celled—organisms, the protozoa, reproduce by binary fission. An amoeba is the living model of the atom. The cell is huge, like a molecule . . . Which of them undergoes fission, divides itself? Everything divides. Endlessly, in one direction or the other.

But what if everything that is were simultaneous, concurrent? The past, the present, the future, space, speed, time, the void, thought?

Pulse, explosion! Silence.

Fearlessness—that's what is frightening. That's what life is.

Life is more frightening than death, because in death there is no you.

"For in death there is no remembrance of Thee . . ." That's a good line.

Only I don't agree. Because memory is all that remains of God.

That is, everything is always simultaneous.

Lord! When did I get entangled in these gray fibers?

Already as a child. As I chased the fugue reluctantly to and fro on the violin. I imagined it as a nauseous infinity, and the string snapped. It curled into a ringlet in the joy of release. I sneaked outside for a walk, too, so I wouldn't get spanked by my father.

When I walk, I don't think about anything at all. What's more, I can think about nothing at all for hours on end. I feel surprised if, on occasion, I realize I'm hungry, or I'm freezing cold, or it has started to rain. And then I start thinking for the first time—what have I been doing all this time? Doing or thinking? Well, I do love reading signboards: a peculiar sort of inventory of the world.

On schools it says SCHOOL; on a hospital, HOSPITAL; on a store, STORE. As if one would otherwise never know. After all, it doesn't say TREE on a tree. Same with clouds.

Wandering around at night, I filched a lot of them, these signboards. It's like a collection. I even have a sign from a police station.

When I tried to court the fair one (the brown-eyed girl), I was in the throes of jealousy regarding her interest in a rugby captain. I suspected her of being unfaithful but couldn't prove it. Just when the indirect and incoherent evidence started to seem incontrovertible, my attempts to pin it down caused it to unravel all over again.

During the sleepless, jealous nights, I would lay out my collection on the floor like a game of Patience. Suddenly, a map of the city appeared, overlaid with a map of the starry sky. Playing cards were laid out for the next layer, but I couldn't remember their fortune-telling values. I had to resort to the Tarot. At least they say what they mean: the Fool, the Hanged Man, the Empress . . .

What else?

I arranged all the elements by their atomic weights, then shuffled them around. Suddenly, it all fell together: the Table of the Elements— very elegant. The guilt of the unfaithful lover seemed to be established beyond the shadow of a doubt. The Table had been devised already: by some Russian, or some Austrian—a Mendel, or a Mendeleev. I always mix them up—though they're not like two peas in a pod. Is the weight of one seed equal to a carat? They're used for measuring diamonds, apparently . . . Ah, so that's what the seed is called; a "carat."

Only once did Tishkin cast a glance at the audience. He saw Toshka's eyes, vacant as two soldier's buttons, and the languid gaze of Manya, who had unbuttoned her blouse and was using his manuscript to fan herself. By the time he had finished reading, Toshka was fast asleep and Manya was gone.

This was the very evening when she pushed off on the ferryboat in the direction of the railroad station, accompanied by a visiting baron, or some merchant; or was it a tenor? Or perhaps a singing merchant.

Guessing where she might be headed, Tishkin decided to go west, and to send the loyal Toshka east, on the understanding that if he failed to catch Manya he would do some moonlighting in the gold mines in order to continue his work on the flight to the Moon.

Anton knew nothing about Tishkin's adventures in the capitals; but he himself had no ambition to catch Manya, and set out for the mines. He didn't make any easy money* there, but he did make the acquaintance of a certain genius of Buryat extraction who worked in an office as a ledger clerk. The Buryat had just then discovered integral calculus, so he entrusted his manuscript to Anton and provided him with some money for a trip to Vladivostok. There Anton was to present the manuscript to the Far Eastern division of the Academy of Sciences. But no division of this description (nor any "Manya") did he find in Vladivostok. However, a mathematics teacher that he met in a local bar explained to him that this calculus had been discovered already in the seventeenth century by the one and only Isaac Newton, and was not likely to come as a surprise to anyone. That was the moment when Lieutenant Bruce turned up in Vladivostok, looking for someone who knew a thing or two about horses.

Then there was Antarctica. What happened, happened, including our getting acquainted with each other in the pub. Anton tried to return

---

*Because Anton writes all three words—"money," "Manya," and "mania"—the same way in English, even with the help of Slavists it was difficult to distinguish them in context. (A noteworthy note written by the author himself! A. B.)

to his homeland, with the goal of "soaking" (revenge by drowning?)
the "Finn," Amundsen, for having deprived Scott of his "first."* The
First World War intervened, however, and Anton was called up for active duty. Although he didn't perish, he was one of the victims of the first
and only gas attack.† Then there was the revolution in Russia, followed
by the civil war, in which he sided with the Red Army. He wandered
around from front line to front line, and ended up in Murmansk, where
he "hunted the American." (It turns out that some sort of landing, if not
outright intervention, did take place in northern Russia.)

It is still a mystery to me, this simultaneous openness and secretive-
ness of Russians. Anton inundated me with the most intimate details of
his life, details that no one in his right mind would dare to divulge here,
even to a friend. At the same time, he refused to show me his "gift from
the Queen," lest he "jinx it." I found his use of this expression inappropriate and chose not to believe him. As it turned out, I had doubted not
only him but Her Majesty herself. Now I am proud of both of them:
Anton was awarded a lifetime retirement allowance, which he continued to receive until 1927, when the Soviets broke off diplomatic relations
with our country.

That was when he had to return to his Fathers, where he assem-
bled a bicycle out of an old sewing machine and some other mechanical device, and joined the local postal service as a mail carrier. Then he
caught wind of the plan to organize collective farms, and he was the
first to support such an idea. I answered his letter in the eager hope
that his connection with the postal service would facilitate communi-
cations, but I never received a reply.

About a dozen years later, my own letter was returned to me. It
floated up out of time, like a memory. It had been opened at least once,

---

*Some clarification is called for here. This is a subject in the most Western sense of that term. Roald
Amundsen (1872–1928), on board his ship the *Fram*, which was rigged to sail to the North Pole, suddenly, "by a dramatic surprise" (a strange turn of phrase for the *Britannica*, and containing too many
nuances to convey in translation, including the suggestion of a military maneuver) redirected the expedition toward the South Pole (1910–1912) and managed to reach it first. Captain Robert Falcon Scott
(1868–1912), with a crew of four, reached the South Pole on January 17, 1912, only to discover that
Amundsen had preceded him there. The members of Scott's team all perished on their return journey
home. *(A. B.)*

†According to the eyewitness account of Russian writer M. Zoshchenko (1895–1958), who was also a
victim of the attack, it did take place. That is already a Russian subject. *(A. B.)*

and seemed to have spent some time in a puddle. Still, all the pages, despite having gone for a little swim, were in the correct order. Pressed between them was a beautiful butterfly, preserved better even than the pages themselves. Someone had written a message in red crayon, slant-wise across the first page, in big fat block letters. It looked like a resolu-tion. The same Slavist friend helped me to decipher it:

MESSAGE ABROAD TCHK PERISHED ALONE
TCHK KILLED BY LIGHTNING TCHK*
(signature indecipherable)

Killed by lightning . . . No, Russians can't have a subject! They can only have a fate.

The year was 1932. It was still just the beginning.

I remember that when Anton was asked, "Whither Russia?" he would just shrug. "A Russian is not capable of choosing between two things: he always chooses what is more, and not what is better. That's why autocracy is easier for him to live with. But it has become dilapi-dated, so there will be a doubling of autocracy. It's no coincidence that the two-headed eagle is split and looks in opposite directions." He clearly meant something by this.

At the time, I didn't understand.†

Tishkin? Ah, yes, I completely forgot. I forgot about our protago-nist. So the plot fell through.

Yet a good half of Anton's letter was about him. I couldn't make heads or tails of it. In it he set out a new theory of time—my friend

---

*"TChK" turned out to mean not "Tobolsk Cheka" (*Chrezvychainyj komitet*) but "STOP," or "period" (*tochka*), the issue which so preoccupied Anton: the end of the sentence must be marked by a period. Just like the draft of a telegram—addressed, very possibly, to the infamous Cheka . . . (*Translator's conjecture. A. B.*)

†Anton Lukich Omelchenko was born in the settlement of Fathers (Batki) in Poltavshchina in 1883. When he was training racehorses in Vladivostok, he accompanied Lieutenant Bruce to Harbin to se-lect Manchurian horses for Captain Scott. He became part of the expedition crew, met and accompa-nied those who were setting out to the South Pole, and reached 84 degrees south latitude. After the expedition crew returned to England, he was awarded a medal and a gift by the Queen. He returned to Russia not long before the First World War, and was inducted into the army. During the civil war he fought on the side of the Red Army. Upon his return to his native settlement, he worked as a mailman. He was one of the first to join a collective farm. He died after being struck by lightning in the spring of 1932. (*The Mountain Climber's Handbook*, 1972.) (*A. B.*)

translated it the best he could on the fly, without understanding much himself. There were several beautiful, even lyrical, passages about the nature of time, which were somehow reminiscent of the conversations Anton and I had had in the pub. They concerned not only the celebrated boundary between time and space but also touched on the notion that the boundary is being moved about by a sort of piston, or a Higher Power—which is, itself, time. That the space behind the piston is rarified, and that's what is called the past, or memory. That everything has memory: crystals, metals, water, and, to a lesser degree, people, who limit themselves only to a hole-ridden history and allow bandits and swindlers (that was Tishkin's attitude toward the powers-that-be—he was a bombist, after all) to cheat them out of the present time. That there was, therefore, no future at all, because it was always being hollowed out of time.

At that point, it all becomes vertiginously incomprehensible: time was likened to some kind of membrane, like an eardrum, letting sound into itself but not reproducing it.

Even more interesting was the claim that time is not whole or unbroken but discrete. That it bursts, it sparks, so to speak, like a tiny garland of micro-explosions invisible to the eye, and that all this is a complete catastrophe, which we can only sense but never capture with our minds.

These ideas were also grounded in mathematical formulas appended to the manuscript, with many references to someone by the name of Forehead.* Tishkin attempts to deduce a formula of the crevice ("Tishkin's Crevice") as a part of a Universal Theory of Nausea— for the effort to work with time, as with infinity, results in no more than faintness, dizziness, and nausea.

How, may I ask, could I be expected to present this to the Royal Society? However, I did show the mathematical section of the work to a mathematician acquaintance of mine at the Club.

At first, he laughed out loud. Then he frowned, and cleared his

---

*Nikolai Ivanovich Lobachevsky, perhaps? ("Forehead" in Russian is *lob*.) In the *Britannica* he is assigned a fourth of a column, although he is the only Russian who is granted the status of "first." I never suspected that he was born so early—in 1792! Stephenson had not yet traveled on his locomotive, and Nikolai Ivanovich's rails already crossed somewhere in infinity! (*Translator's unchecked rejoinder. A. B.*)

throat, now approvingly, now with indignation. Then he perused it again, this time without betraying any emotion at all.

"Where did you get all this gibberish? Ah, Russia. Well, that explains it. Although, come to think of it, they have quite a reputable school of mathematics there now. But what you have shown me here is a very peculiar porridge." That's what he said—porridge—and I immediately thought of Anton. "On the one hand, this is stuff that every schoolchild knows; on the other hand, however, the approach taken to these truisms is stunning in its originality. Do you know what all this reminds me of?" he said, rejoicing. "Naïve painting. I am a great admirer of Henri Rousseau . . . Is Rousseau from Russia? Of course not, he's French. Mathematics in France was also quite good . . . None of this"—he tossed the manuscript carelessly on the table—"has the slightest bearing on science, however. Only the last part. What did he call his theory?"

I read out the title and translated it as faithfully as I could.

"Hmm, *durnota* . . . Nausea, you say? Yes. Figures. When did you say he wrote it? In 1905? But that's impossible! Why, you ask? Because it was in 1905 that Albert Einstein published his theory of relativity."

I would be hard-pressed to explain why, but I was truly upset.

"Porridge," I muttered. "Stone soup. Or, as they call it, *soup iz to-pora*," I said, recalling another of Anton's favorite expressions.

"What is '*soup iz topora*'?" the mathematician said.

"*Topor*," I said with vulgar cruelty, like a Russian, "is what they used to cut off the head of our Charles, in the seventeenth century. An ax. Hence, 'ax soup.' It's full of surprises."

Ah, yes, Tishkin. I keep forgetting about him. In that same letter, the last one Anton wrote, the one I am spinning this tale out of, there was something else about Tishkin. The last thing.

The Soviet authorities impounded Tishkin's rocket ship, and sent him away somewhere under convoy, even farther than Tobolsk. Anton (Toshka), crushed by sadness and emptiness, set out for his native Fathers to join a *kolkhoz* (collective farm).

When I think about Anton now, I realize that however strange it may seem, he loved his homeland deeply. He liked England, true, but primarily for its pubs and Robert Scott (Robert Falconovich, as he called him affectionately, insisting that he was just like a Russian. Why? Because he arrived too late, then perished). "Scots," he used to say, "are different. They're similar to us, though we don't have red hair. Don't you understand, you wise men who know so much, that people want to live not only in their own country but in their own time? In their epoch. And so they struggle: not the strong with the weak, the backward with the advanced, the old and the new, the white and the red, the Catholic and the Protestant—but the age with the age! All the epochs at once, simultaneously. Time wages war on time before our very eyes, the living with the dead, seizing us up and leaving us in its wake like dust." Tishkin claimed that time is a single instant, the instant of a blast, an explosion drawn out and delayed many billions of times. And Russia has been time's firing range.

After writing this "thing" (I don't know what else to call it), I looked out the window and discovered that the weather had cleared up a bit, though it was still as gray as ever. I began waiting for the dawn. But instead of the sun, a cargo ship appeared, enormous, like the *Britannica*, moving at a rapid clip, as though an invisible thumb was pushing it along the horizon from north to south. This incongruity of scale prompted me to think that I had mixed up the ends of the Earth, and, where I had assumed I was getting nearer to Russia, I was in fact sitting in front of a window that looked out toward Sweden, the West, my England; and not toward the East, toward St. Petersburg, toward Russia . . . As though I had turned my back on them. Suddenly I realized how cold and numb it was, my back. (The landlady who rented me the room warned me not to smoke in the house, and I had flung open the window . . . This, it seems, is how *Moby-Dick* begins.) While I was writing, the cold crept in and now I was frozen stiff like Anton at the South Pole, or even in Siberia . . . Siberia had somehow arrived here: we had not had such a cold May since, I daresay, the Battle of Poltava ([*sic*], Fathers is in Poltavshchina [*sic*], the Tobolsk Kremlin, not unlike its Moscow counterpart, was built by Swedish prisoners captured by Peter the Great at Poltava—cf. the *Britannica* [*sic*], this cold was driven here by a powerful cyclone from northeast Siberia [*sic*], wasn't this island considered to be Russian not so very long ago? [*sic*] And what if there is in all of this a glimmer of something—if not of a subject, then at least a temporal cross-connection?).

"Go ahead and smoke," the landlady said, slamming the window shut fiercely. "We'll never have enough firewood for you."

Then she smiled tenderly. Instead of the sun.

No matter what I had written, my mood lifted.

"I'm going to a pub to warm up," I told her, somewhat shamefaced.

"Good for you," she approved. "Otherwise, what you've written there might end up . . ."

And that's the truth. It's good that on some islands there isn't any time, either. Only weather.

The wind shifted in exactly the opposite direction, from north to south, and it became much warmer after my third . . . Today it might even be possible to see the sunset, and I left the pub to watch the sun go down. But the clouds were now floating in another direction, from the west, gulping down first the sun, then the sea, then the town, then my little house, then me, leaving only the last stroke of the bell to melt away.

"They can't prevent you from living well," I said into the void.

"Or poorly, either," from out of nowhere, in a thick accent, came the reply of the Talking Ear.

PART II

THE ABSENTMINDED WORD
(A Couple of Coffins
from a Cup of Coffee)

TO SEÑORA SIMONE N.

The verses stalled, and then gave way;
But what a price I had to pay!
—H. H.

. . . And here I break off the translation and begin my recollection of the forgotten text.

The prose in the original left something to be desired, too, and I'm afraid I can't improve on it in my own narrative. Evidently, Tired-Boffin also wrote his now forgotten book absentmindedly, taking long breaks (in much the same manner as I'm translating this, which gives me a convenient excuse). There is too great a difference in the thickness of plot between "The View of the Sky Above Troy" and "The Absentminded Word." ("Absentminded"—yet another justification of the Russian penchant for renaming, and not just the untranslatability of the dubious English pun.)

It seems that in this chapter, Mr. (or was it Mrs.?) Tired-Boffin was bent on taking revenge on all women, not just his protagonist, for Dika's death. However difficult it is for me, as well, to reconcile myself to her death, it is in this part of the book's rather intricate structure that I am particularly annoyed at its professionalism—at the "plotfulness" and "belletrism"*

---

*Belles lettres—"fine letters" (Fr.). (A. B.)

so alien to the tradition of the best Russian prose. Here the translator cannot help but heave a bitter sigh.

For the alleged Russian plotlessness itself prods you to think. I will not take it upon myself to discuss the merits of non-Russian belles lettres, of the endless dialogues with allusions to subtext (for what sort of subtext can there be in the absence of a text?), the alterations with a view to a potential screen version, the adjustments for ease of reading and translation—this is commerce, the marketplace (fee by the word, or the page?). All of this uproots belles lettres from its native French soil and removes it an infinite distance away.

Narration without the slightest nod to a plot is impossible, however— the text would have neither end nor beginning. The Russian subject is feeling (Chekhov); the fantastic (Gogol); and, more infrequently, thought (Pushkin). Hence, the shimmer of mystery that a careful reader cannot help but discern in it; not to mention the vaunted impossibility of translating it into Western languages (with the notable exception of Chekhov, for some reason). Only Dostoevsky, perhaps, that universal Russian "brand" (along with vodka and bears), excelled altogether in plot, in literariness, in readability, and in translatability. Then again, he was the only one who took instruction from the West: from Alexandre Dumas, George Sand, and even Eugène Sue, though he didn't know much French, and wrote haphazardly in Russian—whichever way the spirit moved him (which not only facilitates translation but also accounts for the charm his style holds for the Russian reader—despite the jealousy of Turgenev and the envy of Nabokov).

I have tripped over Dostoevsky, too, however . . . What I'm saying is that we have no subject in our classical Russian literature, at least in the sense that it exists in English literature. Those infamous three hundred years of the Tatar-Mongol yoke can never compete in significance with the fact that our Pushkin emerged two hundred years after the death of Shakespeare. Yet it was Pushkin alone who narrowed the gap between us and Europe by at least a hundred years. It was Pushkin who attempted to cultivate a European plot on Russian virgin soil, if one understands a plot to be a certain elemental, even ultimate, product of experience—a grasp of the structure of life. Was Pushkin merely hurrying to catch up, or have we not yet fully understood him? *The Queen of Spades* is an opera, *The Captain's Daughter* a children's story . . .

(Children's stories! I had forgotten about fairy tales. That's where plots are developed. It is only fitting that Pushkin was so enamored of fairy tales. What if "The Gingerbread Man" or "The Giant Turnip" predated the Tatar-Mongol yoke?)

To wit, not a hundred years of the great tradition of Russian literature had passed (from the mature Pushkin to Alexander Blok) when the Revolution of 1917 erupted, drowning all the emerging literary subjects in the blood of all too real ones.

So we do not have a subject. It has never had enough time to crystallize into any sort of continuity over a span of even three generations. All our subjects are still contained in the dictionary of our "great and powerful, truthful and free" language. We are still living in language, and not in the subject (in the soup, and not in the main course), although we taste our bread and sip our vodka like truth. The subject for us is still a fairy tale, lies, falsehood—"that's not the way life really is." We always want more honesty. We're waiting, sir. For the time being we prefer to read books in translation. Because they are allowed, because it's not the truth; it's not about us but about them. Though it turns out that they're people, too. The same double standard.

Is our Russian language really so free? However many foreign words it has borrowed along the way, it is still lacking in terminology (the "term," as a word, is also the end of a subject of thought; its distillation, its specificity, its very point). Thus, our plotlessness is also the absence of a certain final thought, or model. (Although the Western subject, elaborated upon until it has become automatic, a "stock" notion, is probably the absence of a thought model altogether.) Thus, Shakespeare and Dostoevsky, but not Tolstoy and Proust—because the former transferred models of life onto the stage, and the latter onto a spatial plane. Why *Hamlet*? Tolstoy fumed. One wants to extend one's experience, and to accept the alien as one's own. But although it is possible to translate prose, and to translate poetry very approximately, translating one mentality into another, the seventeenth century into the twentieth, is not possible. Again, Pushkin was the only one who managed to overcome this dilemma in his own era.

My lament about the difficulties of translating this chapter is concerned, above all, with terminology referring to what we call sex. This is a matter that people in all countries are more or less equally preoccupied with, and Russians all the more. "Everyone, who isn't too lazy, f——ks," as Barkov said. This is not amenable to translation into literary language.

Is our Russian literature really so true to life, then, if we permit ourselves all kinds of things in life that we do not allow ourselves to commit to paper? "The pen is mightier than the sword"—or is it? True, no one has inundated the reader with so much inner psychology as we have. Evidently, the complete absence of civilized notions of privacy and private property in our totalitarian society forced all private life underground. On paper we don't carouse, smoke, lie, steal, or anything else (exactly what everyone is thinking just now). We don't fawn, cheat, or die. Our life is free as a bird's. (This is why, and for no other reason, we need relentless censorship, that selfsame "sword"—for fear the secret that nothing human is alien to us might, God forbid, be divulged.) And yet we're surprised by the guarded attitude the rest of the world adopts toward us (though we are flattered by the notorious mystery of the "Russian soul"); we are filled with indignation at "double standards." Say what you will, but hypocrisy is the main rudder of the powers-that-be.

Therefore, there is not a single Russian book (poetry not included), with the exception of the *Dictionary of the Great Living Russian Language*, written by the Dane Vladimir Dahl, that I would deem true to life. Verisimilitude is to be found only in the language as a whole.

I must conclude that Russian literary speech has not yet earned the degree of freedom achieved by our language. It is by nature as timid and chaste as a provincial young lady of the nineteenth century—which is why everything concerning our bodily functions is banished to a very specific and remarkable form of taboo speech or foul language known as *mat*. But it is censored. Thus, in our literature, too, you will not find anything about that which interests all of us most of all. A word like "stimulating," in this context, already smacks of impropriety, like any literary substitution or euphemism. It bears repeating that *mat* is far more decorous and seemly than any substitute, that what is ugly is not its apt usage, but the pathological need to perceive a corresponding visual image behind every word. All these "intimate parts," "laps," "loins," and "manhood"; all this "taking advantage of," "penetrating," and "knowing"—all this is far more unnatural than our *mat*, far more repugnant, and even bawdy (now there's a word that stands as a sentinel between one and the other realm of language). In the case of Tired-Boffin, I derive comfort from the somewhat dated style of his descriptions. It remains for me, together with him and his hero, to peek under the skirt, and, together with the heroine, to offer myself (in the given instance, to whatever happens in the text).

As a result of my own translation of all this foreignness, I arrive at the patriotic conclusion that Russian literature is unsurpassed, that no other literature offers itself with such sincerity of oft-mended chastity to its native tongue (like a houri in the Islamic paradise). Thus, the so-called untranslatability is dual-natured: it is untranslatable not because a language is incapable of conveying something in another language, but because one's own language is not amenable to translation into any other.

(Yours forever . . . You see what my computer has just done? It's guilty of co-authorship, like a true kindred spirit. I wanted to write "yours, and yours alone," but it began to swallow letters at every turn, and finally prompted me, unasked: "yours forever." These words were the furthest imaginable from my mind! Well, maybe the computer is right. Maybe it will be forever. Either I'm tired, or it is. Tiredness is also contagious.)

1. Ris

> I thought the heart
> forgot
> the easy art of suffering.
> I said of what had
> been—
> nevermore! nevermore!
> —Alex Cannon

Urbino Vanoski, twenty-seven, an English poet who had received some acclaim but was not yet well known, of mixed Polish-Dutch-Japanese ancestry (second, third, and fourth generations, respectively), who didn't know a single one of these languages and had never once traveled to any of these ancestral homelands for any significant length of time; author of an almost sensational collection of poems titled *The Night Vase* (an untranslatable phrase meaning something approximating "The Vase in the Night"), which, however, found only a scanty readership, except perhaps for the poem "Thursday," which was subsequently included in one of the respectable anthologies—a sad poem that seemed to express the personal experience of the author, in these lines, for example:

I'm a one-woman man
as a matter of fact
I'm on the lookout for a wife
(husbandless, of course)
to meet at the cinema,
under the marquee
in the rain
the past reveals no guarantees
we cannot say that what happened
truly did (happen) . . .

. . . and so on, and so forth, i.e., that same Vanoski who decided to end not simply life itself but his own life, rather than to endure infamy or drama, changing it at the very root, including his own name, in the manner of the Japanese poets, who, nearing forty, having achieved everything they wished to achieve, abandon everything, disappear, and, after assuming incognito and voluntary poverty, begin a poetic path from scratch as completely unknown, unsung, but indisputable geniuses. Enamored of Bashō and quoting him right and left, Vanoski twisted his own name this way and that, until he finally reached a combination of letters that was more or less tolerable to the human ear: Ris Vokonabi. (It reminded him of the Japanese culinary arts.*) The first collection of poetry he published under this pseudonym enjoyed great success with select readers, and favorable reviews from the critics. He became a "discovery."

---

*A typical example of back-(re)translation, or gaining in translation . . . In English the name Ris (spelled Rhys or Reese) bears no associations with "rice," as it does in Russian. *(A. B.)*

And so Urbino became Ris.

One fine day (fine days are the weather of choice in our age; stormy days are already outmoded)—one fine day, or even hour, Ris's life, which had until now seemed to be his life in spite of everything, i.e., its belonging to him was never in question, seemed suddenly like non-life. That is, it was not life in its unbroken and unconditional meaning but only a means of living through (reliving) one more clearly defined segment of time. Thus, life broke off and seemed now to be a remnant, a fragment. It experienced the tragic sensation of continuing in a void, as though it were an ellipsis. And this nonexistent continuity of a broken-off fragment ached—a peculiar case of causalgia, or pain experienced in a lost extremity.

Struggling over Dika's death, oppressed by an ever-increasing sense of guilt, Urbino devoted himself to spirits with typical Slavic extravagance. He stopped washing, shaving, and cutting his hair for the forty days of mourning, and then for a whole year, so that he truly forgot who he was. After that, his friends forgot him, too. Bashō became his sole drinking companion. He began to acquire notoriety under the nickname "Bashō." People had already started turning around to stare at him in the street.

At the same time, his publisher didn't even remember that there was such a person as Vanoski.

That was how he finally understood that fame is not achieved through hard work but through serendipity.

He decided to leave his beard and his shoulder-length hair as they were. It was the easiest way to conquer his past.

He began to flourish: an unanticipated but welcome surge in his creative powers, newfound success with women, a sudden passion for travel . . . After Vladivostok he made his way to New Zealand, where he stayed for a while, following the trail of Anton, his Russian drinking companion, who in his turn was trailing behind Robert Scott's expedition to the South Pole. Actually, he refused point blank to follow Anton to the "island of penguins." He needed some place that was warmer and more uninhabited.

In a private sanitarium where he attempted to rid himself of the "scent of death" that continued to haunt him, a certain baroness, who was also a psychiatrist, wrote him a letter of referral for a "virtually uninhabited" island.

"You'll like it there," she said. "Just don't let anything surprise you."

That was when Ris consented to become Urbino again.

In Taunus, a coastal fishing town, he met (as his letter instructed him to do) Midshipman Happenen, a veritable Hollywood Scandinavian with long blond hair tied with a pirate's bandana and a scar across his forehead and cheek, who was building a yacht not far from the pier. With his taciturnity and sternly handsome looks, the midshipman immediately appealed to Urbino. He sized up Urbino at a glance, as meticulously as a carpenter sizes up a plank of wood.

"An inch shy of six feet," he said.

"Do you build coffins here, too?" Urbino said, making light of the comment, and estimating the midshipman's height in his turn. He exceeded him in all dimensions (he was at least an inch taller than six feet), not to mention in pounds.

"Well, it's a straightforward craft." The midshipman flexed his facial muscles so that his deeply etched cheekbones stood out and invited him into his boat. "And there was no one else around to do that kind of work here. They don't die too often in these parts. Unless they drown."

And he rowed silently across the strait. He pulled up onto a sandbar. A dog bounded up to them in greeting, splashing them from head to toe. Its behavior contradicted its appearance: excessive in size and coloring, like a mixture of a wolf and a sheep—a Baskervilles hound that whimpered like a puppy.

"Easy now, Marleen!" the midshipman commanded, and the dog obeyed, calming down immediately but still yelping now and then. "This man is our guest."

The Scandinavian's at home here, Urbino had just managed to think, when the Scandinavian scooped him up along with his rucksack, carried him from the boat, and set him down on shore as if he were as light as a feather.

"Show him around," he commanded the dog. And without giving Urbino any chance to take offense or to settle the payment, he began rowing back. Thus, Urbino went ashore, to see what he could see.

The beach rose up at a sheer angle, the height of about two men, and obstructed the view. Marleen led him along a path trampled in the sand, overgrown with pleasant, fleshy grasses (he seemed to recall that as children they had called it saxifrage). The island spread out above and in front of him, appearing to be a single enormous sandbar covered with crooked, stunted trees, on the apex of which stood a sailing frigate sunk in the sand up to its waterline. It's not for nothing the camel is called the ship of the desert, Urbino thought, staring in wonder.

This was in fact a hacienda. It resembled a camel, but it was called The Bermudas. Of which he was informed now not by Marleen but by the landlady.

2. Lili

"This is a present from the last tsunami."

"It's the best memento of the elements imaginable," Urbino said ingratiatingly. "A monument to the sea. I've never seen anything like it before."

She stuffed his letter of introduction carelessly into the pocket of her apron.

"I know what it says. The Baroness has already told me everything about you."

"How did she manage to get here ahead of me?" Urbino said. "I've been trying to reach the island for three days, and from what I understand, you have no means of communication here."

"Are you so weary of communication?" the landlady said with a wry grin.

"That's why I'm here."

"Come with me into the stateroom. I'll feed you, show you around, and tell you about everything. Marleen, go lie down!"

Urbino was startled at the sudden change in tone, from polite and conversational to peremptory. The dog wasn't surprised, but hurt: she obeyed, reluctantly but without hesitation.

●

The stateroom was very cozy. Everything had been preserved in the condition in which it was originally found. At the same time, there was evidence of a woman's touch: pots and pans and skillets, scrubbed like the railings on deck, hanging bunches of local herbs . . . Suddenly he saw a stuffed beast: it looked like a beaver or a hare, with webbed goose's feet and horns like a goat.

"What the devil is that?"

"An ordinary hare with horns."

"Are they really found in these parts?"

"Not anymore. They died out. Foundered," the landlady said, smiling.

"Hmm. Amusing."

"Not me, it was my sister, Marleen. She's the punster. Devil take her."

"They foundered. Just like your ship," Urbino punned in his turn. "Still, it's very cozy here."

"Thanks to Happenen. He was the one who restored everything."

There was a crash down below, as though something had fallen. What do I care about that fair-haired devil, Urbino thought, bristling. He said:

"I'm confused. Where is this Marleen of yours? Who is Happenen?"

"All right. Let me explain. Marleen is downstairs, where she belongs. She had to be isolated. Did the Baroness really not tell you? Marleen is under her care. We're twins. No, not the Baroness! Identical, but different. Perhaps because we were raised differently."

"What do you mean, differently? You both have the same mother and the same father, don't you?" he said.

The landlady pondered. So did Urbino.

"I didn't want to go into all of this right away. Apparently the Baroness knows how to maintain professional secrecy . . . Father left us, and Mother died in childbirth. We were abandoned as babies. The Gypsies took her, and I was raised in a convent. When we reached the age of eighteen, an attorney located us. Our parents had left us a small inheritance. So we were reunited."

The landlady's face looked dreamy, or perhaps sorrowful.

"I don't wish to talk about it anymore. Happenen . . . It was a training vessel." Here she lapsed eagerly into an explanation. "He was a midshipman, but like a captain. After the wreck, the cadets who were saved all scattered, but he couldn't abandon the ship . . . He's a skilled carpenter, and managed to adapt it for conditions on dry land, while preserving its romantic marine ambience."

"It looks absolutely sailworthy. Fine windage," Urbino quipped, at the same time parading some vestiges of one of his abandoned courses of study.

"'Windage.' A pretty word. I've never heard it before. Not even in crossword puzzles."

"Windage is the air resistance of the vessel in full sail. Didn't your midshipman explain something as simple as that to you? You're waiting for a tsunami, but your fortress will keel over at the first squall."

"It's possible," the landlady said evenly. "This is a very dangerous spot."

"How so?"

"It's not really here at all."

"??"

"It could disappear at any moment."

"???"

"This is not really an island. There's no land underneath us. It's just the bottom of the sea that has emerged for a time, like the back of a whale. After the last big tsunami, I suppose."

"And how often does this whale sink back into the water again?"

"Judging by the trees, it hasn't gone under in at least half a century."

"And what is the forecast?"

"The meteorologists try to scare us, year in and year out . . . But my sister and I have lived here a long time. We're still here."

"Do you get bored?"

"Not at all. Even when I find my way back to civilization to do errands, I want to return after just one day. And I can't leave my sister alone for too long."

"Is your civilization very far away?"

"No need to scoff, Ris. You just came from there! From Taunus."

Urbino grinned, recalling Taunus: a shop, a pub, the police station, and the post office, all in one building. Plus a moorage.

"Ris? Is that what the Baroness called me in the letter?"

"Isn't that who you are?"

"Well, yes, I am who I am; but Ris is my pseudonym. I'm Urbino."

"Interesting." The landlady's expression became secretive and romantic. "Then you may call me Lili."

"And the dog?"

"The dog . . . Better not confuse her. Just call her Marleen."

Sounds of rumbling and growling, even the clanking of chains, came from downstairs.

"An island that's not an island. Is your sister not really a sister? She sounds like a bear."

"You just about guessed it." Lili laughed out loud. "It's the seasonal spring aggravation of her condition. Don't be alarmed, though, she's not dangerous. In a week she'll calm down, and stay like that through summer. She'll be sitting in front of her radio transmitter day and night."

"You mean to say she's also a ham radio operator?"

"Well, you can't accuse her of not having a broad range of interests. Actually, she was the one who put me in touch with the Baroness about your arrival."

"So, a radio . . . But doesn't anyone ever come here to visit you?"

"They do. But they don't hold out for too long. They get bored."

"I already feel like I'll never want to leave."

"There was someone like that once. It ended badly, though."

"What happened?"

"Marleen fell in love with him."

"What's so bad about that? Did she eat him up or something?"

"Precisely."

"What about the bones?"

"She gave them to the dog."

"The beast!"

"Are you referring to Marleen?"

"No, your dog is quite imposing . . . What do you call it?"

"That's her name. Marleen."

"They have the same name? How do they know who is who?"

"The dog doesn't understand words, just intonation. Whether you call her 'dog,' 'bitch,' or 'Marleen,' it's all the same to her. She always knows whether you're talking to her or to a person."

"Still, it's strange . . . And she doesn't feel hurt?"

"That we call her by a human name?"

"No, that you call your sister by a dog's name!"

"Why should she feel offended? She is a dog."

"Huh?"

"A bitch if there ever was one."

"But she's your sister!"

"Ris . . . I mean, Urbino, do you have a brother?"

"Yes," Urbino lied without skipping a beat.

"Do you get along?"

"Not much these days."

"Why is that?"

"He drowned."

"Oh, dear! How did it happen?"

"It just did."

My God, why on Earth was he making all this up? He was having fun.

"I'm sorry to hear that. My sister didn't drown."

"Is this why you . . . ?"

"She didn't drown. She tried to drown someone, though."

"Who?"

"Well, I mean it figuratively. Although he still has a scar. But you saw him yourself."

"Not Happenen?" Urbino recalled his scar. It couldn't be anyone else.

Lili fingered her cup with a preoccupied look.

"Shall I tell your fortune?"

"How, by reading the coffee grounds?"

"No need to be snide. The past always works out."

"Well, all right. Do tell."

"I see a faraway land . . . See how the air shimmers in the heat? An animal, perhaps a two-humped one . . . Were you ever in Arabia? You don't know Arabic, do you? I don't know much of it, either. That's where I learned tasseography, though. With those . . . what are they called? Oligophrenics? Oligarchs? No, no, not spongers, not pillagers . . . not dramaturgs . . . You know, the poorest of the poor, almost primordial . . . but very kind, very sweet people . . . and not dromedaries, those are their camels . . . and definitely not Druids.

There aren't any trees there at all, it's the Sahara . . . Who were they again? Dreadnoughts? What, a battleship, you say? Heavens no! I came across it just recently in a crossword. Oh, drat! Now that's an absentminded word! Oh, it isn't? Forgetful? Did I say that right? Or just forgettable . . .'"

"No, no! The first one was perfect! It was already poetry."

He knew the word. It started with a T. But something (or some-one?) prevented him from saying it out loud. He had been in the Sahara. And, truly, they were very sweet people . . . Dika had wanted to buy something from them, just out of the goodness of her heart, and the entire throng of them began talking her out of it: "Don't buy that, don't buy that! Look at this one, it's much prettier, and far cheaper!" thrusting God knows what under her nose. Urbino pushed back the memory, and, strangely, the word vanished from his mind the moment he resolved not to say it to Lili. Trilobites? No, those are fossilized remains. The word. One moment it was on the tip of his tongue, and the next moment it was gone. That had never happened to him before—that a word simply evaporated. Like a drop of water in the Sahara.

"So you don't think I'm such a dimwit? I don't have much educa-tion, and I haven't chatted with anyone in ever so long. Please excuse me if I misspeak sometimes."

"Not at all. You are very sensitive to the word."

"That's nice to hear from a poet. But that's Marleen's domain. She pens verse herself. Take a look."

"'And the Angel slipped on his wing' . . . Hmm, not bad. Not bad at all," Urbino muttered.

"What can that she-devil possibly know about angels?"

"'The branch sways inside the room . . . if I only knew why— what to ask, and of whom?'* Now that's quite something."

"I'll be sure to pass on your favorable opinion to her," said Lili, pursing her lips.

"I wrote something similar once. I can't remember it now, though," Urbino said, warming to the subject. "Something about how, in wind-less weather, the trees go to sleep at sundown. All their branches shiver

*Translated from the verse of Inga Kuznetsova. *(A. B.)*

before they go still. It happens of its own accord, not in sympathetic movement, the result of some outside force. I was especially struck by a sunflower field . . ."

"Like van Gogh?"

"He painted individual sunflowers, but this was a whole field, as wide as the horizon. I even made a discovery, only not a single biologist would believe me. On the sunny slope . . . Well, never mind."

"Why not?"

"I said it better in a poem."

"Read it."

"I'm afraid I'll mangle it. A decent poet knows all his poems by heart. If you can't remember it, it means it wasn't any good. I'm afraid to disgrace myself in front of you."

"Is that what you really believe, or just what you think?" She blushed and cast her eyes down into his cup. "I see here a very beautiful young woman . . . She turned away from you, she's averted her gaze . . . But how strangely she has turned away! She's wearing a long, Eastern form of dress, like a sari. Is she Indian? By the way, a camel in the cup has a very specific meaning."

"How could it fit into the cup? Never mind the camel, let me hear about the Indian woman." Urbino had already begun to believe in the fortune.

"Were you so much in love?"

"I didn't have time."

"But she's happy now. See? It's like she's on a cloud. Like a film set. There, next to her—a tall, respectable sort of fellow. A director, or her husband? And around them are little tykes, like putti. She's wearing costly jewels. Where is she now?"

"She betrayed me."

"How could she do that to you?"

"She drowned, along with my brother."

"I'm sorry. Was she an actress?"

"No, but she looked like one."

"Oh, I'm so sorry."

"It's all right."

•

It's all right . . . Urbino never imagined he could be so nonchalant.

Having arrived with a heart full of grief on an island of his own choosing, as close to being uninhabited as he could find so as not to disturb that grief, could it be that he had forgotten everything so quickly and easily, that he had slipped so sweetly into oblivion and temptation?

First, Lili had a genuine ear for poetry (for which his own provided the evidence). Second, she was such an adept at tasseography, and he was already eager to begin writing on the subjects that had been generated so arbitrarily and capriciously in the coffee grinds. And, third . . .

"Let's make a game of this," Urbino said, intrigued. "In the evening, you tell my fortune in the cup, and in the morning I'll bring you a poem inspired by the previous evening's coffee grinds. I won't need to make anything up: life itself has given me my next book. Let it be called, accordingly: *Poems from a Coffee Cup*. First, your interpretation, with a picture . . . I wonder how I could draw it, though? Do you draw? Or perhaps you have a camera?" Urbino's eyes glittered.

"I can't draw, and I have no camera, either." Lili pondered for a moment. "Marleen used to draw, though."

First, second . . . Third: Lili was lovely.

Ash-blond hair, a bit over thirty, with dark-brown eyes and a face untouched by anything but a natural suntan, she resembled a slightly faded tea rose. Urbino would not deign to describe her in verse—it wasn't to his taste, and he had no mind for it. A madrigal had already begun to ripen there, however . . .

"And can you tell fortunes with tea leaves?" he couldn't help but ask.

"I probably could, but I don't know how," she said with a shrug of her tanned shoulders.

"I can," Urbino said.

Naturally, they switched to tea.

Urbino swirled around the tea leaves in her empty cup and muttered under his breath. Then he blushed, and blurted out:

Though I don't read, to my dismay,
like you, the script of coffee grinds,
the dregs of your teacup, I daresay,

(although a monk, I am not blind)
I cannot help but read this day.
And if, till now, I may have pined,
it's you I dote on, when I pray,
and from my heart, make bold to say:
I'll give you verses, if I may.

"Well, that was very sweet," Lili said, nodding in approval. She blushed, too, looking even more like a tea rose. "But let's put the cups aside. The sun is already setting, and I still have to show you to your berth."

When they went up on deck, the sun was already disappearing behind the sand dunes.

"I still haven't gotten a good look at your sea," Urbino said.

"We must hurry, then, before the sun goes down."

They disembarked from the beached ship just as the sun hid itself completely behind a dune.

Lili kicked off her sandals like it was her living room floor and started scrambling up the dune. Urbino followed right behind her.

The sand rained down on his head, kneaded into motion by the fine soles of her feet. He found it rather pleasant, truth be told. The landscape that opened up to him from his vantage point underneath was worth any number of sunsets . . . Extraordinarily slender legs, and nothing more (under her skirt, that is).

Lili was used to the trek, and she made her way to the top with ease and grace. The heavier Urbino was falling behind. He kept getting stuck in the sand and dropping down on all fours (possibly not so much from the difficult climb as from the desire to see more of the "landscape" from below). In any case, he had hardly reached the pinnacle, puffing and perspiring, when he realized that this, too, was worth the effort.

The sun was sinking down to the horizon. It seemed to elongate, and the red deepened to crimson as it approached the nadir. All of a sudden it seemed to flatten out and then drop into the sea.

"Strange that the sea doesn't sizzle," Urbino said, mouthing his own tried-and-true phrase.

"That surprises me every time, too," Lili agreed.

The sun sank ever deeper. The upper part of it stuck out, looking more and more like a ship floating on the horizon, its searchlights ablaze.

"There's another ship that will founder." Urbino, don't be so eloquent, he berated himself silently.

"Tomorrow it will come back on the other side, over the bay."

"How can you be sure?"

"I'm here to greet the sunrise every day."

"Strange," he said. "I suddenly realized that I have watched far more sunsets than sunrises in my life. But surely they are equal in number?"

"Don't be so pessimistic. It's just that you are a social being and a poet."

"Should I be offended by that?" Urbino said coquettishly.

"Why? You are most likely a night owl."

"Most likely. And you?"

"I'm a lark."

"That means we're birds of a different feather." Urbino sighed.

"But the sun belongs to both of us," Lili said, proprietarily. "Look there, above and to the left. The Moon! That's truly a thing of beauty, isn't it?"

"Never a truer word. Would you like something apropos?"

"Certainly."

Urbino sighed more deeply and focused his gaze on the last crimson ribbon, no longer blinding. Then he began to recite:

The sunset was not aware of its own beauty.
The mirroring sea did not dim for its own sake.
The wind did not see itself ruffle the calm surface.
The tree did not watch at all.

They stood, imprisoned in the night,
invisible to themselves, ablaze, at play.
Neither wave of sound, nor wave of light,
did they discern, though they possessed them both.

The sky did not know that the Moon had risen,
that the sun had hidden. The darkness thickened.

All around, ignorance abounded—
no one knew. And that was the point.

What is there on this shore for myself?
A bird in the sky shows crimson—what is it to me?
Where have I fled to? I tripped on the run,
I stand here alone, remembering nothing.

The dogs yelped. Lying prostrate before the
pitch-dark sea, a shadow trembled,
and mutely merging with the songs of birds
my soul reflected immortality.

The shadow of clouds, the hum of pines, the rustling grass
and harnessed wind—the evening sensed them with its skin.
And died away. And "conquering death through death,"
arose again. And again did not revive.

Who rejoices in one's own creation?
Whoever does believe, he holds the keys to Heaven.
And the wind just ruffles the hair of the fool
playing with a tiny mirror.

Whoever builds a house is not the one who lives there.
Whoever created life does not look for meaning there.
Thought from above does not understand itself.
Take to the road, and on it, overtake yourself.

"Beautiful!" Lili gushed, grabbing his hand. "Did you compose
that just now?"

"I can't lie," Urbino demurred. "But I happen to like it more than
the others."

Bashful and flattered at the same time, he kept hold of her hand.

As carefree as children, as though on swings or taking giant steps,
they tumbled down the dunes toward the sea.

"Let's go for a swim," Urbino suggested without any guile.

"Not after sunset," Lili said.

"Why not?"

"You might catch fever."

"As you wish. I'm the imperialist of water. I have to dunk myself whenever I arrive at a place for the first time."

He stripped down, then, working his broad shoulders, his small, pale buttocks gleaming from behind (he knew what he looked like from the back), he dove into the water like a torpedo and swam toward the horizon, doing a furious crawl. When he was completely spent, he heard a gentle splash behind him: Lili was swimming silently in his wake, like a little fish, easily keeping up with him.

"Why are you so afraid of the water?" Lili said, grinning at him.

"Me? Afraid?"

"Yes, it's like you're afraid you'll swallow some."

Urbino was unmasked as the boy he no doubt still was.

Just as silently, she yielded to him in the strip of surf. Her meekness confused and aroused him.

"My sweet little fish," he murmured, licking salty droplets from her shoulders and nipples. But something held him back from any bolder caresses; he didn't want to risk it (though she seemed so compliant and willing). He hesitated at the stage of stroking her silken (*bah! —trans.*) pubis.

"What do you think she's singing about, this little bird?" Lili said, countering his "little fish" with her "little bird."

"It's a he. And he's calling his mate."

Oh, that timidity, that chagrin, that discomfiture, the seeming inaccessibility, like the very first time . . . and for you, you alone . . . it is a pause, an intermission . . . Yes, that's what it is, a pause—what people later call love, when they're searching for what has been lost—Urbino thought, relaxing in the intermission, smoking and looking up, now at the sky, now at the ceiling of the attic berth that had been assigned to him for his creative isolation.

"So you claim that I have a fear of water. Perhaps I am afraid, but not like you think I am. Yes, I'm afraid of drinking it: it's alive! I might not be able to swallow it all of a sudden. I'm less afraid of the sea. I haven't had much luck with ships. True, I forced myself to cross the equator, but so what? A convention, but not a goal in itself."

He embraced Lili to prove to her that she was not the equator, that she was a goal, not a convention. Lili responded in her own unique way:

"To each his own . . . Have you ever wondered about that? Why different people get different things? You know, poor and rich, beautiful and ugly—that's understandable. Talented and ungifted, that's more complicated. Intelligent or dull-witted—that's just altogether unclear. Or, say, a man and a woman—why? Why are you a man, and I am a woman, and not the other way around?"

"Well, do you want to swap?"

"I didn't ask which of us is which, did I?"

"What about cats and dogs?"

Pondering the sequence of his subsequent actions, and the ones after that, reentering the realm of his previous experience and discovering in it a certain unity of principle, Urbino became aroused again merely by the thought that a wonder was lying next to him, just as insensate and immobile as he, but already warm . . . The wonder of another human being!

Honestly, you're just like a child, he thought, surprised at himself, as if for the first time discovering that another person could be another body, too: other breasts, another stomach and hips, another . . . Precisely! Not this awkward little tail of his, Urbino mused complacently. His "little tail" took offense and pouted, swelling until it resembled an old cannon on wheels. And Urbino took possession of the submissive Lili again and again. He even wanted her to conceive . . . Just then she peeped feebly, like a little mouse.

"Did you finally come?"

"How could you say such a thing! You—a poet! Never use that terrible expression with me again."

And she turned to the wall, sobbing softly.

"It was an unfortunate word choice, I'm sorry. Please forgive me. It won't happen again."

And this pleased him. And he made use of it: licking the tears off her cheeks touched him, and he *reiterated* (and she, it seems, did, too).

In the morning, now on the other shore, he greeted the dawn, which was rare for him. The sun peeked out, by now no longer crimson, then rolled out above the horizon on its golden rim, for some reason far more slowly than it had set. Urbino was overcome with feeling . . .

Lovely sun, so round and yellow,
are you shining for this fellow?
Yesterday she called me dear.
Did she think I wouldn't hear?
Water's blue, the sky is, too,
The sun shines bright, and I love you.
Sunlight, moonlight, sand and sea,
Life's a mystery to me.*

"When did you write that?"

"Never."

"Whom was it meant for?"

"You."

"When did you manage?"

"Just now."

"Then let's go swimming!" Lili cried.

"So it's all right to swim at dawn?"

"Everything's all right at dawn." She threw her arms around his neck.

And they were as naked as the first day in Paradise.

Then they did crosswords together. It turned out that Lili was a cross-word puzzle buff. She dragged out a huge pile of them, most of them already completed.

"They're often rather dull, but on occasion the words and phrases are exceedingly curious. Look . . . what are *maps in a binding*? Five letters."

Urbino thought hard.

"Atlas!"† Lili called out gaily, before he had time to venture a guess.

"I should have known that!"

---

*Here the translator cut some capers, trying to cope with the untranslatable alliteration and assonance of the English text. In the original, for example, "sunny" rhymed with "funny," "I" with "bonsai," and so on.
†Here, too, the translator relied on personal experience of the native tongue.

"And this one? *Where do fools fall to Earth from?* Well? Four letters . . ."

"The Moon?"

"Good show! Moon. Where did you fall from so you could be with me?" Lili embraced him. "You can't imagine how boring and tiresome it was here without you . . . What finally got me was *a psychic current.*"

"Me, you mean?"

"No, of course not! Nine letters."

Urbino had been about to give way to vanity, but his spirits slumped.

"Well, and what is it, then?"

"Emanation. I really had to struggle over that one. Here, help me out now! *Gas that blows its top.*"

"Explosion!" Urbino bellowed.

"No, no *x* in this one."

Urbino was stuck. There was no such gas . . .

"Do you memorize every single crossword?"

"Not every single one. Just the ones where I dispute or concur with the author. Sometimes there are really cool* ones."

"Did you say 'cool'?"

Lili laughed out loud.

"There are cool ones, you'll see. 'Cool' is a word that Marleen likes."

"Do you work on them together, too?"

"Sometimes. Here's one, for example—*the most beat-up thing on a nail.* Don't even try, you'll never guess! It's a hat."

"True," Urbino said, casting a sidelong glance at his fellow wordsmith. "But that would be for a woman. For a man it's a head."

Lili blushed.

"Here's a nice riddle I had never heard before: *Accepts the hand of all who come in and go out.*"

"I have no idea what that might be. The hostess of a salon? A debutante receiving her suitors?"

"My, what a ladies' man you are! A doorknob, of course."

---

*Pardon me, if you insist, as Zoshchenko remarked (2008 edition). *(A. B.)*

Finally, she found a fresh crossword that she hadn't tackled yet, and they began to work on it together.

An occurrence that elicits surprise—this was phenomenon (Lili guessed it, and Urbino disputed the phrasing in every possible way, then started quibbling about *ph*, and why the sound wasn't just spelled with an *f*, and finally concluded that in our crazy times the phenomenon is in fact the norm).

He did know without thinking twice that *politics with bloody methods* was terror. Lili showed no interest in that one.

The crossword certainly was a "cool" one. Urbino was especially proud of knowing that *ascent in ancient Greece* was descent. So he easily forgave himself for not knowing *ancient Greek goddess of fate*. Who knows who Moira is nowadays? They talked a bit about differences in mentality, then took a little breather. They were happy about descent. They needed the *t* for the next word: *time-pusher.* They thought of all manner of ways to measure time: calendars, watches, chronometers. They measured, but didn't actually push. History was too long, birthday even longer. And the letters didn't match up.

They thought of piston—a piston would have been far-fetched, but it did speed things up. Still, there were two letters too many. Last? No, no, that was for shoes. Shoes are timeless (though not as timeless as bare feet). Pram? No, the *t* was lacking.

Planet in the solar system . . . If Urbino could excuse himself for not knowing *satellite of Uranus* (they had to leave that one blank), he couldn't afford to be so sanguine about a planet in our solar system. No siree! He combed his memory, trying to dredge up the dormant contents of his schooling; but Uranus, Saturn, and Pluto were no go.

"Perhaps they recently discovered another one?" Lili ventured to say.

"Perhaps," Urbino said glumly. "I'm trying to finish one of my many unfinished novels. It's called *Back from Earth*. It's about an unfortunate Russian scientist who's always a step behind in his breakthroughs. On top of that, he's also an astrologer. He's convinced that directly opposite Earth, behind the Sun, there is another planetary system, exactly like ours. We never see it, because its period of rotation around the Sun is parallel to that of Earth's. So it always remains invisible to astronomers. It has a planet that is exactly like Earth, and it's at the same distance from the Sun, but it's always hidden behind it. Whether there is life on it or not we don't know, but, astrologically speaking, we are linked to it and dependent on it. All of our disasters, our whole history, could depend on the state of affairs of that unseen planet."

"I don't believe it," Lili said, wearily. "We already tried Venus, but it didn't fit."

"Not Venus; it's Nevus—a birthmark. You see, Russians are very superstitious. They believe in all manner of signs and portents."

"How do you know all this?"

"I have a Slavist friend who's helping me."

"Fine. We'll put two of them on hold. There's just one left."

"Which one?"

"That planet."

"What a cretin your crossword author is!"

At this point they began discussing the character of the author of the crossword. It became a kind of game for them to conjure up his personality. He was so ambitious and enthusiastic that he signed with a highly unusual name: Goreslav Kitsey.

Urbino suspected he was a Pole.

They fashioned a portrait something like this: he was rotund, bald, wore a sort of Tyrolean hat and checkered knee breeches, with a ski pole instead of a proper cane—some kind of half-Scotsman, half-Bavarian from the Austro-Hungarian Empire. A widower. He kept canaries. He was a great beer lover, that was certain. They even started to like him.

"I could write some poems about him and his crosswords."

"By all means, write! Don't you think he must write poetry, too?"

"It's possible." Urbino scowled.

He went up to his berth to work. In fact, he collapsed onto yesterday's mattress, still lightly scented with Lili, and fell asleep on the first line: "Move your mind, stir your heart, lift your pen . . ."

He was awoken by Lili.

"I discovered a new planet for you."

"All the same, it's food I want. I'm starved."

"Dinner is ready. Here's your planet with spaghetti."

"Hey, you're already rhyming!" Urbino said with his mouth full. "So, what's the planet?"

"Earth!" Lili said.

"Earth!" Urbino laughed. "The word came up so many times in our conversation and we couldn't see it. He's simply a king, this crossword man. He pulls words out of thin air. Now you see them, now you don't. The world is his playground . . . Or should I say Earth. Maybe that's why we didn't guess it right away. There's no earth under our feet here—you said so yourself. We're on the bottom of the sea. Still, we do have another letter—*a*."

"So what do we get?"

"In what sense?"

"The time-pusher. Think."

"I'm stuffed. I have no more appetite for words. Fine, fine, just give me some coffee. Let's see . . ."

Urbino gulped down his coffee and examined the bottom of the cup.

"Well?"

"Well what?"

"The word!"

"The past. A time-pusher: what propels time forward is—the past. Your crossword man is a genius!"

And Urbino fell into a brown study.

"Don't look so dejected. You can't be the only genius, you know."

"A genius, eh? Well, how about this one: 'Earth and the past crossed paths'—that's already a line, isn't it?"

"Then write it down."

"I already have."

"Then read it."

"Not yet . . . Later."

"I see here some sort of rain cloud . . . and lightning . . . Like a change in the weather," Lili muttered over the evening's cup.

"And I already began writing about yesterday's 'cup' . . ."

"Recite it."

"Well, it's just a rough draft."

"Recite it anyway."

"It's called 'The Death of the Bride.'"
"The bride? Let me hear it!"

1. ROUGH DRAFT
but death, as death, is easy,
and life cannot be mended . . .
river . . . hand . . . soft . . .
a piano without strings or keys.
(the river is dubious)
a hand without strings or keys . . .
lifeless hand . . .
but quicksilver is alive . . . (it can't be alloyed)
and death, like quicksilver, lives—
the piano has no keys
and life is dead, like you—
you steer a rudder without a boat.
here's a broken thermometer
and a small mirror in the hand—
blind quicksilver trembles,
like a sunspot on the ceiling . . .
(not "at" but "on" the ceiling)
the piano leads to a scale,
like a beam, the string vibrates,
and there is quicksilver in the amalgam.
one line is alive—
in an unclear drama:
"but death, as death, is easy" . . .
bright. round. and—amen.

2. WORD-FOR-WORD TRANSLATION
so, did he die?
(no one could think this—yet everyone did.)
a small plain daughter-mirror
she raised to her lips,
so that no one would begin first.
        she looked into it
        and

was reflected
in a dispersing cloud
and saw
herself—
but she did not recognize
herself.
no, it wasn't a mirror she raised to her lips . . .
it was his life that looked in the mirror for an instant
and was reflected in it simply
as a girl,
sure that no one, not ever, would pass by,
and that it was not possible
to be younger and more charming,
so . . .

she only glances, almost unwillingly, to see
that everything is so
(and could not be otherwise).—
her shoulder flashes in it
like a beam
(or the chance flight of a butterfly),
and so flies past,
hardly touching its own reflection
leaving the shadow of its transparent movement
in the air,
like a falling veil,
that she weaves with her every moment
(each—a wreath,
together—a shroud) . . .

even now,
when no one was in the room
and there was no one to reflect off,
even for her,

because she was gone already—
there was only mist where she had just been,
because she had only just left,
and she can be found now in the garden
(a note made by the breeze of the curtain
was left in the room saying this,

an unread book
and a nibbled apple)—
she was there already
among the trees, under the stars
outlined
like cuneiform
on birch bark—
  thus
  she was not reflected
  but
  abandoned
    the mirror . . .
no, the mirror was not touched by his breath
(or the breeze of her motion . . .)
    it's the mirror
    they brought to the lips
    it's his life
    for an instant
    reflected in the mirror
    and,
    recognizing himself
    recognizing
    that it was she
    who left him
    with the same ease
    as
    breath on a mirror.
My God!
how brief!

This time Lili's fortune-telling was very accurate and came true immediately: at first she grew gloomy as a storm cloud, then her gentle eyes flashed lightning. And there was a peal of thunder.

"You still love her!"

Wearied by the thought of trying to reproduce the contents of the rambling and lengthy dialogue that follows (it spans two or three pages), I will get right down to the gist of it. In fact, there wasn't much substance to it, anyway.

"I can't drink any more coffee," Lili said. "These cups . . ." She was about to fling one to the floor but thought better of it and stayed her hand. "They are driving me mad! Do you want a drink?"

Urbino did.

To his delight, it turned out that she had half a bottle of whiskey. She preferred a glass of white wine.

Urbino was so relieved at the possibility of a truce that he quickly became tipsy, and at her sympathetic prompting, he told her without holding anything back how things had been between himself and Dika. He didn't notice how carried away he was by his confession.

"Is that all?" Lili said evenly.

"That's all. It was a sunny spring day, there were many birds, like there are here."

"Like here?"

"Yes. Children were playing on the vacant lot in brightly colored jackets. I read a strange word on a fence: BIRDY. I made up a poem."

"Read it!"

Urbino sobered up a bit and pondered, like he was trying to remember. Should he?

"I'm very drunk."

Lili pursed her lips.

It was windy and birdy
Children blossomed in dust
Morning shining and dirty
Building Future from Past
We were left in the Present
With yesterday's ties
To forget the last lesson:
How to die.*

---

*Of all the poems, the translator liked this one most, and he gave his all trying to translate it. It turned out twice as long, and the poetry may have escaped altogether:

There was wind, and birds.
Children blossomed in their jackets.
Yesterday's faces were unable
To recognize us at all.
Not much remained

"Birdy? Is that what you called her? The way you call me Little Fish!"

"No, of course not! Her name was Eurydika, and I called her Dika."

That night was a sleepless one. She didn't come up to his attic, and he tossed and turned in expectation.

At dawn he didn't find her on the shore they'd visited the day before.

Of you and me,
And a road rose up
Out of yesterday.
So the blinding taste
Will stay. Drink it all.
And taste,
How full you are, and how empty.

The translation of this poem, however, allows me to date this place in my work on the larger translation of the book: January 28, 1997. At Princeton, the news reached me of the death of the poet Vladimir Sokolov (which is where these "faces" came from). A victim of taste, his whole life he worked on a long poem with the title (not easy for the Russian language) of "The Plot." He never finished it. His subject converged to a point by a coincidence: this day, January 28, 1997, was the first anniversary of the death of Joseph Brodsky.

Oh, the 28th of January! Pushkin, Dostoevsky, Blok (if we take into account "The Twelve") . . . Brodsky and Sokolov were certainly in good company. What is this? The stars? Or is it "the heavens mocking the Earth"?

This footnote leads me synchronically to another memoir, which allows me to establish another date, connected with the very beginning of my work on this "translation," my first test of the pen.

"The spirit of sad idleness . . ."—the Russian always strives to start with what is easiest. And I began with the poems. I didn't dare write them in my own name; but under the name of the protagonist, and all the more since it was a translation "from a foreign tongue" . . . "Thursday" seems fairly decent. Still feeling the momentum, I drafted "The Death of the Bride." Just at that moment, I ran into Joseph on Nevsky Prospect (in other words, he hadn't yet left for good). Knowing that he earned his keep as a translator and was celebrated for his "Elegy for John Donne," I described my project to him and asked for a professional consultation. "Sure, why not?" he said. And we went up to my place for a cup of coffee. I explained to him that coffee grounds were the inspiration for my literal translations. He glanced at "The Death of the Bride," and praised the last line: "My God! How brief!"

"Still, it's not quite the thing," he concluded. "Oh, by the way, I've got something here on the same subject." And with a magician's gesture he pulled out of his breast pocket a sheet of paper casually folded into a quarto. "I wrote it yesterday. Did you know Bobo? No? Strange. Well, she died."

And in his rich, gingery voice he read: "Bobo is dead, but don't take off your hat . . ." His dandyism turned out to be justified: not only did Inga and I like it, but he liked it himself.

"You've convinced me" was all I managed to say to him.

I don't know whether this was the premiere of the poem. The next time I heard it, I was at his home, already very drunk, at his send-off. (A. B., February 10, 2008.)

There was no one on the whole island—as if the island wasn't there anymore, either.

Although he felt he might lose his mind over these matters of the heart, hunger got the better of him and he decided to visit the stateroom on his own.

3. Marleen's Island

A very different person, the complete antithesis, met him at breakfast.

"Ah, the guest! You're late."

There could be no doubt that they were twins, although she looked significantly younger. With an almost clean-shaven head, excessively made-up, she was a blowsy brunette in a canvas robe, with a neckpiece like a dog collar. An unkempt little girl.

This was Marleen.

"Are you looking for Lili? You won't find her. She weighed anchor this morning."

"Why all of a sudden?"

"There was a storm warning on the radio. She was in a hurry to make it before the typhoon."

"Make it for what?"

"First, to stock up. And second, to see a friend."

"What kind of friend?" Urbino couldn't help asking.

"Just a friend. Like most people have. Did you think you were the only one in her life?"

Urbino started hating the sister immediately. His love for Lili flared up in him with all the power of jealousy.

"So, did she let you out?"

"Of course not. I gnawed through the chain." And with a monstrous smile, Marleen bared a row of blackened teeth.

The day was uncommonly still, as if a storm really was in the offing.

"Just don't read me any poems," Marleen said categorically. "They're terrible. Especially those off-the-cuff numbers."

"And I quite liked yours . . ."

"What, she showed you mine? The traitor!"

"What surprises me is that she showed you mine. When did she find time?"

"I was eavesdropping." Marleen laughed raucously.

"How was that even possible, when you were locked up in the hold?"

"I have a special pipe, like a ninja."

"What do you mean, a ninja?"

"You really don't know?"

Marleen launched into an ecstatic account of this remarkable sect, to which she herself seemed to belong—according to Urbino, at least.

"And you already know that I can breathe underwater and escape from any chains. Hey, don't be offended. Your poems aren't all that bad. Only the impromptu one was atrocious."

"Which impromptu one?"

"The one you dedicated to her."

"Which of the two?"

"You dedicated two of them to her?"

"Well, yes. Although you wouldn't have been able to overhear one of them."

"I'm sure it was terrible, too."

Strangely enough, the more he missed Lili, the more he enjoyed Marleen's company. Being with her was simpler, more natural, as though she were not Lili's sister but his own. That's because I'm not trying to make her like me, he realized.

"I wish I had a sister, instead of the brother," he said. "Life would be much easier."

"If I only had a brother . . ." Marleen sighed. "One like you, in fact."

"What would you do with him?"

"We could drink together, for instance."

"Would that make me the girlfriend?" Urbino said.

"One more shot, and then—off to bed!" Marleen resolved.

He didn't understand what happened next. Didn't understand, or couldn't remember?

"That's just my variation. An overture. A variation on a theme from the overture to *The Magic Flute*. No, Mozart was just the beginning. Now this is going to be my flute. I am merely the performer, I just blow it."

"You're a true virtuoso!" Urbino cried. "I bow down before your rendition!"

And he fell to his knees at the slightest touch of her finger.

"And now, Wagner!" she said. "Which overture will you perform? I want *The Golden Rhine* . . . No, even better, the whole *Ring of the Nibelung* . . . Yes, just like that!"

"Listen, why do you shave it?"

"So you can see my tattoo . . . My turn: *The Flight of the Valkyries*!"

And she thrust her tattoo in front of his eyes.

But he saw nothing—he drowned.

The womb that had once borne him devoured him now by force of will.

It was something both similar and contrary to being born, the memory of which, it turned out, was hidden so deeply and irretrievably that this was the only way to reach it. "Mama, I want to be unborn!" How unchildish, in fact, this sentiment really was. You had to shrink, become a baby again, a newborn, completely diminish yourself . . . No, even more minute (which is larger—a microbe or a spermatozoid?) so that you could finally be swallowed up, dissolved in love!

"And now, *The Twilight of the Gods*!" Marleen screamed in a frenzy. "All together now!"

First the strings went quiet, then the woodwinds died away, and only the timpani remained.

Urbino got lost. He wandered around backstage, he flung aside the backdrop and yanked the curtains apart—it was a theater in which a fire had just been extinguished.

"What do the Gypsies in restaurants sing?" he murmured weakly. "'Kiss me, then I'll kiss you, then we'll both kiss together' . . . Is this what were they singing about?"

"Didn't you know? What else?" Marleen said in a low, husky, Gypsy voice.

•

She tried to attack, but instead she only flattered him.

"Now I see the effect you have on dames. They can't stay away from you. You make it seem as though you have nothing to do with it, that they're the ones who started it. And so they fall prey to you, poor things."

Urbino was genuinely offended. No, she's wrong! he thought. Things weren't like that with Lili. He was the one in control, not her. He would never spurn Lili, his final choice.

A bird was singing in a bush. Another one perched next to it, turning away in silence. It set off a faint echo in Urbino's head, and he couldn't keep it to himself.

"What are they singing about?" he said.

"Only one of them sings. The song is hers; his song is silence."

"Makes no sense. It's always the male who sings."

"Sing, then."

"I don't know how."

"You see? She's the one who's singing."

"Why is she singing?"

"She's horny, that's why," Marleen said in a low growl. In the same throaty voice, she broke into a song that went like this:

Milenkii ty moi,
Vozmi menja s soboi
Tam v kraju daljokom
Nazovjosh menja zhenoi

The song moved Urbino, though he didn't understand a word of it. Thoughts of Lili and Dika, Dika and Lili, merged and flowed into the melody.

"Did you learn that from the Gypsies?"

"Did Lili tell you that?" Marleen bared her fangs to bite. "Lucky for you, I get all wound up by the soft and gentle . . ."

"What about Lili?" (He missed the punch.)

"What about her?" Marleen barked. "You should know. I think she has the hots for musclemen. She's into force."

"Well, then Happenen is just the guy for her."

"She's scared of him."

"Oh, and not me?"

"You're a girl to her, Urbino!"

"What do you mean, a girl?" he said.

"Because you wake up the man in women. You're a vampire! You drain the energy out of their desires. That's what broads do, not men."

He didn't want to admit it to himself, but things were both simpler and easier with Marleen. And even to himself he couldn't say which one he liked better. His sense of guilt when he thought of Lili was intertwined with jealousy, and it grew so strong that he hoped that she would return soon, and that she would never return at all, both at the same time.

"Does it not seem incestuous to you?"

"You mean with Lili? With that Medusa?"

He didn't want to continue the conversation in that key.

"No, with me, with a brother."

"Well, you're quick today! No, I've never tried it with a brother. Get over here, on the double!"

"You're my Gorgon," the brother gushed.

"Little bro'," Marleen said tenderly. "What, did you want to make it with your little sis'? With both of them? How about with both of them at the same time?"

Urbino was gripped with horror at just the thought of Lili's return.

"Did you take fright? Let's go out and get some fresh air."

Everything looked different to him now: the air tickled his nostrils and the sand touched the soles of his feet in a new way.

"What's wrong? Are you confused again about where you've ended up? Climb up to the top of the mast."

"Why on Earth would I want to mount it?"

"You didn't have second thoughts about mounting me, did you? Go up and take a look. You get a pretty good view from up there."

Climbing up the mast proved to be a long and arduous process: the rope ladder (what was the term from the crosswords? halyard? rigging?) swayed precariously and cut into the soles of his bare feet. Looking down, he was terrified, but it was already too late to turn back.

Reaching the top was worth the effort, though. He really did see everything differently from up there. It was a different island—Marleen's Island.

It stretched out like an oyster. Two rows of dunes, like folds, like those very lips . . . The woods were like a pubis. All around, to the very horizon, stretched the loins of all life: the sea. And he, atop the mast, was like a stake plunged into the loins.

Two or three liters of that same sea, but from back in the Mesozoic era, sloshed around in the brain. Into it swam the little fish of a single thought, and thrashed its little tail. Pubis, little fish . . . He was seized with yearning for Lili. That's it. I'm lost . . . I'm lost in pussy . . . This is how the island landscape appeared to him now.

At the same time he felt the urge to climb down and avenge himself on that bitch Marleen who had severed him from Lili, who had cunningly passed her (he was now convinced of this, after witnessing the unruffled calm of the sea all around) a spurious radiogram about an approaching typhoon. He wanted to wreak vengeance on her, to take her roughly, violently, from behind, like a bitch. But climbing down turned out to be even more difficult than climbing up.

My God! What have I done!

"Well, did you take a good look?"

Instead of carrying out his crude intentions, he pushed Marleen away so roughly that she fell in the sand and began to whimper and whine like a puppy.

He locked himself into his cabin and refused to open the door.

Never in his life had he found himself in such a bind. He had only to set foot on an uninhabited island for it to become overpopulated— overpopulated by him. That's an idea: exporting your Bermudas to the farthest corners of the globe.

He tried to express this in the best way he knew how . . .

THE DEATH OF THE SEED
To think something through to the end!—
No wreath more hapless or more gratifying . . .
Four operations of arithmetical passion,
An integer of one—alone, alone!

Irrational delirium is the experience of a multiple fraction:
Twelve-eighteenths . . . zero point six . . .
The row of sixes extending to infinity,
Wagging the tail of the apocalypse . . .
If only once to understand and divide the remainder
By itself—what joy!
Not to live with the carelessness of life and hope:
Division by one is reality . . .
Death is an integer.

But madness does not threaten reason—
And scientists dispose of the kernel of the irrational
With terrible composure:
"Well, it never tallies."
Thus, the freedom to think falsely is the right
of a human being, to be beside his thought his right.
Thus madness does not threaten reason.

As though, ostensibly! There are degrees of loneliness
That no one knows besides oneself,
If only because to taste and know them
Is a riddle: the code conceals
The possibility of continuing. No matter how paltry,
The remainder is your day tomorrow.
How otherwise would the Savior drive the Creator
To continue the mistake of generations?
What logic is there in Creation—
It is equal only to itself!
Luring us into ourselves is easier by far
Than luring seeds into the earth . . . and we ourselves are the
     seed.

Fatal is our rupture! It's vulgar
Not to understand that life is only in us!
It is not for us to boast of poverty with you,
Holding fast to a plan of universal fate!
Not to unlock us with a slavish master key

Of fear to be spurned . . .
Relinquish and *Take* have a common meaning:
NO ONE takes ALL. No one needs ALL.
It fell to my lot already . . . And the measure of loneliness—
Is the reserve of love, never revealed.

I must die every second!
Burying myself thus is as safe
As a tree burying its seeds . . .
Their immortality is genuine: without rupture
From death to life. The existence of the soul
Conceals rupture within itself. Through what
Abysses one must fly to achieve
What the tree is able to do effortlessly! To regret
This, truly, is not futile for us:
One day to stop trying to be understood—
And to understand, at last, oneself.

"Now that begins to resemble something," Marleen said, finally expressing approval.

"What does it resemble?"

"A spermatozoid. 'The row of sixes extends into infinity . . .' How does it go?"

"'Wagging the tail of the apocalypse.' Hey, you're right!"

"There, you see? You can, if you try hard enough. Come to me."

"We'll see about that. You come to me, my bitch! Any news from Lili?"

"Don't be so uptight about her or I really will start getting jealous. Did she tell you how horrendous I can be? Anyway, I sent her another typhoon warning. Don't think she's going to miss you."

Marleen shouldn't have said this.

He pushed her away and stormed off. But how can you escape one another on such a tiny speck?

Lord, save us!

The mast suddenly appeared to him as the only secluded spot.

Already more deftly, and with greater confidence, he scrambled up. Rather, he flew.

The crow's nest felt very cozy to him, almost lived-in: a warm and trusted treehouse. There was plenty to look at—in all four directions.

It was worth the effort. He saw what he had never seen before.

On the left, an enormous full Moon (perhaps not quite full—but in a day or so it would be), pale turquoise. On the right, the sun, even larger than the Moon, was easing itself down into the sea. So the Moon was in the east, where it belonged, Urbino's schoolboy imagination told him.

He recalled a Muslim fairy tale from his childhood about a young man who dreamed about the sun and the Moon at the same time, and a Sufi had interpreted it for him: You will have two equally beautiful wives . . . and that dream came true. When the young man grew up, he remembered the dream, and was happy that his fate had been fulfilled.

Urbino clung to his perch, between the slowly fading sun and the exultant Moon, measuring the distance between them: between Lili and Marleen, between love and passion.

And, while admiring this marvelous equilibrium, he recalled that it was not only among Muslims but among followers of other religions, perhaps the Hebrews, that a widower had an obligation to marry the unmarried sister of his deceased wife. No! He was not wishing for another death. What if Heaven is a place where another life, as yet unrealized (but deeply desired), unfolds? . . . And it turns out to be the embodiment (in practice) of Hell! The West becomes the East, the slave a tyrant, the homely girl a beauty, the pauper a rich man, the sensualist an ascetic . . . and vice versa. Equality as retribution, he thought.

Thus, turning his rapt gaze now to the east, now to the west, he almost missed the moment when the sun began to plummet into the sea. From up here, he could see it didn't flatten out but remained perfectly round, and sank like a solid, dense orb. In no time at all, it was gone.

The Moon hung motionless in the sky as if nothing at all had happened.

What if they're lesbians? Urbino wondered with a childish sense of sweet apprehension. Marleen the active one, and Lili the passive one?

It would make it easier for me, he thought selfishly. The notion that he was the third party amused and distracted him for a while. He began imagining them together, as though he were observing them from his vantage point atop the mast, or from the side, as if through a window . . . They pass by, their fingers entwined . . . two blossoms. The lines of the poem "Two Blossoms" began to compose themselves . . .

Two girlfriends, Heaven and Hell,
a blonde and a brunette,
choose a skirt to go with a blouse,
and become cross-pollinated.

They stand before a mirror
and don't see themselves—
each gaze reflects the other girl
in her best light.

"Strange," Urbino thought. "The lines are thinking themselves; I have nothing to do with it."

Yes, everything is simpler when you're on the mast. You're at the peak of loneliness in the most literal sense.

A cool breeze blew up. It grew darker, and he had nothing to jot down the poem with.

When he had managed to clamber down the mast, it was already twilight. He locked himself in his cabin, then wrote down the lines that had recently come to him. When Marleen gets here I'll have her take a look at them to see if they're any good, he thought. He waited for his Moon, as he had awaited, long ago, his sun. But Marleen didn't come knocking, either.

Time seemed to stretch out endlessly before him; it became unbearable, and he went off in search of her. The Moon cast a brilliant light over everything. Her hold was locked up, however. He knocked, and called out to her—there was no response.

4. The Bermudas

I water invention with my tears . . .   —Alex Cannon

In the morning she was nowhere to be found, either.

He went out onto the shore to greet the sunrise and contemplate what to do.

As the sun rose, he saw a boat approaching.

He caught himself feeling glad—not because it was finally Lili, but because at least she wouldn't be catching him with Marleen.

He expected it to be Midshipman Happenen transporting Lili, and was confident in him.

Though not in himself. He intended to show every possible restraint, no more, no less.

And he was completely taken by surprise when he saw that Lili was alone in the boat, rowing powerfully toward shore.

He was overcome by a mixture of delight and fear. It was his Lili, only she was wearing the midshipman's pirate bandana.

She could have at least taken it off, he thought. Still, she probably didn't expect me to get up so early.

"Oh, it's you." Her voice sounded both careless and guarded.

Damn female intuition! he thought, amazed, but said:

"What do you mean?"

"I mean what I say. You didn't miss me at all. Give me a hand, will you? This stuff is heavy."

"What about the midshipman?" he said, his voice cracking as he heaved canisters of kerosene onto shore.

"Oh, you mean Happenen?" Her voice betrayed alarm. "He wanted to come, but I said no."

"Oh." Urbino was equanimity itself.

"That kind of emotional strain is not good for Marleen."

"I see, you were worried about Marleen."

"If they renewed their relationship, blood would flow."

"Are you saying"—Urbino knew he was saying too much, but he couldn't stop—"that Happenen is not your lover but hers?"

"Well, well, well . . ." Now she sounded angry. "Did she tell you that? So you let her out."

"She broke out herself."

"How did she manage that?"

"She said she gnawed through the chain. I thought it was a joke, that you had set her loose in case of a typhoon, or who knows what." Urbino was struggling to keep afloat in a morass of half-concealed lies, some of human nature's muddiest waters.

He bobbed up for a gulp of air. "Do you know what the primary task of our intellect is?"

"What?"

"To hide our own natures from us."

"The truth, you mean? Quit beating around the bush. Are you talking about Marleen?"

"She is quite a strange girl, I must say."

"Strange? Girl?" Lili snarled. "So you slept with that bitch! How could you?" She was crying.

Her tears were her strongest argument. Urbino was defenseless against them. He tried to assuage his guilt by putting his arms around her. She tried to push him away halfheartedly, and refused to let him touch her head. Then she slapped him.

"What was that for?" he said. It was the weakest possible argument. Then again, the slap she had given him wasn't all that hard.

The simplest solution now was to read her some of his new poetry.

I dreamed the naked truth
with a braid down to her naked rump,
and suddenly she was someone else—
with a wolf's bared teeth, her braid a scythe.

All night she stalked me
with a curved blade of sleep,
now tempting, now repelling,
beauty and death in one.

"The one about Birdy was better. Is that about Marleen? Did you write it for her?"

"Marleen? With a braid? She's bald! You're the one with hair for braiding."

"So I'm your death, then?"

The similarity in intonation startled him. Something pierced his brain like a stroke of lightning. He heard the sound of one hand clapping. Was a slap in the face the answer to the riddle of the Tao? Makes sense, he thought, their teachers are in the habit of striking their students for obtuseness.

"Is that the midshipman's bandana? Take it off. Now!"

"It's not his, it's mine! I bought all three of us the same kind."

"Oh, all three . . . Well, where's mine?"

"I haven't gotten around to getting you one."

"But I'm the third. Give it to me!"

Lili tried to put up a fight but feigned weakness at the same time.

Finally, he managed to kiss her. His hand strayed over the bandana. The bandana was too tight, and the head underneath it was too smooth. His hand guessed what was wrong. He yanked the bandana off. It was Marleen, sans makeup. And yet it was Lili, her head shaved clean.

"Who are you now? Lili or Marleen?"

"It doesn't matter anymore. What matters is who you are now."

"'Whoever I was then, I still am now,'" Urbino quoted from memory.

"Precisely. You've always been alone. Good job, now keep it up!"

"Take your own advice!"

"Are you just pretending, or does your elevator not go all the way to the top?* Do you really not understand that there's only one of us?"

"I've never had any experience with real twins. I heard that besides their physical likeness they can have a heightened affinity, be very close to one another—a spiritual bond, so to speak . . . But you are so different . . . Listen, if you and Marleen are really the same person, then there are only two of us!"

"What are you going to do about Marleen now?"

"Who's Marleen? I only have you. You're my Lili Marleen!"

"That's a song, not a person. And I'm here alone; except for Marleen."

*Begging your pardon (again). *(A. B.)*

"What Marleen?" Urbino was losing patience.

"The dog, of course."

"Oh, thank God! Then we finally are alone, just the two of us. We're happy, aren't we?"

Lili didn't speak.

"Two people in a boat, to say nothing of the dog." The joke didn't fly.

"The dog has nothing to do with it."

"So there definitely are just the two of us. We are one whole, I mean . . ." Urbino mumbled.

"You disgust me. Don't you get it? We're never going to forgive you for this. I'll never forgive you about Marleen, Marleen will never forgive you about me, and neither of us will forgive you about Dika."

"Leave Dika out of this. I've been waiting for you! You are my fate."

"Fate is what you got, you slithering dirty reptile, you! You've never loved anyone. Your poems are trash. You're a man split in half. Do you think you're smack dab between Heaven and Earth? Well, like hell you are! Between the soul and the body. You know what you are? You are a callus. A callus doesn't hurt, it only causes pain. Oh, how the dead cling to the living! You are an invalid. Your capacity for love is atrophied."

"If I'm so bad, how come you seduced me?"

"Me? Seduce you? It required no effort on my part. If only . . . If only I had . . . It would have meant at least something to me. And to you, too. But no, you melted like wax from the word go. Never in my life have I seen such a milquetoast."

"You haven't seen much, then, I take it," Urbino spat back at her, not without jealousy.

"None of your business what I've seen. To think that I had gotten my hopes up. The Baroness had wasted no words describing the power of your feelings, your inconsolable grief over Dika, and I thought: There's at least one real man on Earth. I liked your looks. All is not lost, I thought. I'll save him, I thought. I never suspected that the Baroness would saddle me with such a swine of a man!" She shook her head in disgust. "I should have guessed right away! Maybe she really is a good psychiatrist. She saw right through you, and for that reason, instead of going after you herself, she forwarded you to me. She spread out the net for me by painting a glowing image of you in her letter."

"Stop it, you mutt!" Urbino said in a fury.

"Well, I may be a mutt, but right now I'm ready to barf, not bark. It hurts between the horns I'm wearing now because of what you've done to me!"

"Horns are also a kind of callus," Urbino retorted.

"That's right," she continued, "because you're a bull. It makes no difference to you whom you cover. What made you pass up the Baroness? Was that fine, upstanding woman not good enough for you?"

"She's a psychiatrist. Their lot has dispensed with romance."

"Perhaps it's so they won't go mad themselves. Yet she did . . ."

"How so?"

"Revenge is a kind of mania."

"Revenge?"

"She was head over heels in love with Happenen."

"What about him?"

"He was in love with me."

"So whom did she want to avenge herself on by sending me, you or Happenen?"

"Both of us."

"But why?"

"To separate us."

"To separate you? Are you engaged?"

"Halfway."

"Which of the two of you, you or Marleen?"

(Urbino hadn't noticed that he had already chosen Lili over Marleen.)

"To him, I'm the only one."

"And he to you?"

"I'm the one who persuaded him not to kill you. He sensed danger. He's a real man, a pillar of support. Perhaps he was more aware of the danger to him than to me."

"Care to elaborate?"

"It's simple. He loves me. He needs only me, even if I don't love him back."

"So he allowed you to have me?"

"Why not? He said he'd kill you either way."

"For what? It was his idea to begin with."

"For me! Because you would cheat on me."

"But you set it all up! Why did you pretend to be Marleen?"

"To prove him right."

"Oh, so you conspired against me together."

"No, he's not capable of that. It was just me and Marleen."

"But there never was any Marleen!"

"Yes, there was. And I'll marry him."

"Did you promise yourself to him?"

"Yes, but on one condition."

"Do go on."

"That he never be jealous of my infidelity again."

"Again? You're one lowdown scum. You've got quite the nerve to mistreat two men at the same time."

"Why two? There's just one. And he's still the only one."

"I'm speechless."

"Don't worry. He's not going to kill you. Provided one condition is met."

"You dare set the terms for him?"

"No, this time it's him. He set the terms for me."

"Curiouser and curiouser. And the terms are . . . ?"

"That I marry him."

"Damn you, Lili! You're worse than Marleen. You're a monster!"

"Go to your Marleen, then. Damn right I'm a monster. Because I'm a woman, and I know how to love. I'm bound to love one who does not love me back. You told me yourself that one can't split the magnet into a negative and a positive pole. You can't split me with love, either. Just like the magnet, just like Marleen and me. No, you didn't say anything about a magnet, that wasn't your idea. It was your lovestruck Russian scientist Tishkin, whose story you can't finish writing. You know why you can't finish it? Because you don't know how to love."

"'The less we love a woman, / The more the woman loves us. / And thereby we destroy her.'"

"Now, that's good. Did you write that?"

"No, it's by another Russian. Pushkin."

"Someone else's stuff again. Tishkin, Pushkin . . . Do all Russians have the same names?"

"No, not all of them. Just Pushkin. That's a joke. Mine."

Lili laughed, and Urbino attempted to draw her to him again. No go.

"It's my translation, too. My Slavist friend translated it differently: 'The less we more a woman, the more she lesses us back.'"

"Are you saying that you're more and I'm less?"

Urbino sensed the change of tone and changed his tack. "If you and Marleen are the same person, it means you stayed on the island the whole time and couldn't have gone to see Happenen. Where did the kerosene come from, then? Where's the logic in that?"

"Logic is all that's left. I have a storehouse on the other part of the island, behind the woods."

"Okay, fine. But how on Earth did you manage to transform yourself into Marleen?"

"That one is even easier. When we were being brought up in the monastery, we put on wonderful puppet shows at Christmas. I always got the role of angel, and Marleen played the devil."

"Oh, come off it. You've told too many lies for just one person."

"There isn't just one person. There are two."

"What?"

"Marleen and me. Which one do you prefer?"

"Lay off."

"No way! What if we both like you?"

"You'll take turns, then," Urbino said, scoffing.

"Wrong again. Make a choice. I won't settle for less."

"And this is why you shaved yourself head to toe?"

"I planned to do it long ago, before you got here," Lili said in Marleen's voice. "Besides . . ."

"What?"

"I was embarrassed."

"In front of whom?"

"You. Myself."

"Yourself meaning Lili or Marleen?"

"Obviously it's all the same to you. But I'm ashamed!"

"Just ashamed?"

"Yes; but not 'just.' Idiot! Shyness is the foundation of feeling. It is the bedrock of . . . *s-s-s* . . . I can't bear that word."

"Sensibility?"

"No, of course not! *S-s-s* . . . No, I can't."

"Oh, you mean sex?"

"Well, yes. Except that men and women express shyness differently. For us it's embarrassment, for you brutality."

"Brutality, eh? So it's Happenen. Fine, but where's the embarrassment? In your tattoo?"

"What tattoo?" (Innocence itself.)

"The tattoo. The one you have down there."

"Oh, that? That's Marleen. She did it when she was a kid, a silly prank. What is it, by the way? I haven't seen it in a long time."

"Talk about shyness. You're two of a kind."

"So, two?" (Another clapping of one hand.)

"Well, let's take a look, shall we? Maybe it's a fleur-de-lis, like Milady de Winter's brand!"

"Milady? What Milady? What are you talking about?"

"You must have read *The Three Musketeers*. Go on, show me!"

"No way!" Lili said, spurning his readiness.

"Yes, way!" Marleen screamed, grabbing it roughly.

Suddenly, everything in Urbino seemed to go limp.

"Why don't both of you just go f——k yourselves!" he shouted. "I'm going to get my things."

"No, you go f——k yourself!"

"Enough! I'm not Happenen. You're a monster. This isn't Hollywood. There are just two of us. You and me. No Marleen, no Happenen, no Baroness, no . . ." He broke off.

She understood.

"Oh, so there's no more Dika, either? You see, now you've betrayed her, too."

"I'm going to kill you."

"Thank goodness, you still have some feelings left."

"I didn't betray her while she . . ." He broke off again, and again she understood.

"While she was alive?" She finished his sentence. "But you did betray her while she was still living."

"How would you know? Who could I have betrayed her for?"

"I just know. Otherwise the snake wouldn't have bitten her. You betrayed her for the snake that stung her in her heart."

"With a snake? You are so cruel! You're a snake yourself!"

"Finally! Now you're getting it. It was me. I was that very one."

"I'm going to strangle you! No, I'm going to see your tattoo! What have you got there? A snake?"

Urbino threw the full weight of his body on her, all the while continuing to grope and fondle her . . . Before they realized it, it was all over.

"How could you! You rapist! I'll never forgive you for this!"

"Marleen said you were into this kind of thing."

"She's a bitch, your Marleen."

"Pot calling the kettle black."

"*The Kreutzer Sonata*!" Lili-Marleen moaned.

A shadow fell across their bodies. Happenen loomed over them.

"Ready yet?"

The goodbye was cool and restrained. Urbino handed her a carefully sealed envelope, with no addressee, and no return address.

"I wrote this just for you, Lili. Not for Birdy, not for Marleen. For you."

On the envelope was scrawled:

THE LAST CASE OF LETTERS

Happenen splashed the oars impatiently, like Marleen wagging her tail.

"Hurry! We'll never make it before the storm!"

And it was true. Something unimaginable was brewing in the sky. It was still and quiet, but the waves were starting to surge. The edge of the sky was charred and turned upward, like a Chinese pagoda, inside of which a bright transparent ring took shape. In the middle of the ring, as though directly over the boat, a storm cloud appeared. It condensed and grew steadily blacker toward the center. Darkness was pouring into it, and it sagged like a bomb.

Everything anticipated his imminent departure.

Their boat had already crossed half the strait when the black bomb tore off like a droplet and began to fall. An orifice just big enough for a full Moon to fit in opened up in the morose skies. The Moon illumined the rearing waves that crashed over them.

"Lili! I remembered!" Urbino cried, choking and gasping for breath, paddling back to the island with all his might. "I remembered the word from the crossword puzzle! It's TROGLODYTE!"

"Troglodyte?" an echo resounded.

But this was Happenen, bobbing up and down in his boat on the crest of a wave.

"Rape her!" Urbino burbled, taking in another gulp of seawater. "She likes it!"

"Can do," said Happenen, trying to brain Urbino with the oar.

A military patrol boat picked him up. When they had pumped all the water out of him and he had started breathing again, the first word he uttered was "Happenen!"

"There was someone else with me! Where is he?"

They gave him some whiskey. He took a swig, and began undulating to the rhythm of other waves . . .

The more we live
The more we leave.
The more we choose
The more we lose.
The more we try
The more we cry.
The more we win
The greater the sin.
To reach the aim—
Obtain the same.
The only law—
Lose Waterloo.
The only way—
Just run away.

THE LAST CASE OF LETTERS

(Pigeon Post)

FROM *Lines from a Coffee Cup*, A COLLECTION OF POEMS
BY Ris Vokonabi

I.
In my sleep I was forewarned
of your impending visit . . . What the devil?!
I woke up too early, and arrived
almost too late at the station,
cursing to high Heaven (though dark
as Hell it was) the sluggishness of servants:
couldn't they have brought the news on time?
At the appointed hour a ladder was in place: I descended
into a flock of waiting Vietnamese. "Get lost!
Begone! I'm no gourmand!" The flock scattered.
The ship left, I was ungodly late, and thought
up a just punishment for the trusty servant
who managed to wake me up on time:
For Promptness. What dismal failure
in the task at hand—to wake me up,
and by ticking, to measure out the time of life,
depriving life of—time . . . What do you mean "what for"!?
Because, you scoundrel, you didn't pinch the maid,
did not drink an extra mug, and managed to
shun the realm of dreams—
behind the door, out shivering with the roosters!

II.

Thus, wrenched out of my delirium at last,
I sat upright and glanced around me groggily:
"What a night! Thank goodness it was all a dream."
In the night, someone had reupholstered the divan
and moved the walls around. There, across from me,
where I fell asleep the night before was now a rectangle,
overgrown with a flora of dust . . . within this thicket—
another, geometrically similar shape: a letter,
the address facing downward, two diagonals crossing it . . .
Two threads from the corners came together in a knot—
a little kite! . . . a fragile thread
stretched over to the window. The window was grayish
and looked just like an envelope . . . amidst the dust a window
    gapes,
a letter shines bright in the window sash
and strains to fly off to the sky. Such wondrous
ties and connections are completely understandable.
I'm tired of guessing: defining the circle of loss is always helpful.
The window is torn open. Barefoot, shivery handwriting.
A scrap of fog is hanging from the windowsill . . .
"I arrived yesterday
too early at the station;
don't wait and don't be late
kisses, sleep, goodbye
—Marquise Méranville" . . .
Oh, drat it!
I tore it up. Untied the laces.
Who in our day and age writes letters, really?
The letter flew up in the air, nodding to the wind,
The sky above the former Prussian town grew rosy pink,
anticipating sunrise, signifying
that *today* had finally come!
I smiled and wiped it from my face:
"It's all right now," the nonsense went,
reminding me of dreams.
I rummaged in the upholstery—

flowers of a southern genus, perhaps Italian . . .
how had they grown here?—
on a small, neat, dusty glade
the letter lay.

III.
As always, a carelessness may be observed in space:
here is the chink in the floor where light squeezes through—
what's down below? An ominous, raucous feast;
thank God they don't have time for me.
Suddenly—a spat, a quarrel, untuned voices
rise, and doors are slammed!
                         Then vulgar laughter:
"Don't mind him!"—and they leave forever.
It's fine this way, they say.
                         My objects sleep,
they borrowed shadows from the places of the past . . .
Like light, extinguished, hurries into shade!
A cry trembles somewhere near the throat!
Your objects harbor so much inner horror,
changing unaccountably:
then return and take their seats again.
There on the nail hangs my overcoat,
there is no person in it, and yet,
hostile velvet lines the collar
and the shadow of the nail basks in the light . . .

I fathom not the world of my salvations!
Frightened so by various trifles that
betrayed me imperceptibly and subtly—
a mailbox, found all of a sudden
instead of a bedside table
                         did not surprise me in the least
but rather touched me . . . I smiled
and in the chink I stuck a finger,
                         "That's that,"

I thought calmly,

            and, not taking off my shoes,
flopped down on my back, arms folded:
"Is it possible to spit up to the ceiling?"
My head was filled with simple thoughts:
whether to put the kettle on, or steam the postage
stamps, a present for my daughter.

            "Yes, yes. Come in!"
But no one's there.

            The letter's missing. Gone. Whereto?
In the dust a flattened trace, a distinct letter-shape—
but it's not there. The subject, quite amusingly,
lay down to sleep some more . . .

            It's time for dawn to break,
for me to yawn: how crumpled is the envelope of the bed!
The lamp hangs like a seal
from the envelope of the ceiling,
the stove is closed up like a letter,
the hardwood cracks form oblong letters . . .
and a crazed pigeon sits atop the windowsill,
where the return address of sleep is written.

IV.
A scientific fact: the epistolary genre
gave birth to the novel in days of yore . . .
Oh, there were ways in the Dark Ages
to know the gift of life and understand the game:
to perish or to die—

            and savor
freedom of choice,

            while leaving it all up to chance . . .
As if they knew it all, as if
they read the book of life before their birth
and knew the novel written about them
during their lifetimes . . .

            Fortune is unique!

The words FATE and PASSION are about them, them,
                                        and them!
For us! For us!—the theater of their movements:
an alcove destiny, the airy handwriting of swords,
the fall—finality . . . the novel
Notes of a Homing Pigeon—marvelous!

V.
A picture from my childhood: "The Unfaithful Wife
Slain by the Final Kiss."
The shoulder is bared diligently,
a blossom falls from the corsage
and the waving of the captive's handkerchief—
for the future medium of film—
here the "little bird flies" into a prison window,
a dove, its wings beating feathery clouds . . .
The convent wall, smothered with ivy,
a wafer drops into the wine,
and all grows dark before your eyes,
but jealous steel sweats underneath the cloak—
in the shadow of the wall, covered with ivy,
the jangle of spurs and clatter of feet on stairs . . .
The visuals here gain in strength
(so our cameraman would have the time)—
so long lasts the kiss of the parting lines . . .
And life is worth the death! The gaze is worth the risk
right now! right now! Then—obliging poison . . .
What in this ritual is the life span?
Oh, knowledge that life is happening right *now*!
The impossibility of division into parts,
happily called by the name of "passion,"
which until now still makes you ache with woe:
"You?" "Me." "When? . . ." "Now!"—
This is the buried root of the word *happy*.
The time is nigh for me to leave for home, or from the same—
the road is "happily" all too familiar.

VI.

We will live in the past! And this is Heaven—
knowing in the future that the mistake of
our lives we commit just once—
and that is all.
Life is rude and death is courteous
if only in the sense that it does not
leave us, like pain.
Death is true to us, and our infidelity to it
does not deter it. It is patient. It waits for us.
How much longer before we meet? An eternal instant—
to grow younger, back to the initial smack
and become the nothing that looks at me . . .
with such profound love . . .
                    I will not be the worse for it.

POSTHUMOUS NOTES
OF THE TRISTRAM CLUB
(The Inevitability of the Unwritten)

FROM *A Paper Sword*, BY U. Vanoski

Others rigged the sails . . .   —Alex Cannon

There were three of us. Together we didn't row, together we didn't finish
Cambridge, together we didn't make our careers, together we planned
to become writers. Together we never became them. One of us received
an inheritance that was too generous. Another received an education
that was too fine (at Oxford) and then opened a shop in the tradition
of a Dickensian curiosity shop, but the other way round—the same
kinds of inconsequential odds and ends, only modern. However strange
it might seem, this shop became fashionable, and business took off. Then
the business expanded, he stopped going to the store himself, entrust-
ing it to his managers and executives, and continued only to rummage
through catalogues in search of his one-of-a-kind, sometimes outlandish
wares: an umbrella *cum* chair, a nostril-hair trimmer, a bottle opener/
cigarette lighter, and so on. Myself, I learned to live without everything
except disorder—in other words, I didn't do anything, either.

The moneybags was called William; the shopkeeper, though he had
the most aristocratic roots of all of us, was called, simply, John; and I
am myself. Ernest, that is.

Although we had not become writers, we did become—I am certain of this—very talented readers.

I think that this was what united us: the more stringent our tastes
grew, the less frequently we differed in opinion. Oh, I forgot to mention (and this may prove to be important in the future) that we were

inveterate, dare I say committed, bachelors. I won't try to account for how this happened to the others—those are their private affairs. Instead, I will tell you how it happened to me.

Gerda Uvich-Barashkou (of Polish-Romanian extraction) was the epitome of beauty, and a highly intelligent epitome of beauty, I might add. I confessed my everlasting love to her, and she answered me in kind. Happiness and good fortune should not exceed their proper measure either, however. In her somewhat peculiar English she told me, "I will marry you"; yet I shied away from the suit, and hesitated to accept her hand right away. Moreover, John and William tried to talk me out of it. As a result, she later refused me thrice, even though we were living together all the while. I wouldn't go so far as to say that John and William were not in love with her themselves, but by the time it had become awkward for me to bring up the subject of marriage a fourth time, she had already become my dearest friend—as she was John and William's. She was the only one of us who had professional commitments: she translated all sorts of unlikely languages, including her native Romanian and Polish, wrote critical essays, and reviewed new books. So it was only natural for us to propose that she become the president of our Club.

But I'm getting ahead of myself. Allow me to begin with an account of how our Club was born.

The Club was born quite naturally, by means of *degeneration*.

At first the three of us met at William's to read each other what we had written.

"Come on, you go first!" we told each other, and all of us balked. "Well, I only have fragments, just a few sketchy notes really." "I just started on it." "Mine is just a vague concept so far." Those sorts of things.

"Go ahead, we're waiting," two of us would say, ganging up on the third. "But it isn't ripe yet, I'm afraid to read it out loud." Or: "I'm superstitious. If I tell you the plot, it will dry up." Or . . . In other words, there was always some excuse, until, after the second or third glass, one of us felt inspired, and, convinced that he was more talented than the others, began to regale us with another in a string of ingenious gambits. "I could never wrap my mind around how Shakespeare and Cervantes, clearly not knowing anything about each other, contrived to die on the very same day. Be that as it may, one day . . ." and he was off and running.

The upshot was that it did *not* seem so improbable to us as it did to him, and the narrator retired, dispirited and perplexed, while the spirits of the other two, on the contrary, soared unaccountably. The unlucky fellow was dubbed "Oneday," which thereafter became his nickname. It was all the more fitting since all the letters were contained in his middle name and surname. Who among us was Oneday? Why, William, of course!

Our system was of a strictly closed variety, and outsiders were no less strictly forbidden entry.

One day William Oneday ran into an old friend of his father's, Jerome K. Jerome,* and invited him to dine with us. We revered the venerable old man for his wonderful book, the heroes of which we were wont to compare ourselves to. Among ourselves we also admitted that we admired him for the fact that he never wrote anything so outstanding again. So we could not refuse Oneday.

Oneday coughed up the money for a lavish spread, and we ate our supper and sang away before the Maestro.

The novel that John was "writing" (*Tea or Coffee?*), and which he now recounted in a somewhat abridged version, was about an unhappy love affair between a man and two sisters, about the flaming jealousy of one sister for another, and the jealousy they triggered in him. The Maestro was digesting. Seated in a soft armchair, he snuffled quietly, his magnificent silver mustache hovering above the ivory knob of his cane, on top of which he propped his chin solidly. His face was frozen in a mask of unwavering benevolence. His opinion about John's composition, however, was unequivocal.

"You shouldn't marry either one of them, not to mention both."

Then he heard out the next story.

Oneday's novella (*Hamlet's Legacy*) was devoted to the idea of patronage as a vocation and purpose in life. Two prominent manufacturers meet at an annual trade fair in London and argue about why they are amassing money, and on whom they should spend it. One of them, who was from Barcelona, spends his on the architectural follies of

---

*Jerome K. Jerome—author of the book *Three Men in a Boat (To Say Nothing of the Dog)*. (A. B.)

young Gaudí, and the other, who was from Germany, spends his on the healthy, mature, and farsighted ideas of Karl Marx. Both of them consider their protégés to be geniuses.

At the word "genius," the old Maestro started:

"First off, I've never heard of them. But then again, I've never understood a thing about economics, much less architecture. How about you, young man?"

The young man in question was Yours Truly.

"Not a word about music, though!" he warned categorically. "I'm tone-deaf."

I decided to flatter the old man, comparing him to my beloved Sterne. My story was called "Sterne's Laughter" and told about how an admirer of *Tristram Shandy* travels back in time in a time machine to record the jokes and laughter of the remarkable writer on a phonograph, and how he manages to meet him. But when he returns to his own time, the apparatus, instead of laughter, reproduces only snorting and unadulterated snoring.

At the word "snoring," Jerome K. Jerome woke up with a start.

"Who is this Sterne? And where is he? Is it you?" he asked me.

I didn't deny it.

"We've had enough of your Wellses and Conan Doyles," he said, struggling out of the armchair with some difficulty. "You're good lads . . . Go ahead and write, if you must."

"Well, whose story do you think he liked best?" John snapped at me with unjustified venom.

"Yours, of course," I retorted.

"We need new blood," William said, when he came back after seeing the old man out. "I have someone in mind who inspires hope."

And so we introduced the post of corresponding member, appointing Jerome K. Jerome our Honorary Chairman. (I can't vouch for whether he would have agreed, had he known about it.) We hung his portrait on the wall (though to this very day I'm not sure we didn't confuse his picture with that of Nietzsche). The number of corresponding members increased, but our hopes did not.

First a physical chemist joined our ranks, then a defrocked priest, then there was either an astronomer or an astrologer, and once we even had a hope-inspiring politician. That was when we came up with the idea (lest all our discussions be in vain) for our Club to sponsor something called the GNRP: the Great New Reader's Prize. Everyone was in favor of it, this cockamamie idea.

"It's getting crowded," Oneday said morosely. "We need to expand."

He had just come into another inheritance from an aunt, who left him a small house, and he was faced with the difficult choice of either selling it or keeping it for his own use.

As a consequence, the idea of moving to his aunt's until such time as the legal rights to the inheritance came into force presented itself. The prospect of a dedicated space could not but bring with it questions about the organizational structure, that is, who would be in charge of all of this.

I proposed our mutual lady friend as a candidate for acting president, and the motion was carried with as much unanimity as enthusiasm.

Gerda agreed, but in view of the large volume of work that would be expected of her, she demanded there be a position of executive secretary created (she had someone in mind for the job). Murito Pilavut was also of mixed ancestry, but with Asian roots: he hailed from one of the countries squeezed between the English and Russian colonies with the commonplace ending of "-stan." He wrote and spoke English even better than Gerda herself, and agreed to the most paltry compensation, with the proviso that we rename his post general secretary. We acceded to this small demand, and so he was appointed. His responsibilities, in addition to the unavoidable official ones, included recording the minutes and preserving confidentiality (for which we acquired a safe, the only key to which remained in Gerda's hands).

And so, we moved our base of operations to the aunt's residence in a quiet, leafy part of London. After we lit a fire in the fireplace, as well as in our pipes, we began to discuss, over port and sherry, what was new on the literary translation scene (so as not to become embroiled in the local literary process), with the aim of choosing the worthiest candidate for the Best Foreign Book award. During our deliberations we again veered off into a discussion about the prospects for our future unwritten works.

It all ended, invariably, with our getting out a jigsaw puzzle, solving a crossword, or playing a game of charades, and before long we had hatched a new game that was a version of anagrams.

The point of departure was:

THERE IS NO IDEA THAT CANNOT BE
EXPRESSED MORE SIMPLY.

The principle boiled down to this: every complex word consists of many simpler words that together contain its letters. The first example we came across was so convincing that we *got personal*. It turned out that a great person was embodied in the letters of his own name (given name and surname)—thus, his entire fate and character are encompassed in one or several key words derived from it. (How delighted I was to discover that both *sense* and *sentence* were contained in Laurence Sterne!) Leaving the ranks of the great, we had the temerity to start right in on ourselves. Now we wrestled with our own names, trying to discover the various ways in which they could be twisted and rendered.

Our own names didn't yield such a bountiful harvest as the names of the famous and celebrated: we had to content ourselves with simple nicknames.

Oneday already had one. John had become Barleycorn—Barley for short. I plucked a suitable one for myself out of *Tristram Shandy*: Shydream. The others were envious and objected, however. Ernest *must know the vital importance of being Earnest*! Thus, Wilde's verdict prevailed.

And so we became Oneday, Barley, and Earnest. "We are alive until fate *falls into place*," we concluded. Whether to use the results of our tinkering as pseudonyms in our writing was still a hotly debated topic among us.

Everyone was satisfied, however. After all, that's what the Club was for—so we could feel like gentlemen, rather than half-wits.

Murito carefully recorded the progress of the performance, then hid the minutes in the safe as we looked on, locked it up, tugged the door to make sure it was fast, and handed the key to our president, Gerda. (I should note that these two, as official personages, appear under coded names in our minutes. These code names mean nothing from the perspective of anagrammatical Fate.)

•

Thus, there were five of us: Gerda, Oneday, Barley, Earnest, and Murito (not counting the corresponding members). A quintet, as it were. We had now become far more demanding with regard to the choice of corresponding members.

The priest who had broken with the Church, for example, we refused from the outset, and not because we were so devout. We simply didn't like him or his novel. *The Gospel According to the Tempter* was its title, and it fully deserved it.

According to the story, along with the canonical gospels, others were found in a secret cave. These were the gospels of Thomas, Phillip, and other apostles, including Mary Magdalene, and even Judas. Now, the Gospel of Judas suggested that Jesus was an ordinary extraterrestrial, an intelligence agent, and knew beforehand that he would either be saved or resurrected. He was certain of this. Judas knew that Jesus' origins were extraterrestrial, rather than divine, and he sacrificed himself to maintain the authenticity of the myth of Jesus, not to undermine the Teachings, which he believed more implicitly than anyone else.

In this sense, it was Judas who sacrificed himself and thus deserves the worship of all humanity. The author played up trivial contradictions and discrepancies in the canonical texts to substantiate and further develop his subject. Suddenly it became irksome and boring to listen to all of this. We advised the defrocked priest to repent before it was too late and return to the humble service in which he had been ordained. As for ourselves, we decreed that introducing an extraterrestrial into the plot was unworthy of a self-respecting author.

The hope-inspiring politician did not live up to our standards, either, but for completely different reasons. (I'm afraid we may have envied him: he was wellborn and well-fed, like Hamlet, but was absolutely unconcerned with the problem of whether "to be or not to be." He *was*—perhaps even too much so. He wore his suits well, he sipped his cognac elegantly, and he smoked his cigars with aplomb.) Although his unwritten novel, *The History of the 2Xth Centuries*, was, to be honest, not altogether bad, I couldn't help but object to the fact that his novel, like mine, involved time travel.

In his book, a schoolboy from the end of the twenty-first century disobeys his teacher during a history lesson. He plucks, and then eats, a forbidden fruit during a school field trip through the twentieth century. He begins to experience terrible abdominal pain (imagine the trouble a product that had outlived its shelf life by a whole century might cause), and strayed from the strictly regulated, neutral path for a moment to answer nature's call. After relieving himself in the last century, he was forced to use the only thing that came to hand—namely, a page from the textbook in which everything about the twentieth century had already been revealed. This page was subsequently picked up by some secret service agent or other, and since they took an interest in the events at the end of their own century, they tried to deflect them. This unleashed catastrophes connected with the fracturing of time and gave rise to a host of undesirable regimes that might otherwise have been avoided. Trying like the best of them, the secret services thus managed to make the history of the twentieth century even worse. In other words, the novel made visible the polysemic vicissitudes of the future and the role of chance or blind Fate (though not Providence) in determining the subsequent incontrovertible course of events.

I began to dispute this principle of indeterminacy, insisting on the role of Providence; the highly educated Barley supported me, prompting me with a corresponding term (*determinism*). Gerda, however, was the one who really rose to the occasion, saying that a subject that was so dependent on gastroenterology was sorely lacking, if only on aesthetic grounds, and that if history was really like this, then history as a subject was similarly dubious, aesthetically. (In hindsight, I think we rejected the hope-inspiring politician for another reason—for his recently published book, which enjoyed great success.) We advised him to devote himself to politics, which he did. (He was successful there, too, perhaps because he was so familiar with the laws of digestion.*)

After such a charismatic politician, it became easier for us to dismiss the other candidates. The professor of physical chemistry wearied us with a concept about the concept—i.e., with the plot of how his plot refused to take shape (and that's what the novel, dispiritingly, was called: *The Plot*). The professor tried to tell the story of how a Russian saw the

---

*Whether he had read the great author of *The Butterfly That Stamped Its Foot*, the forgotten A. Tired-Boffin, is open to question. *(A. B.)*

Periodic Table of the Elements in a dream. The narrative was packed with detail—interesting primarily to the specialist—as well as with incomprehensible Russian jokes. We dozed off, and considered the whole dream to be highly improbable.

Another professor (an astronomer and closeted astrologist), with his "almost finished" novel *The Centennial of Abolishing the Calendar* (we nixed the title without a second thought as being too complex for a pun), tried to restore Kabbala to modern consciousness, reuniting letters with numbers again. We sensed that he was encroaching upon our monopoly of anagrams, and we made a feast of him, then spat him out like a bone, telling him he should finish his novel first, and *then* not come back to us.

We grew sad.

"It's about time that one of us, at least, finished something." Barley sighed.

We bristled.

"Have you perhaps become too exacting?" Gerda said acrimoniously.

"Isn't it time we lit the fire?" I suggested.

"We need new blood," Oneday insisted.

"Aren't we becoming too bloodthirsty?" My voice sounded strange in my own ears. "Because I have someone in mind."

"We need a charter!" we all said in a chorus.

And so we charted new territory without budging from the spot, in our new . . .

CHARTER

1. *Complete freedom of the word! (That is to say, no working on the word—let the word work on the author.)*
2. *The responsibility of the author to his characters cannot be less than the demands he places on himself.*
3. *An orientation toward authenticity of imagination—i.e., a ban on any subjects involving great people (there are already enough of them), and also on so-called science fiction.*
4. *Difficulties in writing the text signify not laziness but the complexity of the task.*
5. *Everyone is free **not** to write whatever they wish.*
6. *One may write only what actually allows itself to be written.*
7. *Books and manuscripts are **not** read, and **not** returned.*

8. *An unpublished author who submits to an examination by any of the active members of the Club is considered to be a corresponding member.*

9. *A member of the Club is permitted to publish a work only when all other members of the Club consider it to be finished.*

10. *Upon publication of a work, the author's membership in the Club is automatically annulled.*

11. *The decision to admit a new member to the Club must be unanimous.*

12. *The Club will dissolve itself if one of the members raises himself or herself to a level above the others.*

   NB:

   a. *The General Secretary does not have the right to vote.*

   b. *The President has a consultative vote.*

   c. *A decision may always be postponed until the next meeting.*

Points two and three inspired a great deal of argument.

"Hold your horses!" Oneday said indignantly. "You mean to say I can't kill my own character? Perhaps I'm not even permitted to let him lose his mind or to commit suicide? What are we supposed to write about, then? About ourselves? How can one discern a subject in the plotlessness of one's own life? In that case, this vaunted 'freedom of the word' turns into a ban on writing anything at all!"

Barley agreed and suggested that we banish from the ranks of literary protagonists all monsters and maniacs, who are too apt to unbind the hands of the author in constructing a plot.

Gerda, sensible as always, suggested that the name of the Club be tied to its charter, and that it henceforth be called the Society for the Protection of Literary Protagonists from Their Authors, thus linking it to more socially conscious themes like the preservation of cultural heritage and environmental conservation. Somehow, things always came down to birds with Gerda . . .

Numbers four, five, and six did not give rise to any controversy among us. It was, effectively, the same idea, formulated in three different ways by each of the three founding fathers of the Club.

We had the sense not to wrangle, and to judge each formulation on its own merits.

This was not uppermost in my mind—I didn't really listen, but pondered how I was going to rescue my work on Laurence Sterne from the prohibition on writing about great people.

"But look," I said, "how can Sterne be considered great if everyone has forgotten about him? He is better known in some backwater called Russia than he is in his native England. In the *Britannica* he got less than one column. Who's running that outfit, anyway? I'm dedicating my novel, *Rule Britannica*, to the bureaucrat who two centuries later settles his personal accounts with a genius. Imagine, he called Sterne an 'eighteenth-century English humorist and son of an officer,' while some paltry Jerome K. Jerome was deemed worthy of being called 'Author'! I happen to think that Sterne was the genuine forefather of our movement—after all, he never finished anything he wrote. He even succumbed to a self-induced illness and died, after demanding too much of himself so as not to have to finish anything . . . A tragic, heroic fate. I propose that we take this Nietzsche off the wall and replace him with a portrait of Sterne, and that our Club adopt his noble name."

I sat down, my heart pounding, unable to see or hear anything in my agitation. And it was all for nought, for it was instead article C in the notes that resulted in the most lively discussion.

Changing the Club to a Society was desirable, argued Gerda, from practical motives, as well: taxes, publicity, etc. (There was some suspicion that this proposal came at the instigation of Murito, who didn't have the right to vote himself.)

As a result, my point was not discussed at all (everyone had already read *Tristram Shandy* on my advice, and adjudged it favorably), and I was entrusted with the task of and that I was just one step away from transforming my friends from mere admirers of Sterne into true Sternians. Article C of the notes to the Charter was reformulated thus: *To continue the discussion of the question of renaming the Club.*

At the next meeting I brought in a portrait and hung it up. No one noticed.

Insofar as the goal of the Society was now formulated as the "protection of literary protagonists," it was decided to adopt the name not of Sterne but of Tristram Shandy for the Club. This suggestion originated with Barley, and no one objected, least of all me.

We really had grown a bit tired of our bloodthirstiness. In spite of our rigorous Charter, the examination of *my* candidate went exceptionally smoothly.

Everyone liked him immediately: a former musician, very flighty and fidgety, resembling a red-haired Negro, who had never read anything, he showed up without his instrument (the last thing we needed in the Club was a double bass), armed with not one but two unwritten novels, and another one that had just occurred to him, and thus was simply "premature." We were won over by his fecundity; but the main thing was that a "fateful" anagram could be derived from his names. He started out as, simply, Michael, and became M. Viol de Clavier (thereafter simply "Viol"). His curriculum vitae *suited the anagram, too.*

He was the beloved and stubborn protégé of a famous old organist, who had placed great hopes in him; but Viol managed to break his hand in a motor-racing accident. It lost its former flexibility, and Viol set off to study philosophy at a Swedish university in Uppsala, but never found anything pertaining to Swedenborg there, and so set out for Japan to learn the language, for which he very quickly had no time, and then returned home to his father, mother, and music, adapting himself to the double bass as an instrument that required less two-handed dexterity, though he still considered, nevertheless, the option of buying a small hotel in hopes that he could play before a select public. The fact that he was the author of three unwritten works could not help but appeal to us, but we advised him to focus on not writing just one of them.

Viol chose the title Fathers and Sons—*the father being Johann Sebastian Bach. The novel was rejected in compliance with rule number 3 of the Charter. However much Viol tried to prove, addressing his pleas for some reason to Gerda, that the novel was not about the greatness but about the disparagement of Bach, belittled by his own children, who shunted him aside as a has-been for more than a century, right up until his "discovery" by Mendelssohn, that the novel would be about the children, who flouted their father as God, and, thus, God as the father—for all of us, Bach remained God, and we declined to accept the novel.*

"Come on, I'm the organist, and not you!" *Viol looked beseechingly at Gerda.* "I'm the one who betrayed my old teacher, who was like a father to me, and not you. I know from my own experience what I am writing about: I'm the one who saw Bach alive, and not you!"

"What do you mean, you saw him alive?" *we all asked in a chorus.*

"That's how I will begin my novel, I think." And Viol took a sheaf of papers from his pocket.

We were unable to stop him—he had already begun to read. That was not our way, but we were too late. We had no choice but to listen.

A certain "I" (the author?) wanders through an old, unfamiliar city, and suddenly senses inexplicably that behind this little door lives Bach himself. Without any deliberation, he knocks, and a venerable old Frau opens and invites him to wait. He waits, and hears how behind the door fragments of the St. Matthew Passion are coming together. As he is himself a musician, one can imagine what he must have been feeling at that moment! Finally, the door opens, and a strange man emerges, completely bald—still not Bach yet. Then the narrator realizes that he doesn't speak a word of German and starts repeating "Bach! Bach! Bach!" over and over again. "Ich bin Bach!" the old man says obstreperously, and this is when our hero realizes that this is indeed Bach, only without his wig. He wakes up in horror, and finds himself back in our own time; but he knows that he saw the living Bach, because that single detail—that he didn't wear his wig at home—was not something he could have thought up himself.

"So it's a dream!" Oneday objected.

"I quite liked it," Barley said.

"The wig part was very convincing" was Gerda's response to Viol's presentation.

And we changed the wording of our judgment: the novel was not rejected, but—its state of unwrittenness was approved.

The difference was significant, but Viol didn't accept it.

He was all the more persistent about his second concept, which was about Rossini.

Which we rejected just as strenuously, in accordance with the same rule number 3 of the Charter.

"Don't you understand?" Viol fumed, now addressing himself solely to Gerda. "First, Rossini is certainly no match for Bach. Second, I am only interested in Rossini after he gave up music for good and devoted himself heart and soul to the culinary arts. Third, it's not even a novel; it's a libretto for an opera."

We were indignant about that. Bringing us some sort of libretto!

It was decided that we would introduce an addendum to the Charter banning plays and scripts, to say nothing of librettos, from consideration.

"*And what are you going to serve us for dessert, what with your fascination with cookery?*" *Gerda said, smirking.* "*Mozart?*"

"*How did you guess?*" *Viol turned a dark red.*

"*The third one suggests itself,*" *Gerda said secretively.*

"*Besides,*" *Barley said with a sneer,* "*can you really consider Mozart to be one of the Greats?*"

"*Strictly speaking, the novel is not about Mozart but about Salieri,*" *Viol murmured.*

"*The poisoner?*" *Oneday said.* "*But, then—poison and cookery are certainly related . . .*"

"*Not at all! That is precisely why I had my doubts about the poisoning.*"

We sighed, and poured ourselves another glass of sherry. Since we had already listened to two, we might as well hear the third.

Viol built his hypothesis-novel on two assumptions: the suddenness of Mozart's death, and the reason for that suddenness.

The description of Mozart's death is truly intriguing: he did not take ill, but suddenly and mysteriously lost the life force. He melted away like a candle, faded like a heavenly body, set like the sun ("*deflated like a balloon,*" *as Viol put it), as though he really had been poisoned.*

Viol did seem to agree with the story that Salieri had been the poisoner, though not in the literal, dastardly sense that had been passed down in legend. Salieri's poison was far subtler, far more refined and lethal than any alchemy: his poison was enlightenment.

Mozart was more brilliant, but Salieri was more competent. For more than thirty years (beginning when he was four) Mozart had been without peer (and thus remained a four-year-old), never thinking about who he really was: whom he had surpassed, or who had gone before him. If you are the one and only, you have no need to compare yourself to anyone. Salieri, who admired Mozart more deeply than anyone else, understood the difference between first and second only too well. He enticed Wolfgang with various fashionable novelties, but Wolfgang knew everything beforehand: there could be nothing entirely newfangled to him.

Salieri, however, was patient, and waited to seize his opportunity.

Mozart really did accept the grim commission of a requiem mass from a mysterious stranger; as always, he was in need of cash and couldn't resist the down payment. The task oppressed him; at first, work proceeded slowly and with difficulty, while the deadline loomed. Salieri got wind of a first performance of a certain mass by some forgotten composer, and lured Mozart out to hear it. "You'll enjoy it; it will shake you out of your doldrums," Salieri said. He was able to persuade him. And as soon as Mozart had agreed, he felt his mass begin to inch forward, and then to gather lightness and speed. He felt himself approaching the limits of his strength, and this always heralded the same inscrutable something: the singularity and uniqueness of creation! Either you die, collapsing onto the pages of your manuscript, or you soar ever higher until you reach the apex and finish by drinking away your joy in the first tavern. He desperately wanted a drink.

Enter Salieri. It turned out that three days had passed like a single day, and now it was time.

"Time for what?"

"To hear that mass. You promised."

He had caught him at a moment of utter exhaustion.

And Mozart followed Salieri as though on a leash. Like a sacrificial lamb.

Salieri knew where he was taking him, but he had no idea what Mozart would hear, what he would drink in with his ears.

It was the St. Matthew Passion.

On the way home, Wolfgang had too much to drink and didn't say a word to Salieri. He recalled how they, together with his friend Carl Philipp Emanuel—all of them carefree, clever, and ingenuous—drank up a trifling sum that they had received in exchange for some ancient and decrepit clavichord belonging to Philipp's father.

When he returned home, he plunked himself down at the clavier and started to compose, unable to accompany himself with his left hand, and hardly able to hold the pen in his right.

But the ink ran out. He tried to call someone to replenish it . . . and slowly slumped down in the chair, then fell over and sank to the floor.

And it is true—however brilliant Mozart's mass is, it is the only piece in his whole oeuvre that bears the imprint of influence, and that influence is Bach's.

Two suns cannot rise at the same time on the horizon of our planet!

Oh, if only he had known about this earlier! Such a thing might never have occurred.

Now, however, we have both of them: Bach and Mozart.

We were silent, waiting for someone to speak first.

"*In your hypothesis you claim that Mozart knew nothing about the elder Bach, but what about his* Well-Tempered Clavier?" *said Gerda. "After that piece, Mozart's own music acquires a new impulse and develops apace, leading right up to his great mass.*"

(I never knew that she was so well-versed in music.)

Viol looked defeated.

"*You're right, there is that piece. Why didn't I make the connection? That kills my subject.*"

"*It's quite all right,*" *said Oneday with a flourish of the hand. "Such a novel is not even within the power of Dr. Mann. And you're no Faustus, either.*"

And we decided, all the same, to approve this unwritten novel of his, on the strength of which we accepted Viol as an active member of the Club.

Only on the condition, however, that the mediocre Salieri be promoted to main character, and that the genius, Mozart, be demoted to a minor character. As always, we spent more time deliberating over the title than anything else. The Man Who Never Heard Bach *didn't work for a number of reasons. First, it was a bit long, and already refuted by Gerda. Second, because of Chesterton.* Third (and everyone applauded the unexpected subtlety of this remark by Barley), the contents of the work are already revealed in the title. Another title, which Viol proposed at that point—*The Seeing Ear—*was categorically rejected by Gerda, giving me reason to suspect, yet again, her feelings for me: she knew very well how long and hard I had not been writing my novel* The Talking Ear. *In the end, a decision was made that Viol continue working on the title.*

He looked inspired by our decision, and we were satisfied.

But that was not why he exulted.

"*You can't begin to imagine,*" *he said to Gerda, his eyes burning with excitement, "how perfectly you have rescued my poor plot! Bach was belittled and abused by his children a bit too much, and Mozart, metaphorically speaking, was like Bach's son born out of wedlock. But Mozart was the first of them to hear the authentic Bach already in* The Well-Tempered Clavier—*and then he went further, spurring himself on to catch up with him, and then to surpass him. What gardener had led him to this powerful trunk, that everyone already considered to be a dead tree! It was in the*

---

*G. K. Chesterton, *The Man Who Was Thursday.*

mass that they melded together and became completely conjoined. How-
ever tragic it may have seemed for Mozart to hear the Passion *for the first*
time, he heard his own music, and no one else's. He blended into it, co-
incided with it, never feeling the influence of his predecessor, because the
Teacher of both of them was one and the same."

"Would you look at that!" Oneday burst out. "He has already crossbred
both his novels. What about Rossini? Perhaps he abandoned music after
hearing Mozart for the first time?"

"That would be wonderful, if it were true." Viol sighed. "Then I could
unite all of them under the title The Three Masses*!"*

And so, we became Oneday, Barley, Earnest, Viol, Gerda, and Murito.
A sextet.

But enough is enough. Suddenly, something ended. Something
happened.

Murito received urgent news from his homeland and had to leave
us at once.

Talking without a record of the proceedings had become dull.
This was how we explained to ourselves the disappearance of Viol,
although he himself explained it differently: he was returning to his
project of running a little hotel.

He promised to return as soon as he had found a suitable place for it.

All of a sudden, Gerda found a convincing reason for which she
had to leave us, as well: some matter or other in Poland.

There were now just three of us in the boat again, under the portrait of Sterne, with the same names: William, John, and Earnest. We
felt sad. At the same time we also felt how wonderfully pleasant everything had again become.

"How about we finally finish writing *something*, at least?" William
said solemnly, and we all burst out laughing.

I was probably the only one who took his joke halfway seriously: I
couldn't understand why I was suddenly in such a rush . . . but things
began to *fall into place* for me.

I intended to get even with this so-called editor at the *Britannica*,
the nonentity who wreaked vengeance for his personal failures on the
reputations of great people; but the result was something very different.

He turned out to be an honest and just ruler, burdened by his authority, governed by ultimate mercy and *modernation* (a good slip of the pen!) toward those creators tormented by their own powers into producing at least something in our world. He was a warrior against oblivion, a knight of immortality . . . I suddenly started to love my protagonist, and it all went like clockwork.

I don't think that John and William betrayed themselves in the same way I did, but all it took was my putting the final period to it for a literary sensation to erupt. An unknown author from Kurdistan, or perhaps it was Pakistan, published a novel called *Kill Wolfgang!* that astonished the critical establishment.

He even had the temerity to use one of our anagrams, ambitiously flaunting his authorship on the first page with only one name: Murito.

His star rose, and did not set. One after another, his novels appeared: *The Gospel According to the Tempter, The History of the 2Xth Centuries,* while we were still plowing through his novel about Mozart.

It was ghastly, this intellectualism for the poor! In his book, Salieri saved up some money, dressed up like a Black Monk, and, concealing his face with the hood of his robe, commissioned a requiem from Mozart, already aware that Bach's *Passion* would destroy his soul. He just had to wait for the moment when Mozart was at his apogee to shoot him down like a bird in flight.

William tugged at the door of the safe. It was securely locked. Gerda had the keys.

The thought that Gerda and Murito might be conspiring together against the rest of us was terrible! I imagined to myself the horror of Viol (Michael) when he found out he had been robbed, and rushed off in search of him. Even his parents did not know where he was, however: he had left with some girl to find a property for starting a hotel (this much, at least, seemed to be true), and had gone missing. I came back with nothing.

Suddenly, Gerda appeared, it seemed, out of thin air, having returned from Poland, and without so much as a greeting she rushed over to the safe. She jangled the key around in the lock and opened it up. It was empty; no minutes whatsoever.

"Bastard! Traitor!" she said.

And it seemed to me that I heard more than just curses in her rage.

The story has a happy ending, however.

While all this was going on, William decided to sell his aunt's dwelling, and no one tried to dissuade him. At that point I also ran into the elusive Michael-Viol. He was hurrying somewhere with a cake in his hand and greeted me as though nothing at all had happened. Without going into too much detail, he told me that he was taking the cake to the cleaning lady at his hotel on the occasion of her birthday, that he was not satisfied with the hotel accommodations and was looking for something else, but that he *was* satisfied with the cleaning lady, and intended to keep her on.

I persuaded William not to sell his aunt's property, and he agreed to lease it to Michael.

Oh, if only William knew that Michael had come to us in the first place with the intention of renting the house, and not out of any love for literature! I was surprised to learn that he and Gerda were working together on the staging of his new opera, but was happy that she was with him and not with Murito. Well, it was my own fault I'd lost her. I take my hat off to her. (On second thought, I need to wear that hat.)

Murito made it onto the Booker shortlist for the third time, and was now hard at work writing his next novel (I wonder whose?) to qualify for it. But time had run out for him to write *The Battle of Alphabetica*. That battle had been won by me. (And did I not deserve it?) And although according to the Charter I could no longer be a member of the Club, I deployed a powerful counterargument: that what I especially liked in my little piece was what I *did not* write about—namely, the battle itself. That what had at first appeared to me to be the greatest lacuna in the story turned out to be its greatest merit: the subject of revenge was not realized in it. And this was more likely a virtue of my protagonist than of me. It was my protagonist who rose royally above insult, and scorned his carefully planned vengeance, which consisted in making a laughingstock out of his antagonist (Adams, the viceroy, who was he again? . . . Sir Poluzhan). Sir Poluzhan, who promulgated his own hypothesis about the person of Shakespeare while promoting himself for a peerage. And it was my noble Bartholomew who could not sacrifice his love for Shakespeare, using him to settle accounts with all manner of nonentities, and instead pretended that he was too busy, that it wasn't proper on Christmas . . . In short, that I was *unable* to write this. My speech made an impression, and they granted me the status of corresponding member until such time as I *did not* write something else. For this purpose, John passed on to me his unwritten novel *A Doctor for Freud*, and I scribble away at it now and then under the working title of O: *Letter or Number?* It's all turning out to be shorter, and sadder.

I managed to see all three at the premiere of A Bundle of Herbs—"An Opera for a Trio and One Silent Singer," *as the poster announced. It was certainly worth it!*

There were no programs, and no one had any idea what was in store. The number of firemen in chef's hats worn over their shining helmets was bewildering. The overture consisted of the very appetizing aromas of food being prepared.

On the curtains, on an Italian background, was depicted a house. There was one illuminated window, through which it was possible to descry a large kitchen. The curtain rose, revealing the kitchen, which occupied the whole stage; the sumptuousness of its props was astonishing. A puffy, slovenly-looking man in an apron wandered about the stage, clearly upset with the servants, who were nowhere to be seen. Who was this? There was something familiar in his expression, but I am in no way, shape, or form a theater person, and I don't know a single actor by face. The man was not only angry, he even cursed very colorfully, using musical terminology, such as "Crescendo-fortissimo-barbaro-furioso! Ta-ta-ta! Rum-pum-pum!" Right there on the stage stood a stove, in which he lit a real fire (hence the firemen), and began clashing and banging and rattling frying pans, cutting boards, and various other utensils, in order to shred, slice, boil, and fry. These random sounds of knives, spoons, ladles, hammers, frying pans, sauce pans, the hiss of steam, and the sizzle of oil, made the strange cook now sniff the air, then prick up his ears; or prick up his ears, and then sniff the air; and he had good reason

for it. Suddenly, all this kitchen clatter and din settled into a distinctly delib-
erate rhythm, or the beginning of a musical theme, wafting out from the
wings, now from one side, now from the other. It was possible to make out
percussions, then strings or woodwinds. Once the music became more de-
fined, the cook seemed to become particularly enraged, and he changed the
culinary procedures; but to no avail, because the cacophony he created settled
down into a pattern that repeated over and over again.

This was the opera, and short it was not. If anything evolved and de-
veloped in it, it was the aromas of the unknown dish being concocted by
the man incensed with the music.

He stirred, tasted, and added spices, but each time something was
missing, until it became clear that what was missing was a very particular
something. The cook pinched samples from a bundle of herbs that hung
picturesquely on the wall (string solo) but couldn't find what he was seek-
ing. Finally, he gave up with a dismissive wave of his hand. He grabbed a
large sprig without even looking at it, and, cursing (percussion solo), tossed
it into the cauldron. Now he began stirring and sniffing (woodwind solo),
and then he tasted it . . . Oh, wonder of wonders!

"Bravo! Bravissimo!" the cook exclaimed, savoring it (the entire trio
began to work together), and at this moment, outside the window, a call
rang out:

"Signore Rossini! Fresh herbs! Celery, Signore Rossini! Basil!"

"Rossini! ROSSINI!" the shouts resounded, now from the hall. It had
finally dawned on them.

"BASIL!" the maestro cried. "Where on Earth, barbaro furioso, *have*
you been?"

In the heat of the moment, he sipped too much from the ladle and
leapt away, scalded . . .

"Diabolo! But this time it was far better! What did I put in it? How can
I ever repeat the performance? Woe is me, yet another recipe lost forever . . .
What theme was playing just now?"

Rossini picked through the herbs in despair, unable to remember which it had
been . . . The music in the wings of the stage, uniting the muffled fragments
that had sounded during the preparation of the opera, grew and expanded
marvelously. Rossini, tasting everything anew and remaining satisfied with
the result, was no longer agitated by the music but even began conducting

it with his ladle. He stepped out onto the proscenium, the curtain fell, and on it was written his culinary recipes. Reading them as though they were sheet music, Rossini conducted his pre-death mass.

Oh, what splendid music it was! The audience went wild. The curtain rose and fell, rose and fell.

From the wings, like apparitions, the musicians materialized—all of them in black. A trio: a percussionist with copper pots and pans, gleaming like timpani; a woodwind player with an unrecognizable wooden pipe that extended down to the floor (a bassoon! finally I'd seen one in person); and our Viol, with a limping double bass.

"Bravo! Bravissimo!"

And they did the same trick over and over again: they took one step back and disappeared, blending in with the black curtains, waiting for a new outburst of applause, and then took a step forward again, delineating black from black.

At this point, the firemen came to life and started bustling about, extinguishing the stove and dragging out a long table, which they themselves began to lay with dinnerware. After that they placed in its center the gigantic steaming dish that had just been prepared by Rossini. The maestro directed the brigade.

The audience crowded up to the proscenium, continuing to clap but uncertain about whether the performance had ended, or whether this was still part of it. Rossini was also puzzled, and had been so engrossed in playing his part that he had truly worked up an appetite. Here our author (Viol) stepped in and finally took control of his narrative. He invited all the participants, including the audience, who had "brought a little drop with them," onto the stage to sit at the table. The audience surged up to the buffet and bought out everything that was on offer there (these proceeds alone paid for the entire cost of the performance). The table was covered in bottles, and the stage thronged with extras.

Gerda finally passed out the programs, which were drawn up like menus, with the recipe of the main dish.

Everyone ate and drank, and thus began the second act of the show: a discussion about why Rossini, at the peak of his talent and fame, suddenly ditched it all and took up cooking . . . And Viol told us about an incident that led directly to his idea for the opera.

In his heyday, when he could write a new piece of music in a fair copy right off the bat (for example, on stage during a rehearsal, even while other music was playing), it so happened that he once needed to finish an overture by morning. Even then he had loved eating, and when he came home late that night, he scribbled down the overture. When he collapsed onto the bed in fatigue, his pages of notation were swept off the table, and they glided under the bed. He was awakened by the director of the opera, who demanded that he hand over the overture immediately. The sheet music was still under the bed. Bending over to pick it up was more trouble than writing a new overture that had nothing at all in common with the one under the bed, which was even more difficult to remember than to pick up.

"And it's the same way with culinary recipes," the author explained. "Because cooking is also serendipitous. The most important factor is the freshness of the ingredients!"

Everyone ate and drank copiously—and that's the true measure of success!

So what *is* a finished work of art? was the question that gripped the collective consciousness of our Club so tenaciously. The work of art is not *that which already was*—but *that which is* (both written, and unwritten). There is, however, the debut performance (a musical term)! The opening night. There is no other definition! The thief will always be second, and the one who is fleeced the first. And the uncaught thief, as the loser, never forgives the one he has robbed: void, emptiness, anguish . . . Try and catch me if you can! But we won't try to catch you. You lose, Murito!

Now we are together again, all of us except you . . . We are sitting in the cozy lobby of My Aunt's House hotel, watched over by the portraits of Sterne and Rossini and the gentle gaze of the landlady.

Gerda pours us sherry or port, and tries to persuade William to rewrite his unwritten novel *Hamlet's Legacy* (before Murito finishes it) as the libretto of a new opera for Viol.

William proffers his empty glass with a puzzled look: What's she going on about?

We don't discuss anything anymore.

We are free, finally, *not* to write.

I have *already* written.

THE BATTLE OF ALPHABETICA

(The King of Britannica)

FROM *A Paper Sword*, BY U. Vanoski

For time does not flow but amasses.   —S. S.

Bartholomew was a king. Not your everyday Sixth or Third—not even the First. He was the Only. His power was vast. Any other king of any other era would find it difficult to imagine how boundless it was. True, Bartholomew could not so easily decide to chop off someone's head, say, or bestow half a shabby kingdom on someone else. But he was able to do something more: he could banish. And I speak not of ordinary banishment. Both banishing from a realm and curtailing a personal allotment of time by separating a head from a body will solidify someone's place in history. No, this was something else: absolute banishment . . . from time itself. From human memory.

His kingdom was neither larger nor smaller than others; indeed, he reigned over all possible worlds—even, to a certain degree, over the Universe. It was not, of course, within his power to extinguish the sun or take the Moon from the sky. Removing from the firmament a trifling little star, however, was something he *could* do; and he could make it shine a little more brightly for people, as well. He could not convince his subjects that the elephant or the lion never existed (the fable, after all, is the most firmly rooted element in the human mind). He was completely capable of eliminating an entire species of flora or fauna from the extra-fabular consciousness, however. And he succeeded in this.

His authority was vast, though not without limits. Then again, no authority, except that of the Creator, is boundless. Any other power is subject to limitation. Even where the Creator is concerned, His power is not really power. For what kind of power can it be when it is equal to itself? It's all one. We have always confused our unlimited dependence— our powerlessness—with the absence of limitless power. Bartholomew had no interest in such power. Perhaps because, in this sense, he had none. Here, however, it is hard to draw a line—was it that he didn't *have* it, or that it didn't *interest* him? Do we need less power if we possess it in sufficiently great quantities? If we endorse the widespread conviction (which we hold less strongly than Bartholomew) that power is one of the strongest human passions, exceeding (when it is present) other human passions (in our view, only because the others can be quenched); if we accept such a conviction as axiomatic, then, of course, we will easily sacrifice a lesser power for the sake of a greater power, and a greater power for omnipotence. Did Alexander the Great not forget about his little Macedonia when he had finally reached India?

Speaking of Alexander, Bartholomew had a bone to pick with him—though in principle he sympathized with him, and was even favorably disposed toward him. In any case, he liked him much more than he liked Napoleon. Toward Bonaparte, truth be told, he felt considerable antipathy. And not only because Napoleon had cut short the brilliant career of his future wife's ancient family, the Dukes de O. de Ch. de la Croix. Bartholomew was able to rectify this matter somewhat, not only by marrying into but also by devoting several vivid pages to the history of the family (for example, its involvement in the attempt to save the ill-fated Carl I).

He disdained Napoleon above all for being the most sovereign of all historical figures, for his overweening autonomy (which amounts to the same thing), for his *independence* (which is quite another thing) from his, Bartholomew's, power. Indeed, no one had been able to tame him, to this very day. Imagine how much fear he must have inspired—that they had to maroon him like Robinson on a tiny island in the middle of the Atlantic Ocean, that for years on end Bonapartists argued with anti-Bonapartists, so that he had to be exhumed and buried again in five coffins like a Russian *matryoshka* doll, and covered with a Russian stone, lest he—God forbid!—return to life and spring out of his tomb like a jack-in-the-box!

To this day, one has to bow down when entering his tomb—the

ingenious architect designed the entranceway to match Napoleon's stature, *sans* tricorne.

Bartholomew could, of course, cancel one or another of his insignificant battles, tinkering with history a bit, omitting and adding something here and there; but there was nothing he could do with the *myth* (something no less firmly rooted than a fable). Napoleon continued to stand on the Bridge of Arcole, and his flag still fluttered unhindered.

While Bartholomew had once humbled Alexander the Great (an attractive and altogether nice fellow) and put him in his place, depriving him of one of his battles in favor of Darius, he had failed to cut Napoleon down to size, even if he had managed to take away a few such battles from him. Bartholomew was not content with the battles of the Nile, Trafalgar, and Borodino . . . The two Cyclopses, Nelson and Kutuzov . . . Even Nelson was not on par with Napoleon. What other commander could suffer such a great defeat, ending up with just the measly island of St. Helena after conquering all of Europe, and still remain the victor in everyone's mind? Only this miniature hot-air balloon!

To this day, his tricorne remains more royal than any crown. Napoleon's fame turned out to be greater than itself—now that's something to ponder! Was it all because of his Hundred Days? No, not only that. Bartholomew even took a liking to the Hundred Days. No, not because of Waterloo, not because the usurper lost unequivocally to Bartholomew's fellow countryman, Lord Wellington. Who remembers now that Wellington even existed? Yet everyone remembers Napoleon.

"Greatness is revealed by distance," Bartholomew said with a sigh. "Is one century really any kind of distance?" The nineteenth century still surrounded the twentieth like an encampment: even the First World War had not managed to dislodge it. Oh, those countless beds in which Napoleon slept a single night! They reproduced by cell division like amoebas, providing income for provincial taverns and wayside inns.

Despite his vast authority, Bartholomew was a broad-minded man. The futility of his efforts convinced him of one important thing—their vanity. And vanity, like emptiness, was beneath the dignity of a ruler of Bartholomew's stature. It was true—it was ridiculous to sacrifice a greater power to a lesser one. For Bartholomew, battling Napoleon was the same thing as Napoleon reigning over the tiny island of St. Helena. Bartholomew grinned at this thought and shrugged: no, his power would not be overshadowed even by that of Bonaparte. Did Napoleon have the power to create even a single tiny bug, a single blade of grass? For these powers were within the reach of Bartholomew, and had even been tested: he was cultivating one enchanting plant from the umbel-liferous family, and he was the one who had introduced the tiny moth *Bartholomeus waterloous*, unknown not only to science but to the Creator Himself, into Patagonia. He had done this only once, on the day of the longest night of the year, the usurper's birthday. Who would dare say that Bartholomew had ever abused his authority? He did not raise himself to the level of the Creator—but that he *could* do what was possible only for Him was not to be gainsaid.

So, Bartholomew's authority ranked second only to that of the Creator. And insofar as it was not strictly about power for the Creator but rather about himself, Bartholomew, in his reign, possessed powers, the likes of which no one in human history before him had ever possessed.

His authority was not onerous for his subjects, since it was absolute. One didn't notice it, just as one doesn't notice air, or water. This authority could not inspire doubt or suspicion, since no one was capable of sensing its coercive power—that's how great it was. (After all, we don't balk at the force of gravity, for it cannot be lighter or gentler—it is what it is.) Time submitted to Bartholomew. He wielded power over the Glory of the World, as its sole heir, its ultimate instantiation. He was the Result of everything. He always stood at the end of every line of petty czars and emperors, looking back from our day to the Sumerians. And not simply because a living dog is better than a dead lion but because the last in line is the Only one. There had been swarms of those who had come before him. Bartholomew pulled the entire world behind him by this string, and the world followed obediently in his wake, as though it had been headed there all along.

Bartholomew awoke to the sound of a sudden banging. He was unable to account for either the noise or its source. It was dark. Of course, the somnolent Bartholomew thought, tonight is the longest night in the year. What time is it, anyway? He turned on the night light and scrabbled around for the alarm clock on the nightstand. The clock showed three, and had stopped ticking. It had been limping along for some time now. The king's alarm clock held such delusions of gran-deur that it deigned to show the time only when its axis was set exactly parallel to the axis of the Earth, which, as everyone knows, is itself at an angle to its orbit. Before going to sleep, Bartholomew spent a long time trying to achieve this astronomical accuracy for the proud mechanism. Now the device refused to revive in any position at all. It was absolutely dead. Evidently, it hadn't been able to survive such a long night. The banging repeated, and Bartholomew, fully awake now, determined its source.

It was the Queen Mother (a widow, of course), banging her scepter on her bedpan.

Despite all his power, Bartholomew never forgot his filial duties. For the epitome of royal duty is the ruler's obligation to his subjects, to his children: What kind of father could he be if he didn't carry out his own filial duties? Bartholomew lowered his feet down to the floor. He groped around with his foot and found one slipper right away. The other one was missing. Then he remembered what day it was. Today was a very important day, one of the most important in the year, and, who knew, perhaps in a whole lifetime. In any case, do we not prepare the whole year for tomorrow, amassing strength, saving up every second to spend on it? And since we also prepare for the year itself, living through our prior life leading up to it, you might even say that our whole lives we prepare precisely for that day which yesterday we called "tomorrow." Is today not the culmination of everything? Today it was within Bartholomew's power to overthrow a small kingdom, or dry up a sea, or dethrone a hero, for today was the day when the annual General Map of the World approached completion and would remain thus for millennia and beyond . . . Today was the day when he did not intend to amuse himself with his power in such a way, for today the moment had finally arrived to settle some personal scores that had long burdened him, casting a shadow on his past—scores with one person who had once rashly gotten in the way of his authority, a certain Sir Poluzhan. And on such a day! Where had that accursed slipper got to? The devil of annoyance overcame him when he discovered it on the nightstand, right by the clock. Groggily, at a loss as to how to get the clock working again, and unable to find anything else, he had stuffed his slipper under the clock, at last achieving the proper angle for it. The memory amused him and cheered him up. His irritation evaporated and he took away the Queen Mother's bedpan, demonstrating the diligence of filial respect.

Shuffling down the hallway with the bedpan in one hand, he heard more unaccountable noises, coming now from the kitchen. They sounded like sobs. Who could be weeping in there? Passing the bathroom and the WC, still holding the same sloshing bedpan in his hand, wearing only his underwear, King Bartholomew, naturally, glanced into the kitchen, where he saw a long-haired, barefooted maiden in a short nightshirt guzzling down cold milk with greedy sobs, drinking it straight from the bottle. (The refrigerator door was still wide open.) The maiden gave a little squeak, like a rat, spewed out milk, and darted off down the hallway to the Crown Prince's chamber. (This was Bartholomew Junior—or Bartholomew the Younger, because there was still another Bartholomew, Bartholomew the Youngest . . . but he wasn't here—he had left with the Duchess for Opatija so she could take a cure for her back.) Bartholomew the king sighed. The girl was another one of the prince's numerous amours, whom he could no longer tell apart. The king sniffed the air shrewdly, and caught a whiff of the sweet pungent scent that reminded him he also had some accounts to settle with Alexander the Great—whom he generally viewed with sympathy, but whom he nevertheless blamed to a certain degree. For during his wars, which eventually degenerated into wanderings, Alexander had conceived a liking for narcotics, and he had blazed a trail for this heady folderol, a direct route all the way to Europe. The Crown Prince had recently taken a superficial interest in the Orient, smoking up all manner of truth serums to the point of stupor. Once again Bartholomew remembered *what* this day was, and the devil of annoyance at the hindrance his kith and kin posed to this Great Thing entered him with new force. What time was it, anyway? His wife's family heirloom, a clock in the guise of the Trojan Horse—pre-Napoleonic, from the heyday of the Dukes of O., a clock whose punctilious striking had given rise to a fierce, unceasing battle for inheritance that had been waged for generations—this clock had also stopped.

He kicked it spitefully. The clock began to strike with its little hoof. Restive after its inactivity, it struck its allotment for the whole night at one go. Bartholomew counted thirty-seven strikes—that couldn't be the time. Bartholomew laughed out loud (say what you will, but the king had a healthy sense of humor). He looked out the window and saw that it was already a dusky gray. That meant that it was after nine! The Great Morning had dawned, and Bartholomew was running late.

After assisting the Queen Mother at her ablutions, and serving her coffee and toast, the "Poor Knight" carefully seated her on the wheelchair-throne, wrapped her in her ermine mantle (which was so tattered and ancient it had lost its tail and paws and now looked more like a mole, though it was still very warm), and wheeled, or, rather, dragged the throne (the chair was lacking a wheel, and had been reequipped with half a broken ski) out onto the terrace, where a little birch tree was withering away in a tub in the corner, and where a view opened up over the damp roofs of Paris, the capital of Bartholomew's place of exile, and the birthplace of his wife, who at the present time was accommodated in his residence. "Ah, the life of an émigré." Bartholomew sighed. He didn't like this city. "If it weren't for my marriage . . ." He sighed again, sending a puff of steam into the damp air in the direction of his homeland, where the shores of Albion were said to lie wrapped in mist.

Now, in his raincoat, and holding an umbrella, he looked into his son's chamber. The prince was sleeping on top of the blanket, fully dressed. Why had the maiden been disrobed, then? the king wondered with a sad grin. But the girl was already gone; she had slipped away when the king wasn't looking. The chamber was stuffy and smelled strongly of that spicy folderol. The king cringed, opened a ventilation window, and covered the prince in an afghan. The prince didn't even stir. He lay there almost lifeless, his sharp nose turned to the ceiling. His nose was followed by his sharp Adam's apple, and then his sharp rib cage. Bartholomew felt as though he were wrapping up a little bird in the blanket. The king heaved a sigh, placed five French francs on a little table, then sighed again and added another five.

The king was just getting ready to leave the house when Basil the Dark saw fit to wake up (he was named after a fifteenth-century Moscow prince, largely because Bartholomew had not yet been able to discover why that prince had been nicknamed "the Dark"). Basil padded toward him with deliberate, demanding steps, yawning and meowing—an enormous, frosty white cat, blind since birth; not so much a cat as a bear (hence his dark, Russian name). Dropping the umbrella, the king bestowed a little fish on him, stroked him with the hand of a tyrant exhausted by his own power, and sighed once more. Who on Earth possesses more power than a king? His beloved cat.

Now he could leave. The cook would arrive toward noon, and all three of the others would survive until his return.

The king descended via the stairs (the elevator only went up). When he was downstairs, he checked the mail. There was no letter from his wife, but there was a pile of new bills, which occasioned his last sigh.

"Enough!" he said, irate. "It's time I stopped doing this."

"Doing what?" a voice seemed to say.

"Sighing."

"Don't ask the impossible of yourself, Your Majesty."

As we can see, his sense of humor, of which he was so proud, did not desert him. He had already grown to like the new mailboxes that had been installed three days before: the camouflage color, with nickel-plated locks, reminded him of the Ministry of Defense and the Periodic Table of the Elements (many people claimed the Periodic Table was a Russian invention). All the numbers were in the right order, the boxes and the letter openings had been organized and evened up, and only the royal mailbox number stood out, royally disrupting the prevailing order in accordance with its sovereign privilege. The boxes all followed in proper sequence up to number thirty-two, and then came his—twenty-eight. Today, too, he would have to sort things out with Russia. At noon he had an audience with Paul I of Russia himself, and with a prominent Russian military commander. And so, preoccupied by the thought that he would never again have to insult his own dignity by skirmishing with Napoleon,* Bartholomew was running late for work.

He didn't like Paris, either. If it weren't for his wife . . . Well, here history had no alternative: children.

He dreamed of wrapping up his work here (a professional exchange between two great encyclopedias) and returning home to England, to get a promotion and begin work on an abridged *Britannica* for children.

No! Never again would he live in an apartment house, nor in the ministry (even if they offered him a whole floor). He would return to

---

*Only now do I begin to understand Bartholomew. Indeed, what is the modern-day European Union, with its euro (of which Bartholomew could not conceive, even in his alternative history), if not Napoleon's plan, risen to the surface of the present like Atlantis? His Europe, created by fire and sword, disintegrated quickly. The chief architect was dismissed; but his project came to life again, annexing new countries of the former Socialist Empire. Thus, Russia, in retreating, finally inches back toward Europe, like China inching into Siberia. (*A tardy note from the translator, April 28, 2011, 4:00 p.m. The Bartholomiad is complete: "The audience has transpired." See above. A. B.*)

his homeland. His pay would suffice to rent a small house in a leafy suburb, for starters. Then . . . then he would furnish it as he had dreamed of doing his whole life.

Downstairs would be his mother, wife, and children. He would go down only for meals. It would constitute the completeness of "simple human happiness." Upstairs, even if it were just a modest attic, would lie the true realm of Bartholomew.

He would order a long, T-shaped desk and bookshelves from a cabinetmaker. On these shelves he would place only the most carefully selected books, the ones indispensable for his work on the *Britannica*. Right next to the desk, so that he wouldn't have to get up, he would have the cabinetmaker fashion him a revolving bookcase of his own design. It would house the complete works of Shakespeare and everything that had been written about him.

To reiterate, downstairs they would live, prepare meals, clean up, do the wash . . . and he could rest assured that everything was happening in its proper time, in its proper order. Upstairs he would spin his revolving bookcase and take down just the book he needed, without even looking. There would be a staircase leading up to his realm, but it would be retractable, like the bridge over a castle moat. He would be the only one with the right to raise and lower it.

This was King Bartholomew's reverie about what constituted complete royal happiness.

His imaginings induced in him a spiritual equanimity.

Like Harun al-Rashid, indistinguishable from an ordinary official, King Bartholomew, hiding under his umbrella from the curious glances of passersby, glided swiftly along the glossy pavement as though on skates. Today His Majesty's Thief was at long last either supposed to pay off his debt or at least to come clean and admit his wrongdoing.

The Thief had been conferred with a courtly title about five years before, when he had robbed Bartholomew. The story looked simple, from any point of view except the royal one. Though he could rule historical destinies and move heavenly bodies, he was not at all fond of intervening in individual human fates. Because Bartholomew had a brother.

Rather, Bartholomew *was* a brother.

When had Fate mixed them up, so that his brother ended up with

Bartholomew's fate, and Bartholomew with his brother's? His brother had been destined to rule, and Bartholomew to wander; but it turned out the other way round. They were both Twins, the sign of Gemini, but his brother was slightly older, and by the rules of succession to throne . . .

The fact was, that from the time he was in diapers, Bartholomew had enjoyed the rights without responsibilities of the younger. His brother, from preparatory school onward, had borne upon his narrow shoulders the obligations of heir to the throne. By the time Bartholomew had become a C student, his brother had already excelled in school. His brother was the one with a photographic memory. He could multiply three-digit numbers in his head, memorize entire encyclopedia entries, knew by rote the genealogical trees of all the distinguished families of Albion. He learned by heart the schedules and routes of transatlantic liners from the fat reference manual. By the age of five he was already sounding the whistle blasts upon arrival in any port, right on time, by blowing into a toy horn. You only had to ask: Where are we? And he would answer: in Trinidad; or Majorca . . . You only had to look at the clock, and then at the manual—the hour and minute corresponded exactly, his brother was never late. But little Bartie no longer heard him. He was already standing in the very prow, staring out at the contours of an unfamiliar bay, and his heart leapt ashore before he himself did, although he jumped out before the entire ship's company of mulattos, coconuts, and white trousers.

When his brother was still in his stroller, he could read all the signboards on the street backward, without faltering: *pohsrebraB! snosdnarevooH! Zeewhyexdoubleyou!* He rattled off the ABCs, or, the *deeceebeeay*. But Bartholomew no longer heard or saw his brother, because in the thick jungle, amid the shrieking of parrots and the chattering of monkeys, he had been surrounded by savages. They were aiming their arrows and spears into his broad, bare chest, uttering threats in their incomprehensible native tongue: *azneulfnI! niripsareyaB!* Three fingers away from his heart, the cold, glittering blade of a thermometer plunged into his armpit. A caravan wended its way endlessly through the heat of Strepthroat, the Patagonian desert of death—Bartholomew rocked to the slow tread of the dromedary and the monotonous jingling of its bell. Through this unbroken din, a string of mirages emerged—palms in the ocean—Tangiers, Bangkok, Sydney . . . Now his older brother jangled the ship's bells above his ear, announcing the departure of the *Queen Elizabeth* from Singapore at exactly 1:30 p.m., local time. A week later, the ship docked safely in the Bay of Health. Bartholomew jumped ashore, and his older brother climbed on board.

In the oceanic maternal bed, they were sick by turns—first his brother got A's while Bartholomew was sick, then Bartholomew got D's while his brother lay ill. Once, while they were sick, a children's map of the British Empire had been hung above the bed. Actually, it was a map of the world, at that time still three-quarters green. After that it wasn't removed again. His older brother covered it with routes and minutes, and that was how Bartholomew remembered him for the rest of his life: sick in bed, with a scarf around his sore throat, genuflecting before the Empire, multiplying inches by degrees in his head.

The brothers grew, the Empire fell apart and faded: in the corner, by the pillow, Tierra del Fuego and Patagonia became especially tattered. Until old age they would appear before his eyes as the first symptoms of the onset of illness. His gaze would venture farther and farther up as he convalesced, toward Europe, toward the Italian boot, and still higher, to the kneeling Baltic Sea, begging Russia to accept the Gulf of Finland from it . . . And on the last day—a pillow fight, slippers flying, head over heels and upside down: the New Zealand boot a perfect match for the Italian one, but flung into the opposite corner of the world as though in a fit of temper, as though in proof of the predetermined division of the world . . . The brothers didn't get sick anymore, and their mother was aging under the weight of the Empire, now grown decrepit.

O Empire!

While his brother took precedence in this life, while he was finishing Oxford after Cambridge, language after language, degree after degree, stringing them together like a hunter strings his trophies, like a savage strings his beads, did I not string my own necklace of islands, in my own fashion, too, O Empire? Your Bahamas, your Philippines, your Antilles . . . Did I not collect your grasses in the savannas, and catch your snakes in the deserts? Was it not I who, saving up a little something on the grasses and snakes, tried to grow rich on your diamonds and emeralds, on your tusks and your gold? Was it not my habit to joke, when asked "Why do you need gold?" to answer "To find more gold"? Was

I not the one who sank everything I had extracted from you into you again—into your bordellos, your taverns and opium dens, in Singapore, Melbourne, and Delhi? Was it not I who was stroked by your Negresses, your Malays, your Indian women? Where art thou, O Empire? What have you done, Brother? Why is your life mine, and my life yours? Or are the Japanese right, that life has two halves, and after forty one must change one's name? Are these two halves of life sisters? And are they sisters in the same way that you and I are brothers? Why are you sick with fever on the outskirts of the fallen Empire? What do the liberated Zulus need with your Catholicism? Why are you chasing after my cross, having thrown your own onto my shoulders?

Thus lamented the present-day Bartholomew, looking at the map of the world, already one-fourth less green in his time, and half as green in the time of Bartholomew the Middle, his already grown son, and reduced to almost nothing for Bartie the Youngest, by which time the mature emerald sheen of the Empire had faded to a pale, childish salad-green, and amidst its Cyclopean debris young states burst forth like tiny spring shoots. Only by its tatters did the map of the world remind Bartholomew of this world—the map of his childhood. But it was tattered now in the other corner, as well—the corner of the far-flung New Zealand boot, still slightly green; for the Crown Prince's illnesses were of a different nature and his pillow lay on the other side.

O Son! Three photographs hung side by side—the king's pride and joy: the first slightly more yellowed, and the last glossier than the middle one. All three of them looked like Bartholomew: the king, the prince, and the youngest . . . it was the same face. As if the king had not aged, only the sailor's shirt he wore. No one wears them now. No one wore them then, either. It was a hand-me-down from the older to the younger.

Bartholomew missed the youngest, looking at the son of the eldest.

O Son! My curly-haired one in the faded photograph, from which you still look at me with such immense, astonished eyes, as though this world were too small for you. Why did you start balding so young, why did your eyes lose their luster, like the Empire? Why do you want nothing that I want, nor what your uncle wants? Was it not you I saw recently with our Turk? You sidled past me like a shadow, like smoke. You can't fool me with that smell, I can pick it up a mile away! Is he palming off that folderol on you, is that the reason my books keep disappearing? Watch out, Turk, you ill-starred thief! Watch out that you don't pay with your head! The books, don't forget, aren't just valuable, they're priceless—they are my father's—your grandfather's—books.

O Father! I never understood you. Only now do I begin to guess, but you recede from me like a star the more I am able to surmise. You shine for me with a backward light, as though from that little seed out of which the light originally flashed for me. Now you are no longer here, and your light has finally reached me. If only you could see your Bartholomew Junior! Who was it who believed that the Milky Way was like God's seed, that each of us comes from our own star in the firmament? I don't remember. You would know the answer immediately. You remembered everything. Knowledge was your empire.

These were the present-day Bartholomew's tender thoughts, the same Bartholomew whose pranks had been such a trial for his father that he had suffered a heart attack. He took a volume of his father's 1911 edition of the *Encyclopædia Britannica* off the shelf. His father's favorite volume . . .

O *Britannica*!

Like a genuine king of the encyclopedic universe, Bartholomew's father sat in state over the uppermost height of this lofty ridge of volumes stretching out along the entire shelf—over the "Sh" volume.* And Bartholomew had inherited from him this awe. He didn't immediately open the volume just to the place where . . . where he . . . where the most . . . where the one who was found under "Sh" . . . He opened this, the most tattered volume, as though he had all the time in the world, as though he were ascending with measured tread the steps of words to the yearned-for summit.

SHAGREEN . . . How strange that the path always began with this kind of leather, as though alluding to the profession of that doubtful father of the one under "Sh"—a butcher, or perhaps a glover . . .

SHAH—the title of the King of Persia, the sham independence

---

*A conundrum for a translator. The Russian language devotes a single character, or letter, to this sound: "ш." Similarly, English needs two letters ("kh") to represent the Russian sound and letter "х" (as in "Anton Chekhov"). And in French—just imagine!—"onion" and "ostrich," "anchor" and "bee" and "spider," "lamb," "jester," and "lampshade" all begin with the same letter! From here on out, the translator will be confronted with many such difficulties, and will not be able to cope with them. (A. B.)

of which always concealed the cherished interests of the Empire, and from its root . . .

SHAHABAD, SHAH ALAM MOGUL, SHAH JAHAN SHAHJAHANPUR, SHAHPUR, SHAHRASTANI, SHAHRUD, SHAH SHUJA . . . The long shadow of the Empire: a province, then a ruler of its province, then its sphere of interests, then its sphere of influence . . . And through this armored, impenetrable rampart, suddenly a weak sprout of the literary word, like a little chirp: SHAIRP, John Campbell, Scottish critic. How absurd! How ludicrous and presumptuous this proximity, this antecedence . . . As though they were in the same class, as though the Teacher might call him to the blackboard, with a finger hovering over the letters "SH," and expect him to name this one first, not that one . . . Still, how lucky he was that the first three letters of their names matched, and brought them so close together . . . And following SHAIRP, out of the blue, as always with the Americans, these incongruous SHAKERS, intent upon jumbling up the whole world. That is the essence of independence, the only way were they able to free themselves from the Empire, as flesh of its flesh . . . Shakers, what nonsense! They're only good at mixing everything up: communism with the second coming—some "children of truth" they are. Monte Cristo sandwiches, cheese with ham . . . The French were right— what can you expect from a nation that loves cheese with ham? But the SHAKERS, too, are in their place, for the rain cuts through, there's a shiver in the air; one only has to turn over the already trembling page and . . . there he is, under "Sh" . . . WILLIAM!

Here it stops making any sense, from the very first line. The 23rd of April. Is that the day he was born, or the day he died? And why at the same time as Cervantes, on the same day? And why did he die on his birthday? Or was he born on the day of his death? And who was his father, a butcher or a glover? And who were Bacon, Marlowe, Lord Southampton? Did they even exist? Were they not all one and the same William? And which of the twenty-six portraits is genuine? Well, of course, Jansen's, the father would say. Why? Because it's the handsomest. Certainly not the Hampton Court portrait: a sword, a belt, a ring on his finger, a glove in his hand—a Christmas tree, yes; but certainly not Shakespeare! It's the glove that clinches the matter. They say it was his father who sewed it for him.

This argument about the authenticity of the portraits was the last thing that Bartholomew remembered about his father. For his father died of heart failure, unable to cope with Bartholomew's most recent escape, while Bartholomew was sitting up to his neck in a swamp on the isthmus of Panama, happier than he had ever been in his entire life. O Wife! . . .

This time Bartholomew had fled on a large-scale oceanographic expedition. Commissioned as an artist to draw grasses, skulls, and nests, he was especially absorbed in the task of drawing cephalopods (or was it *Hymenoptera*?) for a charming naturalist. And so they were sitting together in the pitch-black night, up to their necks in a Panamanian swamp, straining to hear the mating call of a unique frog, in order to record it on a phonograph for her professor, one of the world's foremost experts on *Coelenterata*—a professor who was far less excited by arthropods than by his hobby: the mating calls of precisely this frog, who sings once every hundred years, at that very hour, in that very pond. In other words, the entire future of the budding naturalist depended on this mating call, which was synonymous with the happiness that occurred at just such rare intervals, on which depended the entire future of the budding naturalist, both professionally and on terms that Bartholomew could set. Nine months later she gave birth to a son, but refused to take Bartholomew's name, as she hailed from a patrician family with three lilies in its coat of arms. And on the next day, Bartholomew received the news of his father's death.

After WILLIAM, Bartholomew didn't close the volume right away but descended the steps of words to the bottom, more quickly this time, as happens when going downhill. SHALLOT (*Allium ascalonicum*), already cultivated in the early Christian era, widely used in the preparation of meats (his father had most likely been a butcher, after all, not a glover), of which there are two varieties—the common shallot, and the Jersey, or Russian, shallot (somehow we can never stray too far from Russia). SHAMANISM—the religion of the Uralo-Altaic tribes (Russia again). SHAMBLES—an abattoir for the preparation of kosher meat (well, perhaps a butcher, but certainly not a Jew). SHAMIL—leader of the Caucasian tribes in the war with Russia (again!). SHANGHAI, finally (out there, beyond Russia).

Today was the day of the Thief and the vizier. Bartholomew didn't realize right away that he had tried to combine these two burdensome affairs into one. The Thief was supposed to pay off the remainder of a sum he had stolen from Bartholomew, and the vizier was supposed to increase the budget of Bartholomew's court. Bartholomew was supposed to find time to see both of them, and at least not miss his audience with Paul I.

In the space allowed by this sheet of paper, it is difficult to explain at all clearly how Bartholomew had formed such an uncommon relationship with his Thief. Though that, perhaps, is another story. For the sake of coherence, suffice it to note that on that day, when news came of the tragic disappearance of his older brother, and the Queen Mother took to her bed in grief, Bartholomew decided to renovate her room to create an atmosphere conducive to recovery. Amid such dramatic family circumstances Bartholomew was not quite himself, so he hired the first person who showed up, a Turk without references, and left him alone in the apartment. In Bartholomew's absence, the Turk stole from his grandfather's desk, which was never locked, a small number of securities (shares, to be exact) that Bartholomew had received as an inheritance from his father, and which he, only for that reason, had not yet sold. That was, in fact, the whole, and the sole, family fortune. He robbed Bartholomew, but he was not caught redhanded. Only on the following day, and then only by chance, did Bartholomew discover that the papers were missing.

Distraught over the excess of calamity, Bartholomew neglected to alert the police, for whom he had had no special liking since his roving days, but summoned the Turk, and two of his own friends for moral support. One was an Orientalist, who (he thought) would be able to speak to the Turk in his own language. The other was more experienced, a comrade who had taken part in his youthful journeys, and who would be able to deal with the legal side of the matter. The Orientalist was of no help, because the Turk turned out to be a Yezidi; the experienced friend intervened just at the right time and threatened to hang the Turk or the Yezidi (or both at once), privately, with no interference from the police; and, moreover, to hang them not by the neck, nor by the feet. The Thief, however, stood firm and wouldn't spill the beans, retreating into a deep sulk. It would have been impossible to extricate him from that state, were it not for that same *Britannica*.

Looking up "Yezidi," Bartholomew came to understand a peculiarity of theirs, namely that they were considered to be devil-worshippers, and that the most terrible thing one could do to them was to curse the Evil One in their presence. That was precisely what Bartholomew did, and, most unexpectedly, this experiment had an immediate effect.

Although he didn't confess to the theft, the Turk-Yazidi, whining and lamenting, promised to return the above-mentioned sum because the evidence was so dramatically stacked against him, but only as a "debt of honor," to salvage his good name. For he had a fiancée and planned to marry her and to have children by her (as you can see, devil-worshippers are no different from the rest of us). But, considering the magnitude of the sum that had gone missing through no fault of his own, he would agree to hand over one half of it the next day, he said, and the other half in installments over the next month. And on that note, they parted.

"Forgive me, Bartholomew," said his friend with the checkered past, "but I don't think I've ever met anyone as gullible as you are. And if he brings you half the money tomorrow, go straight to the nearest church and light the biggest candle you can find—because it means that you're not alone. There's someone else in the world even more gullible than you are: your Thief. But no matter how great a blockhead he turns out to be, don't ever expect to see the other half of that money for as long as you live."

The skepticism of his friend with the checkered past was not justified with respect to the first half of the money, which fortified Bartholomew's faith in people; but the second half of the oracle's prophecy turned out to be true, thus fortifying Bartholomew's faith in his friend's wisdom.

But it is one thing to believe in someone else's wisdom, and another thing altogether to follow it. Bartholomew continued to visit the Thief from time to time to inquire about the second half, and the Thief never refused, even a single time, to promise to return it—it was always "next time without fail!" The Turk never deceived him, that was the point. He did get married, and even came over to invite Bartholomew to be an honored guest at the wedding, which Bartholomew, though flattered, declined. Now when he showed up at the Thief's for his "debt of honor," the Thief, sincerely eager to discharge it, tried to remove his wife's wedding ring from her finger in lieu of the money, and Bartholomew withdrew, filled with shame.

Once it happened that the Thief came to invite him to a feast in honor of the birth of his firstborn. Just at that time Bartholomew had received news that his brother was alive, found somewhere in South America. Happy for his mother's happiness, Bartholomew was moved to tell the Thief that if he confessed to the robbery, all would be forgiven and he would be released from his debt. The Thief, strangely enough, was deeply offended, and left. Although deep in his heart Bartholomew was certain that the Thief was, indeed, a thief, sometimes, stealing a glance at his grown son, he still experienced a tremor of doubt. Oh, if only he knew what kind of abyss he had plunged himself into with his own generous—speaking juridically—special ruling!

The Thief paid him the respect due a king. And, truly, his joy at seeing Bartholomew would be hard to overestimate. Sometimes it seemed to Bartholomew that his brother and the Thief had changed places. He couldn't quite claim that his brother had become a thief; but that the Thief had become a brother was very close to the truth. He still didn't pay back the debt, but he gladly volunteered for small errands. True, he didn't actually carry them out, but his eagerness always warmed Bartholomew's heart. It had been a year since he had promised to procure a new wheelchair for the Queen Mother, and now he was going to bring over a Christmas tree, tomorrow at the latest . . . Each time, the Thief had a weighty excuse for why he had to postpone payment of the second half of the debt: his mother was ill (a circumstance Bartholomew understood well himself). The Thief's older brother vouched for this, even putting in an appearance (also a Turk, possibly his brother, too). Then there was trouble concerning that same brother, who had to go to court (Bartholomew could relate to this circumstance as well).

This time the Thief rolled a barrel of honey into the middle of the room as a conditional guarantee of imminent payment: his relatives had sent it; he had only to go to the bazaar to sell it. Then he would rush right back to give Bartholomew the proceeds, only there was no time—too much work (though every time Bartholomew dropped by, the Thief happened to be at home), and if he didn't believe him, he could take the barrel with him right now—there was plenty of honey there to cover the debt, with interest. Bartholomew didn't take it.

The eldest little thief, Bartholomew's pet, was already sitting on his knee. Not limiting himself to the candy he had already been treated to, he had set his sights on the ballpoint pen or the cigarette lighter, so Bartholomew gradually turned into a juggler, catching in midair first the one, then the other, then a handkerchief, then a watch, and then restored them to their places. The youngest crawled on all fours with astonishing speed, like a little cockroach. The wife trundled her enormous third belly from the kitchen into the living room and back again. All this progeny had been conceived and born within the span of Bartholomew's memory. He was freezing, and he stayed to warm himself at this hearth, forgetting why he had come. In the kitchen, something bubbled and exhaled a savory Turkish aroma, and it would be ready in a jiffy, Bartholomew must stay and taste it . . .

As proof of his candor, the Thief showed Bartholomew, finally, the king's own fur coat, which the Thief had volunteered to repair back in the summer, and had snatched out of Bartholomew's grip almost by force, in spite of his timid protests. The coat had been an object of especial pride for Bartholomew. It was wolf skin. He had brought it back with him from Alaska—no one else could boast of such a prize, and no one but Bartholomew would dare to wear it. A fur fit for a king! He donned it only on very solemn occasions, though those occasions seemed to have become increasingly less solemn, or . . . When Bartholomew finally brought it out to wear, time itself seemed to fly out of it, like it was giving up the ghost, in the familiar guise of the clothes moth. The Thief, seeing his dismay, made fervent offers to come to the rescue: he had a cousin, a Turk, first class, it would be just like new again. Bartholomew mumbled something about how it could never be new again . . . in vain. The Thief grabbed it under the arms like a living creature, and it even seemed to resist, like a dog that was being hauled away from its master.

Now, along with the subject of the debt, the subject of the fur coat took root and grew until it had assumed equal proportions, and already it was unclear which matter was more pressing—the fur or the debt? (Bartholomew was sure that the fur had made it to the bazaar, where someone's barrel of honey hadn't.) One seemed to supplant the other, so that returning one of them canceled out returning the other.

"You've halved it again!" It suddenly dawned on Bartholomew, and he laughed in delight at his own shrewdness and insight. It seemed he even said this aloud. This time the Thief was offended, as deeply as only thieves can be.

"You insult me, Your Majesty," the Thief said, reaching behind the honey barrel and producing an untidy bundle. "Here!" the one so recently maligned said triumphantly. "Here!" His arms and back looked like he might be sobbing while he unfastened it. His sharp shoulder blades worked furiously beneath his tank top.

Finally the wrappings dropped away, revealing the remains of what had once been Bartholomew's fur coat.

"We tried everything we could," the Thief insisted, scooping up handfuls of furry scraps, and letting them fall back down again, as though he were fingering priceless jewels in a treasure chest like Ali Baba. "But you can see for yourself, it's the inner side of the hide, it didn't survive the process . . ." With these words he plucked out a slightly larger scrap, one that still looked whole, and commenced tearing it into tiny strips, like paper, to prove his case. Poor Bartholomew reached out to stop him.

"But we'll think of something," said the Thief, comforting him. "I know a furrier who says he will trade these odds and ends for an almost new chinchilla jacket. A woman's jacket, sure, but it's chinchilla! And the surcharge will be minimal."

The Thief's ingenuousness moved Bartholomew, and he laughed, relieved that his sense of humor had returned to him. "Fine," he said, "but when will you return the money?"

He didn't mean to upset the Thief. It was sly on his part—waltzing so lightly over the problem of the fur coat. The Thief shook his head at him as if in reproach, as if to say, "Oh no, here we go again."

Bartholomew left with a wave of the hand. "I'm running late!" he said, and rushed downstairs, skipping every few steps.

"Wait!" the Thief called out to him. "You really won't make me give you the money back if I confess?"

Bartholomew seemed to hang in the air in midflight. Finally! he thought. It's too bad I won't ever see my money again, but oh, what a relief it would be!

We could leave them like this forever: Bartholomew, frozen in midflight, his head turned back over his shoulder like a playing-card king, and his court Thief, in a tank top, hanging over the bannister of the stairwell. If the story had ended here, they would have made a perfect chiseled image: it captured their relationship like a curious and apt monogram.

"I swear by my cross!" cried Bartholomew, unprepared for such a turn of events. Bartholomew's oath, however, made no dent in the demonology of the Thief. "I gave you my word!" Bartholomew was exasperated.

"Okay, I believe you," the Thief said with conviction.

"Well?" said Bartholomew, landing finally and stamping his foot. "Come on, I'm late."

"I have so much respect for you," the Thief said in a voice filled with emotion. "You're like my older brother."

Bartholomew shuddered and jerked his shoulders back, like he was trying to fend off the cold. Hadn't he had the same thought only moments ago?

"You're like a father to me," the Thief continued. "Do you think I don't know what you've done for me? You got me out of jail, you didn't let my children become orphans . . . I'd do anything for you . . . If you ever need anything, anything at all . . . call on me . . . I'll be there . . ."

"Wait, is this a confession or not?" Bartholomew said, distressed and overjoyed at the same time. The Thief began to writhe, the promised word was about to tear free from his lips. "What's wrong? You don't believe me?" Bartholomew thundered, his foot stamping the floor again.

"Of course I believe you! How could I not believe you?" the Thief reassured him.

"Well, then, yes or no?" Bartholomew yelled.

"Don't get mad." The Thief stepped away from the bannister. "I was just asking, just to be sure . . ."

It couldn't get any more certain than that. Bartholomew finally slipped out of these "Thousand and One Nights" he found himself in and started off at a run, smiling bitterly as he ran: it was nearly word for word the same as the last time, and the time before that, except for the fur coat. That was new. (Bartholomew regretted what had happened to the fur.) He knows, and I know, too, he thought, as he always did. And he knows that I know, and I know that he knows that I know. And he knows that I'll keep my word. And I will keep it, though I need the money, what with Christmas coming up . . . Why do I keep pressuring him? He is simply unable to utter those words. He wants to, but he can't! And this seemed to Bartholomew to be some special kind of honesty unique to the Thief.

Bartholomew sighed as he shook his wet umbrella and entered the loathsome office of Sir Poluzhan, where he was to have the audience with Paul I and a serious talk with Adams the Vizier.

The daily royal routine had begun.

Bartholomew was late for his appointment with the vizier. The vizier was no longer at his desk. His annoyance with the Thief was short-lived: as soon as Bartholomew found out from his secretary that the vizier hadn't come to work today at all, never mind about being here at the hour for which his meeting with Bartholomew had been set, his annoyance was transferred to the secretary. Bartholomew did manage to occupy his own desk on time, however.

"Shirkers," he grumbled, entering the reception hall and opening out his umbrella to dry, so that it took up the whole room. He took off his coat and his jacket and hung them up carefully. He donned his black sleeve protectors, like an accountant, gave the pillow on his chair a few punches to put it right, and sat down on his throne. He reached for a thin folder containing urgent matters of state, and assumed an air appropriate to the seriousness of the task. Then, saying, "You may enter!," he opened it.

A Russian field marshal, covered in decorations from his neck to his belt (and something below the belt dangled on a sword), lay topmost in the folder. It was a color photograph, and although nobody on the editorial board had heard of the field marshal, the photograph turned out to be the most impressive of the entire Russian collection. He overshadowed the greats, Peter and Catherine, and later Russian leaders, and the editor-in-chief insisted that he have a place in the publication. It remained only to invent a biography for him, since even the field marshal's name was not known with any degree of certainty, and according to the stipulations of the publication the article could not be smaller than the portrait itself. Judging by the number of decorations alone, he must have lost a very large battle.

Of seven articles and three illustrations for which there was no room in the layout, it would be necessary to choose five, or two. Or to abridge the articles so that they *all* fit. And this was within Bartholomew's power.

If he were to abolish one, which would it be? Bartholomew arranged the photographs in front of him. The field marshal would stay, never mind that his battle was unknown. His rivals were a certain little fish and a certain locknut that bore the name of its inventor. What a fate! There was no article about the inventor, only about his locknut. But the field marshal would be granted an article, although his battle was far less successful than the locknut. Not to mention the fish. The fish was extremely quaint: transparent, with a beak. And what's more, it was terribly old and rare; but despite the millions of years of its triumphant survival as a species, no one had ever heard of it. The field marshal's defeat was more famous than he himself was. The locknut eclipsed its inventor. In fact, the locknut was the most famous of them all.

Bartholomew put the field marshal in the middle, between the fish and the drawing of the locknut. There was no way the locknut entry could be shortened, for purely objective reasons; the field marshal had to stay, for he was under orders; and the little fish was the dearest of all to Bartholomew. So, an altar dripping with medals, an ancient fish, or an ingenious locknut?

O Encyclopedia!

Bartholomew laughed out loud in the consciousness of his power.

This was the incarnation of all his exotic experiences! As a former expeditionary artist, he was not only the literary editor but also the art director. Although clearly underappreciated by the managing editors, this rare combination did put a crust of bread on his table (though he would have preferred it with butter, too). For this reason he occasionally visited the Chairman of the Editorial Board on Mount Olympus. The chairman, on the one hand, regarded Bartholomew's merits as an employee very highly; on the other hand, he largely avoided him.

Bartholomew's last name was a hindrance to him. Especially here, in France. It was not so much a name as a nickname. A London telephone book alone contained no less than thirty pages of others like him. Even in his beloved *Britannica* there were at least thirty of the greats with his name, from Adam (the economist) to Sir William (the admiral), whom Bartholomew particularly admired.

When he was still working at the *Britannica*—which gave him his first steady job out of kindness, in recognition of his father's legacy after he passed away, and after Bartholomew had married, his brother had disappeared, and his mother had lost her legs—he promoted this admiral, who brought up the rear of this list of eponymous figures, to a place higher on the ladder of the encyclopedic hierarchy. He fostered a kinship between him and a minor religious philosopher, whom Bartholomew himself had included as one of his own great-grandfathers once removed. He had managed to devote almost an entire column in the encyclopedia to the admiral, and had achieved a convincing kinship with him, when he had suddenly found it necessary to cease this innocent abuse of power due to his brother's Catholicism, which had acquired a scandalous, almost political, character. Thus, instead of a kinship with Sir William (the admiral), diligent colleagues on the editorial board discovered another undesirable relationship, besides that of his brother: an all but Irish relative (through the maternal line). Taken together, this was enough for him to feel unwanted in such a respectable and upstanding institution, and to deprive him of his crust of bread (still without butter). He was forced to move to his wife's native France; one might even say, to emigrate.

Bartholomew sighed and banished this bout of nostalgia. Now he swapped the locknut for the fish: the fish became higher, and the locknut became lower than the military commander in rank, though strictly alphabetically it was the other way around.

How marvelous the alphabet is! Bartholomew thought. Everything submits to the letter. BARTHOLOMEW, Smith is a king, an admiral; SMITH, Bartholomew is a D student and a soldier. If you're in the middle, fingers point at you more often, you get called to the board. The middle is much more densely populated, it's harder to struggle free and make your way in the world. A Smith has to be a genius. A Smith needs a Wesson, otherwise it won't shoot. How much better it is to be the letter *A*! You automatically head the list. They are less inclined to reprimand you. They hit you only when they miss someone else. An *A* is almost exempt from failure, thus facilitating an easy career. Who is better suited to be chairman than an Adams? (Bartholomew's dissatisfaction with the vizier, as with everything else this morning, now grew.) But being the last in the alphabet has its advantages, too. Watch your back, Zuberg is sneaking up on you! In the shadows, tailing behind, closing out the list. He doesn't have to watch his back; no one can get behind him. You can't rise higher than the letter *A*, and you can't turn back, either. But Zuberg can see the whole chain, from *Z* to *A*. When the flock turns around, the last sheep becomes the first! In the manner of revolution . . .

Bartholomew's reasoning may seem somewhat haughty, but he had experience on his side. The view from on high, from his encyclopedic Olympus, on all of our earthly hustle and bustle, from ancient, prehistoric, and even pre-geological times, made certain things clear to him.

The career ladder, for example. In his own eyes, Bartholomew passed as a great prognosticator. His experience as art director helped, of course. Glancing at a photograph of a newly formed government cabinet, he didn't pay much attention to the central figure, pushed forward by history. His attention was drawn to the sidelines—those who were to the left and to the right. They were the ones who had a free shoulder. They leaned in from the margins, pushing out the central figure beyond the frame of the photograph like toothpaste from a tube. Bartholomew divined the future ten years ahead: the one on the left would move to the right, the one on the right would move left, and they would collide in the middle in a preelection struggle. They stood there, modestly and unobtrusively, hardly distinguishable from one another: the left somewhat younger, the right a bit older, but both still in their prime. They are dressed almost identically, like the central figure; it is barely visible, but if you look carefully you will see that the jacket on the left one is a bit narrower in the waist, and the trousers are flared (or the other way round, depending on the generation). Also barely visible, but in the latest fashion, the haircut is nearly the same, but not quite. The right one, on the contrary, though it is barely noticeable, clings to a style that is already out of date—the jacket is wider, the trousers narrower—and clings to a government that is already out of date. It would not seem to be to their advantage; they hang there in an uncomfortable pose on the periphery, at the farthest point of the pendulum. But in two years they'll accelerate toward the center: now the second from the edge, now the fourth . . . faster and faster, until they knock heads in the middle. Bartholomew knew a thing or two, and he even understood it. Except . . .

They overtook him, left and right. His concrete experience proved to be of no practical use to him. Ten years he had slogged away without a promotion. Bartholomew grew angry again, and again he flew up to the peak of Olympus, to Adams, in the glass elevator . . .

And caught him. At the very last moment, when Adams was looking forward to his imminent lunch. Adams's self-command prevented him from showing his vexation: his face beamed too cordially, he bent over backward to show how democratic he was. Who was Bartholomew, that Adams should try so hard to please him? Ah, a king, the salt of the earth. Undethronable and eternal. The entire encyclopedia—the entire universe, that is—rested on him. And who was Adams? Decay, dust, nothingness. One minute he's here, the next he's gone, in a puff of smoke. He knew his place; he trembled before Bartholomew. He was the cat that had swallowed the canary. Adams was afraid, though he wasn't even aware of it himself. He wasn't afraid of, say, Zuberg, but of something in a way more terrible. As though the future lit up Bartholomew's face: only look into his eyes and you'll see that you are doomed, that soon, very soon . . . That is why Adams averts his eyes and can't look directly at Bartholomew. He only imagines that he can't stand Bartholomew; but it's himself he can't stand. He only imagines he is able to conceal his confusion under a guise of simplicity, shyness, and sensitivity toward his subordinate. He wouldn't want to show his superiority, or injure someone's self-love inadvertently. But he's the only one who imagines these things. All the others, the ones below, see him for what he is. And for the Adamses of this world, being seen is *death*.

Bartholomew saw him, and Adams knew it (he was shrewd, you had to hand him that). He began to make excuses: how he had presented Bartholomew's request, and had even gone all the way to the top, to the Man Himself. If he didn't believe him, Bartholomew could ask the secretary, she'd show him the paperwork. "In a month, you can count on it," Adams says, but in his own mind he is already going down in the glass elevator, and the door of his limousine opens, and he's spreading the toasted bread with Russian caviar. "Come back in a

month, and I will personally take care of it. I'll go straight to Him."
And Adams was gone. Vanished.

Well, what do you know! Bartholomew thought, overcome with
admiration. By golly, it's the very same thing. He's just the Turk all over
again. Six of one, half dozen of the other. The undeniable accuracy of his
discovery buoyed him up. Adams, the Turk; the Turk, Adams . . . Could
it be just by chance that he had combined them on the same day? No, it
turned out there was a reason . . . and the reason was that they were one
person! A thief and the Thief. Their gestures, the little expressions they
let drop—they were from the same script. Only the Thief's acting was
better. More honest. Bartholomew's heart warmed with the memory.
And he became still more attached to his court Thief.

Only when he had returned to his own office and assumed his
throne did Bartholomew realize that Adams had again passed him
over. The Turk and the fur coat? That was nothing by comparison!
The Thief had halved his debt (again); but the vizier had doubled his.
And as soon as Bartholomew had sat down, he realized that he had
returned to his place. No, Adams had *put* him there, in his place. With
empty promises, casual flattery—"You're the only one . . . Only you
have the qualifications . . . All my hopes rest on you . . . Help us out,
rescue us, for God's sake . . . [The Thief prays to the devil, and only in
private, keeping it to himself; but this one appeals aloud to God, without so much as blushing] . . . A great responsibility . . . Only with your
experience and expertise . . ." He foisted it off on Bartholomew, and
Bartholomew didn't notice that he had accepted it, and that the wool
had been pulled over his eyes. That the burden had fallen on him alone,
he was up to his neck in it, and now up to his ears . . . all the work on
the entire supplementary volume!

Adams was still strong, after all; Adams was still Adams.

Nevertheless, Bartholomew was still Bartholomew, too. The king
grew irate. With one hand he extinguished a star, with the other he
tore a tree out by the roots. On Osman Pasha he conferred a defeat in
the nineteenth century. That was for his Turk the Thief, and for the
Armenians to boot. The innocent Adamson was executed—abridged
into oblivion—that's for Adams. Take that, Sir Poluzhan!

All those who had been summarily executed he buried immediately in crosswords (one of his drinking buddies gladly printed them,

then stood him a bottle for a fee). All the crossings arranged themselves elegantly, without the least coercion on his part. The last one
was *carat*, from an article about diamonds ("*carat*, see: *diamond*"). Now
there were some job openings for disadvantaged concepts . . .

On a liberated spot he was going to furnish a picture that hadn't
made the cut: a breaking wheel in fifteenth-century France. It was a
good picture, very detailed: one criminal, already processed, already
hung up on the wheel, his broken arms and legs dangling from it (that
was Adams); another one, spread-eagled on a scaffold, is being blud-
geoned by the executioner (that was the Turk: he could still beg for
mercy, and Bartholomew could still pardon him). But that wasn't all.
He got rid of a picture of some kind of centrifuge, and in its place he set
up a gallows so he could hang Adams, as well. The picture of the hanging man could serve as an illustration for a lesson on extreme disciplin-
ary measures. And as his blood cooled and slowed down, the king didn't
even notice how he had suddenly adopted a more charitable frame of
mind, carrying out more merciful acts—how he himself had begun to
draw. He drew an invalid in the entry for INVALID, and it seemed
that without any obligation he had drawn another unfortunate victim
for the article on LEPROSY. On the chest of the invalid hung military
honors and medals, and on the leper he had drawn—a heart. Both of
them had the faces of good people. One had a crutch, the other a staff.
They got by. They lived. They limped onward.

Bartholomew got carried away, lost in his pastime. Who could
have known what joy . . .

Who could have known what joy it was, this supplementary volume! What fun. It was a cornucopia of shortcomings and oversights.
The entire one hundred volumes of experience fit within its pages. All
the provincial narrow-mindedness of our notion of the world. All the
failures, all the victims of encyclopedic injustice, all the latest upstarts—
from *A* to *Z*. What a motley, absurd throng! The ARC LIGHT ("Ya-
blochkov's Candle"), which helped earn Paris the name of "City of
Light," had been omitted before, as well as the absolutely innocent
ÅLAND ISLANDS. Who had left them out of the first volume? Now,
however, for moral compensation, Bartholomew even bestowed a map
on them, an honor that even mighty archipelagos had not received.
Here was someone else who would see his luck turn at the very end of

the supplementary volume—JOSEF ZUBATY, Czech philologist. Bartholomew pushed out some newly hatched minister (he should have known his days were numbered). "Don't be timid, Zubaty," he said, nudging the philologist gently toward the volume. "Climb aboard."

Bartholomew was now completely absorbed in his work. The choices became ever easier and more mechanical; he replaced a gulf with a mountain peak, an exploit with an honor, a wrench with a cathedral— the index cards flashed through his hands like those of a cardsharp. He was never once tempted to hold the trump card behind his back. And all of this for the sake of harmony and justice, and all of it to the detriment of chaos and evil.

That was just the beginning—the main battle still lay ahead. There, between *A* and *Z*, was his favorite letter. There, he and the enemy were going to clash . . . *Ta-da-da tum-ta-da!* Bartholomew hummed a victory march, savoring the triumph to come and rubbing his hands together. This was not the first year that Bartholomew had cherished this hope. In England it wouldn't have happened. Here, among the frogs' legs, why not? A supplementary volume, this crude appendage, but of the *whole* world, gave Bartholomew a freedom not available in the regular volumes, orderly and predictable. Bartholomew had prepared himself. Bartholomew was ready. The bookshelves were finished, the cannons were loaded, the trumpet was about to sound. He merely had to light the fuse.

Bartholomew reached out for the trump card, the sacred folder . . . Suddenly, instead of the ace he was counting on, he pulled something else out of the deck—a fresh joker. Someone in a red leotard, a regular jester. Illustrating the article on ARLEQUIN.

He examined it. Something was not quite right. Instead of a cap with bells, it had horns; instead of pointed elfin shoes, there were little hooves. "Ugh!" he exclaimed. What a blunder! He had pulled out the wrong card, *D* instead of *A*. Or maybe even *S*? But who believes in him anymore, anyway, dressed up in that red leotard? Now he wears a three-piece suit . . . Adams!

"Ugh!" said Bartholomew again, starting to get worked up. "The devil's on the loose!"

He looked up. Outside it was dark, and the building was suspiciously quiet. Was he burning the midnight oil again? His watch had stopped.

"I wonder what time it is?" Bartholomew thought, alarmed, and straight-away his royal cares beset him again. They thronged around, grimaced and pulled faces, winked at him and nudged him, then scattered, like a deck made up entirely of jokers. Bartholomew spasmodically stuffed the one in the red leotard back under S and started to hurry, shuffling things in his hands, juggling his umbrella and his galoshes, and headed downstairs. The glass elevator was stuck between floors, and it shed the only light there was on the dark stairwell.

"You're the last one here," the doorkeeper mumbled with kindly disapproval, sweeping Bartholomew out together with the sawdust from the lobby. "Telegram for you. Have a good holiday!"

"What kind of telegram? What holiday?"

"Christmas, of course."

"Christmas!?"

BARTIE HURT. HOME FOR CHRISTMAS. CALL SURGEON.

"For Christ's sake!" A sluggish wave of cold washed over Bartho-lomew. "When?"

"Tomorrow."

"What kind of nonsense is this, you dunderhead?" Bartholomew exploded. "How is that possible—tomorrow?"

"It just is," the doorkeeper said indignantly. "Tomorrow is Christmas."

"I'm talking about the telegram!"

"Today, of course."

"Yes, yes, the telegram came today, but when are they arriving?"

Bartholomew turned around and left with a dismissive wave of the hand.

Bartholomew was, of course, a great military commander. But, what with the disarray on the front lines . . .

For some reason we don't allow great people to give in to weakness or fall into despair. Yet that's their right, too. In depriving them of this most paltry and basic of rights, we don't notice that we are also depriv-ing them of sensibility and humanity; and we are the ones to suffer the consequences. We should assume that the great ones of the world expe-rience both great despair and boundless weakness. For where is the guarantee of victory, if not at the bottom of the abyss? We assume that Napoleon lost a single battle because he happened to have a cold. We cannot even begin to imagine *how* he could have contracted the cold, however.

Fear for little Bartie threw a pall over everything. How could such a heap of misfortune land upon the poor king all at once? This king, who raised mountains, swept away islands, and scattered stars, was, after all, just an unlucky son and an unlucky father, no greater than us. The despair that gripped King Bartholomew defied the ordinary meaning of the term—it was infinite. Wet snow mixed with rain lashed his face, and his whole body was racked with a vile, hungry, feverish shivering. Everything in his head became a jumble: micro and macro. Bartie—the Christmas tree; the Thief—Adams; the surgeon—a wheelchair; the devil—the non-devil . . .

How had he so miscalculated? He thought that he would have time for everything tomorrow, and suddenly today morphed into yesterday. That was all he needed . . .

He had no Christmas tree, no wheelchair, and, worst of all, no surgeon. And what was wrong with little Bartie? Poor Bartholomew, horrified, pictured the Duchess rushing home, carrying a bleeding child in her arms. What could it be? His hand? His leg? His eye, God forbid? His ear? The thought of the ear comforted the unhappy king somewhat: without an ear one could still live. Forceps! It suddenly dawned on Bartholomew. But of course—Forceps! How could he have forgotten? Forceps, the brilliant Forceps, famous throughout the world for sewing back torn-off fingers, detached hands, feet, not to mention ears . . .

He dashed over to a pay phone. Forceps was at home, and he was happy as always to hear from Bartholomew. Bartholomew had to come by this instant! Ears, fingers—that was all nonsense, easy as pie. Put it in a cellophane bag and stuff it in the freezer. Tomorrow we'll sew everything back on . . . Scary to *you*, but to us doctors it's not at all scary. What's scary is taking a knife out of someone's heart, if the man is still alive; but if he's already a corpse, no, that's not scary anymore . . .

"A knife? A heart? What are you talking about!" Bartholomew was horror-struck once more and broke out in a cold sweat.

"Remember how we sailed on *The King of Something*? I was just a humble ship's doctor, can you believe it? Relax, everything will be A-okay! Remember how you and I cleaned out the whole ship's pharmacy? And by the end of the journey I was treating everything with kerosene. And we didn't lose a single crew member, nobody got seriously ill. They were all in the pink of health when they went ashore. True, they were inedible . . . Why? Because they all stank of kerosene!"

Forceps roared with laughter. "Get over here this instant! What do you mean, your mother, what are you going on about? A fracture? We'll put *her* on her feet, too. Tomorrow we'll do it . . . Wheelchair? What do you mean, a wheelchair? I've got thousands of them, they're all yours, take as many as you want! What, do you think I'd begrudge someone that kind of crap? Listen, I never thought you were such a fusspot. You'll get your Christmas tree. From where? I'll cut it down on my grounds here. Just settle down—it's my land, I can do whatever I want with it."

Forceps was completely drunk. Bartholomew was trying to wrest away the ax, which Forceps kept aiming at his leg. "Listen, why did you ever marry?" Forceps said, brandishing the ax. "To save you," Bartholomew said, still not managing to liberate the ax. "I wasn't ever really in love, was I?" "Yes, you were." "How lucky I am that I never married, and especially not for love . . ." And thus, while aiming at Bartholomew's leg, with one stroke, professionally, at one fell swoop, Forceps removed a splendid fir tree from the grounds in front of his splendid house built in the Elizabethan style—a little island of Great Britain in the land of frogs' legs. "My home is my castle," he announced to his valet, who wore a slight frown underneath his impenetrable mask of equanimity. "I can burn it down, if I want to. See if I can't. Show His Majesty to the telephone so he can call his residence."

And—oh, joy!—the widowed Queen Mother sounded very pleased about everything: Maggie was back! You can't imagine how wonderful our Maggie is! She washed and set my hair. Charming! . . . No, my voice is fine, it's just inconvenient for me to talk . . . No, they haven't returned. Were they supposed to? I assure you, it's only Maggie . . . It's just inconvenient to talk with a mirror in my hand. No, no telegram, and no one has arrived. Are we having more guests for Christmas, then? Splendid! Come home as soon as you can, you'll never recognize me! Do you want to speak to Maggie?

The situation with Maggie was a bit unclear; or, rather, almost clear. She had found out that the Duchess wouldn't be home for Christmas. The Duchess couldn't bear her, and Bartholomew couldn't understand why. She was by far the loveliest of all the prince's favorites. The Queen Mother adored her, however; and Bartholomew was of one mind with his mother. The Duchess couldn't understand what they all saw in her. Bartholomew, in his turn, couldn't understand something either: What did Maggie see in his son? Such rare disinterestedness! She came just at the right moment, as always; she knew just what to do, as always; as always, she rescued them. Sweet Maggie, Bartholomew thought fondly. But were she and that rascal up to some other kind of monkey business, Bartholomew wondered all of a sudden. No, she's not that type . . .

Bartholomew and Maggie didn't speak over the phone. He left the number of Forceps, just in case, and calmly (only bad news travels fast; and the Duchess was still on the way) proceeded from the telephone to the dining room, where Forceps had concocted a most improbable pick-me-up for the king—the *Limb Resection of the Day*.

The next morning, the ground was covered with frost, and the air was filled with light flurries of snow—Christmas weather. Forceps, upon whom the king had conferred the title of Admiral, pushed Bartholomew in a splendid state-of-the-art wheelchair, its spokes glittering expensively and its multitude of nickel-plated parts, the purposes of which were not immediately clear, gleaming. Across his lap the king clutched yesterday's Christmas tree and the surgeon's bag, with its heavy instruments, some of metal, some of glass, that clattered and clinked. Clean-shaven, with the order of the Legion of Honor in his buttonhole, Admiral Forceps followed on the footboard. Excited subjects the age of children chased after them, hooting and tossing confetti. The policeman on the corner gave a salute.

And so, with a surgeon's bag and a Christmas tree in his lap like his orb and scepter, and a groom with the rank of admiral on the footboard, King Bartholomew rolled into the narrow courtyard of his own residence. Leaving the king's equipage by the elevator door, supporting each other and leaning now on the Christmas tree, now on the surgeon's bag, they made their way upstairs. But the key wouldn't fit into the keyhole.

It was from a completely different lock—this was a French one, but the key was, of course, from an English one. It was possible the key was even from another door altogether—perhaps from Bartholomew's study. He had no other key. And Forceps never brought any keys with him, as he had a steward for that. No one answered when they rang the bell. Nor did anyone respond to their knock.

A wave of anxiety, accompanied by the aftertaste of yesterday's "recipe," gripped the king. He went downstairs again to call on the telephone, but no one picked up, and then he discovered that the wheelchair was no longer by the elevator. Bartholomew trudged back upstairs in despair. On the landing there was no Forceps, and there was no Christmas tree leaning against the door. Bartholomew clawed at the door piteously; from the other side he heard only the mewing of Basil the Dark.

The king started banging on the door and shouting at the top of his lungs: "Hey, is anybody there?!" To his great relief he heard, muffled by distance but recognizable at an instant, the cry of the Queen Mother— either "Bartels, my little king!" or "Where the hell have you been?"

"Why didn't you answer the phone, Mother?" cried Bartholomew, pressing himself against the door.

"Why didn't you call?" his mother answered.

"I left my keys at home!" Bartholomew shouted.

"I don't know where your son has gone," his mother answered.

"And where is your Maggie?"

"Madeleine couldn't come today, her grandsons are visiting her!"

"Did a telegram arrive?"

"Someone brought over some sort of bundle!"

"With what? What's inside?"

"Let me look for your keys . . . I'm going to find your keys, I said!"

"Just don't go crawling around the apartment again!" Bartholomew yelled.

"Your Asian brought it over!"

"What did that scoundrel steal this time?"

"What happened?" his mother yelled. "What did he hurt?"

"In the name of God, don't get out of bed!"

"Is he alive?"

"How will you give them to me? I'm on the other side!"

•

"I've been looking everywhere for you!" Forceps grumbled at him, yanking him away from the door. "Stop shouting. Nothing's the matter, I just commandeered a truck."

From the window on the landing, Bartholomew saw the long metal arm of a truck crane rising into the air. A worker was seated in the winch and aiming straight for the balcony of Bartholomew's apartment.

"You didn't happen to see the wheelchair downstairs, did you?" Bartholomew asked on the off chance.

"Nope. Someone swiped it. Never mind, I'll get you another one. But where's my Christmas tree?"

"That's gone, too," Bartholomew said.

"My, my, you've got your crown on backward, Your Majesty!" Forceps laughed out loud, unfastened his surgeon's bag, and took a swig from it. "That's why I never let this thing out of my hands." With these words he spread a sterile surgeon's napkin out on the floor in front of the door and took out some tweezers, a lancet, a surgeon's handsaw, and a pair of tongs, all wrapped up in an improbable amount of cotton gauze. After he had arranged all of this on the napkin, he took his wallet out of his pocket and rummaged through it until he found what he needed. He tapped lightly all around the lock, bending his ear to it as if to a patient's chest, and inserted a coin into the opening. Then, with a deft movement of the lancet, he removed a superfluous object from the lock like a tumor. Next, he turned the coin, and *voilà!*—the lock clicked obediently and the door flew open.

A frosty draft rushed through the corridor of the apartment, and a triumphant man in a hard hat strode toward them. They were like two mining brigades who had been hollowing out a tunnel from opposite ends and had finally reached the middle. They met in the heart of the apartment, mutually satisfied with their respective efforts and their precision, like people who had been working at a single task but had never seen each other face-to-face.

"It's all right," the Brigadier reported to Forceps. "I had to remove the window frame. Now I'll open your door."

"Please do," Forceps said.

And the Brigadier made his way to the door, an expression of indignation slowly suffusing his face, with which he greeted the Duchess and little Bartie in her arms when he opened it.

It was the foot, after all. Thank God. The little one's leg had been wrapped in scarves and stuffed into a hat with earflaps, and the strings were tied up in a bow at the top, as though his leg were on upside down . . .

"Who are you? What are you doing here?" Her penetrating, silvery voice rang out, instantly recognizable even after her long absence.

"Where's the ear?" Forceps said, getting right down to work.

"Forceps, my dear!" the Duchess cooed, her tone shifting abruptly. "I'm so glad you're here . . . Ear? What ear!" she squealed.

"A plain old ear, the one in the bag."

We'll break off here for a moment. Take a breath. Fast forward a few happy scenes . . .

The arm of the Brigadier's crane got jammed and remained there, sticking up outside the window of Bartholomew's residence like an enormous Christmas tree ornament, delighting little Bartie, the Youngest of Them All, with its siren-red fire-engine color. After becoming acquainted with Forceps's pharmacy, the Brigadier was refitting the window frame with ever-increasing ardor, but also taking his time about it.

Forceps, having finally figured out which was his patient's head and which was his foot, arranged his instruments (including the saw) again, just like he had in front of the door, and with great difficulty extricated the limb in question from its hat, scarves, gauze, and splint ("Who was the quack who made this mess?"). He took the sweet, slightly swollen, somewhat dirty and smudged little foot into his large, scalding-red paws and, tenderly, as though stroking and warming it, suddenly, with a sharp and terrifying movement, seemed to wrench it off and put it back on again. As a certain Yankee once said, nonetheless quite accurately, Bartie "outstripped his own yelp" and flew up to the ceiling, where he drifted around for a time, spinning about among the lights like a little angel. The Duchess fell into a dead faint, and when she came to, she saw that her little fellow had landed and was perfectly healthy again. Forceps, grunting and using some colorful language, was trying to bind the splint back onto the foot—to no avail.

"The door is wide open," said Bartholomew the Younger, leading in a very pretty girl, whom Bartholomew had lost hopes of ever seeing again.

"Maggie!" the Queen Mother cried out in rapture. "I am so glad to see you, my dear! Fix me up again, please. You see, it's started to come undone."

And while the lovely Maggie whipped up her hair into something incredible, something akin to an eighteenth-century tower; while the older son gave an account of himself to his mother (to his father's relief, he didn't reek of anything today—there was only a faint whiff of beer); while Forceps was putting away his instruments in his bag, and taking out some vials, Bartholomew finally turned his attention to a large and dirty bundle, and it seemed to him that he had seen it somewhere before . . . But of course! Those tatters were his fur coat! The king started to undo the bundle with great curiosity. What was all this?

When King Bartholomew entered the common hall in this fur, irrepressible good cheer settled over his entire residence, and it will not disappear for the rest of our narrative, at least not until the end of Christmas; and we don't know what will come after it, because Christmas is TODAY.

Believe it or not, the coat was whole and in one piece again! It was reconstructed like a chessboard, but in a much more intricate manner. The remaining scraps of wolf skin were placed side by side with the fiery-red fur of an as yet unidentified animal—perhaps it was a hare; or was it a cat? In any case, the coat was all in one piece, but it looked very agitated, like a frenzied ball of madly fighting cats and dogs had just rolled into the room—and this was King Bartholomew in his fur coat. Or was it the poor hare perishing in the jaws of a wolf? . . . But it was most likely a cat, for Basil the Dark arched his back and his fur stood on end. Then he sidled off to the radiator, where the Brigadier was warming himself, his hard hat askew. And perhaps it wasn't the coat at all, but Bartholomew himself whom the staid cat had shunned, upon witnessing the loss of his royal dignity. Wearing the fur, having donned the Brigadier's orange hard hat, and grabbing the Queen Mother's bell for summoning the servants, Bartholomew pranced about the rooms like his own court jester, to the general delight and satisfaction of all present . . .

"The door is wide open," said the court Thief, who had long been standing in the doorway and watching Bartholomew's dance, holding a luxuriant Christmas tree in his hand. "So you like the fur, do you?" he said with unconcealed pride.

"Welcome! Come in, come in, dear Samwel!" the king said, inviting

him to partake in the general merriment; but the Turk was more serious than he had ever seen him before.

"May I speak to you for a moment, Your Highness?" he said, beck-
oning him out into the hallway. There, in the corridor, gleaming with
all its newfangled parts and gadgets, stood the wheelchair that had
gone missing in the morning. "It's the latest model!" the Turk boasted.
"It's beyond your wildest dreams. American-made. It cost no less than
several thousand dollars. Accept it from me as payment for what I owe
you, and also as a sign of respect for your honored mother."

Bartholomew was dumbfounded and could only stare at the wheelchair, and then at Samwel holding the Christmas tree, and then at
everything in reverse: the Christmas tree, Samwel, the wheelchair; the
wheelchair, Samwel, the Christmas tree. "All right," he said when he
was finally able to speak again. "We're not going to bargain anymore.
We're quits. Only tell me one thing—why didn't you admit that you
had robbed me?"

A profound sadness, equal to Bartholomew's injustice, filled the
Turk's gaze: it was starting all over again . . .

"But how could I admit it to you, when you might not keep your
word?"

"So you still can't say it?"

"No, I still can't." The Thief sighed a doleful sigh.

"But we're here face-to-face, just the two of us. We're already
even!" It suddenly dawned on Bartholomew. "So it's not proof of anything at all. Come on, what do you have to lose? Please . . . Jesus, Mary,
and Joseph, I beg you! For Christmas' sake."

"Face-to-face, you're right about that . . . Oh, you, whose name I
dare not speak aloud, give me strength!" The Turk's body was racked
with convulsions—still he couldn't.

"Fine. God be with you. You're free," said Bartholomew.

"Really?" the Thief said, brightening.

"Really," Bartholomew assured him.

"For always?" He still couldn't quite believe the one he had mis-
trusted for so long.

"Of course."

The Thief dropped down on his knees and kissed Bartholomew's
hand. Bartholomew leaned down to raise him up, saying: come now,

come now . . . And when he was leaning over him, the Thief whispered rapidly and hotly in his ear. "Yes, it was me, I stole from you, I stole from you that time I stole from you when I stole from you that time . . . But how could I not steal, when you yourself showed me where!" He suddenly grew furious and jumped up off his knees. "You did it! You!" And then they embraced and kissed and sobbed on one another's shoulders, finally absolutely quits, so it could all be left behind.

"Come in, let's celebrate!" the happy Bartholomew urged his newly restored brother, and the Turk was about to refuse, but had already agreed, when suddenly—the Christmas tree . . . Samwel, the wheelchair, Samwel, the wheelchair, the Christmas tree . . . "I say," Bartholomew ventured, taking a step back, "did you happen to . . . borrow . . . that Christmas tree and the wheelchair from me?"

"Me? No way!" The Thief laughed. "You're barking up the wrong tree. No way. My third cousin brought me the tree, he runs a Christmas tree stand. And the wheelchair . . . the wheelchair . . . Well, better not ask what that cost me! Someone on the street just offered me a hundred francs for it." The Thief, or, rather, now no longer the Thief but the Turk, though not even the Turk but the Samwel who was dear to Bartholomew's heart, was on the verge of crying from the insult of unjust suspicion, and might have turned around to leave again altogether in light of this injury done to him, and so Bartholomew found it necessary to apologize to him.

And now the lights of the Christmas tree were burning—Forceps had managed with great dexterity to untie it and free it from its wrappings, and Bartie the Youngest of Them All was pushing Grandmother in her new wheelchair up and down the hallway, both of them squealing in delight. His foot was as good as new, and the Queen Mother's hair was a sight to behold, and the Crown Prince, who did not reek of anything, sometimes left the room with Maggie, or she followed him out under the haughty gaze of the Duchess, or they both came in together. And from the kitchen wafted the scent of pies that Maggie was baking under the supervision of the Thief and the Brigadier, and the Turk, as usual, had used too many spices . . .

Now they were all together, around the pies and around the Christmas tree, and Bartholomew was wondering how it was possible that there could be so much happiness at one time . . . it even frightened him.

"For your information," announced Bartholomew, famous for his encyclopedic knowledge, "according to the Vietnamese calendar, this is the Year of the Cat!"

Everyone then tried to catch Basil the Dark to install him in the place of honor. The Duchess stroked the cat, and Forceps stroked the cat, and Bartie the Youngest of Them All stroked the cat, and Bartholomew the Younger stroked the cat, and Maggie stroked the cat, and the Queen Mother stroked the cat. Bartholomew the King had no place to stick his hand in, since everyone was stroking the cat. Forceps stroked the cat, thinking he was stroking the Duchess's hand, not knowing that he was in fact stroking the hand of the Queen Mother, who thought that her dear son Bartholomew was stroking her hand, and Bartholomew the Younger stroked the cat, thinking that he was stroking Maggie's hand, and in fact stroked Forceps's large paw, and the cat had long before run off, and Maggie . . . Where was Maggie? Bartholomew suddenly felt that someone was gently ruffling his hair, but it wasn't his mother, and certainly not the Duchess . . . Bartholomew smiled happily, and then a new wave of irrevocability and despair swept over him, and he quietly slipped out from under the caresses, as though he had forgotten something, as though he had to go to his study, and there to lock it from the inside.

He sat in his study, sobbing softly: "Why, Lord?"

The Youngest, the Younger, his mother, the Duchess, Forceps, the Thief, Maggie . . . You're getting old, Bartholomew. Your shoulders are sagging under the burden of authority. You're tired. You're just tired, Bartholomew. It happens to everyone . . . Who will carry this weight after you? Whose right hand will bear this orb?

Bartholomew threw a glance at it, and could not take it all in. It was infinite and eternal, from A to Z . . .

When the world had already been created, and the firmament was in place, and the watery depths, and the sky, and the stars, and the grass had been sown, and the trees had been planted, and the fish had been let loose into the sea, and the beasts were in the woods, and the birds in the heavens, and the beetles and the spiders were in the leaves and grasses—not to mention the viper and the mosquito and the cockroach—when man was already walking upon the Earth, when he had lived through his golden childhood, and his bronze youth, and his iron maturity . . . when he had already carved and painted and sung and written everything he could . . . when he had plowed and battled, raised up heroes and thrown down tyrants . . . when this world, finally, was finished, up to today, and no other day . . . when, orderly as grenadiers, chest-to-chest, shoulder-to-shoulder, their leather creaking, glinting with fresh gold, all the volumes of the Encyclopedia arranged themselves on the shelves in the only possible order—from A to Z—no one but Bartholomew would be inspecting the parade.

Like a generalissimo, like a peasant, like the Creator; and if not the Creator, then at least hand in hand with him. They would walk together, only the two of them able to understand each other. They walk solemnly, looking about them with a lordly gaze: what a House! Here they're cleaning up the wood chips, there they're fortifying a plank. Here they allow a forgotten fly to take flight, there they sow some neglected grass . . . Bartholomew is proud to be on such good terms with the Creator and with Creation: what elegance, what might! These were his feelings about the culmination of the volumes. The Creator chuckles to Himself: ah, humans. How did they manage to jumble it all up, to throw it all into one heap: a flower, a soldier, a pebble, a rare tropical disease, a ballerina, a jackal, a locknut? Persephone, Pheasant, Pi, Portugal . . . What a monument to vanity is the Encyclopedia! What practical man would not laugh, beholding this greedy, unruly pile that goes by the name of human knowledge? For the Creator is, besides everything else, a pragmatist.

Bartholomew, although he is only a king, is also a practical man. Earthbound.

The cat, the lock, the thief, the truck crane, the pie, the wheelchair, the helmet, the scalpel, the foot, the hairdo, the ear in the bag, the ax, the bell, the surgeon, the fur, the wolf, the Christmas tree, the gauze, the surgeon's bag, the honey barrel . . . What does it all resemble?

Bartholomew recalled the Creator's fatherly indulgence, when he walked with him hand in hand before the Encyclopedic Guard's Regiment, each man at the ready. How He didn't call him to order, didn't pester him or take him to task. Bartholomew smiled to himself, and understood something he had understood many times before.

Bartholomew was quite an inventor. He brought out a secret box in which he preserved—not so much from others as from himself—an assortment of memorabilia. Out of it he took two tiny tricorne hats—souvenirs from the island of St. Helena. One of them he put on his left index finger, the other on his right (Paul to the right, Napoleon to the left). Then he began acting out his own alternative history.

The audience has transpired!

In this version of history, Russian conspirators did not assassinate their underrated emperor, Paul I, the underrated emperor did not enter an alliance with Napoleon. As a result, the French didn't go to war with the Russians, the Russians didn't burn down Moscow but captured India instead. His favorite one-eyed Nelson did not perish but dealt a fatal blow to the one-eyed Kutuzov, thus recouping India for Britain. Ah, sweet dreams!

As a professional encyclopedist he could not reverse the course of history, as Russians were in the habit of doing, trying to overtake it. One thing irritated him to no end: the popular opinion that the *Britannica* had been written following a precedent set by the French, although he admired both Diderot and d'Alembert.

No, "to write only children's books." Where did that originate?

The idea of an encyclopedia for children beckoned him. There he would have greater leeway. He would have quite a bit to throw overboard, and also to include. Perhaps he would even be able to promote a concept for an alternative history game that would make it easier to master a knowledge of real history. And whoever claimed that history was a science, that it reflected any semblance of reality, when every epoch, every regime rewrites it to suit its own tastes and interests?

His dreams took him far away. Paris, however—here it was, its gray roofs spread out before him. The rain. But it was a far cry from London rain.

And Bartholomew was far away, too. He was still upstairs in his imaginary castle. "Daddy, Daddy!" he seemed to hear the distant voices of children calling him.

He sighed and replaced the tiny tricorne hats where they belonged.

Bartholomew was no longer angry, but he had no strength to go downstairs and join the family.

He put a clean sheet of paper in front of him.

I wonder if there is a language in which the word "homeland" begins with an *A*, he thought. That was not the case in any of the languages he knew; but in all those languages, the letter *A* was the first letter of the alphabet. What does a book begin with?

Why, with a cover, of course!

Look at Bartholomew. He sits here, laughing and drawing. An illumination of the letter *A*. The future *Britannica* for children.

Can you guess from each picture what language it is?

In the middle of the page is a large *A*, standing like a pyramid on thick, sturdy limbs.

In the upper-left corner of the page an aerostat floats near an automobile. Directly under them an Arab wearing a Bedouin's garments is kneeling down and aiming a rifle, having tied up his donkey to one of the traceries, on a branch of which an eagle has perched. The Arab is aiming at an antelope, which is bounding away from him in fright to the other side of the *A*. On top of the letter a hoopoe is nesting. A jester leans with his elbow on the left side of the letter, a bee clinging to one point of his fool's cap like a bell. Halberds, battle axes, lances, and pikes—a whole arsenal—rest against the right side of the letter. In the enclosed triangle of the *A*, a spider has spun its web. The antelope is afraid of the Bedouin and runs away, but next to him are an ostrich and a lamb, neither of which looks at all fearful. The jester looks through the letter at the mountain of weapons and seems to be smiling, as if he's thinking: What is all this junk? . . . And at the foot of the letter is an anchor, an onion, a horseshoe . . .

There seems to be some disequilibrium here . . .

Someone was scratching and breathing behind the door. Was it Maggie? Bartholomew pressed his ear to the door: no one.

He opened it, trying not to jangle the lock . . . and into the room slipped a white cat.

Bartholomew sighed with relief and disappointment. He glanced at the sheet of paper: not bad. Not bad at all.

Something else was needed to balance out the eagle on the left side, though.

On the right side, from the same kind of branch, Bartholomew hung a lampshade. The lampshade shone down on an

AARDVARK

PART III

EMERGENCY CALL

(Doomsday)

> The end of the sentence must be marked by a period.
> —A rule of punctuation

Urbino woke up and realized that it was already *today*. He looked at the button on the wall with equanimity.

The crudeness with which it had been plastered into the wall was equaled only by the precision of the button itself. White, with a slight tinge of yellow, like a cue ball. He traced its outlines gently with his finger but didn't press it. Instead, he examined his hand: nothing occurred to him but its likeness to an autumn leaf. Is not banality the ultimate form of exactitude?

"Lord, have mercy," he muttered mechanically. The Lord pardoned Urbino forthwith: He reminded him that he had to stand up on his left foot and at least try to make the bed ("to square off against the day"—as a monk he once chanced to meet had taught him). Looks like I didn't come across the monk just by chance, Urbino thought blandly. Why should I square off against the day, if *today* has already arrived? He glanced again at the button. It was still there. Fate has converged on me at an unexpected point. This was no longer even a thought, just words. He looked over at his prison window. A little cloud, just like the one in the photograph of the sky above Troy, floated within the frame. Now that's a sign of senility, to see a semblance in every resemblance, thought Urbino, grinning with the living half of his face.

Today that journalist was supposed to come back with the interview transcript. Tomorrow, or today?

Maybe the button is for calling *him*? Urbino grinned again at the vestiges of his creative imagination. What had he not imagined during these past two days of expectation—of fear, in other words! Not to mention the fact that this pimply-faced young man was in fact the devil who had tempted him in his own youth with the photograph from the future.

Fine, say it is the ravings of a panic-stricken old man, but those two boors in uniform who had moved aside first him, then the bed, and then pried open the wall, pulling out its veins and tinkering with a little box . . . and after that had buried all their secrets under a layer of plaster so that only the button remained . . . One thing was certain: they knew what they were doing. They had done this before. They made him sign a paper saying the task had been carried out, and there were no complaints. What complaints could there be, if they hadn't allowed him to open his mouth?

What had he put his name to, and what had he agreed to do? To receive that journalist? Well, then, there's no point in wondering about it now, is there?

Yet again he grinned at the weak surges of his former imagination. To think that an insomniac like himself could even suspect that pressing a button might cause the end of the world, and that he was the one who had been chosen by someone (that very devil) to bear the responsibility and blame.

For some reason he recalled a fat Asian boy on a train who was completely baffled by the toilet in the WC. "Do you know how to make it flush?" "Press the button." A kind smile still played across his face when he remembered this incident. "Just don't be alarmed," he had told the boy. The button looked exactly the same. A terrifying noise accompanied the flush.

They have rules, I have habits. My habits are less aggressive than their rules. I simply exist, and I disturb no one. I am satisfied with the precepts that guide and instruct my experience of my own imperfection, my own sinfulness. They are satisfied with the rules, so they can always be right and never doubt anything, even their own faith. It's easier to go to church than it is to believe. It's easier to submit and obey than it is to discover and follow precepts. I could afford to move into a more comfortable apartment now, but my little shoebox suits me. Here I don't have to pick up after myself, I can sleep late and smoke. No one else would ever choose to live here, anyway, because of the absence of amenities and the noise from the elevator. In what way did I threaten their social contract that they condemned me to this button?

Why did they install the button in *his* room, if *they* are the ones who need to call him?

Let's assume it's for an emergency call to the proprietor . . . although Urbino is already retired and works only on Sundays. Just so they would furnish him with this little hole in the wall . . . On the other hand, the proprietor had been flattered that his elevator operator was descended from nobility. That means it's a bell.

But what if it's simply a light switch, so he can turn the light on and off without getting out of bed? Who would go to the trouble? Granted, the proprietor became very obliging after the announcement of the prize. People are strange, there are no two ways about it.

If it's only a light switch, I'll just give it a try . . . But his hand didn't dare.

How is the installation of the button connected to the visit from the journalist?

However, if it's not the end of the world, and not a light switch, might it not be the end of himself? A rather bizarre means of suicide proffered to him . . . But by whom?

A blue sky was peeping out today. Like a smile.

And the Angels fly under the heavens / A grim purpose still reigns below / Where are you? You must be the judge—/ Until lightning strikes the brain blind / Until that moment, not a day without a line . . . / Ugh, what a graphomaniac!

And what if pushing it brings not the end but a beginning? A simple way to exit this little coffin?

One must shave and put on a clean shirt before the end. He still had a shirt, yellowed and dried, like an envelope. The razor? The razor had always been especially dear to him, even before he started shaving, as a memento of his father. His first Gillette, with the nickel plating rubbed off and the bronze showing through—you could actually whistle with it.

He hadn't been able to find it since yesterday. Who stole it? No doubt it was those workmen who nicked it. They have a soft spot for tools and instruments . . . Or was it the journalist?

What would he need it for? A souvenir? Who does he think I am? A Joyce? That puffed-up, unreadable Irishman irritated Urbino no end. That's right! Joyce stole the razor. The last thing that remained to him . . . Why did he have to take the last one? Back in the day, thieves were much kinder. They took only money, and then only because he hadn't hidden it very well. Urbino remembered with particular warmth his personal court Thief. What is he up to these days? A rich man by now, I'm sure.

Joyce . . . The only thing he didn't steal from me was my last novel—*Disappearing Objects*—and that only because it wasn't written yet. The novel floated up to the surface of Urbino's consciousness, as monumental as the *Titanic* (if only *that* had stayed afloat).

. . . Of course, the old man had known about the *seventh* room since childhood. His mother the Duchess . . . so he would fall asleep. The tighter he squeezed his eyes shut, the more awake he felt. When the colorful flies stopped flitting about under the expanding domes of his eyelids, a black space opened up. He tried to give it a rectangular shape, and the black space narrowed and turned into a corridor that he had to run down as fast as he could, as though he were being chased. Just don't turn around! He squeezed himself through this tightness, he seemed to glimpse a door, or at least a window, a small ventilating pane . . . He found himself in the next empty space, but that wasn't a room, either. He finally fell asleep when he was three or four levels down.

Remembering his childhood intrepidity, the old man fingered the button warily. Today he must get enough sleep: it's already tomorrow!

Tomorrow *that* one would come again. His kind is never late. They're always right on time.

"Well, come on, then. Push!" he commanded his finger. His finger wouldn't hear of it. The old man, by the way, approved. He smiled. "You have to hurry up and sleep . . ." The words made him laugh, then made him happy: one could begin a new life with these words—that is to say, a story could begin that way. What if they installed that button just so that I would write it? I'll just push the button, then write a story! That's what I'll call it: "The Button." There's no escaping realism. My whole life I wrote pristinely, just as I saw things. Why was it that not everyone understood me?

I'll just push it. Take the leap, and start writing! And I'll be more than ready when *he* shows up. He thinks I'm not capable of anything anymore . . . He only wants to stuff me into his own conception, into some sort of Proproustian bed . . . Well, all right, Proust I'm not. But I know how to do things he *didn't*. (The old man's imagination was fired up, along with his ambition.) And so the story will be called: "The Procrustean Bed." "Bed" . . . A nasty word.

He tossed and turned on it a bit longer, and removed his finger from the button. Yes, it now definitely reminded him of a cue ball, orblike and ivory yellow. That's right! Let the hero of the story "hurry up and sleep" (that will be the beginning), before the deciding match of a world tournament.

Out of some dormant habit, the old man's words began to form a chain, reaching out toward the page. The page was rectangular, like a table, but suddenly it turned green. The protagonist was dressed in strict accordance with the code. He wore a tuxedo, black, like a fly. He rested his hand on the cue like a cane, focusing his gaze. A single ball lay on the baize cloth. You can't play with one ball . . . And where was his opponent? The ball wasn't a ball at all but a button for calling the referee. Angered, the player reached out to push it to summon the judge . . . and the old man woke up.

"I'm not writing anything like that!" he said in vexation. "I don't have enough flesh on me anymore to describe a game. At one time, perhaps, I knew how, so that that story of the two opponents diverged from the subject of the game itself . . . But what do I remember now? 'Angle in' equals 'angle out'? . . . A stop shot, a sidespin . . . The best safety is to pocket a ball . . . Chalk your cue before the stroke, not after . . . That's not enough! 'Clueless,' as my first teacher, Serge Wolf, said when I missed a shot. I always wrote better than I played, anyway." The lucidity of this conclusion reassured him that he was in his right mind, in his proper place. *In his bed.* But the button, too—that ivory ball—was in its proper place.

My writing was good, but my *ideas* were even better. Take *Disappearing Objects*, for example. I never got past the title . . . There may have been an epigraph, I recall . . . I'm not sure. Can't remember. Perhaps lines from Edgar Poe: "All that we see or seem / Is but a dream within a dream."

Perhaps something from a Japanese (or Chinese?) ancient? It doesn't matter. What matters is, where is my typewriter? It's gone, too. Could the court Thief have taken it and left that unwieldy Underwood in its place? The other one was so compact, so dear to me . . . an Adler. How much writing I was able to get done on that one! It occurred to him that he might have left it behind in America. Maybe he had. In that case he was again wrongfully accusing his Thief. He thought about him again with fondness: all in all, he had loved the same things as his sovereign. How skillfully the Thief had taken advantage of his absent-mindedness! Two rules sufficed for him to be able to trick his simpleton of a master: that "it's not written all over his face," and that "he's not a thief until he's caught." It isn't right to insult an honest man with unjust suspicions, is it?

How could he demand something back that he had given away himself?

Likewise, wasn't he giving his life away to this journalist? The thought set off another bout of panic, and he glanced with renewed horror at the button: he had only to press it and the journalist would enter.

Maybe the button opened up a hole into the invisible room?

No, he wouldn't press it! Let him wait for the elevator, Urbino thought spitefully, imagining the interviewer in the lobby, shuffling his feet and smelling of eau de cologne, and carrying a book in his armpit to be autographed.

Maybe there *is* an invisible room, though? To press, or not? He stroked the ivory surface of the button again with tender caution. It's his call. How could he not see that what attracted him to this game was not the ball, so like a frontal bone, not the green, roulette-table cloth, not the attempts to pocket the ball in the table's scrotum, but choice! Choosing the right stroke. That's what it was.

The dream, however, was not about that.

He was in a motorboat, accompanied by two lanky young naval officers—a captain and a lieutenant. He was seeing them for the first time *in his life*. It seemed that they were seeing him for the first time, too. In any case, the captain seemed to be scrutinizing him. The motorboat was full of other people, too—ordinary middle-aged men and women. They were traveling as a group of extras in the dream, a crowd, like a new shift at a sanatorium or a resort. He and the naval officers were the only ones who were seated; everyone else was standing.

To what did he owe this honor? Was he under arrest? Suddenly it became clear that the captain was a doctor, and that they were taking him somewhere for treatment. The captain asked no questions, however, and Urbino, too, remained silently submissive. Now and then the captain and the lieutenant talked among themselves. The captain even took the lieutenant by the hand, and, mutely and tenderly, kept hold of it, as though they had agreed on something. Just then the motorboat docked at a pier, and the lieutenant hopped out.

"He is so sweet." The captain was speaking to Urbino for the first time.

"Yes, indeed," Urbino was quick to agree.

"I'm always glad to see him."

Urbino grew indignant.

"What about me?"

"No need to worry. Everything you have is *your own*. The toothache will go away by itself."

The *toothache*? Meanwhile, the passengers were leaving, climbing the ladder one by one. Only the two of them were left.

"But you didn't even examine me!"

"Yes I did. I have my own X-ray machine," he explained.

"How much do I owe you?"

"Not a thing. You're here on the recommendation of Galina L., aren't you? You're one of our *own*."

Your own, my own, our own . . . But what does Galina L. have to do with it?

Urbino was baffled. How did they know? Although these days, more than any of the others, he thought of the woman who had moved in parallel to his life, his wives, his children, his passions . . . As though she had been waiting for him all along—but it turned out she had overtaken him and fled past. Who had fled past whom?

The only thing left to do was to ascend the ladder.

"Where do I go now?"

"Take a cab. Or a rickshaw. It's very close. I must go to a reception."

Urbino still hesitated.

"Everything you have is your own and will go away by itself," the captain said again as he climbed out.

It was clear that the conversation was over.

Urbino woke up in dismay, only to see the damned button again. Now it resembled a tooth. A healthy one, it appeared. How could there be something wrong with it? Why do we always want to press and probe a sore tooth? And Urbino tried to fall asleep again, only to dream another more noble but no less queer dream.

His mother the Duchess, and his late wife, a beauty in an Indian sari, were baking a pie together.

"Well, I agree. Let him have his own study there," said the mother-wife in chorus, both smiling radiantly.

He had always suspected there was a little door under the table. A toolshed in the attic, in the corner, under the eaves of the roof. A storage for stray pieces of lumber and castoff children's toys—wasn't that an apt description of prose?

Then, suddenly, it grew bright. The space around him was clean and empty. The light seemed to come out of nowhere. In the middle of the space was a desk and a chair—not a chair, but a stool; and on the desk was the missing typewriter and a stack of paper. This contrived setup exasperated him, like inappropriate concern about an unfinished novel. Urbino glanced about angrily. The whole room was empty except for a large heap in one corner, as though the room's contents had all been carefully swept into it like garbage. It was a veritable scree, the detritus in a rag-and-bone man's attic. What a hodgepodge of items!

Sweaters and jackets, umbrellas and canes, scarves and caps, berets and gloves, pens and notepads, watches and eyeglasses, wallets (empty) and change purses (with coins from various countries), bracelets and amulets, cigarette cases and lighters, knives and penknives, rosaries and chains, charms and signet rings, and several favorite books . . . everything he had ever lost or been robbed of was found here again. He had never realized he was such a hoarder. There was enough there to supply a flea market in a small town. Every object inspired a recollection of loss, and nothing really took him by surprise until he dug to the bottom of this sweet scrapheap and found his father's razor. It was wrapped in a necktie. A necktie, of all things!

He took it apart and blew on it—it made a sad sound like some Eastern musical instrument. Yes, he had heard it in Greece, in a little Armenian restaurant he had gone to with Dika. She was thrilled about some Eastern garb she had bought for a song (and her song was priceless—that was why he had dreamed of her in the sari today). The tie was Dika's last gift to him. Handmade, covered with a design of round spectacles. The round earpieces looked especially dapper . . . He had forgotten it at Dika's in the heat of their last quarrel, just before she perished at the zoo. He had missed it sorely.

But he was unable to go back to pick it up. It was after the funeral, a soft pink spring morning. Children were playing kick the can in the drying, already dusty, vacant lot. They had thrown off their brightly colored jackets, and birds were wheeling above, making a din and racket as though they were rooting for them. The wind was blowing. Wind, and dust, and children, and birds . . . On a fence, someone had written BIRDY in sweeping, bold black letters. A misspelled golf term? In which case it should have been BIRDIE. A "little bird," or "birdlike"? Or "full of birds" (by analogy with "windy": "windy and birdy" . . .)? There was no such word, though. Perhaps it was the nickname of someone's beloved? He had called his beloved Dika . . . But Dika didn't exist anymore, either. All that was left were little rhymes and ditties . . .

Back then I had wanted to write dozens of stories in all possible tenses of the English language!

He felt chilly, as though a draft had crept in. There was no place it could have come from, however—there were no windows in the room. The walls were as smooth as a bald head. He snuggled down into his favorite Icelandic sweater that he had forgotten at one time in a hotel, its windows looking out over a beautiful view of the Strasbourg Cathedral. He put on the signet ring that Dika had given him, and that had gone missing in a pub in some port city. Then he grabbed the necktie and a random book from the heap, and went over to the desk. He sat down.

In the typewriter there was already a piece of paper with a title in capital letters:

DISAPPEARING OBJECTS

It became repugnant to him that for so long—his whole life—he hadn't written it, this novel. Well, there it was over there, piled up in a heap in the corner—write all you want! Just jot down the history of every object, how it was acquired, how it was lost . . . Don't try to arrange anything chronologically. On the contrary, that would be even better—memories out of sequence . . . What, the sun peeped out? Some snow fell? A horse went by? Little bells jangled? When did that happen?

What was important was how one's nostrils expanded from the smell of the horse! Why aren't you writing, you old fool? . . . It's too late now. Too late.

Here Urbino tapped on the thick stack of clean paper, then yanked the page from the mute typewriter. The page grinned with a crease left from years of sitting idly in the typewriter.

> The page grinned in its search for words,
> With the mockery of an epigraph above.
> O youth, where are those hopes
> That the text was so simple you could step inside it?

> "In the beginning was the word." Easy to say—
> But if it were first, where is it now?
> "Frost and sun"—they're good for the health,
> But they teach hard lessons, lest one forget.

Urbino dashed off the poem, then crossed it out. He had only to describe the history of each newly regained object. But which of them would be first? His father's razor? No, too soon. It would be too potent, too intense if it was about his father . . . The sweater, then. He opened the book he had grabbed from the pile. As if to spite him, it was *Robinson Crusoe*, the copy from his childhood. A first edition. He knew only too well which passage he would want to reread: the part where he salvages all the needful items from the sinking ship. It happened that in his life there had been a shipwreck . . . Urbino had spent a good deal of time aboard the ship, if memory served . . . He didn't even want to think about it, much less remember. The charm of Robinson striking it rich didn't appeal to Urbino, as he stared at the pile of belongings that he had acquired so suddenly. From a distance it looked like a scale model of Gaudí's unfinished cathedral.

Urbino glanced at the other corner and saw a tiny mound there, too. He didn't know why, but it aroused in him a sudden horror; but it was easier to overcome this horror than it was to strike the dusty keys. Urbino stood up resolutely and walked over to the murky corner . . .

Two fountain pens were lying there, the kind with a piston, a curious design . . . He had taken them from his father's study. Their inner workings were already outmoded, and they no longer functioned properly. A bottle with spirits . . . Something he had nicked from his aunt for his older brother, who was already taking an interest in alcohol. (His aunt hadn't had much need for it—she used it once a year to light the Christmas cake.) His aunt searched for it high and low, and naughty little Urbino "found" it, the missing bottle, much to everyone's delight. Several old banknotes, interesting now only to a collector: two of them he definitely remembered, because he had filched them from that same older brother. But these other two, later, issues? How loathe Urbino was to remember them! They were from some poor girl who had wanted to help him out when he had lost at gambling. She had given him all she had, all she earned. He promised to repay her, then went out of his way to avoid meeting her again. What a disgrace! Somehow he had managed to forget the incident all this time . . . How he wished he could compensate her now a hundredfold! But even a hundredfold was too paltry; for she had loved him . . . to the very end.

As though on cue, in the same little pile under the banknotes he found a revolver belonging to his uncle, Count Varazi, who had arrived at his estate on furlough from some war or other. Little Urbino had rummaged through his suitcase when no one was home. The suitcase was almost empty: it contained only some suspenders, hairbrushes (his uncle was bald), an epaulette (only one, for some reason), and a rather heavy, rather compact parcel. Wrapped in a clean puttee was the revolver! Urbino had been especially intrigued by the small bronze circles with a little button in the middle. He aimed at his reflection in the mirror, closed his eyes, and pulled the trigger. The revolver didn't fire. He released something, freed the barrel, and began to turn it, listening to the clicking with particular pleasure. The revolver was loaded. Only one chamber in the cylinder was empty. That was the first time in my life that I played Russian roulette, Urbino the old man thought. But back then, the naughty little Urbino couldn't resist boasting about the weapon to his classmates. At that time, too, his guardian angel was present: he didn't shoot anyone. What an ungrateful swine I am, the old

Urbino thought. I came to fear buttons . . . He recalled how terrified Count Varazi was when he discovered the revolver was missing and thought he had mislaid it himself. It caused an even greater commotion than the spirits had. And again the *resourceful* Urbino left the revolver in a place where Uncle Varazi found it *himself*.

Base acts. But that was all he had stolen *himself* throughout his long life. Or was it? Not much to boast about, if he were a thief. The tiny pile outbalanced the big one. Especially the two banknotes from the girl. Suddenly he remembered her eyes—small, shining eyes, dark and velvety, like two pansies looking out at him.

Even now the revolver was in mint condition, as though no time at all had passed. Urbino put the end of it in his mouth and ran his tongue over it. A Russian kiss, he thought with a crooked smile. But pulling the trigger was no easier than pressing the damn button.

Now it seemed easier to press the keys of the typewriter. Urbino strode over to the desk and grabbed a piece of paper from the stack, intending to write at least the title page, though he considered this to be symptomatic of true graphomania, if not impotence. He inserted the clean page into the typewriter; and while he was rotating the platen, the name of the author emerged, then the name of the novel, already furnished with epigraphs. Edgar Poe and the Chinese thinker were there. Both of them. The Poe—well, let it stay. But the Chinese epigraph was about a butterfly in a philosopher's dream. What tripe! Urbino was indignant, and snatched the page out.

He reached for another. Put it in. Twirled the platen.

TABLE OF CONTENTS

Curiosity already outweighed fear. He spun the platen like the cylinder of a revolver.

Object number one. REVOLVER.

Object number two . . .

After that, everything went according to the list, like an inventory of expenditures.

When he came to the Icelandic sweater, he even pinched himself in it, just to make sure.

Your average sweater. Very thick, unaccountably warm. Urbino shivered.

He forgot about the table of contents. When had he found time to compile all of this?

More of the page emerged, with the heading "Favorite Swedish Spectacles."

They were round, like the ones Joyce wore. He had left them on the little foldout table in a train, together with a book by Joyce, which he had fallen asleep trying to read. He had almost missed his station.

The plot of the book was so vast that the table of contents didn't fit onto one page. Urbino reached for the next page.

An absurd page. It had only one line:

Final Object. FATHER'S RAZOR.

He glanced cautiously at the small stack of pages. The top one was already written and was called "Revolver." Urbino's thumb riffled through the stack of pages like a flip-book, then released it with a snap, like shuffling a deck of cards or running a finger over a piano keyboard. All the pages had been filled.

He glanced at the last one, the one titled "Father's Razor."

There was also just one line on it:

"It's in your room, lying in the same place you left it."

He looked up at the heap in the corner—it wasn't there. He looked at the other corner, where he kept the things he was trying to forget—everything was in its place.

He had long known that everything one describes disappears from life exactly as it does from time.

Since that assemblage of lost things has vanished, it means the novel is written, he thought.

Nothing surprised Urbino anymore. That's how it was. Recently, he hadn't been able to see what was right in front of him. "Where's the salt?" He looked for it high and low, and it was there all along, under his very nose.

Where he had looked for it to begin with.

"I'm still not mad," Urbino Vanoski said firmly to himself. "Since I found the razor, it follows that the novel is written. And if the novel is written, the razor is lying in its place at home. The journalist is waiting for me. I can tell him I finished my novel. But to be absolutely certain about this, I must first make sure the razor really is in the place where it belongs."

He tamped down the stack, evened up the edges, thrust it under his arm, and got up to leave.

There was no exit. They were smooth and unbroken, all four walls.

His frantic gaze darted every which way, then caught sight of another button. It was exactly like the one above his bed, but it was too high up for him to reach.

He couldn't reach it when he tried jumping up to it, either. He only fell down helplessly, twisting his ankle and scrabbling to keep hold of the scattering pages of the manuscript. He had always hated this, manuscripts that slipped out of his grasp and scattered their contents. Somehow, all the pages had managed to switch places. He crawled around on his hands and knees and gathered this unruly Medusa of a manuscript, eventually making his way to the desk. The desk was empty except for the typewriter, the necktie, and the revolver. What a still life it made, though!

Urbino plunked the stack back down on the desk.

He felt injured that he hadn't written anything. "Formula of a Crevice" was one of the favorite last stories he hadn't written. This was the moment. The time had come, Urbino thought, inspired. He pressed Shift Lock to type out the title—but the lock didn't work. He had to hold the key down while typing out with his free hand:

FORMULA OF A CRE . . . ICE

The letter V snapped off. Such an unassuming letter, but so necessary when the time came! From neglect . . . Metal fatigue . . . Metal gets weary, just like letters.

Urbino struggled to remember the story. In it, two people had planned to meet, and they both arrived at the designated place but passed by one another in time. A crevice opened up in space, and the streetcar, in which the father of the main character and his lover were riding together, plunged into it.

The streetcar fell into a canal and sank, with all its passengers. The two of them were the only ones who survived. They had found an air bubble in the end of the streetcar that jutted out above the water. The lover lost her mind; but the hero of the story was beholden to the father for his own birth. And the hero now asks himself: Who am I, after all? Oh, that was a story that begged to be written! But the V . . .

The meaning of the letter was contained in its very outline. Urbino left the letter out to write it in later by hand. He heard a slight crack, and two lines began to crawl along the wall, as though tracing out the fugitive V, but lying on its side. Moreover, the crack started at the base of the letter, at the point where it seemed to end. Then the lines diverged slantwise, ever wider apart.

Urbino was alarmed and tried aiming at the button with the revolver. No, I'll never hit it, he thought soberly, leaning back in his chair. But there was no back! It was a stool. I can reach it on the stool!

The revolver or the stool? Now that's a choice. He grinned the merry grin of a gallows bird. He went to his corner of shame to put the revolver back where it belonged. After he had made his choice, however, he stood in the corner for a time, lost in reverie. He smiled. Then, as cautiously as a child, he wrapped the weapon in the necktie and laid it on the stolen banknotes. He sighed, and reached out for his aunt's bottle. He took a gulp. The undiluted spirits ignited inside him, filling his chest with fire and his soul with an impalpable beatitude that seemed to draw ever nearer.

Now he had the strength to pull the stool over, aligning it with the button. He clambered up on it. His hand stretched out toward the button—it was easily within reach. Still, he hesitated. He discovered that in his left hand he was still holding the bottle. Should I take a drink now or after? he wondered, surprised at the lucidity of his thoughts. But *after* might be too late. He smiled a wan smile, swaying on the stool. Or was the stool swaying under him?

His legs went numb—the stool felt more like a part of his body than his own legs did. The lights began to dim, quite unexpectedly starting from the floor, from which something like smoke or mist was rising.

First it covered the stool, and then his shoes disappeared. Urbino couldn't figure out what there was under his feet, what height he had reached. Now he could only hold on to the button . . . But how do you hold a *button*? You can only press it: either that was the way out, or there was none at all.

To drink or to press? I'll do both at the same time. The decision dazzled him.

Holding the bottle to his mouth like the muzzle of a revolver, he touched the button and licked the rim of the bottle. The burn was already more pleasant, like a kiss, *and he pressed it.*

"It was just a light switch," he managed to think, at the same instant that darkness swallowed him, before he became all-engulfing light.

. . . and he heard music. The music enfolded him like silence, like light, and then like a din and a chiming . . . But his tongue wouldn't obey him. He stirred the remnants of it, like a stump.

"EUR . . . KA!" he seemed to scream, plunging into the embrace of silence and light.

"He's one tenacious son of a gun!" the Guardian Angel said to the Angel of Names.

"Not so much a son of a gun as a warrior, judging by his name. He won the last battle, after all."

"He didn't win it so much as not lose it."

"You talk like it was a game of billiards."

"Perhaps. Is The Sky Above Troy *still hanging over his bed?"*

"Where else . . . would it be?"

"You know, I kind of got used to him," the captain and the lieutenant said to each other without speaking.

"He could have hung on . . ."

"Yes, he wanted to write about all seven deadly sins . . ."

"He didn't get that far."

"What do you think he lacked?"

"Some of them he didn't know, others he didn't understand."

"He got stuck on that novel The Diagnosis.*"*

"What's that one about?"

"About how the author is hunting for a word, and the word is hunting for him. This word is the fatal diagnosis."

"And what is the diagnosis?"

"Diencephalic syndrome."

"What nonsense! Where did he stumble upon that one? Those cretins

just lump together everything they don't understand into a diagnosis like that. Or do you think he died from autosuggestive disorder . . . ?"

"What would that be?"

"He fell out of time. He abandoned it."

"Like in Dante? 'Stripped of the ability to see the future'?"

"On the contrary, he could see the future. It's the present that he had trouble discerning, except in dreams."

"Indeed, he was weary of the present."

"But it is only by depicting the future that one can catch up with the present. For it is always slightly ahead, albeit right under one's nose. The gaze itself, by definition, is directed forward."

"I see you have taken to reading him."

"I have only been following his Name. You follow his fate. So what's the diagnosis?"

"Pride. Mixed genesis."

"Yes . . . He was something of a Pole."

"What does being a Pole have to do with it?"

"Poles say: There's no worse devil than one who believes in God."

"Not bad. I always did believe that a witty saying freed one from the truth."

"Yes, woe to the one touched by temptation."

"Still, he doesn't look like a devil."

"Are you sure that he was able to tell an angel from a devil?"

"It's hard for people: they're trained to believe in halos and wings, horns and cloven hooves; but devils are hard to come by these days."

"Don't sell yourself short! How many times did you save him?"

"I haven't counted. And then it's not me but you. I only made sure his fate corresponded to his name."

"He had risen to the rank of sergeant . . ."

"Yes, he was already prepared for anything."

"Do you think they'll grant him a reunion?"

"It's against the rules for us to take his side. We have already exceeded our mandates."

"Who will fall to our lot now? An uneducated, run-of-the-mill scoundrel with the rank of private?"

"I don't think we'll end up in the same unit."

"Too bad, we made a good team."

"Well, goodbye then . . ." The captain and the lieutenant shook hands firmly.

"Do you think it's a tie?"

"You think he might reenlist?"

"Fortune will sort it out."

"Well, then, maybe it's still

NOT THE END

POSTSCRIPT

"I am the only person in the world who might have been able to shed light on the mysterious death of Urbino Vanoski," I announced at the very beginning. I was wrong.

Darkness.

Of course, I came to him at the appointed day and time, precisely as we had agreed. I rang, but he didn't answer. After shuffling around in the lobby for about an hour, I took the risk of walking upstairs and knocking. There was no answer, so I pushed the door open. It was unlocked, but the room was empty and surprisingly neat. His bed had been made up, almost like a military cot. On the pillow lay a starched shirt with a very unusual necktie and a Gillette razor. This was, so to speak, the head. The body was a typed manuscript of a novel called *Disappearing Objects.* In the place where the button had been, there was now a gaping hole.

I leaned over to peer inside: there was a palpable darkness that seemed to stretch out to infinity. Absolute darkness. Pitch black. A person couldn't have crawled through it. Me, I didn't dare put my finger inside, let alone a hand.

Darkness. He left only books and a black hole behind. How had he put it somewhere, about literature being the most waste-free industry? "A handful of dust in the bonfire of the vanities . . ." I think that's what it was. He had a son, too . . . Unverified, though. Was he from Dika or from Lili? Well, who else? Never mind. He'll show up to claim his inheritance. He had a strange name, like a dog: Bibo.

I scooped up the manuscript and grabbed the necktie without any hesitation; and, with a bit of hesitation, I grabbed the razor, too. My eyes sought the photograph of the Trojan cloud—it was gone.

Where it had hung, only a dark, unfaded rectangle of wallpaper remained.

The matter of the button was both simpler and more complicated. The proprietor of the little hotel turned out to be a sweet man, and even a reader of Vanoski. He had installed this button, together with a fan and an air vent, so that Urbino could at least have some cool, fresh air. Only he wasn't responsible for that hole! Dismantling it hadn't even crossed his mind.

"Every decent writer is supposed to leave a respectable posthumous work in his wake." Vanoski spoke these words during our first (and, it turned out, our only) conversation.

I became the discoverer and publisher of *Disappearing Objects*, the book which launched my successful career.

A. T.-B.

THE FLIGHT OF THE BUMBLEBEE

APRIL 25, 2011, 12:00 P.M.
VISBY, SWEDEN

On Easter, the carillon in the church across the way not only rang out the hours but played *great* music, as well. My room was filled with the buzzing of a large creature: a bumblebee flew in through my open window. It was my first bee of the year, and it was enormous. How had it managed to grow so large so quickly? Did it hibernate, I wondered? I knew little about bees, except that when they stung you, you wished they hadn't. It thudded against the ceiling and walls, looking for a way out. It even flew into the WC. Not finding anything there, it flew back out into the light, where it again found walls and the ceiling. The only place it avoided was my desk, either because it was wary of me or of my ashtray. Which stood to reason: we didn't smell like a meadow.

Its efforts to escape reminded me of my struggles at the computer. I, too, was desperate for a way out of the predicament I found myself in. I was happy to find a distraction, watching its persistent and futile efforts. You'll get no sympathy from me, mister. Its powerful buzzing pleased me. The moron was zigzagging in front of the open window. When it got right up to it, it would shy away from it like a frightened horse and continue beating itself against the ceiling and walls, looking for an escape. Apparently, the ceiling was a sky that had suddenly fallen on it.

In desperation, it landed on a yellow square of the ceiling molding, exhausted. Perhaps it was reminded of a daisy. I took a long look at it—it seemed to have slipped into a coma. I went back to the computer, but the fate of the bumblebee already preoccupied me more than my stalled work. I sat for a good fifteen minutes staring at the screen, which had gone to sleep and was now displaying the lunar surface. I felt so lonely on it! Just like a bumblebee.

I've got to rescue the poor creature, I thought, and began looking around for something I could capture it with. Now here's another appropriate use for a manuscript. I grinned, grabbing a sheet of paper.

As soon as I tiptoed up to the bee and reached out to it with the paper, the bee snapped out of its coma and started buzzing its way around the room with renewed vigor. Evidently it had rested and gathered strength, but also hit upon an idea. It had switched its computer on and was now making more frequent forays up to the window, albeit with caution.

I don't know how it arrived at the decision to struggle through to freedom. It seemed as if it didn't want to use the same broad highway by which it had entered. Instead, it forced its way out through a narrow, much less convenient chink of the ventilating window.

I was happy for it. Its struggles were so reminiscent of my own poor attempts at writing.

It was a true master class.

The bumblebee had a much harder time of it than I had, writing about it.

It's much harder for me to find freedom than it was for the bumblebee.

Its buzzing still rang in my ears. I respected it; but it was indifferent to me. A bumblebee, a bee abumble . . . Bumbling free. Tipsy.